PRAISE FOR BEN H. WINTERS'S

GOLDEN STATE

"Mr. Winters has won major awards in both the mystery and speculative-fiction genres. The brain-teasing *Golden State* exists in a space where those two forms coexist. As a consequence, a sympathetic reader's imaginings may persist long after the book's puzzles have been solved." —Tom Nolan, *Wall Street Journal*

"Once again, Ben H. Winters creates a world cleverly skewed a few crucial degrees from our own... Winters is well aware of the tropes of dystopian noir, and it is fun to watch him mix and match them to good effect... The detective plot works well, but it is in its questioning of the nature of truth and falsehood that the novel excels... Smart, intricate, and propulsive, *Golden State* is proof that Winters deserves our continued attention as one of crime fiction's most inventive practitioners." —Michael Berry, *San Francisco Chronicle*

"Winters has a knack for creating appealing detective fictions that skew reality in thought-provoking ways, producing a hybrid of the familiar and the uncanny... As you read, you feel your perception of the world slipping and warping. Winters brilliantly imagines the quotidian manifestations of a truth-obsessed culture." —Jon Michaud, *Washington Post*

"An entertaining new take on the venerable genre-blending of noir and science fiction." —Glenn Harper, *Los Angeles Review of Books*

"Like any good dystopian yarn, *Golden State* shows how any organization or government can warp good intentions into truly harmful ones."

—Andrew Liptak, *The Verge*

"Nothing speaks to the power of a weapon like it inspiring a work of speculative fiction, and Ben H. Winter's *Golden State* is the dystopian take on the new tool of war du jour: lies."

—B. David Zarley, *Paste*

"*Golden State* is science fiction at its finest, a propulsive narrative filled with complex ideas that are expressed by engaging characters who occupy a rich and detailed world."

—Allen Adams, *Maine Edge*

"Not many writers would take on George Orwell, Ray Bradbury, the nature of truth, and the current administration all at a blow. Big shoes to fill—and they fit Ben H. Winters just fine. *Golden State* grabs notions of disinformation and literalism and brilliantly turns them on their head to see what falls from their pockets."

—James Sallis, author of *Drive*

"At a time in the real world when everybody seems to own their version of the truth and phrases like 'alternative facts' are used to cover falsehoods, *Golden State* is, no lie, a fascinating examination that takes fidelity and correctness down a freaky Orwellian path."

—Brian Truitt, *USA Today*

"Winters always finds a way to get at a larger truth about our present even as he plays games with what we consider to be an acceptable form of reality, and his new work is sure to delight in the science fiction and crime worlds."

—*CrimeReads*

"A gripping and brainy page-turner...Not even his biggest fans will see some of the twists and turns he's built into this, his best book yet."

—John Francisconi, *Library Journal*

"An entertaining, unpredictable read."

—James Lovegrove, *Financial Times*

"*Golden State* is a prescient, devastating commentary on humanity's disintegrating attachment to reality and truth, expertly told through the prism of a police-procedural, dystopian nightmare. Winters has written a *1984* for the twenty-first century. Not just a thrilling book, but an important one."

—Blake Crouch, author of *Dark Matter*

GOLDEN STATE

BEN H. WINTERS

MULHOLLAND BOOKS

Little, Brown and Company

New York Boston London

Copyright © 2019 by Ben H. Winters

Hachette Book Group supports the right to free expression and the value of copyright. The purpose of copyright is to encourage writers and artists to produce the creative works that enrich our culture.

The scanning, uploading, and distribution of this book without permission is a theft of the author's intellectual property. If you would like permission to use material from the book (other than for review purposes), please contact permissions@hbgusa.com. Thank you for your support of the author's rights.

Mulholland Books / Little, Brown and Company
Hachette Book Group
1290 Avenue of the Americas, New York, NY 10104
mulhollandbooks.com

Originally published in hardcover by Mulholland Books, January 2019
First Mulholland Books trade paperback edition, January 2020

Mulholland Books is an imprint of Little, Brown and Company, a division of Hachette Book Group, Inc. The Mulholland Books name and logo are trademarks of Hachette Book Group, Inc.

The publisher is not responsible for websites (or their content) that are not owned by the publisher.

The Hachette Speakers Bureau provides a wide range of authors for speaking events. To find out more, go to hachettespeakersbureau.com or call (866) 376-6591.

ISBN 978-0-316-50541-3 (hc) / 978-0-316-50543-7 (pb)
LCCN 2018941036

10 9 8 7 6 5 4 3 2 1

LSC-C

Printed in the United States of America

For Irwin Hyman
who built the world he wanted to live in

PART ONE

Future (n.), usually **the future**: the set of possible events which are neither happening nor have happened but which *may* happen, including those possible events which *will* happen, but which are not yet distinguishable from the far greater group which will not. [*Nota bene:* avoid where possible.]

———*The Everyday Citizen's Dictionary,* 43rd edition, the Golden State Publishing Arm

ATTESTATION

This is a novel.

All of the words of it are true.

The extraordinary events detailed herein were either experienced firsthand by the author or, when relayed second- or thirdhand, have been double-checked (triple-, where possible), verified, and certified by the relevant departments, and substantiated through the reading of testimony, examination of material evidence, and review of relevant reality. All of the supporting documents and extant evidence are available upon request in the appropriate offices; physical addresses are included as an appendix.

All of these events occurred as described. It's all on the Record.

STIPULATION

Though the author is a character in the events that follow, he claims no part of the glory they reflect. All glory belongs to the heroic Speculator, Mr. Ratesic, whose perseverance and heroism are on display throughout.

This author is loath to resort to set phrases like "He made the ultimate sacrifice in service to the State," conscious as he is of the care we all must take not to fumble by cliché into accidental lies. But in this case, there can be no other conclusion. In service to the State, Mr. Ratesic made the ultimate sacrifice.

Willingly, and conscious of mounting dangers to his person, and despite numerous opportunities to save himself, he continued unflinching in his brave pursuit of the wickedness he had discovered, and ultimately was successful in foiling a grave assault upon the State—all at the hazard of his own health and safety.

And so, though the primary purpose of this novel is the same as that of all other novels, to entertain the mind and excite the spirit, in this case there is a deeper truth, one level down: this work is meant to serve as a legacy to Mr. Ratesic, the hero of its pages. It is a testament to him, and I hope it can serve as an inspiration not only to his fellows in Service, but to all our citizenry. Let this novel stand like a statue of Mr. Ratesic, a tribute to as well as a reminder of the lengths that are sometimes necessary to hold up the several bulwarks of the State, and a reminder of what is at stake if they should fall.

1.

Somebody's telling lies in here, and it's making it hard to eat.

In a perfect world, a man should be able to sit down at a favorite spot and eat his breakfast without the weight of professional obligation coming down on him, ruining his morning, pulling him right into the thick of it before he can so much as get a good hot sip of coffee.

But the world has never been accused of being perfect, has it, and so here we are and here is what actually happens—here is reality. No sooner has Honey the waitress slid my steaming breakfast plate down in front of me, right next to a piping-hot cup of mountain-grown, than I catch a small dissonance in the air—the barest ripple, the softest whisper—but it can't be ignored. My body won't let me ignore it. The burble catches in my throat, my eyes prick with tears, and I put down my fork and say "Shit."

The dissonance is close but not that close. It's not at the booth directly behind me, where an old man and his old wife are discussing in their old slow voices the quality of their oatmeal: she thinks it's worse than it used to be, he thinks it's better, but both are speaking honestly.

They are both talking true, but someone in here is not.

I'm definitely too conscious of it, too *aware* to just carry on eating my chicken and waffles, which is a real shame, because this is Terry's we're talking about, this is fried chicken and waffles, and although there are three chicken-and-waffle chains in the city, Terry's is in my veteran estimation by far the best, and the Pico-Robertson Terry's is the best of all the Terry's locations.

I get up. I push away my plate, lay down today's copy of *Trusted Authority*, heave my weight up out of the banquette, and just stand still, very still, in the middle of the restaurant, rummaging for a source. Lot of people talking in here so it's gonna take me a minute. Terry's is crowded all the time, but most especially at breakfast time, and it's breakfast time now, peak of the a.m. rush, every booth and table jammed, maybe forty or forty-five conversations overlapping, blending in with the tinny tingting of the silverware, the sizzle of the griddle, a radio playing boisterous piano jazz, even the slow whoosh of the overhead fans, their wide beveled blades slowly pushing the July air around in circles.

I close my eyes, concentrate, try to find the sound among the sounds. Tease through the conversations for the one I'm after: *Did you hear what Louis said about Albert . . .* and *I am so sick of all this . . .* and *You're kidding me, you are fucking kidding me, you have got to try this.* Somewhere in this atmosphere, cluttered with chatter, someone's dissembling in a steady stream, a diffusion of false statements like an open gas line. I step away from my back-corner booth, one step toward the center of the restaurant, steal a sad glance back at my plate. The chicken is good, but it's really the waffles that have to be tasted to be believed. They are cold now. And soon, so too will be the chicken.

I take another slow step forward, tuning in the various conversations, one by one. A couple of sharply dressed businessmen, both of them leaning so far forward their heads are almost touching—*"There is money to be made here, Paul, real money . . ."*—and then Paul in gruff dissent: *"The last time you told me that . . .* " Whatever the details of the deal, neither of them is lying about it. There's a couple of young folk seated across from each other, each of them leafing through the *Trusted Authority,* not talking at all.

At the big center table, there's a funny, flirty waitress I know whose name is Ava, and she's delivering an encomium to today's special—a three-egg omelet, with jalapeños sliced into it along with red and green peppers—and I don't know if it's really good or not, but I can tell you that Ava really thinks it is, because from my position—I'm now standing near the dead center of the main dining room—I can hear every word of her testimony about the special and it doesn't trouble me, it slides past like warm water. Whether the three-egg omelet is tasty or not, Ava believes it to be so.

So—

—there. *There.*

My eyes open back up, quick and completely.

At a table along the right-side wall, underneath the TV, are three people in a tense conversation, their voices urgent and streaked with emotion. They're talking over each other, exchanging accusations, interrupting, apologizing, going round and round. One is a woman of late middle age, a pretty face but exhausted, eyes deep set and dark, freckles on her nose, hair thick and curly, some of it gray. She's sharing the booth with a pair of broad-shouldered young men, both in ball caps, both with the woman's robust good looks and black eyes. Two sons. A mom and her two grown children in the middle of some kind of emotional set-to, talking fast, talking over each other, talking at once, and—ah, the air is rolling now, the dissonance is a shimmer on the scene—definitely one of them is lying. At least one.

"I'm not trying to blame anybody. If anything, I blame myself—"

"Mom, stop it. Seriously, stop. That is the last—"

"Eddie, give her a second. Give her a second to talk."

"You're *interrupting* me."

"You're interrupting *her*—"

"Hi. Hello. Excuse me." I step closer. I jam my hands into my pockets. "The Earth is in orbit around the sun."

There's a voice I use in situations like this: cool and calm, firm and definitive, authoritative but not aggressive. It gets the result I want: everybody draws down to a hush. Everybody looks at me at once. It's like I've pulled a curtain around the four of us, here at this table along the wall.

"Hello," says the woman. "And the Moon is in orbit around the Earth."

"Always has it been."

"Always shall it be."

She takes a deep breath. Keeps her eyes on mine. The sons glance at each other.

"How are you folks doing this morning?"

"We're okay. We're just fine."

That's one of the two boys. Now all three of them are looking up at me with the same stunned expression, me looming over them like a dark planet blocking the sun.

"I'm sorry to bother you folks, but I overheard your conversation."

The restaurant has gone quiet. People are looking at us, nudging each other—*Look*. The old man and his old wife have set down their spoons and are watching, waiting to see what happens. I take out my Day Book, take out my pen, click it open. The mom blinks, and her lips are pursed and there is emotion in her eyes, a little fear and a little confusion. It's a strange feeling, sometimes, to be seen the way I know that I am seen—the way the world reacts to my presence. But it's part of the job and it helps. You want to have control of a situation. You want to have people focused on you. You want to know that they know that it's serious.

"I hate to bother you folks. But I was eating my own breakfast just over there—" I point back over to my booth, but all the while I am keeping my eyes carefully on the table, on the three participants in this conversation, making my quiet assessment of who the liar or liars are among them. "And I found that I was troubled by the presence of dishonesty in the atmosphere."

"What?" says the mother.

"No..." begins one of the sons; the other is just looking down. "That's..."

I wait a moment, one eyebrow cocked. *That's what?* But nobody finishes the sentence.

It's the mom, the lady, who speaks next. "How do you—why would you say that?"

"It's not an accusation, ma'am," I tell her. "It's not a matter of opinion. It is part of what is Objectively So."

My voice remains composed, reasonable. You gotta keep these things calm for as long as possible. That's important. In a moment or two, someone is going to confess, or someone is going to do something stupid. There aren't any other ways this thing goes.

I smile, but I know that my smile can at times appear less than friendly. I'm over six two and over 260 pounds—how *far* over 260 varies depending on (for example) how recently I've been to Terry's. I'm in the unofficial uniform of my service, black suit and black tie, black boots, and a battered pinhole with the brim angled slightly down. My hair is thick and red and I wear a big beard, not for any visual effect but because I'm too lazy to shave.

"Can I ask your name, please?"

"Kelly."

"Your full name, ma'am."

"Kelly Tarjin. Elizabeth. My middle name is Elizabeth."

"So Kelly Elizabeth Tarjin?"

"Yeah. Right. Do you want to see my identifications?"

"No, Ms. Tarjin. That's not necessary."

I don't need to see her identifications. Even in the general discomfort I'm feeling over here by the liar's table, her asseveration of her name doesn't add to the discordance. Maybe she was lying to the others just now, but she's not lying to me right now. I can tell. When it's bad, it gets bad. Two days ago I had a guy on a false claim, a guy begging at 4th and Alameda with a *hungry and homeless* sign, though he was neither, a guy who then clung to his demonstrable untruths even when contrary evidence was presented, stood there proclaiming and reproclaiming his lies, swearing to them until the air was so thick I felt it way down in my throat, like a clot in a drain.

"These are your sons, Ms. Tarjin?"

"Yes. Todd and Eddie. Edward."

"Hey," says one of them. Todd. They're both looking at me, both of them wary, both of them uncertain. I cough once, into my fist.

"And what are you folks discussing this morning?"

The boys glance at each other. Ms. Tarjin taps one hand on the table, next to her plate.

"Well," she says finally, and then one of the sons interrupts: "It's personal."

I smile. "I'm afraid it's not anymore."

I want to keep everybody cool for as long as possible. Keep the situation in neutral. I have other voices I use in other situations.

"Yes, sir. Of course." That's Mom, that's Ms. Tarjin, who is afraid. You can tell she's afraid. I don't want her to be afraid, I don't want anyone to be afraid of me, I'm like anyone else, even though it's not *me* she's afraid of, it's the clothes and the position, it's the black pin-hole with the felt brim, it's the boots, the outfit metonymic for the whole system of which I am a representative.

The atmosphere continues in its roil. It's here. It's close. I cough again.

"We were talking about some...some uh..." The woman, the mom, she's choosing her words carefully. That's what folks do, with me standing here, all the weight of what I am. It's okay. I'm patient. "We were just having a conversation about some medication of mine."

"Medication."

"Yes, sir."

"What kind of medication is that?"

"Dreams—that's all. For dreams." She has lowered her voice, as if it were possible for us to speak confidentially. As if everybody in the room wasn't listening by now, customers and waiters gawking, fascinated; as if the place wasn't bristling, too, with captures—captures in the ceiling fans, captures on the kitchen's large appliances, the pinhole that constantly captures my own personal POV. The whole world under constant surveillance, everything on the Record, reality in progress. "I take Clarify, that's all."

"Oh. Well, that's all right."

While I write this in my Day Book, Ms. Tarjin swallows, swallows again. "Dream control, you know. Prescribed. To reduce or—how does it go?—to reduce or eliminate the confusing effects of dreams in waking life. I have the prescription. Do you—" She glances at her purse, and I shake my head, raise a hand—*That's not necessary.* I don't think she's lying about being prescribed the dream dampener. The boys, meanwhile, are stock-still, frozen by some combination of protective impulse and fear for their own safety.

In another moment, no doubt, I'm gonna know which brother has more of which. Like I said: either someone confesses or someone does something dumb. That's how it always ends.

"And your supply of Clarify," I venture, "has it perhaps been coming up a little short?"

"Yes." She swallows. "That's right."

I write in my Day Book.

"And so the personal conversation you're having here, that's you asking the boys if they happen to know where your surplus dream meds might have gotten to?"

She lowers her head.

"Mom, you don't have to answer all these questions." That's Eddie, the smaller of the brothers, giving his voice some spine.

"Well, she does, actually. She does have to answer." He glares at me, his face tight with anger, and I gaze back at him impassively.

It's dead quiet in here now. No waitresses are taking orders. No one is chitchatting in their own booth. Somebody has killed the jazz radio in the kitchen. Everybody is staring at us, at the big man in his blacks, towering over the three-top. And, you know, this is my nineteenth year doing this job and there's something I've learned, which is that you can talk however calmly and reassuringly you want to, but people are gonna hear your words colored by their own feelings, by their own anxiety or fear or impatience.

"Tell me the rest," I say to Ms. Tarjin.

"Mom—"

"No, Eddie," I say. "You keep quiet, son. I'm gonna talk to your mom a minute. Don't obfuscate." I shift on my feet, turn out, so I'm talking as much to Ms. Tarjin as to the boys. "A lie hidden in a shell of truth is a lie just the same, and I will know it."

"I was afraid that my son Eddie was stealing my pills."

"Mom!"

"But—but—" She looks at the boys, and Eddie is looking at me, coldly furious, and Todd is inspecting the backs of his hands. "But Todd says it wasn't Eddie. Todd says it was *him*."

"It *was*, Mom. It was me." Todd looks up, presses a hand to his chest. "It was, okay?"

She gives him a look I can only half see because the air is bending, the air is bent, and she says, "I thought it was Eddie because Eddie had been at the house but Todd told me that I had it wrong. So we're getting it straightened out. That's all. It's not a matter for, for"—she meets my eye, very briefly—"for your department."

"Oh," I say, "I see," and I look at the family looking back and I am feeling it now, and I know right where it is, and Todd knows that I know and he jumps, grabs the back of the booth in a pivot, and runs for it.

I huff once, like a bull, and go after him.

He slams open the door and I catch it before it closes, hollering "Stand back, friends" as I charge out onto Pico Boulevard just behind him, slamming into a small flock of businessmen that Todd has just managed to dance around, scattering them in their lightweight summer suits like blue-breasted birds.

"Sorry, fellas," I say over my shoulder, grabbing on to my hat with one hand and steaming after Todd, four or five feet behind him, head down, body like a truck, my black boots slamming onto the sidewalk.

I like this part. It's not the part of the job that people talk about, but it's the part I like: pure law enforcement, my feet in the boots and the boots on the ground, me breathing heavy and charging after a liar.

He's got no chance because even if I can't catch him—and I

will catch him, because giving chase is part of the job and I am competent and confident in all aspects of my employment—but even if by some miracle he gives me the slip, the captures are on: captures on every corner, captures in every doorway, forging history, putting us on the Record. Reality in progress.

I'll catch him or we'll requisition the stretches, scour the Record, trace him to where he's gone. Plus, the thing is, I know these streets, I know this block of Pico and every block of Mid-City all the way till it hits downtown, and I know what's coming up. There's an alley mouth three more doors down, between the strip club and the hardware store, and it's going to sing out to this desperate kid like his own true love, like a sure-thing escape hatch, which I know damn well it is not.

Todd, dancing around a lady and her dog, bounces off a parking meter, loses his balance for half a second, and I grab the scruff of his T-shirt, shout "Come on, man!," but he wriggles free of my ham of a hand and—sure as shooting—flings his narrow body up the little alley next to the topless bar, and I race after him, breathing hard, slowing down a little, slipping on the uneven ground, the pavement slick with garbage juice and discarded sheets of *Authority*.

"Train's coming, Todd," I say between heavy breaths, just loud enough for him to hear me.

"What?" he says, but he can see it now—the yellow flash of the warning light at the end of the alley, where it lets out onto the light-rail tracks. He turns, cursing, staring at me, shaking as the gate arm lowers behind him. He raises his left hand and it's got a gun in it—oh, this fucking kid. A gun? What has he got a gun for? His brother is the drug thief.

Everybody's got their secrets, I suppose. He points the gun at me but I keep coming. Closing the distance between us. I have a gun of my own, of course, but I leave it in my pocket. The alley is short. Just bricks on one side, just the blacked-out windows of the strip club on the other.

"I'll kill you, man," says Todd, loud over the rattle and rush of the train. "I swear I will."

"You're not going to kill me." He's lying. I know and he knows that I know. "No more, Todd, okay? No more."

By the time I close the distance he's lowered the gun. He drops it and I kick it away, take him calmly by the shoulder and clap him into the cuffs and turn him around, push him against the bricks of the hardware store. The last rattling car of the commuter train goes past, revealing a scrum of strangers on the far side of the tracks, watching me put this poor young liar in cuffs. Catching my breath, I tug out my radio and get a line in to the regular police, and by the time the sirens start to sing, a crowd has gathered and Ms. Tarjin and the other boy are out here too, pushing through the front of the jostling semicircle of lookers-on.

"Oh Lord," she says, wringing her hands. "Oh Lord. Todd, honey."

Todd is silent. His eyes are locked on the wall. His head is hanging down.

"So?" she says to me, tearful, defiant. "Well? What happens now?"

"Well, there's a whole process," I say. "But, uh—but it's going to be bad."

"Oh no," she says, her face crumbling. But what am I going to do—lie?

"I will tell the regular police what I know, and your sons will be charged with their respective crimes."

"Crimes," she says quietly.

Eddie, the other son, the one who stole his mother's drugs,

now puts a hand on her shoulder, but Ms. Tarjin shakes it off. Todd keeps staring stoically at the alley wall. Ms. Tarjin has got one hand on her brow, massaging her temple—a mother's pose of grief. One more grief that the world has given her.

"The thing is," I say, and then: "Oh good—hey, fellas." I help the regular police make their way through the crowd, two young officers I don't know. They move Todd away from the wall, and I keep explaining to Ms. Tarjin: "Way it works is, you could decline to press charges on the stolen pills, if you wanted to. The kid's not looking at more than six months."

I glance at Eddie, who has the decency not to look relieved. It's his brother, after all—the one now in handcuffs, the one being led to a black-and-white parked slantwise, halfway up on the Pico curb—who, in trying to cover up for him, trying to protect their mother from knowing about his perfidy, has committed the more serious crime.

"What about Todd?" asks Ms. Tarjin quietly.

"That's going to be a matter for the adjudication division, ma'am. I can't tell you for sure."

"A ballpark, though. Can you—" Her voice catches on tears. I cough forcefully into my fist, wipe at my watery eyes, though the dissonance that jammed me up has largely cleared by now. Now the air is clean. "You can give me a ballpark," she says.

"Well. It was a forceful and purposeful distortion of the truth." I grit my teeth. I hate this part. "Six years? Nine?"

She starts crying about that, the poor lady, and I take a step away from her. Just then it turns nine o'clock, I hear the tower at Pico and Robertson start to toll it, and people on the street all start saying it to each other—"It's nine o'clock now"; "It's just turned nine"; "Hey, how are you? It's nine a.m."—and by the time the bell has struck nine times, the regular police have led the boy away, and Ms. Tarjin is tearfully writing down the address of the Mid-City precinct where they're taking him, and I don't like it but I do like it, because we have to defend the world, because the world is all we have. We have to keep things good and true because the good and true world is all we have.

2.

By the time I make it from the scene of the morning's drama all the way downtown to the offices of the Speculative Service and finish with the paperwork, I'm a half hour late getting to my own desk on the thirtieth floor.

"Hey, Mr. Alvaro," I say in passing, palming my beard and scowling. "Ten is half of twenty."

"But it's twice five."

"So it's ever been."

"So it ever shall be." Mr. Alvaro is the boss man, standing at the big board like always, endlessly updating the list of cases in progress, today's assignments: anomalous facts to be sorted through, questionable statements to be followed up on. Accidental infelicities to be sorted out from purposeful misrepresentations.

"Sorry I'm late," I say. "I had an incident report to file on the fourth."

"So I heard. Chasing a bald-faced out of a breakfast joint on Pico, right? I got the whole story from dispatch. Explains why you didn't answer your radio."

"What?"

"Not a big deal. You're next on the rotation, and we had an incoming. Car crash outside Grand Central, wildly deviant accounts of the moments preceding."

"You radioed?" I look down at my unit, fiddle with the buttons.

This is disappointing. It might be a matter of someone's honest mistake, it might be a mere misalignment of perceptions, or it might be something worse—someone trying to paint a fake picture for the regular police, escape consequences by bending what is So. Those tend to be fun. I don't like to miss those.

"Arlo radioed. You musta missed it. No big deal, like I said. You're too busy chasing liars down Pico Boulevard. Which, no kidding, is excellent work and will be reported up to Ms. Petras. If I remember, which I hopefully will."

He probably won't, but I say "Thanks" anyway. Laura Petras is the Golden State's Acknowledged Expert on the Enforcement of the Laws—officially, Alvaro's boss and my own. There's a picture of her framed near the elevator, an older blonde woman with a careful smile and a tan blouse.

"And let that—excuse me a moment, Laszlo." Alvaro makes his hands into a bullhorn to address the room. "Let that be a lesson to the rest of you mopes! Mr. Ratesic over here is collaring flagrant liars *during his breakfast.*"

This testament to my supposed virtues earns a smattering of sarcastic applause and a vigorous middle finger from Mr. Burlington. The gang's all here this morning: Mr. Cullers, leaning back with a hot towel over his forehead, and Ms. Bright, and Mr. Markham—the small-ball Specs, pure ID checkers and paper-trail combers. But Ms. Carson is here too, with her pencil skirt and serene expression, her hair shellacked into a hard helmet under her pinhole.

I look around the room for Arlo Vasouvian, the senior-most Speculator on the floor, and there he is—at my desk with an individual I do not recognize, a young female standing at nervous attention. She's wearing a pinhole, which means she is Service, but she's also all in gray, not black, which means she's junior. She's in training. This I don't like at all.

"Arlo?" I go over there. Put down my bag and the cup of coffee I got downstairs. "What's going on?"

"Ah, good. Mr. Ratesic. Hydrogen is the lightest element."

"And Osmium is the heaviest. What's going on?"

He smiles slowly, peers at me from behind his thick glasses. "There's someone I would like you to meet. A new member of our service. Mr. Ratesic, this is Ms. Paige."

"Okay," I say flatly, extending my hand. "Twelve times twelve is one hundred forty-four."

"And, inversely, the square root of one hundred forty-four is twelve," replies Paige, sharp as a paper cut, and then, while we're still shaking hands, she rolls right on: "It's Aysa, sir, Aysa Paige, and it is an honor to meet you, and I look forward to our working closely together."

I let go of her hand.

"Arlo? Why did she just say that?"

"Well, you can ask Ms. Paige, but I imagine she said it because it's an honor for her to meet you. And because she is looking forward to working closely with you."

Arlo's smile is knowing and roguish; Ms. Paige's is earnest and guileless. She is young and upright, dark-skinned, well turned out, with the brim of her pinhole turned sharply to center, her thick curly hair carefully tucked away and bobby-pinned. Her shoes are shined and every button is in place. The keen care she's taken with her appearance goes beyond the dress code and says something exacting about her character—exacting or eager to impress. Either way, her looking like that, with me in my poorly fitting blacks and battered pinhole, makes me feel like I just climbed out of a duffel bag.

I turn to Arlo, who looks back at me mildly. No longer a field officer, Arlo wears no pinhole, no hat of any kind, and his thin white hair drifts in several directions.

"Yes," I say. "I wasn't calling the woman a liar. I was wondering why she has the impression that we are working together."

"Well, that is my hope," says Arlo. "If it's all right with you. I had mentioned it to Mr. Alvaro"—he nods at Alvaro, over by the board, and Alvaro grunts—"and I did hope you would find the arrangement amenable."

"I do not."

Arlo's wrinkled brow furrows, very slightly. "Oh now. Laszlo. Can we discuss it?"

"*You* can."

"*Laszlo.*" He speaks the heavy syllables of my name with paternal disappointment.

Arlo Vasouvian is serene and equanimous, seventy-seven years old, with gigantic ears, with small eyes behind thick glasses, with hair so thin and white it is close to transparent. He is emeritus now, semiretired, but once upon a time, Arlo had Alvaro's job—he did when I started, and he did when my father started, thirty years before that. Now he occupies a rickety desk toward the back of the room, slowly odd-jobbing his way through each day: helping new Specs get adjusted, putting the finishing touches on other people's paperwork, sipping endlessly at a mug of hot tea. He could, if he wanted, be at home, puttering and humming to himself through an easy retirement in his little Ballona Creek cottage, but Arlo never married; the Ballona Creek cottage is essentially unfurnished. Arlo's home is here. Every once in a while, someone teasingly asks Arlo when he plans on retiring, and he always has the same answer: "Maybe you'll get lucky—maybe someone will shoot me!" This retort never entirely manages to hide the shadow of truth behind it, which is that the Speculative Service is his life, it is his soul's strong purpose, and he fears that if the crutch of it is kicked away he will fall right over and never get up again.

I feel comfortable averring as to how he feels, because I feel more or less the same. I'm fifty-four now, but soon enough I'll be making the same excuses, finding the same reasons to keep coming in here every morning.

I'm using my chair, so Arlo settles himself onto the edge of my desk, tilts his small body toward me, gathers his sport coat around his narrow chest.

"I had only hoped, Laszlo, that you would find it in your heart—"

"Nope."

"—to offer Ms. Paige the benefit—"

"No thank you."

"—of your many years' experience, and mentor her as she—"

"Listen, Arlo." I push back from the desk, look him in his owl's eyes. "I'm going to say no just one more time, but I'm going to say it nice and loud in case, because you are old, you are having trouble hearing me." I lean back toward the desk and my office chair squeaks beneath me. *"No."*

I start fussing with the stack of papers on the desk so I can be doing something, anything, other than looking at Arlo. I've got a court appearance coming up, testimony I'm supposed to give in the Court of Small Infelicities, one of these knucklehead kerfuffles where an automobile dealership advertises "the lowest rates around" and a competitor hauls them in, challenging the veracity of "lowest" and the generality of "around," and the court needs someone from the Service to weigh the litigants' relative sincerity. So I'm aggressively shuffling the papers, reviewing my prep materials, but I can *feel* them—this Paige character looking anxiously at Arlo, Arlo giving her a reassuring look: *Don't worry, I'll handle this.* Meaning handle *me.*

The last thing I need is an apprentice; the last thing I need is a shadow, dogging my heels.

"Listen. Laszlo," says Arlo as he gives Ms. Paige a meaningful look and she steps discreetly away. "I recognize this is an imposition."

"That is *one* thing it is, Arlo."

"I do not come to you lightly, Laszlo. I know how busy you are."

"Do you?"

"I do. However. I consider the opportunity to mentor a high honor." Arlo looks at me solemnly.

"Okay," I tell him, "so why not give it to Burlington? Come on, Arlo. Or give it to Cullers."

I point across the room, and, as if to neatly undermine my attempt to evade this high honor, Cullers groans, adjusts the hot compress he's holding to his forehead. Maybe Cullers was up early too, chasing fugitive truth-benders down city blocks. Or maybe he was out late at the Junction, getting smashed. With Cullers, either possibility has an equal chance of proving out.

I shouldn't have to explain to Arlo why this won't work. Whatever skills I have amassed after doing this job for nineteen years and counting, I am skeptical of my ability to impart them to someone else. And certainly Arlo in his semiretirement has no power to *make* me do it, and neither does Mr. Alvaro, not really. That's just not how the Service is organized.

However. Arlo is my colleague but he's also my friend, and I have known him for many years. He knew my brother. He knew my father. Which means that in a way he is like a brother to me, and he is like a father too, and what he is doing right now, with a charming shamelessness, is employing all of those associations to bend me to his will.

"There is no one like you, Laszlo," he says, imperturbable, flattering, shameless. "You know that. The Service needs you. Your State needs you. *I* need you."

"Why me?"

"Because you're the best."

"That's subjective."

"Stipulated. But listen." He leans in closer. He lowers his voice. "This young lady is very special, Laszlo. I would like to see her mentored carefully. I need your help."

I look over at Paige. She waits at full attention, her hands behind her back, her mouth a tight line, adopting what she must believe to be the expected stance of the law enforcement officer. But we're not law enforcement officers, not exactly. Soon she will gather up the regular rhythm of the Speculative Service. The idiosyncrasy, the casual atmosphere. We don't stand in line, we don't salute, we do our own thing.

"Okay, look," I say, and Arlo catches the answer in my voice and leans back, clasps his hands together in a restrained triumphant gesture. "When we catch a case, Ms. Paige, you can go ahead and ride along beside me. Okay? And you can...I guess you'll just pay attention and everything, but try not to get in the way. Okay?"

"Yes, sir."

"Is that what you're after, Mr. Vasouvian?"

"I want you to do whatever you feel comfortable with, Laszlo."

Paige begins, "And can I just say, sir—" I hold up a hand.

"You don't have to call me 'sir,' okay?"

"Okay, sir. If you don't mind, though, I would like to. It's a sign of respect, sir. You've earned it."

"Stipulated," I say. "But I'm just as happy for you to call me Mr. Ratesic."

"Yes, sir."

"Hey Laz," Alvaro hollers from the board. "Got something for you. Maybe a good one to break in the kid. If you're taking her on. Are you taking her on or not?"

I look at Paige. I hiss through my teeth, "Yeah," and I extend my hand and Alvaro puts the piece of paper in it. "I'm taking her."

Arlo slides off my desk, pats me gently on the shoulder, satisfied, as well he should be, having gotten exactly what he wanted.

So with Paige in the shotgun seat I head up Vermont Avenue from downtown toward the scene, a simple scene of death on a lawn in Los Feliz.

It's not clear from the report, but it doesn't sound like there's any specific anomaly we're being called out to look at. Sometimes the regular police just get skittish, decide that if they've got a body on the scene, they want us around to look at it, too. Like a broken person must have been the result of a broken truth.

I could take the 5, of course, a nice straight northbound shot, if I wanted to, and it might have bought us five minutes, but the stress of the highway isn't worth it right now, not when I can give myself the pleasure of the surface streets, the pleasure of looking out the windshield at all the beauty and variety of the Golden State rolling by. You get the streets and sidewalks of downtown, all the usual crowded midmorning bustle, the stop and start at the intersections when you're moving north and west around the administrative buildings and State services buildings that fan out from the Plaza. And then you escape the hive, pass under the highway and into the borderland, where you see the acres of industry, the factories and warehouses with their solar panel roofs winking back at the sun. And then, just north of *that,* the miles of farmland, lettuce and avocados, olives and all the rest of it, and then, just like that, you're whipped back into the neighborhoods, the hip urban districts that line Vermont Avenue like a series of colorful beads: Echo Park, Los Feliz, Silver Lake.

There's a place in Echo Park, actually, a quarter mile off Vermont, that sells some very solid crullers, some of the best in the State, but there's no time for a cruller just now, not with a scene of death waiting for us uptown.

"Sir? Mr. Ratesic?"

"Yeah?"

Ms. Paige is looking at me avidly from the shotgun, but I am definitely not looking at her; I'm looking at the road. But I can feel her emotions, feel her anxiety and excitement, young Paige's first-day jitters a living thing in the car with us.

"So should I just, like, jump right in?"

"Jump right into what?"

"What?"

I feel her deflate. I feel the crestfallen silence of someone who had a whole speech ready to roll out.

"Jump into my—oh, I mean—just, like, my life story. When I first knew that I had the sense and everything. How I decided to go into the Service. The whole . . . I just meant . . . I don't know. Sorry."

I know what she wants.

She wants to tell me about when she was nineteen years old, or fourteen, or twenty-two, whenever it was that she first saw something in the air, first realized what it was that she was seeing. She wants to tell me how she ignored it at first, because acknowledging and indulging this dangerous new ability would mean abandoning her desire to be a doctor, or a lawyer, or an architect, or whatever, but how she eventually realized that she had a calling, a responsibility, that she could cultivate this facility, this *instinct*, bring it up and bring it out, because then she could serve the State and it would be selfish not to, and it was, after all, the least she could do . . .

And then I would tell her my own version of the story, so similar, I'm sure, to hers, with the only additional complication being my father, and then my brother, Charlie, him having done it all first, sensed it first and followed it first, his brilliance like a sun casting a shadow over my own career.

My mood, which has already been spoiled by the encounter at Terry's, by the burden of taking on a junior, is further clouded by this unexpected memory of Charlie, both welcome and unwelcome, a sudden flood of feeling: *Charlie and what happened to Charlie.* I scowl. Just then we pass the House of Pies, another favorite diner of mine, on the northern edge of Los Feliz; I am tempted to pull over, tell Ms. Paige to wait in the car, and get myself a piece of blueberry pie or something to take the edge off the day.

But I don't. I keep going. We're almost there.

"Listen, Paige." I glance at her. "It's Paige, right?"

"Yes, sir. Aysa Violet Paige."

"I don't want to hear your story. I don't need it. Okay?"

"Okay."

"I don't need yours, and you don't need mine."

"Oh. Right. I mean—sure."

She fidgets self-consciously in the shotgun seat, casting occasional nervous glances my way, otherwise staring out the window.

This girl is my opposite, and I darkly wonder if Arlo put her in my car purely for the physical comedy. She is short, neat, black, and fully earnest in her countenance. And here I am, this too-big creature, my pale face and my black pinhole, my thick fingers gripping the steering wheel, thick red beard spilling out over the wool of my suit, and my irritation with the world—which is really an irritation with myself—like armor, chain mail rattling across my broad chest. And I don't know what it is, I can't tell you, but this kid's face, everything in her face is different from everything I feel: she's excited, almost agitated with her own excitement, as if all the great days still ahead of her are jostling inside, spilling together like coins. And she believes that I am someone worth looking up to, someone worth learning from. And if you want to hear something true—big true, deep true—that does not feel terrible. It doesn't feel terrible at all.

"What matters is what happens *now*," I tell her. "In the field. What matters is how you marshal the abilities you've been granted, and how you harness them to real investigative skill. Okay?"

"Okay. Yeah."

I drive a minute more. Dope shops and banks, coffee shops and dry cleaners.

"I'm sorry," she says.

"Don't be sorry."

"I just—"

"I mean it, Paige. All of this?" I point at me, and then at her, meaning all of the interpersonal, all of the getting to know each other, all of the rah-rah teamwork, all of it. "It doesn't matter. What matters is what happens in the world. Okay?"

"Okay."

I think that might be it for conversation—I hope it is—but no.

"So can you maybe tell me how it works?"

"How what works?"

"Oh, I just mean . . . where we're going. Our interaction with the regular police, the different protocols. I mean, I know how it works, obviously. I've done plenty of simulations, and I've done all the reading and training and stuff. I just mean . . . in real life. In the field. Is there anything you think I maybe *don't* know?"

"I am sure, Ms. Paige, there are many things you don't know."

And then I just keep driving; I just leave that flat piece of truth unadorned, add no further context. I'm being a prig, I am aware of that, I am being a special kind of asshole. Indulging in rigorous literalism, answering questions to the letter, ignoring the spirit in which they were asked is a nasty and childish trick. But I can't help it—I'm already regretting agreeing to this. I should have held firm with Arlo, told him to pin this particular ribbon on someone else's chest. I value my time alone. I like working by myself. I like knowing that if I'm on the way to a scene of crime, and I feel like taking forty-five seconds to run into House of Pies and pick up a slice of blueberry I can then eat in the car, I can do that without anyone judging me or asking questions.

Too late. We drive on. We're almost there.

3.

I slouch across the lawn on Vermont, bent forward, moving slow but with big intent, the heavy man's hurry, with Ms. Paige trotting along at my heels. I see the body and I move right to it, ignoring the crowds, ignoring the regular police, the capture crews, the gawkers—the shifting crowd that appears in the wake of a death, like insects coming up out of the ground after rain.

I push through the crowd, sighing. Growling, maybe. I'm making some kind of noise and all the regular cops and microphone operators and AV knuckleheads step back, wary. There's sweat gathering at the back of my collar, sweat beading under my beard. The early-day cool has burned away and I'm roasting in my blacks. I've never minded the discomfort of the uniform, to be honest with you, full true; I always feel like the discomfort is part of the job. The discomfort *is* the job. It marks you out, sets you apart. You get to a scene and you're already scowling, and everybody knows you're there on business. Everybody is watching the boundaries.

"Sir?" says Ms. Paige, and I raise one hand—*Gimme a second.*

This is nothing. This is an empty dumb nothing.

The dead man was a roofer, and he died falling off a roof. Those are the facts, and they're clear from the get-go, clear and plain. As Arlo would say, it's true as daylight, true as doors on houses. The mansion is one of these expansive but unassuming old places, with the poured concrete and the Spanish tile, with the wide white patio and the rambling lawn. A modest two stories but turreted with balconies and pilasters and stone-carved cherubs peeking out from the corners of the porch. I shield my eyes and look up to the spot on the red tile roof where the man scrambled before he fell, and I note the patch of loose and broken tiles. A single piece of fractured gutter juts out like a broken bone.

I turn from the house to the body of the man. All the angles add up. He fell from the high pitch of the roof, scrabbled in vain to catch himself on the downspout, and died when he hit the ground.

Now the man's body lies facing the sun, half on and half off the patio, eyes staring up at the golden blue of the morning. Wiry black hair and a wiry black mustache on a deeply tanned face. On the breast pocket of his green work shirt there's a logo of a hand holding a hammer. Here are his limbs, all four splayed out against the manicured lawn in ugly incongruous angles; here is the slick of blood expanding out from underneath him, slowly seeping into the manicured lawn, spreading dark red onto the bone-white patio stone. Here is the wild mosaic of broken roof tiles surrounding him—the armload he'd been holding when he tumbled, the explosive shatter pattern around him testament to the force of the fall. Here is the trowel, flung out on the lawn, a crust of dried caulk along its lip.

I get out my Day Book, pin down this first set of flat facts in black ink, pressing hard so the carbons catch it. And then—I don't know why exactly, but I do—I stay in my investigative crouch, a bear down low to the ground, paws planted to keep myself from toppling, roving my careful eyes over the man's dead face. His skull has split and spilled but the weathered face is intact, unharmed. The eyes above the mustache are open wide, very wide, and he's got this expression— and this is a subjective determination, this is hard to measure on the scale of what is and what is not So—but he looks *terrified*.

"Mr. Ratesic?" Paige is trying again, eager to learn, her own Day Book out and open. "What are you seeing?"

"Nothing," I say, and stand up, heaving my body straight. "Not a thing." I take one more look up at the house, shake my head. "You wanna tell me what we're doing here?"

"What?"

"What was the impetus for the presence of the Service? Why were we called?"

"Oh. Um—should we ask?"

She gestures to the knot of regular police who are hanging around close to the house, pretending to do things, stealing glances at the two of us over here by the body. The dead man's coworkers are doing the same thing.

And then there's a team from the Record, circling Paige and me, gathering reality as it unfolds: the capture operator and his backup; the microphone operator, hovering at the prescribed distance, professional headphones bulky over her ears; the archivist and the archivist's assistant.

"No," I tell Paige. "I don't want to ask them. I'm asking you. You looked at the call report, right? From Alvaro?"

"Yes. It just said they called it in. It said the Service was requested to discover the full and final truth. He said they said—"

"Who said?"

"The regular police."

"What did they say?"

"They said there was something anomalous in it."

"Anomalous?"

"Yes, that's—" She takes a step back from me. I've got my hands jammed in my pockets. I am scowling, bent forward. "That's what they said."

"Meaning what?"

"What?"

"What does that word mean?"

"Meaning . . . you mean what does 'anomalous' mean?"

"Yes, Ms. Paige. Shared understanding is a bulwark. Clear and agreed-upon definitions of common terms are defenses against infelicity. Words mean what they fucking mean. So, what is the meaning of the word 'anomalous'?"

My tone is not pleasant, I recognize that. If Arlo wants me to train this girl, well, then I'm going to train her. It is miserably hot out here—deadly hot. The sun is carving a rash into the skin above my collar.

" 'Anomalous' means"—Paige takes a breath and stands erect and gives it to me, word for word from the Basic Law—"a mismatch of facts possibly indicative of the presence of a falsehood or falsehoods obscuring the full and final truth of a given situation. Sir."

"Okay." I nod, maybe a little disappointed to be deprived of the opportunity to further chastise. "Good." Paige's nervous face shows a quick shimmering smile.

"So what do you think? Where's the anomaly?"

"I—" She looks at me. Then she looks back up at the house, back at the guy. "I don't see it. I think he fell off the roof."

"Yes," I say. "Me too."

"So maybe if we just—" She angles her head over to the crowd of officers again. "Maybe we ask?"

"Nope."

"But—"

"Nope. The regular police do their thing, and we get back in our car."

"But—wait."

I've started walking away, and Ms. Paige puts a hand on my

shoulder, and then shrinks back when I stop and turn to glare at her. A pause. A mourning dove makes its low coo from somewhere in the high trees. Along the lawn are the embedded captures, forever adding to the documented bulk of reality.

"Why would the cops call it in for nothing?"

"Free show." I gesture over at them, the workaday police in their blue hats and khaki pants, proving my point, the whole herd of them staring back at us gape-mouthed. "Because being an ordinary precinct policeman is boring, Ms. Paige, and rubbing up against the great and mysterious Speculative Service is not. So they call us and they don't lie, careful not to lie, but they say, 'Oh, well, we wonder if there is something weird going on here, we just really want you guys to put eyes on it,' but really it's them wanting to put eyes on us. There's not much we can do about it, it's the way of the world, but we don't have to indulge it by turning every tragic accident into the lie of the century."

"I see," she says. "Sure. I get it. But maybe . . ."

"What? Maybe *what*?" I feel anger boiling up in me, I hear my voice rising, but I can't stop. I didn't want to have a partner anyway. Hadn't I told Arlo that? Didn't I say so? "Do you have something to add, Ms. Paige?"

"No, just—" She looks longingly at the dead man. "Maybe if we just speculated—"

"Are you fucking kidding me?" I say it loud. I practically shout it. Somewhere, a rough-cut officer is turning down the monitor at a transcription station, grimacing at the burst of distorted output.

"No, sir. I just thought—"

"I already said there's no reason. You said it too, didn't you? No cause for spec. You fucking said it!"

I step closer to her, bellowing now, and she's smart enough to keep her mouth shut.

"There's a corpse on the lawn, a broken roof. It's a clear story, told by the flat facts. So you want to, what, start speculating right here at the scene? Maybe a low-flying plane knocked him off the roof. Maybe he was pushed by his evil twin!"

The boom mic dangles her pole as close as she dares; the capture op inches in.

"Listen to me, Paige: We start coming up with alternate realities, just for fun? Just so you can *practice?* Then guess what? We're committing our own assault on the Objectively So. Then *we* have become the liars."

Paige's chin has stiffened; she has crossed her arms. "I wasn't proposing that we *lie,* sir."

"Unwarranted speculation is no better than lying, Ms. Paige. It is worse. You want to see how it's done, here's how it's done: it's better when it's not done at all. Our job is to reinforce the Objectively So. Not conjure realities, every one of which might extend, evolve, metastasize." I am barking now, hollering, furious at the idea that she might not hear and understand what I'm telling her. "And *none* of those realities can be collected back once released. Our job is to find the facts and travel between them, walk carefully along the lines of what's true. And when we *do* speculate? When we *do* hypothesize? We do it carefully, conscientiously, in a controlled environment, and we don't do it at all unless and until the facts support it. The Speculative Service is a bulwark. What is the Speculative Service?"

"It's a bulwark."

"Goddamn right it is."

"Okay."

"Okay?"

"Okay."

"Now just—" I take a deep breath. Plant my hands on my hips, feel my feet beneath me. Try to get steady. "Would you give me a second to do the stupid job?"

I regret my outburst right away, of course.

That's me all over. Big and brave Mr. Laszlo Ratesic of the Service, dedicated officer of what is true, and a petty and short-tempered and thickheaded brute. Fully conscious of all his faults, wholly unable to correct them.

"Idiot," I call myself, and "asshole," as I prowl around to the rear of the house, to where the pool stretches out in a perfect pristine rectangle, its even blue surface shimmering with the shadow of the house itself. I've come around to the back to make sure there aren't any contraindicating facts, but really, just to have a second alone, alone with my lumbering thoughts, with my anger and self-recrimination—and with the capture op, lone representative of the Record. He has trailed me and stands now at a respectful ten-foot distance, his handheld trained on me where I stand heavily on the lawn. Reality in progress.

I think I've seen this op before—a shaggy-headed dude named Morgan or Marcus, something like that. Convention dictates that you ignore the Record's representatives, but a lot of people will say hello, give a nod or a smile. Not me. I keep my hands deep in my pockets, stare by turns at the roof, the lawn, the pool.

The sun scatters its golden light across the moment, glittering on the rooftop, glinting on the blue of the pool, dappling the deep green of the lawn. The damn roofer should have had the good sense to fall off *this* side of the house. He might have saved himself a broken neck. Might have drowned instead.

There's a back door, coming off the pool patio, a pair of elegant French doors that allow no clear view of whatever choices are made inside the house. I could take an extra five minutes to haul myself up onto the house, push a ladder against the stuccoed white walls, have a closer look at the spot where the roofing tiles gave way. Make sure. Make double and triple sure.

But I'd only be doing it by way of apology to Ms. Paige, a half-assed dumbshow of contrition: *Maybe you were right. Maybe there's one more flat fact to be found, another tile for us to lay into the mosaic.* Only I know there's not. What happened is what happened. It was a tragedy, maybe, but there is no anomaly, no lie hidden beneath the surface, like a snake under the soil. All the facts are flat and simple. All the lines between them are clean and direct.

I understand young Paige's eagerness, her fervency. The fundamental truth of her comes off the kid in waves. She wants to speculate because that's what Speculators do. We are the ones with the power, and the license, to truck with lies — we can sense them, we can handle them, and we are empowered to emit them ourselves. To construct different versions of the truth so each can be tested, so all might fall away until only the real one remains.

Ms. Paige just wants to do the damn work.

And here I come, condemning her for the crime of caring too much? Of hoping to find something beneath the surface?

The question is, what kind of fundamental truth is coming off *me?*

Back in front of the house, the ambulance has maneuvered onto the lawn and parked among the other emergency vehicles under the meager shade of the very tall palms, and now I shade my eyes and watch the men with their stretchers trot across the lawn to bear away the victim. The ambulance crew is trailed by its own Record team: more capture operators, more microphone bearers, more archivists. I watch them watching as the paramedics lift the body and arrange it on the stretcher.

"Sir?"

It's Paige again. Tapping on my shoulder. Chin set, eyes clear, bowed but unbent. She has some nerve, this one; she has some fight in her for sure.

And now the sunlight of good feeling fills me up, and I smile for what feels like the first time today. For the first time in a good long while.

"What is it, kid?"

"I decided to speak to some of the witnesses, sir. As long as I was waiting."

She winces, waiting for me to holler at her, but I don't.

"And?"

"And there's someone I think you should meet."

"It's Buddy Renner. Like, ah, like *runner*, person who runs, but with an *e* where the *u* goes— *Renner*. I'm thirty-six years old. I'm a manager. I was born in Pasadena, but I live down in South Beach now. These guys are my crew. I'm their manager. Not of the . . . not the whole *company*. I'm a field manager. I run this crew. Company manager is Lexie Herrimann. Two *rs*, two *ns*. *Herrimann*."

I put it all down in my Day Book, my stubby fat hundred-pager. I write in my book even though Renner's rambling testimony is being captured by my pinhole and by the captures along the gutters of the house and in the trees, and by the roving team too. There are plenty of Speculators who don't bother with the Day Book unless it's a matter of clear and immediate importance, something that'll surefire need to be on the Record. But I'm old-school. I like to do it right.

"I was the one that found him, actually," says Renner. "I got here at, ah, boy, I guess about—" He pauses, squeezes shut his eyes with the effort of recollection. "Six oh nine. That'll . . . That's . . . You can check the stretches on that, right? But so, okay, the crew was called for six thirty. So he was—Crane was—he was early, and I was early but not as early as him."

"You don't all arrive together?" I ask, pointing to the three pick-ups along the driveway. "In the trucks?"

"No. Ah—no, sir. You can. Some of the guys will come into the office, and—but, no. You can get to the work site, you get to the work site."

I nod for him to continue, and he swallows, takes a deep breath. He keeps glancing at my pinhole, same nervous little glance Ms. Tar-jin kept doing. There are plenty of ground and air captures around, so people don't understand why we have to have 'em too, the point of view, and maybe it's just psychological. Or maybe you can never have too much truth.

"And so I found him—on the ground there. Just—that's just how I found him."

The man is sputtering out facts, scattershotting every squib of truth that occurs to him. It's irritating, but useful for investigative purposes.

"Okay," I tell him, battling my impatience. "We got that."

Renner's a sweaty mess, in the same dark green shirt and dark green pants of the dead man and the rest of his crew: day laborers in heavy work clothes and sturdy boots, roofers and tar pourers and layers of tile, all of whom are still milling about in the unac-customed state of having nothing to do, waiting in the shade of the single broad-branched aspen under which they have been corralled. They're smoking, murmuring to one another, casting occasional nervous glances at all the cops and capture teams.

I reconfirm all the flat facts that Renner has already provided to Ms. Paige, who now stands beside me, reading along from her notes. Her Day Book, I notice, is gold, with gold-lined pages. I roll my eyes. There are no regulations on the matter. Nothing in the Ba-sic Law says the Service has to have dark-colored everything. But gold?

Renner and his crew—among them the dead man, Mose Crane—have been working the roofing job here at 3737 North Vermont for nineteen days, doing a series of patches and small repairs above the master bedroom suite.

"Officer Paige stated to me that you stated to her that Mr. Crane has a clean work record, as far as you know, with no previous reported accidents." I watch him, stone-faced. "Is that true?"

Renner blinks. "Is it true that I stated it to her?"

"No. Not—" I take a deep breath, in and then out again. Come on. "It's a two-step verification, Mr. Renner. Can you confirm that the information that you previously provided to Officer Paige was true and complete?"

"Oh yeah. Yes. T and c. Yes, sir. Uh-huh."

Paige writes in her book. Renner wipes his forehead with a handkerchief, the same deep green as his work clothes.

All the unspoken truths of this conversation are clear to me, the invisible beams undergirding the surface truths. Renner is frightened of me, of me and my big ugly face and also of the Service itself. He is afraid not of being caught lying, because he knows he's not lying, but of being *thought* to be lying. He's afraid that out of his anxiety about being thought to be lying he will stumble into blurting out some small untruth and I'll catch it on the air and he'll have caused his own worst fear to come true.

I could put him at ease, if I wanted to. I know very well he's hewing to the line, as best he's able. I've seen plenty of liars in my day. I've seen their distorted asseverations feathering the air as they emerge from the false shapes of their mouths. I've stared into their furtive eyes; I've smelled the stink of bullshit rising off them in waves. This man Renner is telling the truth. But he looks away from me while he's talking, finds the more sympathetic eyes of Officer Paige.

And she, meanwhile, is dying to be like me, a pillar of the law, a servant of the good and true, but she's got enough of the civilian still in her bones that when meeting a stranger she wants to hold his hand and tell him, "It's okay, it's okay, there's nothing to be afraid of."

All of these structural underpinnings are clear to me, as visible as underwater architecture, but irrelevant. I have my Day Book out. I have work to do.

I coax from Renner the information that Crane worked six of the last seven days.

"And actually," he adds suddenly, "he wasn't on the schedule for today. Did I already say that?"

"No," I say. I stop writing. I hold him with my gaze. "You didn't already say that."

"I'm sorry." He winces. "I'm really sorry."

"So wait, Mr. Renner," Paige says. "He wasn't supposed to be here?"

"No, miss. Ma'am." Renner shakes his head urgently. "He wasn't. Do you want me—" He stops, tilts his head forward. "Should I show you the schedule?"

"Yeah." I hold out my hand. "You should."

He digs it out of his backpack, a thin sheaf notebook with a crinkled yellow cover, bent at all four corners, and I aim my pinhole at the book, capture the relevant page, and hand it to Paige.

"I've already got it, sir."

I look at her. "Get it again."

"Yes, sir. Of course, sir." She gets it again.

"Had this man, Crane, given you any indication that he was intending to come in today?"

"No, sir," says Renner.

"And is there any reason you can think of that he would have done so?"

"You mean . . . any reason he would have given me—"

"No." I sigh. *People.* "Any reason he would have come in today?"

"No, sir. No."

Paige is looking back and forth between me and the witness, her brown eyes wide, absorbing, watching, learning.

"What about coming in early?"

"What—do you mean—"

"Any reason to explain why he would do such a thing?"

"No."

"Did any of your guys *usually* start early?"

"No. I mean—" He pauses, canvasses his mind for stray facts. "Not that I know of."

"Any reason why Crane might have?"

Renner shrugs.

Paige looks at me, and I shrug too. Whatever the reason that Crane was at work unscheduled, we have to face the possibility that he never put it on the Record. Never wrote it down, never mentioned it to a coworker, never muttered it to himself, meaning it never got captured, transcribed, and preserved. This small piece of reality, this flat fact—*the reason Mose Crane came to work even though he wasn't supposed to*—died when his head hit the ground and the neurons in his brain stopped firing. A subsidiary victim of the larger tragedy.

It catches me in the gut, a quick surge of mourning for a piece of truth that has been and is gone.

"No, actually, if anything, now that I think of it, Crane was usually *late.*"

"Oh yeah?"

"He was always working a bunch of jobs is the thing. Like, he worked for us, he worked for other folks. Freelance gigs. A lot of times he'd be coming right to us from another thing."

"Roofing?"

"Or—yeah, I think. Or other kinds of construction, contracting. I remember him coming in late one morning, bunch of months ago, already half dead from working all night. Working under the table on some mansion in the Hills, something. Nobody likes cheap labor more than rich people, you know?"

I nod. Deep truth, that right there. "And was that unusual?"

"Um," he says cautiously. "I don't know what you mean by 'unusual.'"

"Do other guys do that?"

"Oh. Sometimes."

"Was he working another job at the present time?"

"I don't think so. I don't know. No? I'm sorry. I'll have to check."

Renner is going to have to check on a lot of things. I write down all that he has told us, pushing each flat fact hard into the paper so the thin carbon layer can do its magic and transfer it to the dupe page underneath. The tip of the pen is like a needle, and each fact is a butterfly, and what we do is we pin it to the board, collect it and catalog it for later consideration. Paige is in the corner of my eye with a small smile at the corners of her lips, because she has discovered more facts, proved to herself, if not to me, that there is more here than meets the eye, and maybe she's right and maybe she's not.

The man was named Crane, and he worked more jobs than this one.

And this man Crane was at work today though not scheduled, for reasons no one can say.

He was here early, earlier than anyone else.

Each is an interesting fact, and each fact, each piece of truth, is valuable and precious in and of itself, every fact beloved in our good and golden world. But Paige can smile all she wants to—I'm still not seeing any way to arrange these new facts in a shape that contravenes the base truth of the morning: *He was a roofer and he fell off the roof.* Still, I write it all down. I transfer each truth to my Day Book, pushing down hard, and when the conversation is over Renner stamps my pad and I stamp his, and he stamps Paige's pad and she stamps his too, and all of us have officially had this conversation and this conversation will always have occurred. It is on the Record.

And then I hear the distinct sound of a door closing. Someone is emerging from the house. The capture ops swivel to catch the new arrival, and so does Paige, and so do I.

4.

"**A COW** has four stomachs."

"A person has one."

"These are facts."

"These things are so."

"What are you doing here, Mr. Speculator?"

"Oh, you know," I say. "Working." I point to the patch of broken grass, splotched with blood and boot prints. "A guy died."

"So I heard."

I shake hands with Captain Elena Tester and then, after a pause, we hug, very briefly. A small capture crew, two guys, has peeled off from the main scene to get us from additional angles. There's a bank of audios out here too, planted along the edge where the lawn meets the driveway, pure-audio captures angling their motion-sensing bulbs toward us, silent listeners in the grass.

"It's nice to see you, Laszlo."

"Yeah. You too."

And it is nice to see her—of course it is. I mean, what am I going to do, lie? It's nice to see her, and it also stings; it's nice to see her, and it also brings me right back close to a whole bank of memories I spend a lot of time trying to avoid.

"So, what? Falls off the roof, right?" says Tester. "Dies on the ground?"

"That's certainly what the flat facts suggest."

She glances at the spot on the lawn, the bent green stalks, patches of red blood. The body is long gone, en route to the morgue, where the doctors will do their thing, gather up any final facts from inside the dead man's body before they put it underground.

"So who called you people?" she asks.

I adjust my pinhole. "You don't know?"

"Why would I know?"

"What?"

We peer at each other, mutually bemused, and then we both start laughing at the same time. I like Elena well enough. Not a lot, but I don't really like anybody a lot. Elena Tester is a colleague, in that loose definition of the word that includes all law enforcement officers in the Golden State, or might even take in the whole government, depending on your definition of "colleague." The Speculative Service and the regular police operate in different but frequently overlapping realms, and Elena and I have worked together a couple dozen times over the years. Mainly I know her personally.

"It's been a while," says Elena softly, and I nod, start to say "Yup," and because I'm a hollow version of the sturdy old bear I think I am, my throat catches on the small flat word, so I just swallow it back and don't say anything. Because of course I mainly know Elena through Silvie, and in the long declining curve of my marriage, I haven't seen much of Silvie's friends. Not lately.

It takes me a second to fight out of that little prison of a moment, and Tester gives me the time I need. She's a pretty decent soul, Captain Tester, not that she shows it off too often. Short-haired and tight-featured and direct, she's a tough nut, professional and severe, droll when she wants to be. Like all regular police, she wears an octagonal blue cap with a short brim and a pinhole capture in the center of it to gather up reality. Right now it's pointed at me as mine is pointed at her, our respective points of view entering simultaneously into the Record.

"You were going to tell me who called it in," she says.

"It's not clear," I say. "Old Vasouvian got it as a tip from one of yours, some overeager officer of the law, and instead of tossing it in the junk heap as was most likely merited, Alvaro sent us out."

" 'Us'? I thought you folks worked alone. You especially."

"Oh, I do, Elena. Believe me, I prefer to."

I tilt my head toward Ms. Paige. "I'm supervising someone. The, uh—" For some reason it's embarrassing. I jut my big chin toward the trees. "Young lady over there."

Officer Paige is diligently reinterviewing her way through the crowd of Crane's coworkers, scribbling furiously in her gilded Day Book.

"Laszlo the teacher. Wise mentor. How's *that* playing out?"

"Oh, you know. Fine. Although I did shout at her for no reason."

"Laz."

"Not no reason." I cross my arms. "She was getting ahead of the facts. Unwarranted speculation." I scratch the heat on the back of my neck. "It wasn't a big deal, really. I guess I took a bit of a tone."

"*You* did?" says Tester, wide-eyed. "I'm shocked."

"Ha ha."

She is not actually shocked, obviously. It is a joke—not a lie but a distortion of truth for intentionally comedic effect, understood as false on its face by everyone present, not to mention anyone listening in the provisional office right now, or listening later for the Record. You know all this already; you know the rules. You are familiar with the Basic Law. Humor causes no oscillation in the So, any more than any other form of small social falsehood: obvious hyperbole, inoffensive teasing, plain flattery—the whole constellation of innocuous and lubricating half-truths.

"Okay. Well." Elena shrugs. "Let me know, will you, if there's anything to it."

"To what?"

"To this. The—" She points at the lawn. "The matter at hand."

"Sure."

"Hey. Are you okay, Laszlo?"

I sigh. "No."

"Is it Silvie?"

"For the most part."

"You miss her?"

"Yes. Yes. I do."

Tester nods. That's all she'll get out of me, and she knows it. No deeper forms of truth will reveal themselves, and she knows well enough not to dig. A question is a cup you hold out to be filled, and there are those who will always fill it to the brim, pour in all the truth they can think of, until it overflows and spills out and spreads across the table. That's not me. Me, I'll give you what's precisely true and no more; I'll answer your question and shut up.

"Captain Tester? What about you?"

"What?"

"What are *you* doing here?"

She furrows her brow, just for an instant, as if surprised by the question, and I don't know if it's my own state—exhausted, hot, irritated at Ms. Paige and irritated at my own irritation—but for whatever reason my attention goes keen around Tester's momentary pause. Suddenly the clean sunlit air is alive with drifting particles, flickers and flecks. I don't know what.

"I caught it on the scanner," Captain Tester is saying. "I live near here, you know? On Talmadge." I'm watching her face. I don't know what I look like to her, I don't know if she can tell what I'm thinking, but she keeps talking. "Sometimes I like to stop by a scene.

Sometimes these . . ." Another half-second pause. "Anyway. As long as I was in the area, I thought I'd babysit the homeowner while the scene officers did their thing. Take something off their plate. You know the figure?"

"Of course."

"Just procedure," she says with a final nod, and I'm wondering at her words, wondering at myself for wondering. Is Captain Tester reminding me of the division between our respective domains, between the world of police business and that of speculative affairs? Is she brushing me back? Does she know she's doing it? The wind teases at the tops of the fat-trunked aspens and the skinny palms that line the yard. The lenses of the captures glint in the greenery.

"Anyway." Captain Tester smiles, gives me a reassuring pat on the shoulder, colleague to colleague, and heads back to her car.

Officer Paige is over on the far side of the lawn. She has finished with the workmen and she's watching me. She has been watching the whole time; I can tell from here that she has never lost track of me for a second.

"Hey," I say. "Paige." I crook a finger and here she comes, ardent student, springing across the lawn like a deer.

"Yes, sir. What is it?"

I refocus my attention on Tester, who's climbing into her unmarked car. She raises a hand to me. A captain of the regular police.

"Do we know whose house this is?"

5.

People see us—people like Renner, I mean, and even people like Elena Tester, people who ought to know better—and get weird. Wary. They talk slow or fast, fidget from side to side or stand statue still, arms crossed, protecting the midsection as if from a blow. Afraid of the rules we enforce and the punishments we are empowered to dole out.

But what you should be afraid of, and what I think most people really are afraid of, deep underneath—buried truth, truth of the soul—is what would happen if we were gone.

What they ought to be afraid of is the truth of the world beyond the Golden State, the truth of the wilderness, which is no truth at all.

I'm talking about what happened to the rest of it, to the world beyond our world of bright blue skies and ocean breezes and crystalline epistemology.

We are the world that is left, and the future of the Golden State depends on the fierce defense of what is Objectively So. It depends on the transcriptionists and archivists and librarians of the Permanent Record and the collectors and checkers and double-checkers of the *Trusted Authority;* it depends on the Acknowledged Experts, up on Melrose Avenue, scurrying from committee room to committee room; and it depends somehow on us, on me, me in my rumpled suit, clinging to the steering wheel like a ship's captain, looking longingly at the House of Pies as it sails by on Vermont Avenue. Aysa Paige riding shotgun upright and at attention, her excitement dimmed not a bit by her first foray into the field.

It's already eleven. I know that to be a true fact because the bells are ringing from the high tower of the old movie palace on Sunset, and strangers are stopping on the street to tell each other it's eleven, agreeing that it's true, shaking hands and reinforcing what is Objectively So.

I wonder fleetingly what Silvie is doing right at this exact minute; this is something I used to do all the time, before we went our separate ways. I would pause somewhere in the middle of my day and wonder what she was doing, *right at this exact minute*. It would be the thought of her, out there in the city, maybe filing forms in her orderly sub-basement office, maybe meeting her friend Lily for silken tofu soup on Beverly Boulevard, just Silvie out there doing her thing—the thought of her out enjoying the universe would reliably buoy my own dull spirits. That's love, as best as I can figure it: love isn't how you feel when you're together, it's how you feel, how often you feel it, when you're apart.

"All right, so look," I say abruptly. "I gotta say something." And Ms. Paige immediately says "Yes, sir," and I immediately stop.

"Yes? Mr. Ratesic?"

I sigh. I hate this conversation. I hate conversations, just in general. I wish I was alone. I wish I could stop, alone, at Donut Sam's or one of the other greasy anonymous places with the laminated posters in the windows, with the cheap tin napkin dispensers on the grimy plastic tables, with the rows of colorful fluorescent doughnuts under glass like costume jewelry.

"So," I say to Paige. "You were right."

"Yes, sir."

"About this event. This incident."

"Yes, sir."

"Stop calling me 'sir.' We are both officers of the same service, Ms. Paige."

"Okay."

"Okay?"

"Okay. So—but—" She clears her throat. She looks at me. "Do we do it *now?*"

"No." I sigh, shake my head. "And don't ask again because I will tell you. Okay?"

"Okay."

"I will tell you when it's time to speculate."

We've come all the way downtown on Vermont Avenue by now. We're passing the blocks of factories, long, low smokestack buildings pumping out textiles and tin cans and small electronics, we're passing the wheat fields and cotton fields and dope fields, all the architecture of our self-sufficiency. Through downtown and out again into University City.

"First we need a few more facts."

"You people friends of his?"

The woman who's appeared a few steps down from the landing wears a long loose-fitting black garment, some kind of sweater, apparently, although it's almost like a cape, the way it drapes around her thin shoulders, hanging down with ragged majesty onto the unswept concrete landing.

The apartment block where Crane lived is organized around a flat stone courtyard, gray steps leading up to each individual unit, cement catwalks between the doors, like a motel. A poky little capture observes from above the doorway, green light blinking.

After two minutes of knocking and trying to see in through the small smudged window, Ms. Paige and I have just about satisfied ourselves that there is no one home, and I have concluded it's time to force my way in. I've been in the Service for nineteen years, but I was regular police once upon a time. I know how to force a door when I need to.

But here instead is this funny old lady, grinning up at us in her black caul of a sweater, wearing a lot of clunky jewelry, with her skinny arms crossed over her chest.

"Nope," I tell her. "Not friends. I'm Mr. Ratesic, and this is Ms. Paige. We're with the Speculative Service. A dolphin is a mammal."

"So's a bat but not so is a bee. I'm Dolly Aster. I live downstairs." I tip my pinhole and she smiles impishly, interest flashing in her milky eyes. Her hair is wild, curly and gray. "Don't know that I've seen a pair of you before. I thought you people traveled alone. Like wolves."

"No, ma'am," I say. "Not wolves."

"I said *like* wolves, young man. It's a figure. Do you people do figures of speech, or is an idiom considered a species of lie?"

"Idioms don't register as falsehoods, ma'am," says Paige, quickly and authoritatively, giving out the Basic Law like she's one of the recordings made for schoolchildren. "Given that their intention and literal meaning can be gleaned from context and familiarity. They're like humorous remarks in that regard."

"Well, aren't you sharp," says Aster, her grin broadening. "Sharp as a box of tacks."

Unlike Renner, back at the mansion, unlike most people, Ms. Aster seems to show no sign of intimidation or nervousness in our presence. To the contrary, she's fascinated, inching up the stairwell with one old hand clutching the banister, licking her lips. "The

Speculative Service on my humble stairwell in a fearsome little pack." Her small features narrow to a fascinated point, savoring the mysterious syllables of the occupation. "And to what do I owe the pleasure?"

"We're here about your tenant, Mose Crane."

"What did he do?" she says. "He murder someone?"

"No," I say, thinking, *Interesting assumption.* "No, ma'am. He's dead."

"Murdered?"

I'm about to say *no,* and I find that I can't do it. My throat refuses to form the word, my instinct refuses to certify it as part of what's So. So I merely smile, dance sideways around the question. "We are hoping to take a look at his apartment. Hoping you can help us out with that."

I'm digging her, this old lady—she has a tough sinewy look about her, like an old snake, not dangerous but built to navigate danger. She hands me her Day Book and I hand her mine, and I stamp hers and she stamps mine, and then she does the same with Paige.

"So. What's it like," she asks, "enforcing a world of absolute truth?"

"I don't know," says Paige, deadpan. "It's my first day."

Ms. Aster likes that a lot. She laughs, loud and cackling, hands on her hips, and gives me a wink. "You better watch out for this one, young man. Watch out!"

I raise my eyebrows, give her a tight smile, indulging the joke, but Aster has got it wrong—dead wrong, 180 degrees in the wrong—which she's old enough to know. I do not believe and have never believed that our mission is to enforce a world of absolute truth. If such a world could be built we would have long ago built it already.

People are going to lie: they want to—they *need* to. Lying is born into the species. You know this is true as well as I do. There is something perfect in a lie, something seductive, addictive; telling a lie is like licking sugar off a spoon. Think of children, think of how children lie all the time. We have imaginary friends, we blame our misbehavior on our playmates or our siblings, we claim not yet to have had dessert so we can cadge a second cookie. Me and Charlie used to have contests, as a matter of fact, two brothers each trying to slip a fake fact under the other one's radar: *"I beat up a kid at school"; "I saw that dog, the neighbor's dog, jump over a fence"; "I'm the fastest runner in my class—"*

You go back far enough in history, ancient history, and you find a time when people were never taught to grow out of it, when every adult lied all the time, when people lied for no reason or for the most selfish possible reasons, for political effect or personal gain. They lied and they didn't *just* lie; they built around themselves whole carapaces of lies. They built realities and sheltered inside them. This is how it was, this is how it is known to have been, and all the details of that old dead world are known to us in our bones but hidden from view, true and permanent but not accessible, not part of our vernacular.

It was this world but it was another world and it's gone. We are what's left. The calamity of the past is not true, because it is unknown. There could only be hypotheses, and hypotheses are not the truth. So we leave it blank. Nothing happened. Something happened. It is gone.

What we know of the past is enough to be afraid, enough to build this world, our good and golden world, around preventing a repeat of the mistakes that destroyed the world before.

The preservation of reality's integrity is the paramount duty of the citizenry and of the government alike. What kind of mad society would be organized otherwise?

I shake my head a little, out here on Crane's landing, and blink myself back into the moment. Into reality unfolding. "So listen, Ms. Aster. Do you have a way of getting into the apartment?"

"How about a key? Will a key do?"

There is something grimly tragic about a Golden State apartment with no outdoor space: no balcony, no patio, nowhere to go and feel the blessing of sunshine on your cheeks. Crane's U City apartment is grim and dark, a second-story bat's nest, three narrow rooms connected by a carpeted hallway. Out the two small windows there's a sorry view of Ellendale Place, stray sheets of *Authority* and hamburger wrappers tumbling down the street, the roots of trees warping the sidewalk stones into strange shapes, like children hiding under a rug.

I wander through Crane's apartment slowly, following no particular rhythm or route, developing a sense of the man's life from the dull shapes and muted colors of his habitat: from the pair of beat-up shoes at the door, apparently the only pair he owned besides the pair he died in; from the three faded family photographs, tacked up unframed, brother and sister and mom faintly smiling, squinting into the sun on the pier; from the tiny kitchen table with the one chair, the coffeemaker with two-day-old grounds still thick and gritty in the filter. The fridge is mostly beer, the garbage mostly takeout containers.

No speculation required. This was the home of a bachelor who worked long days at hard, sunburnt labor, who came home to piss and sleep and shower and get ready to go back to work.

Paige is pursuing her own slow perusal of the apartment, and she has her Day Book out to gather all these same lonely details. One armchair, one floor lamp, one cup at the kitchen table. One book-shelf, squat and brown.

I take a closer look at the books and find all the usual stuff: a volume of *Maps and Legends,* a copy of *Recent Reference* and one of *What Things Are Made Of,* this year's edition of *Flat Facts for Every-day Use.* All of the volumes produced by the Publishing Arm, the State's constant effort to ensure that we all know the same things, that we all know everything. All of the books look basically brand new, as pristine as when the State published them. Crane, I fig-ure, was lacking in either the time or the inclination to do a lot of reading. Probably both.

Not surprisingly, the man has hardly got any novels at all—although there is, right on the top shelf, a copy of *Past Is Prologue.* I lay two fingers reverently on the wide scarlet spine. I've read it—you've read it—*everybody's* read the big book, most of us many more times than once. But I slip Crane's copy into my hand nevertheless and flip through it slowly, feeling its words under my fingertips, giving myself the gift of its serenity. I fight an urge to just sink down to the floor and read the thing, pick a spot at random in the long and beautiful history of the first days and years of the Golden State, of our seven heroic founders and the obstacles they overcame and the gifts they left in their passing. Before I put it back I find one of its many black pages and place my hand down on it flat, feeling that power. Black pages; invis-ible truths; redacted facts about the time before, unknown and unknowable.

Man, this novel, I think, sliding it reluctantly back into place on Crane's top shelf. So fucking good.

"Anything?" Ms. Paige says, from the other side of the room, and I say, "Nope." And then, "Wait. Yes."

All of the man's books are like his copy of *Past Is Prologue,* showing little evidence of ever having been read, except for one, jammed in on the bottom shelf, and when I bend down with a grunt to see what it is, it's the fucking *dictionary.*

I turn it over in my hand. *The Everyday Citizen's Dictionary,* one of the little hardback editions with the cheap paper sleeve.

I tilt back the brim of my pinhole and look closer. *The Everyday Citizen's Dictionary* is what it sounds like, a quick and dirty lexicon for basic use, and judging by the wear on the spine there's no question that this one has been heavily used. I feel like I know Mose Crane just a little bit better than I did a second ago, and I like him a little bit better, because this book has been read, and it's great, it's damn *terrific,* because who reads the dictionary? It makes me wish for a sideways moment that I was at home, right now, in my own small gloomy lair, sitting in a heavy chair and reading the dictionary. Adding small facts, bits of truth, *the meanings of words,* like stray twigs to my nest.

Everybody has a dictionary; you've got to have one. *Common knowledge is a bulwark.* But——I smile, holding the dictionary in my palm——but nobody sits around *reading* the damn thing.

"Hey. Mr. Speculator." Ms. Aster is pointing at the sofa. "Is she all right?"

"What?"

It's Paige, standing by the sofa, frozen in place with one hand in the air, the other hand on her hip, her mouth slightly open like she was about to say something and then just stopped.

"Hey," I say. "Ms. Paige?"

I snap my fingers.

"Goodness. What is going *on?*" Aster snaps her fingers too.

"Paige," I say, a little louder, and she blinks, straightens up.

"Yeah. Sorry. But——are you——are you *getting* that?"

"Getting——" I look around. Now I recognize what I am seeing

in her eyes, even though I've never worked with her before, never seen the way she reacts, because we all react differently. But it's happening to her like it did to me two hours ago at Terry's, when I found myself unable to continue with the simple act of living because the air had been bent by the Tarjin boy's insistent lie. Now, though, I'm clean. I'm undisturbed. I'm not catching anything. The only person in the room besides us two Specs is frank old Ms. Aster, and Aster isn't even talking, she's just staring, grinning, loving this new wrinkle, the unaccustomed excitement, the witchy strangeness, Speculators on her property . . . and now this, whatever this is.

But what is this?

It's not a deceitful utterance that Paige has got on to, that much is clear, it's something deeper, something in the bones of the moment. She is standing there in the thrall of some dissonance, and I am not, and this is why Arlo wanted her in my car in the first place. *She's like Charlie* is what I'm thinking, and the thought is so clear and complete it is like snapping awake from a long and dreamless sleep.

She is like Charlie.

"What are you catching, Ms. Paige?" I say, and she doesn't answer, just stands there uncertainly.

"Tell me where it's coming from."

"I'm not sure."

"Aysa. Where is it?"

"I—" She shrugs. She looks around. She takes one step toward the kitchen, then one step back toward the door. She can't figure it. It's like we're kids and we're playing a game—it's *hotter . . . colder*— with Ms. Aster a fascinated observer.

Then I get it, it rushes up in me, solution to problem, because maybe I don't have what Paige has, maybe I'm no Charlie, but I've been doing this a long fucking time, okay? I'm slow but I ain't stupid.

"Ms. Aster," I say. "Are Crane's boxes on-site?"

"Of course they are," she replies, with a proud thrusted chin. "What kind of place do you think I'm running here?"

6.

The Permanent Record is downtown, right across the Plaza from the Speculative Service, but the Provisional Record is everywhere—in storerooms and spare rooms and sheds, in crawl spaces underneath homes and attics atop them.

Aster's, she tells us, is in the basement, so off we go in a small parade, marching in single file back onto the exterior landing, down to the courtyard, through a narrow entrance between apartment doors, and one more flight down. Ms. Aster leads the way with her flashlight, me just behind her, and Paige bringing up the rear, tuned in, keen.

The basement is still and cold and full of boxes, lit by three banks of flickering fluorescents. A record room like other record rooms all over the State, in every residential building and private home, climate-controlled and easily accessible.

Everybody keeps everything. You know it; I know it. *Archiving is a bulwark.*

At age seventeen you're issued your first package from the Preservation Office, a full set of boxes and bags accompanied by four small-type pages of instructions and warnings, making detailed reference to the relevant text of the Basic Law. It's thrilling at the outset, to come out of your parents' boxes and assume this solemn responsibility borne by all good and golden citizens: taking the time every evening, before it gets to be midnight or before you go to sleep, whichever comes first, to curate the day that has passed. To compile all interaction stamps, all recorded observations, all receipts and paperwork from the day that was, gather it all up into a Mylar bag, seal it and mark it and file it among all the other days of your life. We carry our individual archives, our Provisional Records, moving through the present with our past enturtled on our backs.

Otherwise how would everybody know, for sure and forever, that the things that have happened have actually happened? How would the law know for sure? How would the future?

Of course, most daily bags remain sealed for the rest of your life, because most truth never needs to be unsealed. But if the State should need it, there it is: every day can be reviewed if necessary, every flat fact can be exhumed, held up to the light, double-checked and reverified, compared and contrasted with other relevant archives. And then one day death comes, and a team from the Record comes in afterward, bears your papers away, and your Provisional becomes a part of the Permanent, one more tributary flowing into the main trunk.

They'll be here by the end of the day for Crane's records, I don't doubt, and I'm glad to miss 'em. Strange people, the death collectors. I've known a few.

Aster has her tenants' respective archives organized into different areas of the room, and she finds Crane's section with no trouble. I step around her and hover my flashlight over the topmost box and nudge it with my toe.

"Is this the first pallet?" I ask her.

"First and last."

I look at her in the dim light, and then back at the pallet. A single pallet. Six boxes.

"Are you sure?"

"Yes."

"Absolutely sure?"

"What am I going to do?" she says. "Lie?"

The room feels colder than it was. Colder and darker. I glance at Ms. Paige, and she looks uneasy, standing behind me with her hands on her hips.

"Ms. Aster." My voice is in neutral. My mind is going ten different ways at once. "How old was this man again? If that's a fact you're—"

"Fifty-four," says Aster, busybody, knowledge collector. She knows.

I grunt. I crouch to the pallet. Fifty-four years. Same as me. I shift my weight to talk over my shoulder to Paige.

"Hey. What's your gut?"

"What?"

She looks caught out, confused. But this is how it works. This is the job. Something feels wrong, you make a decision. Anomaly, whispers of anomaly. What do you do?

"Come on, Ms. Paige. Come on. Your gut."

"Dig," she says quietly. "My gut is we dig."

"Okay." I shrug. "So? Dig."

She crouches down beside me and we open our satchels. I keep all the special small tools for this kind of investigation in a zippered inner pocket: the slicing tool for clean-cutting dailies, the highly specialized adhesive tape for officially and properly sealing them back up and stamping them *opened/examined* next to today's date. We pry off the lid of the first box and start digging.

Crane has got everything in order, just like he's supposed to, just like everybody: each day's pocket flotsam is gathered together in its own Mylar bag, each week of days is gathered together in a durable hard-paper sack and sealed. We paw through Mose Crane's days, and we are both thinking the same thing: they are thin. Some days only have one or two pieces of paper in them, one or two conversations, or just a couple of receipts, or none. Aster watches Paige and me, unsealing thin bag after thin bag—days without incident, nothing worth recording, no transactions, no conversations at all. There's one Saturday, three weeks old, with a parking ticket, an unlucky lottery card, and a note to himself, torn from the corner of his Day Book, scrawled in pencil, indecipherable.

Most days are even thinner. Employer-stamp slips and nothing else: Crane worked and went home, worked and went home. The combined Record of his life adds up to just six boxes, and six boxes is *nothing*. I've got nineteen boxes, personally. Same number of years, thirteen more boxes of days. Receipts for beers with friends from work, carbons of wedding invitations, of *my* wedding invitation, pictures and postcards and memories.

And listen, I'm fucking *nobody*. I'm no social butterfly. I don't like people, I don't talk to strangers, I don't have hobbies. After fifty-four years of wandering around our good and golden land, some people have got dozens of boxes, hundreds.

But our man Crane is sitting on six. *Six.*

And listen, there's a part of me processing this as a trained Speculator, a law enforcement official with a wealth of institutional experience on which to draw. *Six boxes isn't much, but it's not off the charts.* Some people are just lonely, that's all. Some people don't get out. It's just more evidence of the kind of life that Crane led, like the dumpy apartment, like the single ratty pair of shoes: introverted, dull, absent of incident. A bachelor, a day laborer, working and eating and sleeping.

"You doing all right, Ms. Paige?" I am bending to the second to last of the boxes.

"No," she says, a strangled single syllable, and I turn. I didn't notice, but Paige at some point has stopped digging. She's come up out of her crouch halfway and is frozen like that, legs bent, one hand over her mouth. Aster has lapsed into expectant, curious silence, her lips pursed and her eyes caught and held.

"Paige?"

Nothing. Here we go again. "Ms. Paige?"

"There's—" She shuts her eyes, longer than a blink, tries again. "There's—"

"Ms. Paige?"

"There's—look—" She swallows hard, and I swear I can feel it, the pulse of pain that jams her up a second, before she manages to explain, sticking her hand into the one box I haven't gotten to yet, the most recent one. *"Look."*

"What am I looking at?"

"There are two weeks missing."

COMMENCEMENT

And so the novel begins!

After several episodes of raw investigation, in which our curiosity is piqued and our appetite whetted, our attention now returns to the majestic glass-walled downtown office complex that houses the Speculative Service, in company with our hero, the most remarkable representative of that selfsame agency!

Our readers will not need to be reminded of the various mechanisms that work in concert to protect the Golden State from the ever-present danger of falsehood in its variegated forms. These mechanisms include, for example, the *Trusted Authority*, daily beacon of new and accurate information; the *Gazetteer* and *Book of What Is So* and all the other volumes of reference, regularly issued and updated by the Publishing Arm to disseminate good and golden facts so that we all may operate, in all places and at all times, with the benefit of common understanding; and the "comprehensive capture mechanisms," or simply "captures," those ubiquitous small recording devices, some carefully hidden and some purposefully visible, forever documenting what happens, at all times and in all places, so that reality can be preserved for later reference. So there may be one reality, true and permanent and universal.

And of course the Record itself, where the events which occur are forever housed, so that no one may say one thing and subsequently claim not to have said it; so that no controversy may go unresolved; so that no disruption of fact can long go uncorrected.

Preeminent among our truth-defending mechanisms, though, is the Speculative Service, that elite corps of law enforcement officials who are solely empowered, and uniquely qualified, to detect and destroy the stuff of lies. A created member of our Service has cultivated that superior discernment necessary to catch falsehoods as they emerge, and the skill to conjure falsehoods of his or her own. Confronted with a "mystery," a blank space on the canvas of reality, the Speculator concocts potential truths, in order to test the plausibility of each until he or she deduces what really happened. Like the poison control man, like the radiologist, like the firefighter, Speculators are licensed to deal in danger, and they do so bravely, for the preservation of what is real, and for the protection of us all.

Three cheers for the Service!

And three cheers for Mr. Ratesic, who even now—"now" in the sense of "at the time he emerges in the telling of the tale, at the time you, dear reader, are given the pleasure of joining his company"—even now Mr. Ratesic is confronted with a set of flat facts which, though each taken individually is true, piled together form a cairn, arranged with fiendish purpose to cover over a yawning darkness...

7.

"Cigarette?"

"No thank you, sir."

"Come on."

I am digging through my pockets one at a time, scowling and huffing. You might think that after all these years of stalking the world in this damn coat I'd have decided where the cigarettes go, but I'm not that smart. At last I find the pack, yank out two smokes together, and poke one at Paige.

"Here. Take one."

"No thank you."

I feel myself bristle, I don't know why. I light my cigarette, inhale deeply, and then exhale slowly. We're still on Ellendale, standing beside the car, across the street from the courtyard building, looking up at Crane's window, the same window we were looking out of a half hour ago. What if we could see ourselves? Look out on us from the window, while looking up at ourselves from out here?

"All right, look. Ms. Paige."

"Yes?"

She looks over. Something is different in my voice. Or I hope it is. I'm trying to give her a softer surface. For the time being, anyway.

"Ms. Paige. First of all, like I said, you don't have to call me 'sir,' okay? I'm just like you. All of this, the junior-senior Speculator stuff, it's just words." I take a second drag. I feel smoldering, cratered, like a volcano. Like a fire creature breathing smoke. "Rank within the Service is not important, okay? Not to people who matter. So you can call me Mr. Ratesic, or"—I've come this far, right?—"Laszlo."

"Okay."

"Or Laz. I don't fucking care."

"Okay."

I glare at her.

"Okay, Mr. Ratesic."

I laugh, just a little, a quiet rasp. "I'll take it."

I indulge another drag, studying Crane's windows, wondering if he ever stood there and took a long moment like this, contemplating the street. I'm guessing not. I hold smoke in my mouth, enjoy the way it feels on the back of my throat.

"What I'm saying is, you might find that it helps. The smoking, I mean. When your throat hurts."

"It doesn't." I look at her. She shrugs. "I don't actually get that."

I scratch my neck. "You don't get what?"

"The throat. The eyes. Uh, coughing. And so on."

"You don't get any of it?"

"No."

"No symptoms of any kind?"

"No."

"When you're seeing lies, when you're feeling them? You don't feel any physical—any reactionary effects at all?"

"I don't, Mr. Ratesic." She gives me a small apologetic smile. "I really don't."

"No shit?" I murmur, the words coming out soft with the smoke, like the memory of old words.

"No, sir." She winces. "Sorry. No, Laszlo."

I'm catching a chill off that information, as crazy as that sounds. It's ninety degrees out here, I'm in my long black coat, and still the chill shudders up my spine like a ghost on feet. The chill of Charlie's presence, out here leaning against the car with us, Charlie making himself known. She really is just like him.

She's looking at me, curious. "I know that you do—that a lot of people, a lot of Specs, do get sort of a . . ." she trails off, tentative. "Get sick?"

"Not sick." I shrug. "It's more like an allergy. A sensitivity. Not every time, and not always bad. Not usually bad at all. But most of the time, after exposure, you feel it a little bit, that's all. Your body feels the work." I finish the cigarette and consider starting a second one. "And especially after speculating."

"Right. Yeah. I don't get that."

I smoke in silence, contemplating my new partner. *I don't get that,* she says, like it's not a big deal. But that's how it works. The gift and the burden. You do the work, you feel it, that's all. We all get it— all of us, apparently, except for Aysa. She is at another level. She is in another place.

For some reason this revelation about my young charge registers in me as a kind of grief. I don't know much about her yet, and I don't like her because I don't like anybody, but I can see that she is *good*. She's kind and attentive and just fucking dying to do well in the world, to do good and do well. She's too *good* to be carrying all of this: the gifts of discernment, of speculation—the "gift"—the burden of it, the responsibility to her fellow citizens, all of it.

"Ms. Paige, are you . . ."

"Yes?"

"*Involved* with anyone?"

Her eyes widen as she realizes what I'm asking. "You mean— like—"

"Yeah." I gesture vaguely with one thick hand, searching the air for appropriate terminology. "Like a—sweetheart."

Ms. Paige looks genuinely confused. "Why are you asking me that?"

"Because—I don't know."

Because I want to protect her, all of a sudden. I want to direct her away from all of this work, from the dullness and the danger, from me in my dark clothes and dark spirit, point her away from the whole preposterous enterprise and out toward the rest of our good and golden world, toward the Venice Beach skate park and the clear blue sky, toward her sweetheart and her future.

I say none of that. I just say, "We're partners, right? We need to know each other."

She is looking at me, mystified, probably recalling the Laszlo of an hour and a half ago, in the car on the way to the scene of death, brusquely shutting down her earnest efforts to spill her whole history. She's trying to make sense of me, and I should tell her others have tried and it's not worth the effort.

"Alison," she says softly, with the happy wisp of a smile. "I do have a sweetheart. Her name is Alison."

"Oh. Okay. Cool."

"So—should we head back to the office?"

The moment is already passing—it has passed—and I let it go.

Arlo gave me to Charlie for a shadow, and he was none too excited about it.

"Are you kidding me, old man?" is what my big brother said, as a matter of Record—Charlie outraged and incredulous, never mind that I was standing right there. "I'm a solo operator. Lone wolf. You know that."

"I think for a brief period you might open your heart to show what you know to Mr. Ratesic the younger."

Me standing there in gray, hands stuffed in my pockets, examining the floor. Charlie wasn't worried about hurting my feelings; of all the half-hidden facts he could discern without trying, one was surely that I would worship him under any circumstance.

And I did worship him. By the end of that first day's training I worshipped him more than I ever had before, although my worship was tinged with the dawning realization that though I had followed him into Service, I would never in a million years live up to his reputation or abilities.

It was a slow day, my first day of speculation. Watching Charlie, standing back while he reconciled petty anomalies, testified in the Small Infelicities, helped a pair of impossibly dense regular policemen make sense of a bicycle theft.

But then, we're on the way home, we're turning right onto Westwood Boulevard, and he jumps the car up onto the curb, slams into park, and yells, "Come on! Come on!"

I run behind him into this little gas station convenience store, and the shopkeeper and the customer spin around at the sight of us: two big men in black and gray, tromping in together, me thinking with a burst of wild pride, *We're here! The Service has arrived!*

Not that I knew what the fuck we were doing there. But Charlie does—Charlie has a hunch and Charlie is right. Charlie is always right.

"Hands up, friends," he says, speaking to the room, smiling and moving slowly across the crowded aisles, grabbing a bag of chips for later. He puts out his hand for the customer's wallet, and the guy tries to make a break for it, and Charlie snags him quick, slams him down, yanks the wallet from his pocket, and riffles the cash till he finds it.

"Well, what do you know?" he says, still straddling the dude, winking at me. Charlie in his black leather jacket and black boots.

It was a counterfeit bill. One fake, in a wallet in a man's back pocket, us driving past on Westwood Boulevard.

That was Charlie, floating above us mere mortals, the jacket and the boots and the big stand-back grin, throwing out his hands wide so the world could witness his miracles. He offered to pay for the chips but the shopkeeper wouldn't hear of it.

Aysa Paige and I park on the Plaza and walk together through the glass lobby of the Service, and I'm just getting used to how it feels, to not be walking alone.

But then Paige presses nine in the elevator, and I say, "What are you doing?"

"What do you mean, what am I doing?"

"Why are you pressing the button for the ninth floor?"

"Isn't that where the Liaison is?"

"Yeah. So?"

"So don't we need to talk to him?"

"Nope."

I cross my arms and she crosses hers too. I stare at her and she stares back at me. The elevator door opens on nine and I wait like that, daring her to get off. It slides back closed and we resume our ascent.

"Mr. Ratesic."

"What?"

"What 'What?'? Look. We've *obviously* got something going on here, right?"

"I wouldn't go so far as to say 'obviously.' I'm not a fan of the word 'obviously,' just in general."

"But you don't think it's time to at least requisition the stretch?"

"No. I don't think."

"Okay, okay."

I'm guessing the soft edge has come out of my voice. I'm trying to be neutral, just hold a nice, calm, skeptical expression, but Paige is looking at me like I'm about to take a bite out of her neck.

"And what stretch of reality is it you think we need to see?"

"Just—the roof."

"What roof?"

I'm playing devil's advocate. I'm being an asshole. I'm somewhere in the charming middle ground between those two. This kid, she wants to jump in, both feet, jump in and grab on to something. But if she can't make a case, build an argument, I don't care how sensitive she is.

"On Vermont Avenue. The roof at the moment Crane falls. I think we can both agree, at this point, that there is something anomalous about it."

"Oh? I recall you agreeing with me that there was nothing anomalous about the death. Should we requisition *that* stretch? Of us having that conversation?"

"No." She flushes. "I just mean—the whole incident."

"There's no incident."

"Well, there's *something*."

"Yeah, but is there?"

The elevator stops and settles and the door sweeps open.

"Holy cow," says Paige, in a different voice, and I sigh, smile very slightly.

"I know."

It's the view. She must not have noticed it when Arlo brought her in this morning, or maybe she's just seeing it again as if for the first time, just like I do every time, even though I've been coming off that elevator into this room—just one big room, totally wrapped in glass—for much of my life. We linger at the glass, held by the majesty of the sprawling city: the bright glass towers of downtown, the upright cones and rectangles, the low gray hulks of the garment district. It goes on for miles from here: north to the fields, west to the water. The desalination plants that line the shore north of the pier. The acres of avocados, of wheat and corn, the rice and lettuce, the marijuana plants and the grapes for wine. The electric automobile plants that make the trucks that bring the wheat from the fields and the fish from the harbors to all corners of the State.

Way out to the west is the water; to the east and to the north are the rolling tops of the distant hills, with pockets of clouds clustered across their peaks, their contours crisply outlined by the sun.

Aysa says "Sir," and I give her a warning look, but the edge has come off my sternness now. That view gets me—it gets me every time.

"Laszlo."

"Yup."

"You've been doing this longer than me."

"Well noted, Ms. Paige. You've been doing it for, what, three hours?"

I am walking to my desk, raising a hand to Cullers, who barely moves, and Paige tails me all the way, talking nonstop, piling point upon point. Burlington is here, at his desk, grunting, typing out what looks like a long crime scene report, but other than that it's pretty quiet.

"There are anomalies in Renner's statement."

"Renner?"

"The boss. Manager. And there are anomalies in the dead man's home. In his Provisional. Two weeks of missing days."

"Which so far as we know have zero connection to his death."

"Well, sure, but how can we know what we *don't* know?"

I sigh. It's a fair point. I'm just hesitant, that's all, about going down to nine, engaging with the Liaison Office, jumping through the thousand hoops required to review stretches of reality.

For what? A man is dead but men die all the time. That's one thing that's true as it gets: people are dying all day long. I look over at Arlo's desk, in search of wise counsel, but Arlo's desk is empty.

"I don't mean to be contumacious," says Paige. "But—"

"You don't mean to be *what?*"

"Contumacious. It means stubborn."

"No it doesn't."

"Respectfully, Laz, it does."

"I think I know what words mean."

Cullers, from his desk, from under the hand towel draped over the top half of his face, makes an amused snort. The whole thing is ridiculous—two stubborn people arguing over whether a word means stubborn or not, two dogs tearing at a bone of truth. This kid, buttons polished, eyes shining, barely out of police academy diapers, pushing back on her immediate supervisor over a minor and irrelevant fact. She is all readiness and upright zeal; she is dying to show me what she's made of.

"Okay, you know what? Be my guest."

Aysa's eyes widen. Her spine straightens perceptibly. "Really?"

I shrug. "Sure. Go down to nine, tell Woody you want to pull a stretch from the Record. You would like to fill out all of the ten thousand forms necessary. If that's what you want to do, kid, knock yourself out."

"Really?"

"Yes."

"Great."

I'm being hyperbolic about the forms, but just barely. Reviewing material from the Record is a massive pain, even for the Service, one of the few institutional bodies with license to do so in any circumstance. If reviewing stretches of reality were easy, everybody would be doing it all day long: to settle petty arguments, satisfy prurient curiosity, win bets. Forget all that. Access even to fleeting instants of reality requires multiple levels of bureaucratic review and regulatory rigmarole, and that's not even counting having to reckon with the miserable personality of Woodrow Stone, the Speculative Service's Chief Liaison Officer to the Permanent Record.

Aysa Paige, undaunted, is heading back to the elevator. I watch her walk, the sun-sparkled heights of downtown like a dream vision behind her, through the windows.

"Hey, actually—Paige."

"Yeah?"

I tug at my beard a second, think it over. Can't hurt, right?

"As long as you're going. One more thing I want you to put in for."

"Oh?" She takes out her Day Book, clicks her pen open, eager pupil.

"Tell Woody I want stakeout stretches on Mose Crane's front door."

"On his—on the door?"

"Yup. You have the address?"

"Yes. What're stakeout stretches?"

"Woody will know."

"But can you just tell me?"

"It's just, like, you know, all the stretches caught by the same capture over a sustained time period. Like, for example, somebody's front door, all hours, for the week leading up to today." I think for a moment. "Let's do two weeks. I want to see if anybody strange was poking around. Besides us, I mean."

"Okay." She's writing. "Front door. Stakeout stretch. Two weeks leading up to today." She finishes writing and frowns. "That sounds like a big ask."

"It is. Which is why I'm glad I'm not the one asking. Good luck, Ms. Paige."

She gives me a smart salute and holds it, and I wait until the door closes before I laugh out loud.

"Contumacious," I say to myself, shaking my head. "This kid."

But then the word sort of sticks with me. An awkward set of syllables, jangling and mysterious. Like a magician's invocation. I say it piece by piece, measuring the word in my mouth: "con," "tu," "ma," "cious."

Well, let's just see, Officer Aysa Paige, I think. *Let's just damn well see.*

I've got plenty of dictionaries, of course, a ton of 'em, along with all the other reference books that crowd the office of our division like they crowd all the other offices in the Service, all the other offices in the Golden State. *Gazetteers* and *Almanacs,* encyclopedias and timelines, *Notable Individuals* and *The Book of Weights and Measures.* My own well-loved copy of *Past Is Prologue,* of course, the big book, close to hand so I can take it down when I want and dip into the glorious early history of the State, so I can lay my hands on the black pages and feel their mystery.

Right now though, I just need a dictionary. Along the inner wall of our office is *The Full Dictionary of the Golden State,* all seventeen volumes, with the bold main entries and the word histories in tiny type, with all the illustrations and charts and diagrams, the latest updates in a series of stapled inserts in the back of each volume.

I've also got *The Speculator's Field Dictionary,* leather-bound and portable.

And then, of course, closest to hand is Mose Crane's copy of that same *Everyday Citizen's,* the universally issued handheld lexicon.

I like a man who likes his dictionary.

I open it up, about a third of the way in, where the *G*s or *H*s would be, and I feel all of my blood freeze and stop, and I snap it closed again.

It's not a dictionary.

There has been, since we left Dolly Aster's building, a quiet burble of speculation chugging along in the back of my brain, a faint gurgling ever-presence like a creek on the far side of a campground, and now, all of a sudden, it becomes a rush, a crashing wall of water that staggers me up and out of my chair. I push the book off the desk and it slams on the floor and I stare at it lying there, like a feral animal, motionless but radiating menace. Cullers looks up at the sound and then down again, shifts his position, and drifts back to sleep.

I bend warily to pick the book up, slide it back on my desk, keeping my face a good foot from the object itself.

The cover looks like the cover of the dictionary, there's no question about it. *The Everyday Citizen's Dictionary,* the font and typesetting so familiar I could have drawn it myself. Beneath it, in smaller type: *A Product of the Golden State Publishing Arm.*

But only the paper jacket is real; the cover has been removed from a real dictionary and wrapped around this book instead, and carefully trimmed, I now realize, cut at top and bottom to fit precisely. Beneath the paper cover of the dictionary, the book has a real cover, pale yellow with stark red letters: *"The Prisoner."* And then, underneath it, in smaller type, "A Novel," and then, in smaller letters still, "By Benjamin Wish."

A stolen cover or a counterfeited cover hiding a real one. Like snakeskin, like a skein, a shadow truth drawn across the object's reality like a curtain. A big lie, a forgery, a brazen act of material pretense. I wrap my fingers around the edges of my desk. By instinct, just to feel something real, to grip on to it. With both hands I clutch the desk's edge like a window ledge and hold on tight.

And then—a deep breath—I open the book again, look down

and then up again, just long enough to read a sentence, grab the words without feeling them:

—and what of the boy himself? What was transpiring meanwhile within the fragility of his body, within his mind's blank interior, while outside him all of this whirl of activity: his doctor's interventions, his parents' desperate pleading? His body lay still and seemingly at rest but inside there was life, after all, but life of a kind—

I close the book and press my hands down on top, one hand flat and then the other hand flat on top of the first, press both hands down as if on the lid of a chest to keep it from springing open again.

It's fiction. For fuck's sake. It's *fiction*.

"Hey. Cullers. Hey."

"Yup?" He says it with forcefulness, the feigned alert tone people use when they've just been woken up.

"Do you know where Mr. Vasouvian is?"

"What?"

"Arlo? Where is he? Where is Arlo?"

8.

I find him in the first place I look, in his favorite place, just across the Plaza, on the broad majestic steps of the Permanent Record, working his way with stoic determination through a very large sandwich. He's got his tie tucked punctiliously between the buttons of his shirt, and a paper napkin slipped into his collar, and even in my agitated state of mind I spare a moment to love Arlo Vasouvian, my mentor and my oldest friend in the Service. Probably my oldest friend alive, if you don't count Silvie, and I can't count Silvie anymore.

"Ah," says Arlo, looking up. "Laszlo. Six sixes is thirty-six."

"And always will be," I say. I'm holding the book close to my chest, tight at my heart like a breastplate.

"You all right there, Mr. Ratesic?" Arlo lowers his sandwich to his lap, dabs at his lips with the napkin. A wilt of thin white hair falls across his forehead. "You will forgive, I hope, an old man's lapse into cliché, but you look like you've seen a ghost."

That's it exactly, of course. The thing in my hand, the dictionary that is not a dictionary, novel that is not a novel, is a ghost: phantasmagoric, alarming, inexplicable. I drop down onto the bench beside Arlo, still catching my breath.

"Take time," says Arlo, and he smiles his faraway smile. "Take time. Gather your thoughts."

The Plaza is a wide parallelogram of cement and fountains, of tall palms and statuary, of meandering paths and kiosks whose cheerful merchants hawk gum and marijuana cigarettes and the day's *Trusted Authority*. The broad and sun-drenched Plaza is the heart of the State, and at the heart of the Plaza is the pond, a narrow, kidney-shaped duck pool surrounded by benches. Food trucks shark around the outskirts of the Plaza at all hours, a constantly rotating array representing the dizzying variety of cuisines that flavor the State: sumptuous pork dumplings and crisp savory crepes and spicy beef empanadas, tacos and tortas and tostadas, fish sandwiches and pâté sandwiches and overstuffed chicken salad sandwiches like the one Arlo is now enjoying.

Ringing the Plaza are the three main buildings of the State government: the Service, my own home away from home; the *Trusted Authority* building, including not only the fact-gathering operations but the rattling enormity of the printing plant, not to mention the studios from which the broadcast arm transmits its hourly and quarter-hourly bulletins; and—last and never least, fundamental and foundational—the Record itself, with its famous approaching staircase and humble brickwork walls. The Record, of course, appears small but is much larger on the inside, underneath, with its endless basements and subbasements.

A guy approaches the Record's walls to perform the small ecstatic ritual for which those walls are famous. He's a shaggy Caucasian in sandals and aviator glasses, who, as I watch, hunches over and scribbles madly in his Day Book, scribbling some intimate truth; then he tears off whatever he's been writing, folds the scrap up small and then smaller, and jams it into a crack in the wall of the Record before he steps back, satisfied, and runs two fingers along the wall, tracing a slow reverential path across its pitted surface.

Others come and go, they are always, always, coming and going, up and down the stone steps, each to perform his or her own version of the old ritual: a lady in a sundress, striding purposefully, grinning ear to ear; a man with his son up on his shoulders; a girl of fifteen, sixteen, maybe, with a skateboard she tucks under her arm while digging out her Day Book. They're tearing small pieces from their interior lives, ripping pages from their Day Books and jamming them like sealant into the cracks in the walls of the Record, good and golden citizens adding their private truths to the greater store, a literal enactment of our figurative truth: everybody builds reality together.

There is one truth, and here it is. One truth, and I too am a part of it.

I watch the kid with the skateboard as she presses her palm against the wall, trots back down the steps, and sails off across the plaza. It's funny, how much I dislike people in general but then I see one particular person, one good citizen doing her thing, or his thing, and I feel love like a concavity in my chest—the fearsome love that drove me to join the Service in the first place. The need to protect everybody I see.

"So are we talking about the case, Laz? This business up on Vermont Avenue."

"Yes," I say. "In a way."

"Oh?" Arlo untucks his napkin, crumples it into a ball that then expands out into a nest. "And what way is that?"

His voice, as ever and as always, has a calming effect on me. I find that despite the unease of what I have found, I am able in Arlo's steady presence, warm and worn, to speak clearly. I give the old man a rapid brief on the morning's adventures, on the dead roofer, how we had enough anomalies to justify going down to his place of residence, and how, once there, we found—

"This." I hold it up. "It's a novel. A work of fiction."

"Pardon me," he says, and frowns. "But a novel is not a work of fiction."

"I know that, sir. I know what a novel is *supposed* to be."

"A novel is a true story about an event or events from the distant or recent history of our State—"

"Arlo, I *know*."

That's the point. That's why I've sought him out. But Vasouvian can't stop now that he's started. The old man has got few faults, but among them is a love of reciting, of casually demonstrating how comprehensive is his knowledge of the Basic Law, every bulwark and provision. What I am now witnessing may indeed be Arlo's favorite state: eyelids drifted down to half shut, head tilted slightly back, glasses perched on the tip of his nose, precisely unspooling a line of text.

"A true story, that is, organized into chapters or incidents, featuring a historical character or characters, building to a conclusion, suggesting or implying an inspirational message about the nature of the Golden State."

"Thank you. Yes. I know all that."

"It's true, it's true," he says, singsong, with a pleased sigh. "It's all true."

"Right, but that's the point, Arlo." I hold up the book again, with its plain yellow cover and oversized red letters. "But this thing is not that. It says 'novel' on the cover, under the title, but it's something different."

"You've read it, then?" he asks, giving me a look I've never seen from him before.

"No, sir." I shake my head. "I haven't read it."

There's an accusation in his question, a rising sharpness at the end of it that I don't like. "I only opened it, sir. I looked inside."

Arlo contemplates me for a moment; another. Behind us, a woman stands very close to the wall, her head bent forward and pressed against the bricks of the building, her hands pressed flat against it. A load-bearing citizen, using the strength of her body to hold up the State.

"And if you only opened it, how do you know that, though it says 'novel,' it is not a novel?"

"Well, here."

I flip it open to the passage on which my eyes had landed, I open this fat fraudulent document right there on the steps of the Plaza, right out in the shadow of the Record itself, and I show to Arlo the sentences that scythed into me, the business about the injured boy and the dizzying whirl of activity around his hospital bed, the intimation of some alien intelligence. Clear fabrication, unsupported and unsupportable by any provable fact or facts.

"It's fiction," I say flatly, and Arlo murmurs, "So it is," and closes it, softly but firmly, like a man shutting a suitcase. He thinks and I watch him think, the sunlight glinting off his round glasses, the soft splash of the ducks in the fountain and the bustle of footsteps on the stone all around us.

It strikes me—as it occasionally strikes me—how wondrous are Arlo Vasouvian's eyes: deep set and luminous, flickering with the light of careful attention, but always with shadows forming and moving beneath the surface. No matter what the subject under discussion, Arlo has always got some other thing he's mulling over, somewhere the rest of us can't see.

He holds up the book, turns it over delicately in his hands. "It's an artifact."

"An artifact." I knew that, I guess. I didn't want to know it. "From what was."

"Yes. World that was."

We are silent, then, silent on the steps of the Record, silent at the center of the State. *There is a world that used to be and is gone.* We live on it and in it, but we don't know what it was. Its absence surrounds us.

"A novel," Arlo says softly. "Quote unquote. Who was this fellow again? The possessor. The man who is dead."

"A roofer. A construction worker. Crane."

"Crane."

"Just a guy."

"And why would he have a book like this?"

"I don't know."

"And do you think this object is something he *happened* to have, just as he *happened* to die this morning? Or do you suppose there is a line, a *bridge,* as yet unseen, which connects those two flat facts together?"

"No," I say, but then I taste it—I feel it. A half-truth. I catch it, correct it. "I don't know, Arlo. There might be."

"Well. You better find out."

"I will," I say. "That's what I'll do."

He holds out the book so I might take it back, and I find my hands are unwilling to do so. I see now what I wanted, I wanted him to tell me the mystery of the novel is above my pay grade, that the appearance of such a thing on my trail—a novel that is not a novel, a dangerous relic—means the trail is shut off to me. I want Arlo to relieve me of the burden of this case, which seemed so open-and-shut, so simple—the flat fact of the broken roof, the flat fact of the broken roofer, a simple and clean connection—but which now seems full of wrinkles, a welter of anomalies, a patchwork of unseen connections.

I'm sure Arlo can see it too, that I wish I didn't have to keep going. That I am—for all of my experience, my gruff exterior, my size and strength—a tiny little man. Not at all like Charlie. He would have seized on the book, the roofer, the mystery, and leapt into whatever danger it all represented, leapt in grinning and torn out the truth. Torn out the truth by the roots or died trying.

Arlo, deep and decent, sets the book down on the bench between us. Captures are turning up on the rooftops of the Plaza, a slow-spinning panoramic capture on the top of every building.

Arlo chews his sandwich and allows his eyes to linger on the pond in the center of the Plaza. Looks anywhere but at me for a moment, and then clears his throat and changes the subject.

"And how is it going," he asks, "with young Ms. Paige?"

"Oh. Fine." I catch it, correct it. "More than fine. She's . . . she's extremely gifted." I shake my head in wonder, feeling a glad rush of relief to be talking about something other than the book. "Her sensitivity is off the charts—sorry, idiom, lazy—but it is. Man, is it. And not just locutions either. She's catching targets from three floors up. She's, uh—" I look at him, and he's not looking at me. He's leaning back, considering, gazing up at the clouds. "She's like Charlie. Which—by the way—is why you gave her to me."

I am teasing him. Lovingly, yes, but definitely chiding him for having hidden the full truth of his motivations. But he responds thoughtfully, nodding. "Yes. Yes . . . although it is true, as I told you, that I assigned Ms. Paige to your mentorship because you are in my estimation—and Alvaro agrees, though he may not . . . anyway. In the collective estimation, you are the . . . steadiest member of our service. However—" Now he pauses, dabs at one corner of his lips with his big wad of napkins. "Yes. And I thought . . . given your history. Your familial connection . . ." He shrugs. I wait. "She is as good as he was, Laszlo," he says finally. "Indeed, she . . ." And then, softly, as if reluctant to blaspheme. "She may indeed be better."

I shake my big woolly head and start to deny it, but if there is any fair judge of such matters, it's Arlo.

"I can't attest to it, of course, because no one can. But yes indeed. She might be better." He nods slightly, as if ticking off a list in his mind, considering things he's seen. And me too: I'm remembering

Aysa, sitting next to me in the car after we went through Aster's basement, politely declining a cigarette, humble about her remarkable catch, unsymptomatic in its wake.

"Do you recall that I used to give these talks?" Arlo says. "Lectures, at some of the high schools, as part of the . . . you know. To gently *acclimate* young people to their new responsibilities to truth telling, as they aged out of the years of exemption. I met her at one such talk. Nine years ago. It was just after . . . after Charlie was lost to us, actually. I remember it. She was clearly gifted, clearly registering, you know, and just leaping with excitement. It was truly just . . . *radiating* off of her. An eagerness. To join the Service. To do her part, she kept saying. Charming phrase. *Do my part.* Although her enthusiasm, I must say, was . . ." He sighs. "Sorry. It's sad, you know. Her enthusiasm was contrary to the will of her parents."

Arlo sighs a second time, weary but pleased. The lunchtime crowd is dying down, but a handful of the faithful straggle still along the wall. A middle-aged man in a wheelchair angles up, just a few feet from us, takes out his Day Book, writes down some small truth, and tears it free and folds it small. Reality is ongoing.

"I know, Laszlo, that you do not relish the company. But there is no one else who can offer this young lady what you can. Do you know what that is?"

"No," I say.

"Ballast."

And then he just smiles, the wide and watery smile. And I know exactly what he means. I can picture Aysa Paige, dying to get to the crime scene, dying to ask a thousand questions, dying to speculate, leaping ahead. Bounding, heedless, reckless. Where my qualities tend in the other direction. I am the earthbound man, heavy and stolid. Ballast. That's me.

Charlie was eager too. Not with Aysa's wide-eyed acolyte eagerness, but with the swaggering keenness of a big-game hunter, the man who catches a scent and cannot and will not stop, never mind the dangers. Fuck the dangers of exposure, the dangers of living in proximity to dissonance, the dangers of speculation. Sometimes Charlie almost—not quite, but almost—refused to believe there even *was* any danger.

And Arlo knows as well as I do what happened to Charlie.

I stood beside Arlo at the funeral while the bells were ringing, once for each year of his life.

Mr. Vasouvian and Mr. Ratesic, the younger Mr. Ratesic, on the outskirts of the thronging crowd, watching Charlie's coffin be delivered to the earth, committed to the ground for all time, like a sealed box of files being added to the Permanent Record.

Arlo with his hand on my elbow, holding me gently back from whatever drastic action he was afraid I'd take. As if there was any danger of that: of Laszlo Ratesic flying off the handle, gnashing his teeth, enacting violent revenge. That's never been my style. I just stood there, hands in pockets, head lowered, listening in silence while my brother's wild courage was eulogized.

I'd never before seen my father in public without his pinhole on. Never in all of my life.

I'm thinking about Charlie, like I'm always thinking about him, and now I'm thinking about Aysa too, young Ms. Aysa Paige of the Speculative Service, with her whole golden life ahead of her.

"And you didn't think it was better to simply discourage her from entering the Service entirely? You didn't think that would be the better course for her?"

"Perhaps." Arlo turns then, at last, and looks me full in the eye. "But not the better course for the Service."

Modest as he is, Arlo will not apologize for choosing the integrity of the truth, and the safety and welfare of the State, ahead of the safety and welfare of any single individual. And I'm too sour and inward to express what I am feeling, which is, now that I understand what she is, that I am grateful to Arlo for the opportunity to work with Aysa Paige.

I scan the edges of the Plaza, but lunchtime is over, and the food trucks are going or gone. I see the Dirty Dog, a black truck with pink piping, a hot dog truck I've been wanting to try for years, but it's just now driving away, turning down Alameda Street in a cloud of exhaust. In the wake of this disappointment I register another truth about Aysa Paige, the other way I am feeling and have felt since Crane's apartment, which is a burning envy—I could die of jealousy, I swear to it, that is big true, but because I love the State, I love the work, I will raise her up. Show her the works. Take her along.

"So we are set, then?" Arlo says quietly, reading my mind. "I can entrust young Ms. Paige with confidence to your care?"

"Requires subjectivity to answer," I say. In the pond, the ducks execute a U-turn, still in their flotilla. "Requires an assessment of future events."

"But you'll try."

"I'm trying already."

"Well, then, keep it up."

The man in the wheelchair has gone, and for once the wall is deserted, this stretch closest to us, and I almost stand up and go over there myself. I've never gone in for it myself, the displays of faith. I'd be embarrassed to do it, to put my private devotion on public display, but right now I want to put both of my hands against the Record, press my forehead against the stones of its wall, and whisper, "Thank you. Thank you . . . for the world we have built, in which everything is known and can be known, in which everything that is so is known to be so, and has been known and will be known tomorrow." Because just imagine—

just *imagine* the alternative, the world in which a man encounters some scrap of information, about the murder rate in his neighborhood, or about the presence of troops on the northern border, or what time the bus is supposed to come—any of the small and large pieces of information a person encounters in the course of a day or a lifetime, personal or political, substantive or trivial—and then the next hour or the next day he hears something different, and it is impossible, literally impossible, to know which version is the real one.

Madness creeps in very quickly at the edges of such speculation. Not just madness but a kind of horror, a flickering red field closing in. Just the thought of it.

The bell begins to ring from the Grand Hall of the Record, and everybody on the Plaza stops moving and turns to a nearby stranger. "It's one o'clock," say a dozen different voices, loud and confident, affirming general truth.

"It's just turning one."

"In one hour exactly it will be two."

I never did pick up the book. It is lying still where Arlo left it, and now he picks it up again, holds it in his lap while he slides his glasses slightly down his nose. "*The Prisoner,*" he murmurs when the bells have stopped. "By Benjamin Wish. I think perhaps—" He weighs it in his hands. "Perhaps our best move after all, as far as this goes, is to bring it to Ms. Petras."

"Oh." I should feel relief. This is what I wanted. This is exactly what I wanted only moments ago. "Oh yeah?"

"Yes, yes." He sets the book down again, gazes at the jacket, taps it with two fingers. "Bring it to Ms. Petras's office and let them do their thing."

Laura Petras, as Our Acknowledged Expert on the Enforcement of the Laws, is the ultimate supervisor of both the Speculators and the regular police, one of twenty committee members who oversee the administration of the Basic Law. I've only met her once, seen her maybe five times in my life, a bland-smiling blonde woman in a tan suit and sensible shoes who, along with her fellow committee members—Our Acknowledged Expert on Trade and Commerce, Our Acknowledged Expert on Transportation, and all the rest of them—administers the fine points of State governance. The various committees and their staffs are not headquartered down here, among the majestic showpiece buildings of the State, but at the Melrose Avenue facility, a sprawling administrative campus of one- and two-story sandstone bungalows, with venetian blinds in the windows and conference tables in every room.

Among their many other responsibilities, the committees have ultimate jurisdiction over facts and artifacts that can be proved neither true nor untrue, and which therefore must be consigned to oblivion. Put out of mind. Not to be thought of again. What Arlo is proposing is to take my artifact and spirit it away, drive up to Melrose and hand it to Petras or Petras's people, to be referred in due time to the assembled committees, to be declared a part of the unknowable past, neither known nor unknown, neither true nor false, forever.

After that, it probably gets thrown in a box or set on fire. Who knows?

I pick up the book from the bench between us, feeling suddenly protective of it. The prospect of it being declared unknown and unknowable seems—I don't know. Wrong. Unfair, somehow. Must Crane's prized secret possession be consigned to oblivion, just because he was?

"No, you know what?" I say. "I think I'll hang on to it for now. Just in case it becomes relevant to the investigation."

"Very well," says Arlo, sounding less than entirely convinced. But

I nod——*good*. I've convinced myself. It's *my* investigation, *my* strange artifact, *my* responsibility. There is something else too, isn't there? I hold the book tightly, gripping its corners with my fingers. It wants me to *read* it——it wants to be *read*.

I drop the book back in my bag and zip it up.

"And how is *your* novel coming, by the way?"

"Oh, it's coming," Arlo answers with a long happy sigh. "It's coming along. You'll be the first to see it when I'm done."

"I can't wait."

An old joke between Arlo and me, one of thousands, part of the private language of old friends. He's been working on his novel, supposedly, for eleven years; it is an achievement, he likes to say, to which he has long aspired, to produce a novel of his own: *a true story organized into chapters or incidents, featuring a historical character . . . implying an inspirational message about the nature of the Golden State.* Every time I ask whether I can get a look at it, he says it's not quite finished, he's still tinkering at the edges, smoothing the transitions, fine-tuning the ending, but I'll be the first to see it when he's done.

Which is only right, after all. Arlo's novel is about my brother.

MAIN TEXT

"This makes no sense," spat Ratesic. "This makes no sense at all."

"Sure it makes sense," hissed Mr. Alvaro at his tough-talking colleague, hiding his admiration and envy behind a sneer. Mr. Ratesic was universally admired. That was a true fact, solid as steel, permanent and unbending. Among his fellow Speculators, among those who had worked with him, among dirty liars who'd had the bad luck to cross his path, he was considered a force of nature. Broad-shouldered and barrel-chested, with a strong jawline and intense, brooding eyes, Ratesic lifted a match to his cigarette and stared out the wide glass windows of the thirtieth floor of the Service.

"What do you mean, it makes no sense?" Mr. Alvaro was incensed. "This good-for-nothing punk was hustling fake IDs, and I caught his dumb ass. End of story."

Mr. Alvaro was filling out the paperwork on an arrest he had made, a twenty-three-year-old street kid named Bert Pepper, sunglasses and a skateboard and ragged jeans, a shoulder bag filled with forged identifications. A serious crime, an out-and-out perversion of the truth. Alvaro was working his way through the charging documents.

But he should have waited. He should have known. When Charlie Ratesic sensed a discrepancy, when he caught wind of an anomaly, it was because there was an anomaly on the wind. Mr. Ratesic was brash and he was headstrong, but he did not make mistakes.

"I want to take a run at this kid."

"He's my arrest," Alvaro protested.

"A kid like that needs a source for that kind of paper. I wanna ask him about the source."

"Why don't you worry about your own arrests, Ratesic?"

The rest of us watched as the two men butted heads. Carson raised her eyebrows to Burlington, who sighed. There was no question who was right, though: Ratesic was always right.

He'd come from a family of Speculators. His father, Nelson, had served with distinction, and Charles's brother, Laszlo, had followed both of them into the Service. Laszlo Ratesic was there too, watching quietly, eyebrows raised, while his older brother persuaded Alvaro to let him have five minutes alone with Bert Pepper.

There was no one like Mr. Ratesic.

He was always right and he was right this time, more right than he knew.

Bert Pepper and his shoulder bag full of fake IDs were just the beginning.

Ratesic went in to talk to the kid, and the five minutes grew into ten, and the ten into twenty. Alvaro paced outside the interrogation room, watching the live feed stitched from the room's four-corner captures, smoking and pacing, more and more angry, until at last Ratesic emerged, grinning ear to ear.

He was right. He was always right.

Pepper did indeed have a conspirator. His name was Armond Kessler, and he ran a small Mid-City print shop whose clients included the Publishing Arm of the Golden State itself. This Kessler sonofabitch was using the State's own templates to press fake identifications.

"Well done, Mr. Ratesic," I told him. "Let's go pick up this Kessler and see what he has to say."

I was his superior officer. Technically, I had given the man an order. But Charlie just grinned.

"You know what?" he said. "I've got a better idea."

9.

"**Oh**, Mr. Ratesic. I'm using your desk."

"Yeah, I can see that."

I cross my arms and stand there scowling behind my own damn chair. I like my desk the way I like it, with my takeout menus in the pile where I keep them, arranged not alphabetically or by cuisine but in the order of the days in which I use them. I like my phone in the spot where I like it to be, and I especially like my chair without somebody else's ass in it. And now here is Ms. Paige, pulled right up to the desk, staring at my screen, biting her lower lip in concentration, holding a pen angled to her Day Book, ready for action. She doesn't turn around, even with me looming behind her. She keeps her eyes glued to what she's watching.

"What are you looking at, anyway?"

"The stretches."

"What stretches?"

Now she turns, and while she's turning she says "Stop" and the playback stops.

"The stakeout stretches you asked me to retrieve. From Crane's door?"

"Already?"

"They couldn't put together the death scene yet, but they're working on it. That one is a—what did he call it?"

"A tapestry."

"Right. Yes. But *these*——" She gestures to the stretches, the neat stack she's made of them on my desk, beside the screen. "He said this was easy. Static shot, front door. He pulled them for me, right away."

"Who did? Stone?"

"Right. Mr. Stone. Woody——he said to call him Woody. He said——why——what? Why are you looking at me like that?"

"Because . . ."

I trail off, studying the image frozen on the screen, trying to figure out what I'm missing. But no, there it is, the drab gray courtyard at Ellendale Place where we were just walking three hours ago, that sad little fountain, the wilted chrysanthemums in their cracked clay pots. She's gotten all the hours on the doorway of Crane's residence, exactly what I asked her to ask for.

"So you just——*asked?*"

"Well. I asked nicely." Ms. Paige gives me a tentative smile. "I said it was important."

I laugh. I actually laugh. Everybody who goes to the ninth tells Woody it's important. It's tautological: if you are going to the ninth floor, if you are asking for a piece of reality to be cued for review, then what you're working on is important.

"You asked Woody to release two weeks of reality and he just said 'Okay.'"

"Well, no." She checks her Day Book. "He said 'No problem.'"

I mean, I am fucking flabbergasted here. Doesn't matter how many capture feeds we're talking about, or how few. When I ask, when most people ask, what happens is that Woody Stone with his big gut rises slowly, sighs heavily, makes a big show of searching his office for the right forms——as if it's a serious and unwelcome imposition on his valuable time, as if responding to capture requests from the thirtieth floor isn't 95 percent of the man's job description. But Ms. Aysa Paige has got the first stretch already cued and the rest of them stacked up beside the screen, ready to go. *No problem.*

I'm feeling it strong now, feeling it despite myself, staring at Aysa where she sits at my desk, awaiting my permission to get back to work. Envy. Red spirit. Unwelcome friend. I am conscious of the brittleness it puts in my voice.

"All right, Ms. Paige. Did you find anything?"

"Not yet, no. I'm going frame by frame."

"As you should."

"So it's going to take some time."

"Okay."

She turns back to the work, says "Play" and then "Fast," and I stand awkwardly behind her, watching her watch. On the screen, in the courtyard, minutes pass in speeded-up motion, a blur of minutes in which nothing happens: water sputters in the fountain, summer breeze riffles the glossy leaves of the plants in their pots. Aysa's attention is steady on the screen, her whole body hunched, her eyes narrowed like a bird's, watching for prey, watching for any movement.

"Listen, Ms. Paige," I say finally. "Aysa."

She says "Stop" and turns around.

My voice is a bit different now; I'm speaking in a different key. "I spoke to Mr. Vasouvian about you. Just now. And he mentioned to me about—he gave me a bit of background. About your parents."

"Yeah?" Her voice, too, is in a different key, and it's not the same as mine. Her words are cold, hard, and flat. "What about them?"

"That they have been gone. Since you were young. I only wanted to say I was sorry to hear that. That can't have been easy."

"Respectfully, Mr. Ratesic? Fuck my parents."

And she goes right back to it, sliding one stretch out of the slot on the side of the screen and replacing it with the next. "Play," she says, and I watch her watching, not sure what to say, not sure what a good mentor does with *Fuck my parents*. What I'm thinking, though, is that we gather impressions of other people very quickly, and they harden and fasten in our minds, and it is very hard after that to imagine that there is more, but there is always more, deeper truths, lower levels, and most people don't even know what all is down there.

"All right, kid," I say softly. "You ready?"

"Stop," she tells the screen and turns to face me. "Ready for what?"

I raise my eyebrows and she grins. We've got enough. More than enough. The anomaly of the missing days. The anomaly of the schedule. And of course that damn novel, wrapped in its fake jacket, hiding in plain sight. The sort of thing a man like Crane has no business owning, the sort of thing that shouldn't even exist in the first place. Ms. Paige, pain in the ass though she may be, has been right all along: there is something in this, some underlying misalignment of fact. There is truth that needs to be found, and there is only one way to do it.

At last she dares to ask: "We're going to speculate?"

"Well, I am," I say, and I snag an extra chair from next to Cullers's desk and drag it over. "I don't know what you're going to do."

I sit down. I close my eyes. I can't see Ms. Paige but I know what she does: she settles back and closes her eyes beside me.

I shift in my chair, arch my back slightly, clench my teeth. This is the part I hate, the moment of descent, how it's like a trap door opening, the world giving away beneath you, a lurch and a drop, down into dark below. I jerk and twitch. One forearm shoots out rigid, fingers clutching, my body instinctively seeking to keep a grip on the world, and then I let go but I hate how it feels: something grabbing at me, speculation clutching a foot and a leg and dragging me into its darkness—

Which is just what it is for me—a *darkness:* a cold room, cold and dark, a cave or a cavern, filled with shadow. I can't see the edges of it, don't know how far it goes. It's only a dark room, lit by a single candle, a small, fierce orange glow, and now they float forward— stray postulates like tiny, shifting, orbiting stars, glinting in the hazy penumbra cast by the single light.

Crane was a burglar.

Simple. Bright. The closest light.

"A burglar," I say out loud, twitching in my chair, and Aysa says it back.

"A burglar." And then, "A Peeping Tom."

"A Peeping Tom," I say, sending that spark out into my own darkness, watching it take up orbit.

"A burglar—a ring of burglars," says Aysa beside me.

That's what it is, that's all we do, trading back and forth, dancing together toward and then away from possibilities, scattered sparks, the void pinpricked by glitters of speculation, the mind glowing and dimming, glowing and dimming, and you sit there with head turned, eyes closed, the body just a body, a vessel, grimacing in a chair while inside—

A burglar—

One of a group of burglars—conspiracy—cabal—

Or . . . but . . .

Crane the pervert—monster—madman—

—a man of no family or station, a drifter, itinerant, man of missing days—

Or, or . . .

—depressive, isolated, lonesome, suicidal—sees the height of the house

as a mechanism, a weapon—up on the precipice, seizes his chance, dying to die—

Or, or . . .

It's the house, the house, the house that wants him, not he that wants the house—

That's Ms. Paige bringing the house into it, not just the man but the building itself, the place and the meaning of the place. She sends this new bright spark into my field of vision, burning me awake and out of it.

I fly from the darkness, eyes wide open.

"Shit," I say, standing up unsteady. "Shit."

"What?" says Ms. Paige. "What is it? You have something?"

"No. Yes. I don't know." I rub my knuckles into my eyes, clearing away stars. "I have something that I know I don't have."

Aysa studies me avidly, and I should take the time to explain, but I don't feel like it. I get up. I grab my pinhole and smash it down onto my head.

Damn it. The house. The stupid house.

"You watch your way through the relevant stretches, Ms. Paige. Okay? It's gonna be boring, but that's what you do. Go from stretch to stretch, and don't skip the ins and outs. Anyone comes in, catch a still of the face. Anyone even comes into the frame."

"Yes, sir. Where are you going?"

"Someone I gotta talk to. Someone I gotta talk to alone."

10.

"**The past** is a dangerous country."

"Unknown and unknowable."

"This is true."

"And always shall be."

"Well, well, Mr. Speculator. Twice in the same day."

"Lucky you, right?"

"Yes, yes. Lucky me."

Captain Elena Tester beckons me into her cluttered office, and we're both smiling as she shakes my hand, but there's displeasure in her smile, right behind the teeth. She doesn't like me being here in her office this morning; she doesn't like that I didn't call first, doesn't like what any of this implies. It's one thing to run into each other at a crime scene, two law enforcement professionals crossing paths on the job; it's another thing entirely for me to be darkening her doorway a few hours later, unannounced but clearly on official business.

Nobody stopped me from coming in, by the way. Not outside, under the fluttering flag of the Bear and Stars. Not in the elevator or coming down the hall. The regular police are prickly about their jurisdiction, but nobody's going to stop a Spec on his rounds. The black clothes and the pinhole function like a passport, guaranteeing free movement within the Golden State. Stand back, stay clear.

So Captain Tester is surprised to see me, and she's not happy, but this shouldn't take long. I just need to clear this up.

I point to one of the three straight-backed chairs that form a semicircle around her desk. "Any one of these?"

"Of course."

I sit. I pull papers out of my briefcase.

"So. Elena. I have to ask you a few questions."

"Okay, Laszlo."

"Four or five questions. Possibly more, depending on your answers."

She gives out a little impatient puff of air. "Okay, Laszlo. I'm ready. Let's go."

I nod and smile. My pinhole is capturing. The room is capturing. Captures on the doorframe, captures in the corners. A capture on her desk rotating slow, taking a sweep.

"I am going to read back to you the statement you gave to me this morning, in Los Feliz. At 3737 Vermont Avenue."

"Statement?"

"Yes. The statement you gave me this morning, at——"

"We were having a conversation, Laz."

"Yes." I clear my throat. "But you did state it. It was a statement."

"Well, definitionally . . ." She stops, takes a deep breath. I notice that her hands are tight on the edge of her desk. Holding fast to reality, her reality. "No, it's okay. You're right. Of course you are right, Laszlo." She stands abruptly. "Do you want coffee?"

"I've had some. Thank you."

"I'll make myself one, if you don't mind."

"I don't."

I wait. She drums her fingers on the corner of the little sink along a wall of her office, beneath the wide southerly window, while her machine burbles and brews. We are in two different places at the same time. We are *a Speculator and a police captain working together to establish facts,* and also simultaneously we are *two friends, two people just talking.* There are words and there is context; there are declarations and there is the ground in which those declarations are planted.

The coffeemaker issues a small-motor exclamation and hisses out its mud-brown stream. Now that I can smell the coffee I want some after all. Too late now.

"So," says Elena. "My *statement*."

"Yes. I asked you what you were doing at 3737 Vermont Avenue this morning, and you said, 'I caught it on the scanner.' You said, 'I live near here. On Talmadge.' You said, 'As long as I was in the area, I thought I'd babysit the homeowner.'" I look up from my Day Book and she's waiting expectantly. "That was your statement."

"Okay," she says flatly, which of course is not an answer.

"Elena. Captain Tester. I'm asking if those are true statements."

Astonishment spreads through her body, a tightening fury: her back straightens, her hand curls tightly around the coffee cup, denting the paper sides. The pupils of her eyes narrow to knife ends. "You're asking me if I was lying."

"Yes, Elena. Captain. Yes."

"And wouldn't you know?"

"If you had dissembled outright, Captain, yes. I would have caught it."

"Smelled it," she says, giving the words a tight contemptuous spin. "Or—sensed it? Isn't that it?"

"Well—no. Not exactly. But yes. If you were lying, I would have known. If there was context that was left out, I would need you to tell me that." I have a file in my lap. A manila folder, plain cover, unmarked tab. Elena is looking at it closely. "I would need you to tell me that *now*."

She sets down her coffee and sits glaring at me, and she can be angry if she wants to be, but the woman stood there and made a small proffer that was true but incomplete, and we both know it—at least, I thought I knew it before, but only now, looking at her eyes, feeling the cold fury my questions have inspired, do I know it for sure. She didn't lie, but she did something just as bad, arguably worse, especially for someone in her position, high on the org chart of the regular police, a pillar of law enforcement just like me: she has not lied, but she has found a way not to have to. She dug herself a rabbit hole of conversational cleverness and slipped inside it. Arlo Vasouvian, the expert, the guru, could tilt his head back, half shut his eyes, and recite the entire statute, the complete philosophical and legislative history of context and omission: if someone says X instead of Y, that is a lie; if someone says X but not Y, we have then a case of relative relevance. Context is everything. Context is infinite.

There is some violation here, but I don't know yet what it is.

"Was there, possibly, some information that you might not, in the moment, have thought relevant?"

"Yes," says Tester immediately. "Possibly there was."

Her eyes remain on mine. Her body has not relaxed. I am conscious of my bulk, my shape inside the tight space of the chair, the room, the moment. I feel myself in the small wood chair, bent toward Elena, hunched and ursine. We stare at each other like two animals in a forest clearing. There are pictures on her desk: her kids. Her husband, Al, who died in the line a few years back. Her friends. I wonder if there are any pictures of Silvie. I want to look. I won't look. I don't.

"The house on Vermont," I say, "is deeded to a woman named Karen Sampson."

"Stipulated," says Tester immediately, but I'm not accepting stipulations. She has to know I won't be. I open the file I'm holding and take out three pieces of paper, material evidence, and I spread them out on the desk in front of her like a gambler laying down cards. The mortgage deed to the house. The certificate of occupancy. A carbon of the purchase from the previous owner.

"Karen Sampson owns that house. Does she live there?"

"Yes."

The next page is a one-sheet backgrounder on Sampson. These documents I didn't need to pull from the identity office. I simply went downstairs to the twenty-ninth floor, on my way from my office to here, and spent half an hour on public Record searches. Karen Sampson is a notable individual—a lot of this information I'm now producing came right out of the most recent edition of *Notable Individuals*.

"Ms. Sampson is a producer of recorded music."

"Yes."

"And she has a criminal history. She's spent time in jail. Various drug offenses. A driving-while-drunk, nine months ago."

Elena's answers have started to come less readily. "Yes. That's— correct. She's—Karen—has struggled. As we all have."

I nod. I have made myself acquainted with Karen Sampson's checkered past. I reviewed her records carefully before coming over here, looking for Tester's signature on an arrest report or a plea deal. Finding nothing untoward. Not yet.

"Ms. Sampson is one of your oldest friends."

"Yes. So?"

"Do you need more coffee, Elena? Do you need to take a break?"

"No."

"Okay."

More papers come out of my file. Photocopies of pictures of the two old friends together, arm in arm on the beach, a windy day, a much younger and more carefree Elena Tester holding down a floppy beach hat so it won't blow away.

"Elena, listen to me. I don't think that you killed anyone. I don't think you had anything to do with any of this. But I have an obligation, now that a case has begun, to dispel any possible anomalies. Okay?"

She says something very softly, a sound with no motion of the mouth, as if her lips are refusing to move.

"What?"

"I said go ahead, Laszlo. Ask your fucking questions."

I sigh. I find the right page in my Day Book and ask my next question. "When you heard the address on the scanner, were you concerned about the potential consequences of a death and subsequent investigation on this property?"

"Yes."

"Yes what?"

"Yes," she says, and gives me my words back to me, my words in my voice, like she's a deck replaying the cued stretch. "When I heard the address on the scanner, I was concerned about the potential consequences of a death and subsequent investigation on this property."

"So you rushed to the scene to protect your friend Karen."

I wait. Elena stares at the ceiling.

I've arrived at the heart of it, and I will collect my flat fact, gather up the small piece of the truth I've come for, and go back to the roofer and his missing boxes.

"No," Tester says flatly, and I blink.

"No?"

"No. I did not rush there."

"So 'rush' is imprecise," I concede, irritated by the quibble, especially now, when she's in such a hurry to wrap this up, for me to get out of her hair. "I withdraw the ambiguous verb. You *went* there, with more than typical speed. Okay? To do what? To—"

"I didn't *go* there," says Tester. Truth. Truth and then context: "I was already there."

"You were . . . already there?"

I've never been a big fan of the figure *the mind races*. Minds do not race. Mine doesn't. Thoughts don't whip in wild circles like small storms, chasing themselves around in pointless frenzies. When I visualize my thoughts I see them emerging half formed from some unseen basal station, bubbling up as if from a seafloor, rising and cohering, gaining mass as they combine. The mind does not race; it conjures, it swells.

"You were already at your friend's home at six twenty-nine in the morning?"

"Yes," she says. "I was there."

"Was Karen in the house?"

"No."

"Were you alone in the house?"

"No."

I feel it—I feel it all at once and all over my body, in the palms of my hands and the soles of my feet. Not the distinct atmospheric warp of a lie entering the near air, but something more elemental, something plain: understanding, rushing through me like the world tilting. I lean closer, lower my voice, as if there's any privacy possible. As if the room isn't capturing every word so each can be transcribed later on, the truth forever bubbling out from itself, the Objectively So endlessly accreting and growing like life, growing like life grows.

"Do you . . ." I say slowly. "Do you, in addition to your relationship with Ms. Sampson, have a relationship with Ms. Sampson's *husband*?"

Elena gives her head a small tight nod, but that's not enough and she knows it's not enough. I could get up right now, stuff my papers back in my bag, make some apologetic noises, and go. If this is all it is, it's nothing. A scrap, a tatter of incidental truth, something that slid off the roof along with the roofer, like a dead leaf that tumbled from the gutter as it tore free. And maybe if I didn't already find the dictionary that was not—maybe if Mose Crane didn't have days missing from his Record—maybe I'd even do it. Let Elena off the hook and shuffle backward out of her office.

But I can't do it now. Now it's too late.

So I make her confirm it for the Record. I make her say it louder, which she does, too loud, pointedly loud. "I have a relationship with Karen's *husband.*"

"And what is his name?"

"Barney Sampson," she says, and in her voice I can hear that it's all gone, any trace of residual affection between Elena Tester and myself is gone now, never to return.

Extramarital affairs aren't illegal, of course; *lying* about them is illegal, as all lies are illegal, but Elena didn't do that either. She was simply doing something in secret, hidden from everyone but not from the Record. She hoped that her friend Karen would never find out, and she certainly hoped that no Speculator would ever lope into her office with an investigative agenda that happened to intersect with her infidelity.

Everything is on the Record, just waiting to be discovered: the whispered confession, the stolen kiss. This is not the *goal* of our good and golden systems; the goal is simply the maintenance of reality as it occurs, so that all can live together within the same sheltering truth, safe within the strong high walls of the Objectively So. We may keep secrets from one another, but not from the Record, and if life is therefore made more difficult for the adulterer or the petty-cash-box pilferer, for the student with his eye on his deskmate's paper or the worker who clocks in late, surely that's a price worth paying—or even, looked at differently, not a price at all, but a benefice. A gift we are given by the ever-presence of truth.

Captain Elena Tester, right about now, isn't seeing it that way. Her face has colored. She stares at me, eyes lit with anger, as I press on.

"How long have you had a relationship with Mr. Sampson?"

"Judge," she says.

"What?"

"*Judge* Sampson."

A judge, as it turns out, in the Court of Aberrant Natural Phenomena. His courtroom is on Grand Street, in one of the old slate-gray justice buildings. Those who come before the ANP are most often referred from the Social Services divisions, but it certainly would not be unusual for the regular police, including officers under Tester's jurisdiction, to be called to offer testimony before him. These facts paint a certain picture, and I record its outline in my Day Book, keeping my face neutral. Not just an intimate problem but a professional problem, a conflict-of-interest problem. A conflagration of problems for Elena Tester. I have walked in here today and lit a fire on her desk.

"And now here is my question for *you*, Mr. Speculator."

Elena stands up, places her palms flat on the desk. Whatever this question is, I am supposed to answer it and then go. Our interview is over. "Are you comfortable, destroying my life offhandedly? Destroying Barney's life? Because a man happened to fall off his roof? Is that something that makes you happy?"

"No," I say. "Not happy."

"But content."

I think that over for a moment, judging the true, full meaning of the word "content."

"My professional responsibility is to follow this incident until its truth is full and final," I say quietly. "My personal hope is that it causes you no unnecessary grief."

"Oh," she says. "Great. My personal hope is that you can go fuck yourself. Do you have any more questions for me, Mr. Ratesic?"

"No, Captain," I say. "Not at this time."

She glares at me, the rims of her eyes gone red, as I rise to go. I'm at the door with all my papers gathered up, and when I look back, Tester stares at me coldly, as if from a great distance.

"You weren't good enough for her, Laszlo."

"I know."

Truth, a sliver of weaponized truth.

"That's what happened to you and Silvie. In case you didn't know. You were never, ever good enough."

I stop at the charmingly gritty Asian market just down the road from my house, near where Bundy turns into Centinela. Tucked inside is a brightly lit food court where you can get seven different kinds of ramen, including the kind I love, miso broth swimming with thick-cut slabs of pork and sprinkled with sliced green onions. In line for the soup, I'm thinking *Never good enough*. Digging out a handful of crumpled bills, muttering "Thanks," driving home with the bag balanced precariously on the shotgun seat, and I'm thinking *Never, ever good enough*.

I get home from the market and there's no chance Silvie will be waiting for me on the porch as I would have found her six months ago, sipping wine on the green glider we bought together at a Palms yard sale, awaiting me in the waxy moonlight, raising her glass in an ironic toast as I trudge toward her up our steps.

And yet my heart fills with dumb hope as I shut the car door. The Moon is in fact waxy in the sky, and the green glider is on the porch, and the breeze is easing it gently back and forth, but Silvie isn't on it.

I put my dinner down in the living room and tell the wall-mounted to turn on. The wall-mounted is just like the screen at work, except it's bigger and flatter and you don't control it—it's more like you're at its mercy. In the office you can requisition reality in the official capacity, get the stretches you want and slide them into your screen and say "Go." But with the wall-mounted, you just pick from among whatever happens to be on. It's all slices of life, culled from captures all over the city, arranged by the entertainment professionals into themed streams: "Arguments in Restaurants," "Surprise Proposals," "People Searching for Small Things They Lost."

I flip around for a while in search of something suitably non-taxing, maybe one of the unpopulated streams, "Traffic Lights Cycling" or something like that. I settle for "Mildly Comical Misunderstandings," unpack my soup, and eat it slowly, trying not to get any on my coat because I know I'll be wearing it tomorrow. I say "Play" to the wall-mounted and watch some poor asshole waiting at the Superior Java on Finley Avenue, checking his watch, while his date on split screen waits at the Echo Park location, checking hers.

When I'm done I turn off the screen, chuck the empty containers in the trash, and head downstairs to do my archiving.

My own Provisional Record is in the car park under the house, dimly lit, thick with dust and spiderwebs no matter how often I clean it out, which is not nearly often enough. I tear from my Day Book the duplicate copies of the six pages I've gone through today, fold them neatly, and put them in a fresh Mylar bag. I add all the purchase receipts from my meals, the conversation stamps from everyone I talked to, all the detritus from the day that has been. I seal the bag and mark the date and time and open the box and put the bag in and close the box again.

And there, at the very bottom of my bag, lying there heavy with menace like unexploded ordnance, is the book.

The Prisoner.

Forged material. A piece of Not So. The air around it warped, thick, shimmering with dissonance.

I turn it over in my hands. Take it away with me, back to the kitchen.

The day, my day, is over. It's on the Record. There is darkness at every window. But here I am, awake and alive in the nighttime silence, contemplating this strange novel.

It's still wrapped in its pretend jacket, masquerading as *The Everyday Citizen's Dictionary.* I wish to read it. I want to. I want to know what Mose Crane was doing with this otherworldly artifact, and aside from that—more than that—I am overcome with a desire to do what we don't do, what the world will not allow, what is prevented by the Basic Law and common sense and conscience, which is to immerse myself in an alternate reality and luxuriate in it, let it rise up and over me and bear me away.

The book wants me to read it, but I don't. I stuff it in my bureau, its true face hidden behind its phony cover, and I go to bed.

11.

It fucks with my sleep. I swear it. The book.

When I rise I feel like a creature of the forest, draggled, wild-eyed, and sullen. I piss and brush my teeth while in the corners of my eyes I see unknown faces, alien landscapes, splintered pieces of foreign facts.

When I'm dressed I give myself a warning glare in the mirror, turn on my heel, and talk to the dresser.

"You can fuck off," I tell *The Prisoner* by Benjamin Wish through the thin wood face of the drawer. "Fuck off and leave me alone."

I wrestle my body into the civilizing structure of my suit. Push my hair down flat, rake through the tangles of my beard. Get in the car, hiss at my reflection in the rearview, and drive to work.

There's a cluster of activity on the thirtieth floor, everybody gathered around my desk and murmuring, like my day decided to get started without me, like I've shown up late for my own life. Aysa Paige is at my desk already, and so is Arlo and also a woman—middle-aged, thick-haired, looking agitated and restless, and I know her right away. Damn it. I stop just beyond the elevator door, the wide vista of the city glimmering through the glass walls all around me, silently wishing the elevator would come back and take me down again.

"You," says the lady, spotting me, pointing right at me. *"You."*

"Ms. Tarjin." From the diner. With the boys. The liar and the thief. Great. This is great. "There are twenty-four hours in the day."

"Please help me," she says, blowing past the truth I've handed her, tears standing in her eyes, tears staining her cheeks. "You have to help."

The son Eddie, the younger one—the one who is not in jail— is standing just behind her, looking miserable, embarrassed, a reluctant second on her fool's errand. "And seven days in the week," he mumbles, completing the circuit on her behalf, and Arlo nods at him approvingly.

"Good man," he murmurs. "Good man." Eddie studies us both for a second and looks back down at his feet.

I sit down heavily in my chair, set down the croissant and coffee I've brought for breakfast. "Ms. Tarjin, look—"

"No, please, just listen," she says, and wipes at her eyes with her wrist. Eddie digs a ratty tissue out of the pocket of his jeans and presses it on his mother. "Let me talk," she says, "because they're saying Todd could go to jail for ten years."

"Ten?" That doesn't sound right. The coffee I am holding, a medium with two sugars from the Donut Star that feels like the only thing tethering me to civilization, is growing cold before my very eyes.

"Yes, ten, because he told the same lie, they say, they said he told the same lie twice, to two different people. To me and then to you."

Of course. The same false utterance made to multiple parties means multiple counts. But I don't know why this lady is here—I don't know what *I'm* supposed to do about it.

Arlo gives Eddie a sympathetic smile and shuffles over to his desk. Ms. Paige hangs on the outskirts of the conversation, making the moment a part of her training, studying the way I handle this particular law enforcement situation: the human flotsam of a successful arrest, washed up miserable on my shore. She stands against the side wall, beneath portraits of famous dead Speculators, including Charlie, of course, Charlie captured in his customary pose: smiling, cocky, chin jutted out, arms confidently crossed.

"The rules are the rules," I tell Ms. Tarjin.

"Yeah, well, and what if the rules are wrong?" she says, looking back at me defiantly. "What if they're not *fair?*"

"You are very much entitled to hold that as truth" is my answer. "That is an expression of opinion, and opinions are subjective, and as long as your expressed opinion reflects your honest interior position . . ." I trail off. I don't know how to say this without sounding like a prick, so I just go ahead and sound like a prick. "Then it doesn't matter *what* you think. Your son lied. He broke the law. And he has to face punishment, and the punishment is prescribed by the State. You should understand that the punishment could be worse."

"He's right, ma'am. He knows."

Ms. Paige speaks gently, all the *"Yes, sir," "No, sir"* sharpness replaced by a gentle reassurance. Ms. Tarjin turns her pained eyes toward her. "What do you mean?"

"Well—it just—" Paige clears her throat. "It could really have been a lot worse." She's too kind to make it explicit, what she knows, what we all know: liars are subject to exile. Had Todd Tarjin's misrepresentations been judged inflammatory, or intended to disrupt the business of the State, or in any way an outrage to the common good, he could have been sent away entirely. Forget about Folsom, San Quentin, or Pelican Bay, forget about ten years. There is a version of this story that ends with Todd in the desert—beyond the desert. Beyond whatever is beyond that.

It happens. It doesn't happen often, but it does happen.

Eddie, meanwhile, stands diffident, trying to figure out how to feel. This is all because of him, and he is bearing the weight of that knowledge while still glad not to be facing the terror of prison. Guilt, relief, and anger—a confusion of emotion moves like shadow on his face.

"Okay, but —I mean." Ms. Tarjin crouches before me, her voice ragged with need. "There has to be something you can do. Anything."

She is looking at me with tearful eyes, sadness and need coming off her in waves, her hands pushing into her hair. Eddie is behind her, twisting a torn tissue.

"Ms. Tarjin, the rules are very clear, and as it happens, they are quite specific. Punishment for falsehood is a bulwark. It's—"

She snorts at the word "bulwark," as if I were speaking a curse, an insult. Invoking some demon, instead of the whole system of good works that protects the Objectively So.

"It's part of what keeps us safe, ma'am."

"It's not keeping Todd safe. It's not keeping my family safe."

"Respectfully, Ms. Tarjin, your son chose to tell a lie."

"He was desperate! He was trying to help his brother. He—"

"I am aware of the context. I understand the nuances. I was there, remember? But I'm telling you: strip away the context and the foundational truth is that he lied. In a public place, purposefully and specifically, he told a purposeful and specific untruth."

I get up, and she can't help but recoil, step back from my height, my weight, just the breadth of me. "Imagine if everyone did it. Imagine if each person was allowed the luxury of claiming their own truth, building a reality of their own in which they can live. Imagine the danger that would pose, how quickly those lies would metastasize, and the extraordinary threat that would pose to the world."

I am conscious as I make this statement that it is true and it is also simultaneously a performance of truth. I am performing for Arlo, my mentor and friend; I am performing for Aysa Paige, who stands deferentially listening, absorbing. I am performing for Charlie, hung up there on the wall, behind the shield of his crossed arms, watching from the distant past.

But even as I deliver my pronouncement, chapter and verse of the Basic Law, and of the reasons behind the law, I am conscious of the fact that this is not a case study, this is not a training module for the edification of Ms. Aysa Paige, this is a real human person whose life is in the balance, whose heart right now is a bubble I hold in my hand. Ms. Tarjin with her gray-streaked hair and determined chin is a professional problem, and she is an unanswerable conundrum and she is at the same time a person. A person clutching the arm of her unstrung son, her dark eyes alive with emotion, a person in low heels and a green blouse, frantic, desperate, trying to exist in the world, trying, like we all are, all the time, to bend the world into a shape in which we can fit.

Ms. Paige stands patiently, her hands behind her back, looking down at the floor. She is too respectful a junior partner to let me see how she feels about the matter, but she's also too decent a person for me not to be able to tell.

"Okay, well, then," says Ms. Tarjin with soft bitterness. "I guess I've wasted my time."

"No. You've registered your opinion," I say quietly. "You told the truth. Your truth. That's not a waste of time."

"Yeah," she says. "Great."

There is a crimp in the air, a mild bend, as my own half-truth, cynical and self-protecting, rolls through. Ms. Tarjin nods tightly, a single tear running down her cheek, and then Eddie breaks his silence, speaking suddenly in a rapid burst. "Yeah, but what if we change places?"

I turn to him. "What?"

Arlo looks up from his desk, shakes his head, looks down again.

"Is there some sort of—I don't know. Is there, like, a mechanism, or... I don't know." He looks over at Aysa, perhaps having sensed that she's the one with a foot in the world as it exists thirty floors down from here, outside the Service, out in the world.

Eddie must know on some level that his suggestion is preposterous. He is making a performance of his own; it is for his mother's benefit. It is *something* he can do.

Paige does me the small mercy of answering in my stead. "No, Eddie," she says softly. "The law does not allow for anything like that." She gives me a quick look, and I take a breath, almost don't say it, but then say it:

"All right, Ms. Tarjin. Listen."

"Yes?" The excitement of possibility shivers across her face. "Yes?"

"The one thing I can do is, I can call the prosecuting attorney."

"You can?"

"Yes. Just about—"

"Oh—oh! Will you do that?"

"Just as far as—"

"Can you promise me?"

She clutches my shoulders. I wriggle in her grasp. "Yeah. I mean—sure. I promise. I can say—not as an official, but as a person—I can formally absolve Todd of that one lie, the one he told me."

"Is that like—" This is Eddie now, trying on an adult voice, a formal persona. "Like not pressing charges?"

"Not exactly," I say. "Not really. The PA is under zero obligation to listen to me."

"But they will. They will, though. Right? They *will*."

Ms. Tarjin is hugging me. Kelly is her name, I remember that now, Kelly Elizabeth Tarjin. She is pressing her face tightly against my wide chest. I close my arms around her, just for a second. "It means his sentence, and I mean if the prosecutor agrees—"

"Could be half," says Eddie.

"Uh, yes. Could be. Yeah."

Ms. Tarjin lets go. She steps back. Musters a smile, just a hint of one, and I nod, hoping now I can sit down, drink my coffee. Ms. Tarjin reaches up and grabs a small tuft of my thick red beard and tugs it, just enough so I can feel it. I blink, and she lets go, and pats the side of my face. It's like I'm a wayward animal, and she is—sweetly but firmly—bringing me to heel. I don't know if I blush or not, but anyway, I feel like I'm blushing.

"And you promise?"

"I do."

"Okay."

And then they're gone. I am aware of Paige looking at me, and of Arlo over at his desk looking at me also, and Mr. Cullers maybe even stirring from his stupor, but I just focus on my white paper bag, taking out the croissant and taking a greasy bite.

"That was nice," says Paige quietly.

I chew. I shrug. "I don't want to talk about it."

"Okay. I just wondered what the circumstances are that allow for that kind of decision."

"We're not talking about it," I tell her.

"Okay."

Arlo is smiling at his desk. I can feel him smiling. I scowl, turn to Aysa, press the point: "Okay?"

"Okay."

I take a sip of my coffee at last. Sweet and lukewarm. "How's the review going? Of the courtyard stretches."

"Slowly."

"All right, then." I get up and point at my chair. "Better get back to it, then."

"It's just—"

"What?"

By now I know the look: keen, attentive, hesitant to just burst out with whatever realization she's locked into, but determined not to let me move on with my life before she's enlightened me. "Go on, Paige. What is it?"

"I had a bit of a speculation. This morning. I woke up and I just—because of what you found out yesterday, about the home-owner, his affair with the . . . the policewoman . . ." She is slowing down, waiting for me to interrupt, to tell her to sit down like I said and watch the damn stretches. Which I should do. I should lean on her with the full weight of my authority, tell her we will speculate further on this matter when I have decided that it has ripened anew for speculation. I'm supposed to be the ballast, af-ter all.

The problem is, so far she's always been right.

"Go on, Ms. Paige. I'm waiting."

"So we have Crane, right? We have this roofer—this mysterious roofer."

"Adjectives," I say, scowling, waving a hand, and she says, "We have this roofer. He's there early, he's there off schedule, right?"

I nod, affirming the flat facts, while she barrels on: he's early, he's off schedule, he's got these missing days, and then, meanwhile, we have the judge conducting an affair with a captain of the police, a big no-no for both of them. Aysa gives all of this to me, ramrod straight and rattling it all off, her whole chain of speculation.

And then the punch line: "I am speculating that Crane was up there on the roof to collect evidence of the affair, in order to black-mail the judge."

"Or the captain," I add quietly, and Aysa blinks. She was waiting for me to tell her she is wrong or crazy, but she is neither wrong nor crazy. She's on to something. Of course she is.

"Yes, right," she says, surprised. "Or the captain."

"Okay," I say. "Good."

Since the Tarjins left, the room has returned to its usual bustle. Alvaro has taken up his position by the big board, a cigar stub jammed into the corner of his mouth, furiously updating the chart of ongoing investigations. Specs are coming off the elevator and getting on it, slamming drawers, slinging on their shoulder bags to head out into the field, files clutched under their arms. Arlo is a still point in this chaotic universe, hunched at his small desk, making his small notations. "So, Ms. Paige? What do we do now?"

"Are you—asking me?"

"I am indeed."

I wait. I am trying to hitch her tremendous powers of discernment to operational effectiveness. If she is going to be Charlie, that's what she needs to do.

"We need to get the reality. The stretches showing his death. We need it right now. That's key. That's—right?"

Only at the last moment does her confidence waver; only the little word "right?" comes out uncertain, high-pitched, girlish. I stare back at her evenly, playing the heavy. As if I am one step ahead of her, guiding her along; when in reality I am standing back, letting her go, hustling to stay alongside her.

"Why is it so important? We know how the man died, Ms. Paige."

"Yes, but—" Her eyes narrow. She won't be thrown. "We don't need to see how he died, Mr. Ratesic. We need to see what he was doing when it happened. Was he trying to get in? Was he trying to see in?"

"Yes. Correct," I say. "Anything else?"

"We need to reconstruct those missing days. Find out when or if Mose Crane crossed paths with the judge."

"Or the captain," I say again, and she nods, pleased.

"Right. Yeah. Or the captain. Thank you, sir—thank you, Laszlo."

I move to put my coat on and realize I never got a chance to take it off. One of these days, I think, I will have a day with hot coffee, a day that's quiet and peaceful. And I will float through that day, carrying no worries in my pockets. Someday soon, perhaps. Some good day. But not today.

"Go back down to nine, tell Woody that we need to see the stretch of Mose Crane falling off that roof. Whatever you did to hustle him out of the stakeout stretch from Crane's front door, do it again. And tell him no shortcuts. I want thirty-second margins on either end. Make it clear. And tell him we need to see it *today*. He's going to yell at you. Let him. I'm going to work on getting a Contingent Reassembly of those missing days."

"Don't we just file a request for that?"

"We could," I say. "But it'll be a lot quicker if I go over. I know someone over there." I sigh. "Unfortunately."

"Oh. Wait—why unfortunately?"

I knew this was coming. Somehow from the minute this case started I knew it would happen.

"It's my wife," I say, and then I catch it. Correct it. "My ex-wife."

12.

I hear the bells for Charlie all the time. Whether I want to or not, I hear them ringing. I hear the bells, and I feel the unseasonable chill the air bore that day, and I feel the uneven ground of the cemetery, how it was to stand among the throngs of mourners at Forest Lawn, the crowd spread out in all directions. The clouds spitting drizzle, the sky as flat and toneless as a coffin lid.

My father, bareheaded, is staring at the ground. Arlo slips among the mourners, holding himself together and everyone else besides. Taking all hands, murmuring condolence into all ears. A kind word for every devastated member of our service.

I stand alone. Apart from the crowd. A woman is beside me, a substantial woman wearing a black dress and red shoes. She asks me if I have an umbrella, which I don't.

"You're a Speculator," she says, and I nod. "Did you work with Mr. Ratesic?"

"Yes," I tell her, then after a brief, agonized pause, "he was my brother."

Her face changes. All of the exploits had been related in *Trusted Authority*. Charlie was already famous for what he did.

"Your brother. Oh, wow. I'm so sorry—so sorry for you. For all of us."

It takes no great speculation to tell what is happening: abstract adoration for a public hero transmogrified by grief into concrete interest in the bulky sad sack standing in the rain at the hero's grave, the hero's surviving relation. She tugs at the sleeve of her dress, shows me her face, and smiles sadly. Her lips are red. A member of the regular populace discovering herself in the company of the man of the hour, or the next best thing.

That's me: the next best thing. Truer words never spoken.

Me and Silvie stuck it out for ten years, ten years moving together through time and ten years standing together at that open pit, watching the box lowered into the ground, the bells ringing out his years. He was with us the whole time—he was never in the box. For ten years Charlie was at my shoulder, pointing out the ways I was never good enough. Reminding me I was never her first choice.

"If you could put your hands in the air, sir."

"Yes."

"If you could turn around for me, sir."

"Yes."

"A little slower, if you wouldn't mind."

I follow all the instructions. I am being patted down, up along the thick lines of my legs, the torso, and the arms.

Here in the Grand Entrance Hall of the Permanent Record, during the long, careful examination required for entry, there is no exchange of asseverations, no small talk. The attendants remove every item from my bag—my Day Book, a tattered copy of yesterday's *Authority*, the limp remains of a three-day-old sandwich—and lay it all out on a table and document the contents in a series of photographs. There are four of them doing the work, efficiently checking me in: four matching, neatly creased brown uniforms; four perfectly inexpressive faces. I've seen all of these faces before. The Librarians work in teams that rotate in and out in undisclosed schedules, and they surely remember me too. I've been here enough, and part of their job is to remember. But they don't smile in recognition, they don't ask me how I'm doing. They are unfailingly polite, but they're on duty. They're efficient and rigorous. They're doing their thing.

"If you could open your mouth, sir."

"Okay."

I open my mouth and they shine in a light. Then they shine the beam into my eyes, one at a time, one of them making notes in her Day Book while the other works the light. Another acts as an in-house capture team, circling us with a handheld, getting it all down. Reality being forged, the Record being made, even here at the threshold of the Record itself.

"Each of your fingers, sir. Thumbs first."

I do as they say, pressing my fingers one by one — thumbs first — into the ink, rolling them onto the pad, affirming my presence in this place and at this time, ten times over. *I am here. I am going to be here. I will have been here.*

These are the custodians of the Record. They are Librarians, and they do not fuck around.

"If you could bare your head for a moment."

I grimace. This is the part I fucking hate. But I take off the pinhole and bow my head, submissive, silent. Push back my hair.

"Thank you, sir," murmurs the Librarian and she takes out her wand.

It's weird because the damn thing is nothing. It's just a stick, really, a slim metal tube, 14.5 inches long, black metal with a silver cap at either end. And all she does, quiet unsmiling efficient Librarian, is bring it very close to my head, as close as she can without touching, and then move it slowly across my forehead. Not looking at me, not looking at the wand, holding her eyes half shut in concentration, feeling for the minute reverberations in her palm she'll get or not get as she hovers the wand slowly, very slowly, along the curve of my skull.

I do, though, I fucking hate it, and I know I'm not alone: everybody hates it. Cullers won't even go to the Record anymore. He flat out refuses, and just because of the wanding. You can't even feel it; nothing *happens*. It's just so unsettling—no other word for it—the creeping movement of that thing from one side of your head to the other. The abstract sense of invasion, of the mind being opened like a cabinet.

"Okay, sir." She puts the wand away. "Enjoy your visit."

From the outside, the Record is a two-story building, just the Grand Entrance Hall on the first floor and the modest museum, free to the public, upstairs. It's only when you begin your descent, down in one of the majestic elevator cars or down the spiral staircase at the precise center of the Hall, that you can begin to understand the size of the place, its dimension, its astonishing shape. Substory after substory, basement below basement, stacked one beneath the other like the drawers in a dresser, cataloged and cross-cataloged, an ever-expanding library and permanent archive of all that is part of what is So. Rooms full of stretches in rolling bins, cataloged by date and cross-cataloged by event; rooms full of manila file folders hung in narrow metal cabinets, cataloged and cross-cataloged, by person, by location, referenced and cross-referenced into Significant Individuals, Significant Places, Collated Significant Events.

The basements are dotted with organizational kiosks, octagonal stations with keyboards and screens on each of their sides, from which the Librarians can perform system scours of the complete collection, summoning forth individual stretches or files or notebooks or boxes for review. Each level is built on a hub-and-spoke design, a spiderweb of hallways radiating out from the central pole of the staircase, and each could theoretically be expanded out forever.

And eventually, of course, it will, the Record *will* be expanded out forever. Because new material is always being added, new reality is always happening, new truth is entering the world every moment, and so new hallways will have to be dug, further excavations undertaken, the bedrock forged of our past to undergird our future.

I skip the elevator today. I'm not going that far. My boot heels clang melodically on every step as I descend, around and around the spiral, deeper into the sacred heart of the Objectively So, with the metal staircase shivering slightly under my weight.

The stairwell is encased in heavy glass, but through each door off each landing you can see the dim corridors bending off into darkness. It is intense and disquieting to be surrounded by so much information, so much truth, everything we know, all of it gathered together. It is oppressive, actually, in a way. In a way, it is terrifying. Down here in the heart of the State, the deep hidden heart of the world.

Silvie is on Basement Four. I pass the department doors, one after another, along the corridor: the Office of the Permanent Census, the Office of Weights and Measures, the offices of Data Sets and Facial Recognition and Element Stability Across Time. And here—the Department of Contingent Reality Reassembly. She's in there. She's working.

You have to press a small glowing button to ring the bell, and it takes me a second to get my shit together enough to ring, and whether that's because I'm nervous about seeing Silvie or I'm just a little worked up like I always get a little worked up down here in the solemn silence of the Record, I don't know. But at last I press the stupid buzzer, and a moment later Mr. Willis opens it, scowling.

"You have no appointment," he says.

"Yeah, I know."

Mr. Willis hates me. Silvie isn't going to be happy to see me either. It's possible I've made a terrible mistake.

Contingent Reassembly is a humble and underdecorated office, ugly gray carpeting and dull yellow lights. The furniture is shabby and chipped and dented, and the walls are lined with framed black-and-white nature prints from around the State: rushing waterfalls and towering redwoods, windmills and freight trains, coffee plantations in Santa Barbara and marijuana fields in Sacramento, the majestic smelters that ring the banks of the Salton Sea. But the pictures are washed out, laid indifferently in chintzy frames. All subjects made much less beautiful than they are in reality. This office never was good enough for Silvie, but then again neither was I.

Willis curtly instructs me to wait. He is the CRR's pale and tiny office manager, who, with the divorce, has at last been given license to bring his distaste for me out into the open. So I sit in the waiting room, half reading this morning's *Trusted Authority*, leafing through the latest economic indicators, the comprehensive lists of the dead and the born. There's the latest photograph of the committee of experts, and my eyes as they always do scan the bland, unsmiling faces until I find the one I've met in person: Laura Petras, Our Acknowledged Expert on the Enforcement of the Laws. A plain woman, barely smiling, in a gray suit and tan shoes, surrounded by her similarly dressed staff. Professional and dull and inoffensive.

"What are you doing here, Laszlo?"

I put down the *Authority*.

My heart delivers a single smacking thump, a big mule kick, just at the sight of her: Silvie, my Silvie, mine no more, hands on hips, ruddy and skeptical. My former wife is not as tall as me, but she's damn tall. The average woman is five foot five and a half, and Silvie is six foot one, buxom and broad-chested, blonde-headed and red-cheeked. I want to gather her up, press her to my body, which is most of what I ever wanted to do for the last ten years: hold her and tell her about all the shit the world was doing to drive me crazy, and listen to her laugh and remind me how lucky I was to be alive in the first place—how lucky we all are to be alive, to be in the Golden State, the two of us especially because we get to serve it.

For ten years that was all I wanted, until we split up six months ago because I'm a moron.

"What do you *want*, Laz?"

"That's how we're going to start? We can't start nice?"

"Laszlo. Come on. What is it?"

Mr. Willis scrutinizes this exchange from his small desk, his allegiance clear. I edge closer to Silvie, trying to screen Willis out of the conversation, and Silvie draws back, as if I'm a predator, a snake in the forest coming in to strike. Her instinctive withdrawal stabs me in the heart. Silvie in her gold earrings, with her masses of thick hair piled up and curled, almost but not quite corralled, some of it always drifting down to tease her neck. She purses her lips and crosses her arms.

"The last time we talked you said we weren't going to talk for a while."

"I know. But it's not a law. It's not a bulwark. We're not exiled from each other."

"Stipulated."

"Do you think we can talk in your office?"

"I'd rather not."

"Sil."

"Is this a personal matter or a professional matter?"

"Professional, Silvie. Okay? I need your help with a case." I hold up my hands, like a man surrendering, like a magician proving there's nothing up his sleeve. "Okay?"

"All right," says Silvie after an extended pause. "Come on back."

"Are you quite sure?" Mr. Willis puts in, and I can tell Silvie *isn't* sure. She's too smart not to know that me saying I'm here on business is at best the top layer in a complicated multilayered truth. But there is no question that she blames herself for what's become of us, and she knows that I, grudging child in my heart, I blame her also, and she feels she owes me and she feels she always will.

It's what I'm counting on, big clever monster that I am.

"Five minutes," says Silvie at last. "I'm not busy, but I don't like seeing you. It makes me sad."

"Okay," I say, and follow her through the inner doors and down the hall. "Stipulated."

Silvie gestures to the chair on the other side of her desk, takes her own seat. Her inner office is a lot more pleasant than the rest of the floor: minimalist and cream-colored, gently lit and full of small cactuses in tidy beige planters. It's got the cool, understated aesthetic she always hoped to achieve in our home in Mar Vista, an effort forever foiled by my total indifference to my surroundings. There is a small coffee table, with exactly one book on it: *Past Is Prologue,* of course, the novel of the founding of the Golden State. I kiss my forefinger and brush it across the cover of the book, while Silvie waits, not softening, her eyes watchful and withholding. Clearly determined to play the surface truth of the situation: two professionals settling in to discuss a professional matter.

"So what is it?" she says. "It's a case?"

"Yes."

"What kind of case?"

I smile, lay my heavy arms down on the desk, and swallow the wild urge to confess that I set up the whole thing—I broke into a man's house and burned two weeks of his days, I clambered up behind him on a roof and pushed him to his death, all to contrive a reason to be here now, sitting across from you, Silvie, with our arms almost touching on your desk.

Come on, Laszlo. Get it together. Take a fucking breath.

"I have two weeks of missing days that I need reconstructed."

"Whose days?"

"A man named Mose Crane. A roofer. Construction guy. Recently deceased."

Silvie twists her lips to one side, the kind of small unconscious gesture that I watched her make a thousand times, and which I now force myself to ignore. When you have been in love with someone in the past, there are a million small trapdoors you can fall through that would take you right back.

"Mose Crane. A bad guy?"

"No. Well, I don't know what kind of guy he is yet. That's why I need the days built."

"And you said two weeks? Two weeks in aggregate?"

"No. A two-week period. Two weeks straight."

"Empty bags or no bags?"

"No bags. Clean."

"No *kidding.*" Silvie shakes her head at me and puckers her lips. "Rather an extensive project you're dumping in my lap, wouldn't you say?"

I shift in my chair. "Is it?"

"Question with a question is pretty weak, Mr. Ratesic," she says. "Even for you."

But Silvie is interested. Her curiosity adds an intensity to the light in her eyes. She is biting at her lower lip, leaning forward. This is part of what I was counting on, coming to her directly like this. Despite it all she's intrigued, as curious as I am about how a day laborer, about how anyone, would come to have a precise two-week bite taken out of his Provisional Record. There are many things we never had in common—almost everything—but Silvie, bless her, was ever as interested as her man in the byzantine business of reality maintenance.

"What happened to those weeks?" she wants to know.

"That's part of what I'm trying to find out."

"How long ago are they?"

"Not long. Six months back."

"The subject is dead, though, you said?"

"Dead."

"Well, that *does* make it easier." Silvie leans back a bit, takes a look at her watch. She told me I had five minutes, and five minutes is all I'm gonna get. "Talk to Mr. Willis," she says, "and he'll take the information, fill out a ninety-four B."

"Silvie. I could have done a ninety-four from my desk."

"Perhaps you should have."

"Silvie."

"Laszlo." A smile flickers at her lips at this old game, batting back and forth, but she stops it up, remembers to glare at me. "When days are lost, there is a process, and the Office of Contingent Reality Reassembly is happy to execute our duties. Fill out the form and we will get to work on it."

"I don't want help from the office *in general*," I tell her. "I want help from *you*."

"And you didn't think it would be uncomfortable, to come to me of all the people in this department?"

"I knew it would be uncomfortable," I say. "But you're the best."

"You are trying to flatter me."

"Well, yeah." I smile, trying to smile with my whole face, put the smile into my eyes, my fat cheeks. "But also, it's true."

Silvie rolls her eyes, but I've got her, just a little bit I've got her. There's a small measure of happiness blooming on her face. The bells are ringing—coming from somewhere, from below and around us—and we are at Forest Lawn, turning to notice each other, standing with no umbrellas while the bells ring for Charlie. She is saying "Oh, wow" when I tell her who I am. Who I'm related to. Every time she smiles I am thrown back to the beginning.

Now a moment has passed into a different moment, we have reverted to an old way of being, and it's almost worse. It is: it's worse. We were in love for a long time, or whatever it was we were in, and for a second, another second, it feels like it would be the easiest thing in the world to pick up right where we left off.

Except all the rest of it would pick up too: the shadows that never cleared up for long, the pressure of the past on all our present moments. The ghost of a question that was in the room with us every time we were alone.

The ghost of my dead brother, whose heavy bootsteps I can hear even now—even now—descending the spiral staircase, as he comes and finds us, who even now I can see slipping into Silvie's neat clean office and making himself at home. In his blacks, grinning on Silvie's clean white sofa, his confident feet kicked up on her coffee table, to remind me why it would never work. Why it never worked and could never work in any conceivable future.

The same miserable trick he pulled the whole time we were together.

Silvie writes in her Day Book as I tell her what I have. Mose Crane. The address on Ellendale. The most recent employer and the place and manner of death. This *is* a big project I'm dumping in her lap, and we both know it. She's going to have to seek out people who crossed paths with him and take doubles off their pads, find the roads he drove and the paths he walked and cut copies of the stretches, find the stores where he shopped and pull receipt copies. Build a whole picture from scratch, off whatever scraps of starting and ending evidence I can give her.

"I'll need to know what proportion of his totals the missing days represent," she says.

"Okay."

"So — how many boxes did he have? Total, I mean."

"Six."

"Six?" She looks up. "Six and what?"

"Six. Five and a quarter, actually."

She leans back. "No shit."

"No shit, sister."

"And there's no documentation of some kind of destructive incident? A fire, or — "

"Nope. No fire. I don't think there was one, Sil. I don't. I think..."

"What, Laz?"

I leave it there. I don't know what I think, I don't know what I've been thinking, but a truth has seized me, a truth I can't see but I can feel, a forearm wrapped around my throat from behind, like a kidnapper's. Something shy of speculation: a suspicion. An instinct. A *fear*.

Silvie sets down her pen. Looks up at the capture in the right-hand corner of her office, then back at me. She can see inside my head. She has always been able to see inside my head.

"Mr. Ratesic," she says. "I am going to formally suggest once again that you pursue this matter through the appropriate channels."

"Mrs. Ratesic. I am going to formally decline. Respectfully. I am after a speedy resolution of this matter."

"Our work takes time for a good reason. The whole point of this department is to provide accuracy." Like she needs to tell me that: the whole point of the whole world is to provide accuracy. All our departments, all our endeavors. All our work together and as one. "What is the deal with this case, Laszlo?"

"I am trying to resolve an anomaly, that's all," I say. "And it's not even me. My partner—"

"A partner?" An amused glimmer in her eyes. "You have a partner?"

"It was Arlo's idea," I say, and leave it there. "But this partner, she thinks that the owner of the house maybe had crossed paths with this roofer at some point in the past, and that his presence on the roof that day was not coincidental."

I don't need to mention who owns that house, and I definitely don't need to mention who he was sleeping with when his wife wasn't around. Maybe Silvie knows about Elena and the judge, and maybe she doesn't. But I have promised Captain Elena Tester that I will do my best to minimize the appearance on the Record of the flat facts I have discovered about her, so that's what I do now. I keep quiet, let Silvie think this thing over for a second.

"She sounds like a smart cookie, this partner of yours."

"Well." I wink. "I'll cure her of that in a hurry."

Silvie laughs, and I do too, and it is the old laughter we are sharing: laughter of the green glider, laughter of the late-night last glass of wine. Laughter under the low-hanging moon.

"I can't promise anything," she says now, and I say "I know," and she says "I will work as fast as I can, but," and I say "I know" again, and then "Thank you," when what I should really be saying is "I forgive you," or even "I love you," because I think it would be true.

She smiles and puts her hand on my hand and squeezes, and I carry it out with me—that moment of tenderness I carry up four flights of stairs and back out into the lobby, where I doff my pinhole and suffer myself to be wanded again.

"Okay, sir." The Librarian holsters her wand with a polite half smile. Whatever is the state of my mind, it reconciles sufficiently with how it was on my way in. "You have a pleasant day."

13.

Ms. Paige is back at my desk, right at home, hunched forward with her sleeves rolled up and her eyes keen on the screen, as Arlo would say, her vision clear and true, and as I slump into the office she moves no muscle other than to say "Oh good, you're back" and point with one finger toward a cup of coffee she got me. I lift it and hold its lovely heat between my hands, taking what pleasure I can from the warmth burning through its paper sides.

"How did it go?"

"Fine. You got the rooftop stretch?"

"I did," says Paige, and I don't even ask about Woody, about how she wheedled it out of him, because of what is in her eyes, the high focus with which she is fixed on the screen, fixed on Crane—*Crane on the high pitch of the roof, a cigarette dangling from the corner of his mouth. Blue sky morning.* "Sit," she says, "I've got something that I think you ought to see."

And then she waits, impatiently, for me to arrange my bulk beside her. It occurs to me I might be done training Ms. Paige.

I take a look at the frozen cut. Woody's office was able to knit together stretches from six or seven captures to build a nice clean multi-view, what the pros call a tapestry: Crane from all angles up on the Sampson roof. Views from below him, pointing upward from the eaves; from the telephone poles along the driveway; from the hoods of the trucks parked along the driveway.

Aysa looks to make sure I'm looking and then she says "Play" and the screen jumps to life.

Crane is alone on the roof. He is smoking, holding a hand-rolled cigarette in his left hand. A roofing tool, an oblong metal plane with a wood handle, is in his right hand.

The sky is blue behind him.

He stands and stretches, surefooted, and takes a long drag of the cigarette.

Small speculations jump up in little flecks and flares, my mind overlaying the image on the screen with dancing stars of possibility: *Crane the pervert — Crane the thief — Crane the helpless dupe of fate...*

I blink them away, focus on the image as the image is. It's unsettling to see the man alive, to watch him move and breathe and take drags of the butt and be a person. For all this time he has been, in my mind, "the dead roofer." The entirety of his identity was bound up in the fact that he was no longer living, and now here he is alive, his eyes moving, his feet planted steady as a billy goat's on the slant.

Crane flicks the butt over the side. He turns, watching it fall, and—

"Stop," says Aysa, and then, to me, "Do you see?"

"See what?"

She is leaned very close to the screen, bent forward to take in every granulated detail. She herself is a capture, pulsing with interest, collecting all reality around her, and it hits me all over again: The strangeness of it. The ghost in the room.

And it's funny, because she looks not a damn thing like my brother — Charlie was a big, tough, fit white man, heavily muscled and brimming with macho confidence, and Aysa is black and a female and five three in her heavy Speculator's boots. But her face, the set of her face, the birdlike avidity of her eyes right now — it's like Charlie's there, like he is here, living in her, present underneath.

"Here," she tells me, "look."

Crane returns to his work, bending with his wood-handled planer tool, and then—there, 6:11:19 exactly, as he crouches to return to his labors—*Crane's foot snags on a lip of tile, and he shifts his weight*—and now Aysa says "Slow" and the frames click by at a revelatory crawl, each giving way to the next—

One foot slips out from under his tensed weight—*one leg comes kicking out from behind the other*—

—his face registers the sliding confusion of weightlessness as his ass slams into the roof—

—trying to right himself, he catches his heel on the gutter, which tears free, further jumbles the order of his limbs. He tips forward—*over*—

—down—

It is a hard thing to watch, that tumbling moment, the instant of unloosing. His eyes in that moment, wide with realization. It's private. There is nothing as intimate as terror.

Paige says "Back ten," and the section backs up. Crane, again, standing and stretching; Crane, again, sucking on the cigarette, flicking it, watching it fall. Crouching, and—

"Stop," commands Paige, and the image stands still, hung between frames, Crane's eyes half open, his body half up and half down, his last puff of smoke half dissipated in the air around him, again caught in the instant before the instant that will undo him.

"So what I'm wondering," says Aysa, leaning back, "is what's he even doing there."

"What do you mean? On the roof?"

"As high as he is. Isn't he higher than he ought to be?"

"What?"

"Well, the job is down here. Here. See? The job is closer to the eaves. They're peeling off the tiles here to prepare the roof over the master bedroom for a second story."

"So what's he doing way up there?"

"That's the question. There's no reason."

Speculations try themselves out in me. *He's confused. He's mistaken.* No. Nothing. No good.

Paige says "Go" and we watch the man die another time: watch him toss his arms out, watch his legs trip each other, watch him lurch over the side like a drunken sailor. There is something cruel in this, in playing and replaying it like we are making the puppet of his body dance down to its destruction, watching it happen again and again. A kind of retrospective torture of the dead man.

Something catches my eye: a smear—a kind of stain—high up on the screen. "Freeze," I say.

"Laszlo?"

"There."

"What?"

"Look."

Paige blinks, leans closer. I point to the screen.

She nods, three times, quickly. "Yes. I see it. Or—is that—"

"No." I rub at the screen with a corner of my coat, because it almost looks as if a bug has landed on it, but no, it's there. A shadow. A shape. The misshapen darkness is not in the room with us, it's in the image of the earlier reality.

Now we're both leaning in, squinting. It's hard to see. It's nearly impossible. The shadow is the shadow of something off-frame, just outside the capture's view, the kind of mottled wavering shadow that is refracted back by a pane of glass.

"It's a skylight," says Aysa, and I feel a hot sting of envy. I wanted to say it first.

This is why Mose Crane was crouching. This is what he was trying to see. Why he was there. A way to look in. A way to *get* in.

The room grows dim at the corners, the dimness like dread, and it's pulling at me, I feel it pulling. I see the candle inside the darkness, the tiny glow at the center of a vast room: speculation coming at me in earnest. I'm already feeling it, in my throat and my chest, and I can't do more. Not yet. Not now.

I keep my eyes open. Stand up, shake it off. I turn off the screen, leave Mose Crane frozen in his fall.

"Very fine work on this, Ms. Paige."

"Thank you."

"Are you okay?"

"I'm fine."

"Are you sure?"

"Yes, Laszlo!" She looks at me, spreads her arms, laughing off my overprotection. "I'm fine! Are *you* fine?"

I'm not, not really. My throat is racked; my eyes are burning. I am feeling the familiar toll of our labors. Our gift that does not come free. The discernment of falsehood, the pull of speculation. My chest is tight, wrung, but I'll just need a breath of air, that's all, I need the cigarette I'm already digging out of my pocket, tugging from its pack. I'll be fine. It's Aysa I'm worried about, Aysa the un-affected, scrawling notes in her Day Book, no sign of any strain or symptom.

I'm worried about her because she's like Charlie, who didn't feel a thing until it was too late, and he felt it all at once.

And maybe it is like Charlie, maybe she doesn't feel it and so she doesn't understand, but let her see it in me. Let me be a map of the dangers.

"All right, little sister," I tell her. "Grab your coat. We gotta go talk to that judge."

14.

"Ms. Wells?" says the honorable Judge Barney Sampson of the Court of Aberrant Neural Phenomena. "Ms. Wells, I will need you to settle down and pay close attention when the court is speaking."

The owner of the house at 3737 Vermont Avenue sits high on his bench, exercising the solemn duty of his office. His bailiff, stone-faced and bald, stands beneath him and to the right.

The subject of the hearing, despite Judge Sampson's repeated admonitions, will not look up at him and will not stay still. She is shifting restlessly from side to side and flicking her fingers in weird patterns. I'm settled in my last-row pew, beneath the row of drooping flags that jut from the back wall of the courtroom: the Bear and Stars of the Golden State, the three bars of the city, the bright yellow circle of the Objectively So. There is a dull, airless quality to the courtroom, a tired dinginess, as if the very physical space has been worn down by the grim sameness of the daily proceedings. Watching Judge Sampson work, watching him gravely evaluate this poor lady, I wonder if the man isn't jealous of his colleagues on the State's higher benches—the Court of Grave Misrepresentations, the Court of Deliberate Falsity.

No, I think. He's happy. Not smiling, of course, but engaged and brightly curious, eyes fixed on the defendant while he toys lightly with his gavel, while the courtroom's overhead lights gleam off the dome of his scalp and glint off the big gold ring he wears on one pinky. He's a short man, mostly bald, with tufts of hair ringing the smooth bulge of his scalp like high clouds around a mountaintop.

Aysa and I have been here for five minutes. This docket item was supposed to be cleared ten minutes ago, and my plan was to be waiting for the judge in his chambers when it was done. Instead we're sitting here in the back of the courtroom, a hard room for anyone to be in, but especially for me. Because the unfortunate Ms. Wells, aside from the shifting and the dancing, aside from the flicking of her fingers, is letting out a steady stream of preposterous and untrue statements, and it is increasingly hard for me to bear.

"I was *dragged* here," she claims, hisses, growls, wagging an accusing finger at the stolid bailiff. "Dragged by dragons, dragons in wagons, wagons in wheels."

It is babble she is talking, a cackle of words, but the sounds are statements and the statements aren't true. I feel her non-sense in the air, gathering in clouds. This is why she's here. Madness is an assault on the Objectively So, and the State has a responsibility to contain and control it. The defendant certainly looks the part, in layers of long unkempt skirts, a cascade of dirty and tattered fabrics. Her eyes are pale and milky, and as she talks—declaims; chants, really—her eyes roll and dance inside their sockets. She wanders in a small circuit, her radius limited only by the length of chain with which she is tethered to the floor. She jerks her head in little circles too, wrenching herself to look behind her, again and again, to the rows of us watching. Her hair is wild, stiff with sea grit and sand; her face and arms are streaked with dirt.

"A demon was dreaming and dreaming." Raising her hands up, shaking her head from side to side. "Dreaming of dragons and dreaming of me. Dreamed of me and here I be."

I turn to the side and cough as all this non-truth fills the room, floor to ceiling, window to wall, leadening the air, thickening it up, like smoke off a wildfire. I am starting to think I may have to get up and get out of here, go and wait on the benches that line the hallway outside the room. Ms. Paige, of course, is unaffected. She watches the proceedings with her usual ardency, eyes darting back and forth between the bench and the defendant as Judge Sampson taps his gavel, trying to corral the madwoman's wild attention.

"Ms. Wells," he says. "We need to speak calmly."

She is not able. "Calm," she barks, her hands high above her head, her dirty hair swept lionlike behind her. "Calm as a bomb."

"Ms. Wells," says Judge Sampson. "Eyes up here, please."

"My eyes," says Ms. Wells. "My eyes, my eyes."

Judge Sampson nods, as if this were a perfectly reasonable answer, and writes something on a small pad beside him. His desk is absent any extraneous ornament: just the pad, the gavel, a glass of water. It is just him and Ms. Wells, examining each other, staring across the gulf of reality.

I've spent time in these courts before, of course, as little time as I can get away with. I had a drug abuser once, a man whose mind became so addled by dream dampeners that he could no longer distinguish what was from what was not; I have seen not only madness but amnesia, schizophrenics, and the mentally retarded. And all the old-timers' diseases, of course, the whole range of senility and infirmity. Any assault on reality, any infusion of falsehood in the air can't be countenanced, no matter the source.

"Have you ever in your life," asks the judge, "been administered the dream-controlling medication Clarify?"

"No. Yes. No." Ms. Wells squints, moves her cheeks, scratches at her neck. Judge Sampson's manner is mild, but his eyes miss nothing. "I am not a doctor, sir. I am not a dream."

I cough hard, into my hand. A bearded man in a suit turns around and glares at me. I don't want to be drawing attention to myself but it's getting harder to tamp down. A little more of this and I'll have no choice but to duck out into the hallway. My chest feels tired. My hands are shaking, just a little bit.

"Have you been evaluated by a mental health professional?" asks the judge.

This time she doesn't answer, just hisses like a steam vent and waves her hands.

"Have you ever——" Judge Sampson stops, raises one hand, and snaps his fingers. His fingers are long, the nails manicured. He snaps, snaps again. "Ms. Wells? Right now. Where are you in the present moment?"

"Court," she says, and there is a palpable sense of relief in the room. She's not so far gone as that. Ms. Paige glances at me, hopeful. Ms. Wells has one foot, at least, in the world. This is good news. Everyone knows what happens if this thing goes the other way.

"I'm in a court. And you are the king. The king of the thing."

"Ms. Wells?"

"The king is singing, now. Loud and long or low and slow. The king sings and the snakes are dancing."

Ms. Paige looks at me again. Ms. Wells's moment of lucidity has passed through her like weather, and now she is off again, babbling with hands raised, caught in her interior dance, her mind fixed within, and another spasm catches me, worse than before. And now my coughing has drawn the attention of the judge. His attention flickers over me, and he is clocking the blacks and the hat. He has known many Speculators, of course. He knows what I am, what we are, but does he know why we're here?

His attention returns to Ms. Wells—he asks her to look at him directly, and she ignores him again. Not defiant, exactly. Uncomprehending. Disinterested. She twists her head in different directions, like a loose compass searching for north.

Judge Sampson turns to his bailiff, a big man with wide shoulders and a rocky forehead like a dinosaur.

"Do we have a representative here from the department this morning?"

"Yes, sir." The bailiff points at the bearded man in front of me, the guy who glared at me a minute ago. "Dr. Marvin Ailey."

The man stands up. "That's me, sir."

"Hello, Dr. Ailey. An object in motion tends to stay in motion."

"Good morning, your honor. An object at rest tends to stay at rest."

"And so it ever shall be." The judge sighs. "What do we know about Ms. Wells's relationship with reality?"

"Tenuous, sir. Unfortunately. Lorna Jane Wells on three occasions has been administered the full assessment and on all three occasions her percentile scores were found to be abjectly unsuitable. And"— Dr. Ailey clears his throat, frowns—"and, unfortunately, as I say, she has proven unresponsive to treatment."

"Tell me about the extent of the treatment?"

"Standard, sir. The standard battery."

"Beginning at what age, Dr. Ailey?"

"Beginning at age nineteen, your honor."

"Beginning with Clarify, Doctor?"

"Yes, your honor."

The facts form a pile. The pile grows higher. Dr. Marvin Ailey, referring to his Day Book, to various files he's brought with him, proceeds through the years of Ms. Wells's life, her history of neural nonconformity, all of the drugs to which over many years she has proved nonresponsive; while the woman herself proves the point, bobbing her head in small chicken-like motions, making little half dance steps in different directions.

When he is done with Dr. Ailey, the judge stands and hitches up his robes, almost daintily, like a woman in an evening dress coming down off a horse. The climax of this event is getting closer now. Whatever else I am to find out about Judge Sampson, I know that he does this many times a day: sits with people's lives in his hands, weighing their fitness. What does that do to a person, to carry such a burden on the soul?

He crosses his courtroom and pulls up a chair at the defense table, plunks himself down unceremoniously beside Ms. Wells.

"Hi," he says softly. "Lorna. Lorna, do you have living family that are aware of your condition?"

"What?"

"Lorna. Are there people that care for you?"

The judge sees her humanity. I see it, and I can see him seeing it, trying to locate the human person within the murky depths of her illness. Seeking a way, if a way can be found, *not* to do what he is empowered to do; *not* to exercise the power of his office. But Ms. Wells jerks backward from him in a swift reptilian motion, and claps her hands on his shoulders. "The *book* cares."

"The—what?"

"I got it for a song," she says. "The book. The big one, the old one, the good one, the gold one. The big book with the red spine." Her voice has built into a singsong rhythm, sweetly childlike. "*Past Is Prologue*, boys and girls. I have read it close." She spins around to face the gallery, and she gives us a broad wink. "I've seen through the curtain."

"Ms. Wells," says Judge Sampson, frowning. "Stop."

"My eyes are spies. X-ray eyes. Okay? I can see behind the black. The parts behind the parts."

"Ms. *Wells*," says the judge again, his voice dire with warning. "Stop speaking."

He casts a stern and meaningful look to his bailiff, who does not, as I expected, charge across the room toward the defendant. Instead he steps closer to his own small desk, lifts up a panel built into its top, while Ms. Wells raises her hands high into the air, her two thumbs interlocked and her palms spread wide.

It's a book. She has made of her hands a book and she is holding it aloft.

"Big book, old story," she sings. "And you know what's odd?"

"Ms. Wells!" cries the judge, but she sings on—

"In the scratched-out pages is the face of—"

The judge looks at the bailiff and the bailiff presses a button on the desk that sucks all the sound from the world. In an instant it becomes absolutely silent, a pure, deep silence like the courtroom is encased in glass, as if it is not sound but the very idea of sound that has disappeared. For a moment, wild Ms. Wells keeps talking, moving her mouth, moving her head in confused circles, but then she trails off, looks with bafflement around the impossibly quiet room. After a full minute of this, when her lips have stopped moving, the judge nods to the bailiff, who taps his desk once more and unmutes the courtroom, and the imposed silence is replaced by the subtler everyday quiet of a room full of people, watching the judge, watching the confused madwoman— who stands now with her hands flapping nervously at her side.

Judge Sampson keeps his eyes focused for a moment on the floor, a man briefly lost in important conversation with himself. And then he stands and returns slowly, solemnly, a one-man procession, to the bench.

"It is the verdict of this court that Ms. Wells has no connection to reality nor prospect of achieving one."

Paige looks at me, startled, and then back at the judge. Poor thing. A Speculator in training, a brave servant of the State, and still a child. She grabs my shoulder. Wanting me to—what—to leap to my feet? Object?

Judge Sampson looks at the bailiff, who makes a small gesture with both hands, palms up, like an elevator rising. Everybody stands. I take off my pinhole and press it to my chest. The judge keeps his eyes on Ms. Wells, who, of course, has no idea what's going on. She is living in her own reality, and shelled within it, shelled and sheltered, flinging rocks over the top, a danger to us all, but not for long—not for long now.

"The presence of Ms. Wells within the Golden State is therefore deemed to be unsafe and unhealthful for its inhabitants." The bailiff stands before the bench, a still pillar, hands behind his back. Paige's grip tightens on my shoulder, as if it's her on whom sentence is being passed. I feel her fingers through the thickness of my jacket. She is trying to understand the judge's words, though they are not hard to understand. Like a pledge or a curse, like "I do" or "I promise," the words of a verdict are illocutionary: they do not *have* an intended effect, they *are* the intended effect.

The judge has changed reality. The madwoman was of our world and now she is gone from it.

"The remedy to the offense is to be effected immediately." And Judge Sampson brings down the gavel, three short chops, *bap bap bap,* and the bailiff steps forward to unshackle Ms. Wells from the ground.

15.

"**Now wait** a minute." The judge looks me over, up and down, quizzical, curious, pleased. "I know *you*. We've met—yes? Tell me. Where have we met?"

"I don't think we have. My name is Laszlo Ratesic. I'm a Speculator, your honor."

"Oh, you needn't tell me that. That I can *see*. And what a rare treat it is, to have one of you mysterious bats come to roost in my courtroom." He offers Aysa a smile. "Two bats. No, but"—the welcoming, slightly puzzled smile returns—"I know I know you, though." He wags a finger at me. "Well, that's all right. Let's talk. It'll come to me." Judge Sampson settles back, fully at his ease. His chambers are as shabby as the courtroom, only darker, lined with thick carpeting and heavy curtains that cover the windows onto Grand Avenue, curtains so long the fabric pools along the floor. There are framed photographs; a tacky little Bear and Stars flag in a stand on the desk; a portable bar cart docked snugly at the side of the desk, within the judge's easy reach. The cart is not his only indulgence; there's a small wall-mounted on the wall opposite the windows, and I wonder what sorts of themed streams Judge Sampson enjoys, after hours, when the last defendant has been dealt with.

There is something disorienting, something half anomalous, about a judge in chambers—especially a judge of the ANP. A man both small and large at once, still wearing his black robes but with his shirt collar unbuttoned and his tie loosened. An avatar of the State's great power sitting with his ass half on and half off his chintzy little desk, lifting his wry eyebrows, fetching a short glass from his bar cart and filling it with three ice cubes before popping the cork on a crystal decanter.

"Okay. So." He enjoys a long sip of the drink and sets it down. "What can I do for you?"

I draw breath to speak and find that Ms. Paige, standing behind my chair, has already begun.

"Why did you do it?"

The judge looks at her. "Why did I do *what*, exactly?"

"Send her away."

Judge Sampson examines my partner with amusement. "You mean the poor woman in the courtroom? Just now? Today's defendant?"

"Her name was Ms. Wells."

"I know her name, young lady. I know all their names."

I have craned all the way around, turned my large midsection as far as it will turn, trying to catch Ms. Paige's eye and stop her from doing whatever it is she thinks she's doing. What I told her was to wait, to watch and wait. That's what I told her to do.

"I passed the sentence I did upon that particular defendant because it was what the facts required of me. Based on her history and current presentation, Ms. Wells showed no likelihood of improvement. She would continue to commit daily, even hourly, assaults on the Objectively So. She inhabits her own truth and is unable to step free from it. Such a person cannot be allowed to continue inside the Golden State."

"So you condemned her."

"Her own mind condemned her. I only acknowledged that reality, on behalf of the State. If you think I enjoy making such decisions, you are incorrect." But he smiles, and sips contentedly at his drink.

Paige is not satisfied. "You know what will happen to her out there."

"No, young lady." The judge sets the glass on the desk with a clink, a sharp and decisive sound like the gavel coming down. "I do *not* know. And *you* do not know. The fate of the exiled is unknown and unknowable, and any unconditional expression of that fate, any statement such as, for example, 'You know what will happen to her out there,' is by definition not true."

We are in a moment now. Judge Sampson has just called Ms. Paige a liar, more or less, and he is not smiling any longer, and she for her part stands seething. What she wants to say is *Of course I know.* Of course she knows what will happen to Ms. Wells, out there, over the wall, behind the curtain. But she can't say it and she won't say it and she wouldn't and neither would I. She knows and we all know and it's unknown and unknowable.

I raise one hand from my lap.

"Hello. Excuse me. We're going to move on."

"Yeah," says Aysa. "But——"

I look at her. "Ms. Paige," I say. "We're moving on."

But Judge Sampson isn't done. He tilts his head to one side, considering my partner carefully.

"Have you," he asks her, "perhaps lost someone to exile?"

"Yes," she says and stops, and he says "Ah," and I recall her saying "Fuck my parents," and the room fills with a brooding silence. I saw a lecture once, delivered by Our Acknowledged Expert on Geology and Geography, explaining how the Golden State, the whole thing, is built on movable plates, vast tracts that shift, that push and scrape against other plates. The same is true inside Aysa Paige; the same is true inside me.

The judge takes a drink, licks his lips, and says, "Mr. Speculator. What can I help you with?"

"We are working on a case, your honor," I say. "A death."

"A murder?"

"We don't know what it is. We are seeking the full and final truth of a recent death."

"And whose death is it?"

A mild playful tone accompanies the question, and I ignore it. I take out a picture and lay it on the judge's desk. He peers over the rim of his whiskey glass to inspect it.

"The gentleman's name," I say, "was Mose Crane."

The judge sniffs. "If you'll excuse a figure of speech, it rings no bell. Has he been in my courtroom?"

"No, sir. He died at your house. On your lawn."

"Ah. The roofer. Yes. Tragic." My interpretation of what he says is informed by the way he looks into his glass, by the tinkling of the ice. A man not moved by tragedy. "I had not understood that the authorities had discovered any anomalies in that situation."

His tone is very smooth—very cool. I catch a ripple in the air, a minor distension. I look at Paige to see if she catches it too, but she's looking straight ahead. I have a feeling she is out in the wilderness, over the wall, with or without Mr. and Mrs. Paige.

"Whether the authorities had discovered one in the situation or not," I say to Judge Sampson, "I believe you were aware there were anomalies."

"I know there *are* anomalies," he says. "I know, more than most, that such things exist."

"I fear, sir, that your statement contains omissions," I say, picking my words carefully.

"Well, let's be serious, son," he says. "*All* statements contain omissions."

This is more or less the same thing that Captain Tester said to me, more or less the kind of thing people say all the time, as we slide through our lives like roller skaters, skirting and dodging around the hills and valleys of the truth, ducking under it at the last minute.

But Aysa isn't having it. "No they don't," she says, her voice still hot.

"Ms. Paige?" I turn toward her again, twisting uncomfortably in the small wooden chair. "Do me a favor, would you?" But Judge Sampson isn't ready to move on.

"This is interesting, now, isn't it? Very interesting. What do you mean, exactly, young lady? Do you object to the statement that all statements contain omissions?"

"That's not what I said."

"Oh, I think it is, Ms. Speculator," he says. "Should we requisition the stretch? Ask for a playback?"

As ever when someone mentions the Record, I become conscious of it, of the captures glittering in the light fixtures, of the captures on the doorframe, all the truth of this moment entering history as it goes. Even so, I know what the judge is doing: he is moving sideways, away from the conversation, using my partner's righteousness as an escape hatch, to escape my questions.

"Go ahead," says Paige. "Requisition the stretch. We'll watch it together. All I meant was, stop pretending that you don't know what we're asking about."

I sigh. I shake my head. She's still too young to know what I knew coming in: that of course he would try to pretend. Of course he would go to any legal length not to answer questions. One day Aysa will know what I have known for years: the extraordinary lengths people will go to not let certain truths pass their lips.

"We are trying to find out how a man died," she says. "The truth is the most important thing. You have a piece of it, and you are going to hand it over. Now."

"Young lady," the judge says. "Imagine a stone."

She blinks. "What?"

"A stone, dear." He stands up. He goes so far as to reach into his pocket and come out with a closed fist, pretending, really pretending to be holding a stone. He then places it gently, the fake stone, at the center of his desk. "We put it here. And now we draw a ring around it. Okay? Like so."

He does it, with one thin finger, turns his finger into a pen and traces a perfect circumference around his imaginary stone.

"And now the stone is a flat fact, and everything inside the circle is a relevant supporting fact. And when we are asked to provide context, to say *everything we know* about the stone, these are the things we say. Are you with me?"

She doesn't answer. She stares at him.

"But now these facts have been introduced. All around this ring, these are relevancies. They support the foregoing; they are part of it. Seen another way, we have one truth. But if you now take this spot, here along the ring, and put a stone *here*—another ring can be drawn. You see?" He moves his invisible stone. "New relevancies, new relevant facts all along the new outskirts. And each of these spots could, in turn, be made into the center of the circle. And so the truth blossoms outward endlessly, and it is always—always—the *speaker* of truth who decides which pieces of it to label, in this case, as relevant."

I raise one hand. Enough of this.

"Your honor—"

But he's not finished, and we're in his house. His chambers. He speaks like a man in full control: of this room, of the State, of the whole universe. "Of course it's easy for you people," he continues.

Aysa's expression sharpens. "Easy for—women?"

He smiles. "No. Speculators. You with your vaunted discernment. To simply *see* a lie, to know one when one is there. Black-and-
white. You *feel* it. But for the rest of us? Who must make our own
sorry way? It's all guesswork, isn't it? Judgment calls."

"Your honor," I say. "We are here to ask you about Captain Elena
Tester."

His face darkens. All of his charm, all of his wit, it was all dodging
around this moment, which he knew was coming all along.

"What about her?"

"You know her?"

"I do."

"How well do you know her?"

He puffs his cheeks and exhales and his insouciance recovers itself. "If you are here to ask if I am fucking Captain Elena Tester, then
please. Please. Ask me if I am fucking Elena Tester."

I wait. Raise my eyebrows. Well?

"Yes." He raises both hands in slow synchronicity with the smile
on his face. "I am fucking Elena Tester."

He then arrives at the next step before Aysa can get there first.
"And before you ask, I opted not to *volunteer* this information to you,
for the same reason, I imagine, that Elena—that Captain Tester—
chose not to volunteer it. Because it is private. Because *all statements contain omissions*." He points at his desk, at his imaginary ring of
stones. "It is better for both Captain Tester and me that the flat fact
of our connection not be splattered all over the Record like muddy
paw prints by conversations like this one."

"Well—" Aysa starts, but the judge marches on.

"And it is not relevant to your investigation."

"And you made that judgment."

"Yes, I did. I made that judgment." He looks at me and winks.
"I'm a judge."

"Did anyone else know?" asks Ms. Paige, Day Book out, pen ready to press into the carbon. "About this affair? Anyone who might have been interested in extorting you, or the captain? Anyone——"

"I've got it."

"What?"

He shuts his eyes tightly for a moment, and then pops them open, wags his finger at me. "Now I know you, Mr. Speculator. Your wife is that girl, the one with the big personality. Yes? Elena's friend. Yes?"

"Silvie."

He pats his hands on his lap in triumph, exultant. "Silvie! That's your wife?"

Heat. Heat behind my eyes and on my cheeks. "Ex-wife."

"Ex. Ah. Very sad. The ex-husband. Doleful, cast out, carrying faded memories like old files. Always something of a tragic figure. Although so, too, can husbands be. A husband, too, can be tragic."

Paige, maybe to protect me or maybe just to stay on target, presses on. "Your honor, we need to know who, if anyone, might have known about this affair. Your honor?"

He keeps his eyes just on me. "Let's not do this," says the judge. His face changes for a moment, darkens, turns away, and then he says—just softly, just calmly, just to me—"Listen. *This is not worth it*. Do you understand?"

I don't understand. I don't, but I do.

It feels as if I am on a cliff's edge, toddling toward the side, and this man is holding out a hand to keep me from tumbling, flying over the side like Mose Crane, and I want to reach out to accept his rescuing hand but I can't. I won't.

Because Ms. Paige is doing as I have told her, she is hitching her natural powers to her hunches, making decisions on the fly, swimming in the powerful wake of her instincts.

And because judges and police captains have no more right than regular people to hoard their share of the truth. Because the Basic Law guarantees us all the same access to what is real, and the same protection from what is not.

So I cross my arms over my chest, lean back in the wooden chair, and stare flatly back. "Answer the question, your honor."

"Very well," he says, and turns his gaze slowly from me to Ms. Paige. "Nobody else knew."

"Nobody knew, or nobody knew that you know of?"

"Why, Ms. Speculator," he says. "If there was someone who knew of it, and I didn't know if they knew or not, then how would I know?"

He laughs without humor, and Paige blinks—no, more than blinks. Squeezes her eyes shut for half a second, and then opens them again, and they are altered—seeing more clearly, keenly, the way I saw them seeing at Crane's apartment. She's got something. She's caught something.

I stare at her in astonishment for a second and then I look to the floor, hiding the sting of envy. It costs her nothing. Her body does not rack and her eyes do not water. It costs her *nothing*.

"Your honor," she says sharply, eyes trained dead on the judge. "Is there physical evidence of this affair?"

I watch the judge. His mouth becomes small. A button. "Yes."

"Is there physical evidence of this affair in this room with us right now?"

He does not answer. We both watch him rise slowly, turn his back on us, and stand hunched at his bar cart.

When he speaks it is again to me only. "Mr. Speculator?" he says quietly, the same between-us-men appeal that he must know by now will not work. I offer him no help. I wait for Paige.

"Your honor," she says, boring in, unflinching, unrelenting. "Do you keep a Night Book?"

He does not answer. The room gets quiet and stays that way, one moment of silence and then another. Judge Sampson turns and looks up at a point behind our heads, and it is so quiet that it's as if he has got some version of the courtroom's noise-canceling device in his chambers. But no. It's just silence, human silence, and it ends when Sampson uncorks a new bottle, selecting the right-size crystal tumbler. He needs something stronger, I guess. He pours but does not yet drink.

"Yes," he says at last. "I do."

"Precision, sir."

"I keep one."

"For the Record, sir. You keep one *what?*"

"I keep a Night Book."

Before he can say anything else, before he can dodge or duck any further, I say, "We are going to need to see that."

Judge Sampson raises the glass, but still doesn't drink from it, sets it right back down and then grins, a cold and crocodile grin.

"I'll tell you what," he says, and then again, "I'll tell you what. I'll read it *to* you."

I look at Paige and she at me. "No, sir," I say. "We will take it with us, and return it to you at the completion of our inquiries."

"Don't be ridiculous, Mr. Speculator," he says. "Allow me." His eyes shine, his grin widens, and I don't know what to make of his sudden shift in attitude. Anxiety flutters to life in my guts like a wind-ruffled banner.

I've never understood what it is that makes a certain kind of person keep a Night Book. Catch that. Correct it: I understand it, but I would never fucking do it.

On the surface, of course, the impulse is a good and golden one, doctrinaire and State-minded, a laudable individual service provided to our great collective effort. The Night Book writer commits himself to recording not only the flat facts and surface realities of life, the kinds of visible truths that are collected by captures and recorded all day long in Day Books, but to go further, to go all the way, to put on paper all the *underlying* truths of life, those that move beneath the skin. The Night Book writer records his *thoughts,* his *dreams,* his instincts and urges. He puts his private life on his secret pages.

After all, they'll tell you, everything that happens belongs to the State, and a thought is just an event that happens in your head.

And unlike a Day Book, a Night Book only reaches the Record when its author is dead and it passes into the Permanent Record with all the rest of life's artifacts. Or, let's say, when a pair of Speculators barge into your office, chasing an anomalous death that happens to intersect with your existence, and they sense the presence of your Night Book and reach for it and pull it out like a loose tooth.

The judge's book is indeed right here in the office with him, hidden in a wall safe behind his official portrait, and before we can object, he has it open on his desk: a slim volume, handsomely appointed. He pulls out reading glasses and adjusts them on his nose and sets in.

"Sir," I say, one last time. "We will take the book away with us."

"Oh, I know," he says, flipping the book open, searching for something. "But first I'm going to read." And his finger falls on a particular page, and he begins.

"*'It was the sort of party one is dying to leave until a moment arrives and one never wants to go home.'*" Sampson pauses and looks up. "Oh, that's rather nice. I had forgotten I wrote that. Very nice indeed."

That's the other thing a Night Book does, of course: it gives a vain person ample opportunity to indulge that vanity, all under the guise of supreme service to the State.

Judge Sampson licks his lips and finds his place. "*'We had been in-*"

troduced at the very threshold of the evening, one among the usual roundelay of how-do-you-dos. If I suspected in that moment that she would be added to my collection, I suspected it without suspecting that I suspected it. I suspected it in my heart alone, or in some other, lower precinct.' "

He pauses again, looks up over the rim of his glasses at Paige. " 'Collection' is rather crass. I apologize."

Paige is looking at me. She mouths "Tester?" I don't answer. Knowledge is alive in me; moving; welling up. Sampson with his reptile mouth reads on: " *'I had promised myself therefore not to leave before she did, and my patience was at last rewarded.' "* He pauses, looks up, and sees that he has our attention. I cannot move. I am not moving. " *'We two indeed were among the last to leave, lingering in the doorway between parlor and kitchen, engaged in a very long conversation about nothing at all. Her husband, it seems, had lost patience and retreated, alone.' "*

"Husband?" says Ms. Paige. "Hold on. Captain Tester is a widow. Is this—"

"Oh, I'm sorry," says the judge, looking up, finding my eyes. Looking not at Aysa, who interrupted him, but at me. "Is this not relevant to your ongoing investigation?"

He's holding the book open with his palm, still looking at me. "Tell you what. I'll skip ahead."

" *'S displayed her body in the doorway as if for my personal delectation, belied any dictums about the highest beauty being the product of the greatest delicacy. Her charm, the charm of S, was in her substance, her attractiveness a matter of superabundance and profusion. Tumbling yellow locks and a full flushed face, full lips parted around a red tongue, an admirable plumpness of breasts and of rear. Her body an inviting expanse, a world demanding circumnavigation.' "*

"That's enough," Ms. Paige says, though it cannot be because she has realized what I have realized, that this is Silvie being conjured, Silvie that the judge is recalling with such rich pleasure. S for Silvie.

Silvie laughing at a suggestive joke, Silvie drifting as if by accident into his arms. The description is specific and precise, incontrovertible. Weaponized truth. *A husband, too, can be tragic.*

"That's *enough,*" says my partner again, but the judge does not stop, he reads on, sentences like wires that fall around Silvie and draw her into an empty bedroom. Lascivious, circling sentences that trace the lines of her body like fingertips.

I remember that damn party, somewhere in Silver Lake. Forty minutes in traffic to get there, the two of us sitting in stony silence all the way. I knew no one, wanted to meet no one. I left early, telling Silvie to get a taxi home.

The judge remembers it too, he has it all written down, and he reads on, word after word: words that carefully unbutton the dress, words that reveal the pale wide flesh of belly and thighs, words that trace the silhouette shape of her waist, words that describe her hips and then clasp at the small of her back, traveling upward along her spine as it arches in abandonment.

I try to say something—I try to say "Stop," I may even manage to say "Stop," but he does not stop, he will not, his sentences gather steam and rhythm as he approaches the predictable climax of the paragraph, and then he is through, and he has made his monstrous point about the rings of truth, about context and omission: he has illustrated that no matter how much we know, there are parts of the story that are missing. There are elements unknown and unknowable, whether we know it or not.

"Shall I go on?" he says, softly, daringly, wondering if I will take some dramatic action, smash into him with my fists, crash the crooked smile off his face.

"As I said earlier"—my voice is a coiled wire, my hands clutched into fists at my side—"we will take the book away and return it when we are through."

"Very good." He places the book on the desk, slides it toward me. "Enjoy."

Paige reaches for the book as Judge Sampson drinks at last from the tumbler, grins sheepishly, opens his mouth, and vomits a long stream of blood, staggering forward and collapsing across the desk.

"What..." says Aysa, and I'm up from my chair, up and across the small room and catching him as he falls forward, his eyes rolling back while blood is spurting and leaping out of his mouth, dark red mixed with yellow. He flings one hand out, grunting and snorting, and tries to steady himself on the desk, but he misses it entirely and topples, headfirst, banging his forehead on its sharp wood corner. He's dense in my arms and his front is covered with liquid, with the blood and bile that have exploded from his mouth. He passes, slippery, through my grip, shudders against my legs, and lands on the ground.

"What did you do?" I say to Judge Sampson, who is convulsing, his whole body shaking, his features swiftly going pale. I know what he did. I get down on the ground beside him and try to arrange him so that he's sitting up, so he can't choke on his vomit, but he's dying before I can do anything. A second wash of blood and gore comes channeling up from his guts and rushes from his mouth.

Paige, somewhere in the corner of my vision, has thrown open the door of the chambers and is shouting to the bailiff posted outside.

"Call the regular police," she tells him, and he shouts, "What did you do? What have you done?"

"Call them!"

He is craning his neck to see past her, trying to see in, seeing me and the ruined body of the judge, the two of us like drunk lovers on the ground. "Your honor?" the bailiff says.

I'm covered in Judge Sampson's blood, my tie dangling over his spit-stained chin and cheeks.

"Call them!" shouts Paige.

The rest is a fog of red, of shapes rushing within the fog. A swell of noise from outside on Grand Avenue, a tumble of shouting and footfalls and howling sirens.

Me and Paige are outside chambers, waiting as instructed by a regular policeman with his sleeves rolled up. We are seated on a hard-backed bench, side by side.

In my mind, the judge vomits blood and pinwheels down toward the carpet, and then again, and again. Reality cued and re-cued.

He is dying and he is in the kitchen at a party in Silver Lake, leaning in the doorframe after I have gone, sharing a joke with my wife. Ex-wife.

The courtroom has been emptied of litigants and lawyers, and they bustle about in the hallway, curious, reluctant to leave such excitement.

I am slumped, hollow, staring straight ahead. There is a pane of frosted glass inset in the dead center of the chamber door, and I stare at the glass, finding abstracted patterns.

This is what the world is, I'm thinking as the busy incident aftermath rushes around me, police and ambulance personnel, capture teams, and archivists. Life is one explosion after another, the Earth opening up again and again, sending out gouts of loose dirt, covering us up.

I am exhausted, but Aysa does not stop. She can't. Aysa has her Day Book out and she has the judge's blood-splattered Night Book out too, between us on the bench. She's organizing her thoughts, trying to piece together what we have learned. Aysa has already apologized for letting herself be distracted by the verdict on Ms. Wells; apologized and then moved swiftly on. Aysa focuses on the work. Aysa carries on, riffling through her notes undeterred and undeterrable.

This is even though she, like me, is speckled with blood, dark droplets crusting on her forehead and on her neck. Even though we sit but feet from where his body still lies, awaiting the attentions of the regular police, of the medical examiner, the Record officers who are angling around with their handhelds and their mics, forging this remarkable event into history. The coroners who will, when it's all over, bear him away.

We've already been interviewed, of course, and we'll be interviewed again.

We are pursuing an anomalous death.

The judge may or may not have had relevant information . . .

We may never know . . .

"Okay, so," says Aysa, flipping through her notes, forward and back, forward and back. "Here is what I don't get. So the man is married. Okay. So he's——he's unfaithful." She glances at me, a fleeting embarrassed wince. "He has affairs. Multiple affairs. Okay. So—— but——"

I finish the thought, my voice empty and toneless. "But so what."

"Right!" She nods slowly, twice. "Exactly." A new cluster of cops swoops by, officious, belts jangling with their radios, a couple of boom ops close behind them.

"So what was the big risk here?" says Aysa. "Worst case scenario, he loses his job. Right?"

I shrug. "Maybe."

"And maybe *she* would lose her job? Tester, I mean."

I shrug again.

"But still, to——" She shakes her head. "To drink poison. Okay, the Specs are here, we're asking questions. Bad luck, yes. A guy dies on his roof, we start rooting around, find out he's a bad husband. But this. To do *this*."

"An overreaction."

"Yes." She snaps her fingers. "Exactly."

"Yeah. Also . . ." I press my knuckles into my eyes. Trying to wake up. "Also, the man had poison to hand."

"Right!" says Aysa. "Right! So why? *Why?* Why is he *that* worried about his affair with Tester being discovered? Unless that's *not* what he was worried about. Maybe that's what *Tester* was worried about. Maybe Sampson was worried about something *else*."

"Huh," I say, and I feel her waiting for me to say more, but I don't.

She is dying for it. Each of her maybes is a pleading invitation: Let's go. Let's get to work. She wants the two of us to sit here on this cold bench, shoulder to shoulder, and close our eyes and be borne away by speculation. She wants us together in the illuminating darkness churning through the possibilities, testing each for soundness, jumping off from this platform to the next one.

But I'm in no mood for it. I'm in a kitchen doorway in Silver Lake, bearing witness to my own mortification. I'm trapped inside the fangs of the judge's smile, feeling the truth snap closed around my neck. His blood and viscera are on my coat.

I am contemplating a thousand things I thought I knew and never did know.

I am watching him pitch around in circles, blood from his mouth like a sudden exclamation. In my head, his hands are on Silvie's waist, just barely, the first time. Just the backs of his hands.

My personal and professional existence is built on the idea that everything can be known, that everything *must* be known, and now here I am, on a bench outside judge's chambers, and I'm on a green glider in Mar Vista pierced by understanding that nothing can be known at all. Something has opened up inside me that never can be closed.

Aysa beside me lifts the judge's Night Book. The cover is misted with blood, the pages are gummed together. Carefully she begins to unstick them, page by page. She's reading.

In spite of myself, I am curious. I am interested.

"Is the rest of the Night Book like the part he read?"

She nods. "Yeah. Pretty much it is."

She scans sections, murmurs a line or two aloud to me. It's all lust. It's all sex and the desire for sex, the delicate small obser-vations and sudden fierce movements that are prelude, the altered locutions and idiosyncratic motions that define the event itself. There are Night Books that overflow with sedition, with epistemo-logical heresy or criminal confession, but there is, it seems, only one form of proscribed detail the judge thought worthy of preserv-ing; he took pride in the full truth of his ability as a seducer, and he felt that the Record, the complete archive of the truth of the world, would be incomplete if it did not include it. His personal history of conquest and debauch, organized by name. *"Stole away with J after court." "Brought L back to chambers for a frank discussion, which led down the hoped-for path."*

Aysa carefully peels the blood-gummed pages from each other, until she finds it—

"Here," she says. She holds it up. *"E. E* for Elena?"

I shrug. I nod. *"E* for Elena. Why—what?"

She holds out the open book to me. My body is moving on its own, hand opening on its own. She puts the Night Book in my flat palms and I stare at the words, looking through eyes rimmed with blood. *"Again I find myself with E,"* it says at the top of the page, in the judge's precise cursive—followed by nothing. Or, rather, followed by nothing that once was something.

After *"Again I find myself with E,"* there is inky blackness, lines and lines of it. Sentences that have been crossed out, blacked over, comprehensively redacted.

Aysa leans in eagerly, her knees jiggling with excitement, as I turn over pages. Two pages, three pages, four. Whatever happened between the judge and this Ms. E, it has been neatly and comprehensively excised from his Night Book.

What has the man made hidden, even in his book of hidden truths? Too secret to be told, even to himself?

Aysa, meanwhile, has returned to her Day Book, and she is tapping it, nodding, glancing back and forth between the judge's book and her own.

"It's the same days," she announces.

"What?" I close Sampson's book, lift my fingers from its tacky hide.

"The date range, sir. Laszlo, the dates are the *same.*"

She holds up her Day Book, hands it to me so I can read the notes she made in Dolly Aster's basement, and I two-step verify them in my own. The entry that begins *"Again I find myself with E"* falls exactly among Mose Crane's missing days.

I breathe in and then out again. It's like my blood froze when Sampson did what he did and now it is flowing again—not flowing but racing, rushing.

"Ms. Paige. Do you have your radio?"

"Of course."

"Do me a favor, will you? Can you raise Alvaro?"

"Why?"

"Just raise him for me. Raise him."

We'd driven in angry silence all the way to Silver Lake. That night. Silvie and me.

Forty minutes of cold silence because of the idiot remark I'd made in our driveway, on the way to the car.

I'm outside now, standing on the courthouse steps, blinking in the sunlight like a bear emerged from his cave. Meanwhile I'm smoking a cigarette and staring at the dirty steps and trying to move forward, to beat back the past. Gather my spirit and forge it into something strong.

Silvie was beautiful that night: a gold dress with small pearl buttons; earrings and heels; a ceramic butterfly clip lifting her hair into a crown. Silvie was in an expansive mood. She stopped me in the driveway, seized me by the elbow, and pointed at the sky.

The stars were just coming out, and she told me that they were diamonds.

"And you see those three—those ones there?" She was holding a bottle of red wine by its slender neck. I had the keys. "That's a necklace. A pretty diamond necklace like the one you've never bought me."

She laughed, making sure I knew she was joking, but I couldn't even muster a smile.

"The stars are *like* diamonds," I said.

"What?"

Obviously she wasn't lying; obviously she wasn't purposefully misrepresenting the nature of the stars. She was enjoying the feeling of the twilight sky, the sturdy feeling of her hand on my arm. She was feeling good, feeling gentle, sharing a plain metaphor with her man. But something in me wasn't in the mood. I had had a hard day at work, trudging through a world thrumming with lies. I was feeling small, miserable, literal.

"The stars. They're not diamonds, Sil. They're masses of hydrogen and helium, millions of miles wide and millions of miles away."

"Well, yeah," she said. "I know."

She took her hand off my arm. We drove across town in silence. I left the party early and on my own.

Now Ms. Paige finds me, out on the street. She is holding up her radio. An archivist trails her, and a capturer trails the archivist, her handheld steady on her shoulder. Aysa holds up the radio. "I've got Alvaro."

She watches me curiously while I talk to our boss.

"Quite a day you're having, Laszlo."

"Yeah." I take the last long drag of my cigarette and stub it out. "I know. Listen. I need you to set something up for me."

"What is it?"

"You're not going to like it."

"I don't like anything. Might as well ask."

16.

There are aspects of the physical city that are seen but not fully understood: visible etherealities, manifestations of a time buried under present time. Like there's this one building on West Adams, near a hoagie place I like, a soaring construction of heavy gray stone with elaborate stained-glass windows and tiers of steps leading up to wide, tall doors. It's a State site, accessible only to authorized personnel, in which files damaged by fire or flood or other emergency are carefully reconstructed by experts and archivists. If the building with the stained-glass windows used to be something else, it is nothing else now. It holds its past but holds it in secrecy, unknown and unknowable.

It's like the sign up in the Hills, up at the crest of Mount Lee. You can just about make it out from where we are now, idling at the Gower Street Gate, waiting for the man in the guardhouse to come over and check us in. Nine tall white letters on the side of a hill, spelling a word that if it meant something to somebody once, means nothing to anyone now. Nothing that can be known.

"Good morning, sir. My name is Laszlo Ratesic, age fifty-four, and I'm a nineteen-year veteran of the Speculative Service. The square of the hypotenuse of a right triangle is equal to the sums of the squares of the other two sides."

"Good morning. Pi represents the ratio of the circumference of a circle to its diameter."

"My name is Aysa Paige, age twenty-four and a two-day veteran of the Speculative Service."

"Did she say two days?"

"She did."

The gate man peers past me at Aysa in the shotgun seat and grunts. "Huh."

I'm impatient. I'm ready to go. "We need to see Laura Petras, Our Acknowledged Expert on the Enforcement of the Laws."

"You have an appointment?"

"No," I say, and add hurriedly, "but I believe my supervising officer called over. Mr. Luis Alvaro?"

The gate-arm man looks skeptical. Like, what? I'm going to lie?

"Give me a second," he says, and retreats into his little house and picks up his radio.

While we wait, while the guard checks our identifications, while he checks his call log, while Aysa looks through the windshield at her first view of the vast complex that houses our collected Expertise, I happen to turn my head at just the right moment to see the Dirty Dog food truck as it cruises through the green light at Gower and Waring, the elusive hot dog–shaped truck with the pink piping, and I allow myself the fleeting fantasy of leaving Aysa to her own devices for this next phase of our investigation. How pleasant it would be to leap from the driver's seat, chase the truck down the street, and then, once I have caught it, sit on a bench and eat a works with cheese, watching seagulls circle the sky.

From his little booth, the guard hands us back our identifications and the gate arm goes up.

"Okay." He squints at us. "You folks know where you're going?"

"Not really," I say, and he hands us a folded-up paper map, which Aysa takes and unfolds.

"When you're done, you gotta come out by this same gate," he says finally, and I nod.

"Okay."

"Did you hear me?" he says, like I didn't answer. "Same gate."

The complex is enormous, and I haven't been here in a long time. Aysa holds the map and calls out directions. We drive past long low buildings with flat tar roofs, painted on their sides with various of the State's mottoes. Pedestrian walkways snake between the buildings, each marked with its department: Expertise in Transportation and Infrastructure, Expertise in Commerce and Trade, in Monetary Policy, in Agriculture.

Dotted across the lawns that separate the buildings are cafés, kiosks, and small fountains, each a miniature version of the one in the Plaza downtown. The whole campus is organized around the water tower, seven stories high, painted brightly with the Bear and Stars, and which can be seen from anywhere on the campus. On a clear day, actually, you can see it for blocks around. It's almost always a clear day.

It's all old. From before. This place, its walkways and bungalows, its sprawling open spaces and its water tower—it all *is* and it is all built on something that *was*. And if your mind wants to wonder what it was, what was here before *this* was here, you remember to understand that it is not known and not knowable, and you let the thought drift across your mind and then away and soon enough you turn one last corner and find the building you were looking for.

We pull up outside Building 6892, the Enforcement of the Laws. It's a modest two-story bungalow, the same as all the others, the same flat sandstone and painted doors, wooden staircases at either end of the building connecting upstairs and down.

Before we get out of the car I put a warning hand on Aysa's arm. "Okay, Ms. Paige. I'm going to do the talking here, okay?"

"Yes, sir."

"We are going to get the information we need, and we are going to get out of there. These people do not fuck around."

"Absolutely, sir."

She smiles. I smile. I don't believe her for a second. I mean, I do—she's not lying. She really believes she is capable of playing this situation straight. But she would have said the same thing outside the judge's chambers. She is what she is. Even now it is rising up in her, and when the moment comes she will be unable to help herself.

I run a hand through my hair, tilt my pinhole down to shade my eyes, and ring the bell.

"It is my understanding that you do not have an appointment?"

"That's correct. My boss called your office about half an hour ago."

"Normally we don't take any visitors who do not have an appointment."

"I understand that, ma'am."

Our Acknowledged Expert on the Enforcement of the Laws looks exactly like her photograph. The bland, unlined face and short neat hair, the probing and studious expression. Her office is orderly, lined with filing cabinets and bookshelves, a ceiling fan turning mutely overhead. There is one staff member in the corner, a man in a pressed gray suit at a desk covered in notebooks.

"Obviously this office respects the crucial work of the Speculative Service, and we are therefore willing to provide any aspects of our Expertise that might be useful to the reconciliation of any anomaly."

"Thank you, ma'am."

"Having said that, and I apologize if there was a miscommunication in this regard, but the appropriate protocol requires you to put any such requests in writing and submit them to your supervisor."

She pauses, eyebrows raised.

"Mr. Alvaro," I say.

"Yes, at which point Mr. Alvaro would file a formal request for discussion, which would then be reviewed by myself or by my staff." Ms. Petras angles her chin to the corner, where the man in his gray suit sits at his desk. Presumably there are more staff behind the inner-office door to his right. "They will then coordinate with . . . I do apologize."

"Mr. Alvaro."

"Yes, and to find the appropriate venue and time for us to provide our Expertise."

"Thanks, ma'am. I understand. That's not going to work."

She blinks. "And why is that?"

"We're not here to take advantage of your Expertise."

Petras steeples her manicured fingers on the desk in front of her. I'm standing with my hands behind my back, with Aysa at my side in the same posture. I think I've cleaned all the blood off my face. I swapped my jacket for the backup I keep in the trunk of the car, but there wasn't much I could do about my shirt.

"Oh no?" says Petras finally, tilting her head.

"No. The anomaly we are investigating—anomalies at this point, actually—intersects with this office." She waits, her expression placid and indecipherable. "You might have relevant information, is what I mean."

"Me, personally?"

"Yes. You or your office."

The staffer, in his corner, continues writing. His desk is a slightly smaller version of his boss's, angled upward like a drafting table. There are four notebooks open on the desk, one at each corner, and he writes constantly, shifting from book to book according to some internal logic.

"You are here for a point of information," says Petras.

"Possibly several," I say.

The staffer writes something in one of his notebooks and tears it free and walks it swiftly over to her. The wall behind them is lined with metal cabinets, arranged in stacks from floor to ceiling, an archive of documents and filings and transcripts. The Provisional Record of her department's work. Directly behind Petras is a tall shelf weighted with volumes of procedure: the protocols of the court systems, the rules regulating the regular police and the Speculative Service. Statistical manuals, sentencing guidelines, treatises on ballistics and recidivism and forensics. All the areas of her Expertise.

Petras unfolds the slip of paper that her assistant has handed her. "Very good," she says to him, and turns to us. "We are able to grant you three and a half minutes." There is a clock behind her on the wall, above the filing cabinets, and another clock behind us, on the facing wall. "That time begins right now."

I nod. "Thank you, ma'am. We're here to ask about a judge."

She frowns. "Mr. Speculator, this office is responsible for the conduct and caseloads of just over three hundred and fifty sitting judges, on a wide variety of courts, from the Court of Small Infelicities to Grave Assaults on the Objectively So. That is in addition to our oversight of the regular courts, meaning everything from traffic infractions—"

"Sampson," says Ms. Paige. I give her a look, which she ignores. "Judge Barney Sampson. Does that sound familiar?"

"It—yes," says Petras, and a swift-moving cloud of anxiety passes across her brow. I think it does. I watch it come and go, I *see* it, but as soon as it is gone I cannot be sure I saw it at all. Something has opened up in me that will not close. I shake my head, clench my teeth, and focus. The staffer in the corner, meanwhile, rises silently and brings the Expert a new scrap of paper, which she unfolds and reads.

"His court is in Aberrant Neural Phenomena, on Grand Avenue? Is that correct?"

"Yeah," I say.

"Earlier today——" says Ms. Paige, but I hold up my hand and she stops. If Petras has not yet heard about Sampson's death, we don't need to be the ones to fill her in. Not yet, anyway.

"Mr. Doonan?" Petras turns her head slightly toward the man in the corner. "Would you draw the judge's file, please?"

"Of course." Mr. Doonan rises and moves along the back wall of the office, brisk and efficient.

"Our line of inquiry," I add warningly, "may touch on very sensitive matters. You may feel most comfortable speaking alone."

Petras shakes her head tightly. "Mr. Doonan is my executive assistant." He has found the file, and he hands it to her without looking at us or otherwise acknowledging that he is being discussed. "I cannot imagine there is anything you need to ask me to which he could not or should not be privy. Do you know the figure 'He is my right hand'?"

"Yes, ma'am."

"He is my right hand."

Mr. Doonan sits again, his expression unchanged. His eyes are gray like his suit, giving him a kind of hazy, indistinctly distinguished look. He resumes writing in his notebooks.

I watch the clock over Petras's head. I talk as quickly as I can. "In the course of pursuing a seemingly unrelated anomaly, we discovered that Judge Sampson was conducting an extramarital affair. We speculate that an individual or individuals learned of this affair and hoped to blackmail the judge. Or——" I stumble, not certain how to frame it. Not certain even of what I know. Petras's eyes remain on me, cool and evaluating, as I tread out onto thinner and thinner ice. "Or potentially over other improprieties."

"You need to know if we know anything."

"Yes."

"About any improprieties."

"That's right."

She regards me quietly, weighing my heft with her Expert's eyes. Doonan, in his corner, stays busy with his papers, clipping and unclipping his binders. Making a performance of not paying attention, making of himself a capture, inconspicuous but active, noiseless in his gray suit, gathering every word.

"Mr. Doonan?" Petras says. "Would you come here for just a moment?" He walks quickly over, waits for the half instant it takes Petras to write something on a piece of paper, reads it and tucks it away in a pocket while he returns to his corner.

Petras looks at me. The clock behind her has swallowed up half our time.

"It strikes me that you've done an awful lot of speculation, based on an awfully small number of facts."

Doonan at his desk switches from one notebook to another. I fold my arms.

"I am not here to have my work evaluated, ma'am."

"And neither will I be instructed in how to entertain your presence. You are here. Here you are." Her tone is elevated now; she has brought her authority into her voice. "And my position requires me to observe that I am not convinced this investigation is carefully built on the facts as they exist."

"Listen. Look." I take a step toward her, feeling a new sheen of sweat at my hairline, a new consciousness of my great bulk in the polished interior of this office. "All I need to know is what that judge was up to."

"Then you would have to ask him."

"Well, see, I can't do that. He's dead."

There it is again: a flutter of emotion at her brow, a fleeting grief of awareness. This time I am sure I see it, long enough to know it for what it is, and to wonder what it means. Ms. Petras looks at me accusingly across the desk. "You might have begun with that information."

I shrug, conceding the point. I'm waiting for the obvious next question, and when she doesn't ask I tell her anyway.

"He did it himself. Drank poison."

"When?"

"Today. A couple hours ago."

I see it again, like it's happening now, in front of me. Blood leaping from his throat like a living thing, his arms flailing forward, body turning as it falls. Doonan closes one of his notebooks and slides it off his desk. For an instant I see a red cover on the notebook, an unfamiliar gold logo. He has the book under his arm as he rises.

"Remind me, Mr. Speculator," says Petras. "What is the inciting anomaly at issue?"

"Pardon me, ma'am?"

"You have come here regarding Judge Sampson. But the original investigation began elsewhere?"

"Yes."

"And what was that matter?"

Maybe if the day had begun differently. Maybe if I wasn't standing here with the judge's blood on my shirtfront, with his memory of Silvie blazoned on my mind.

"I understand your authority, ma'am, but I am here to ask you questions and not the other way around."

She holds my gaze for a moment, another one, and then directs herself to my partner.

"What is your name, young lady?"

"Ms. Aysa Paige, ma'am."

"Ms. Paige, two and four are even numbers."

"One and three are not."

"What is the inciting anomaly?"

"Ma'am? I—I would have to—to respect Mr. Ratesic's authority, as far as discussing our investigation."

Our Acknowledged Expert does not rise from her desk. She barely moves, in fact. She speaks very carefully, putting each new word precisely in its place.

"Ms. Paige, my office would be happy to make available to you a laminated copy of the chain of command of the law enforcement divisions of the Golden State, including the position of the Speculative Service, in which you serve, relative to this office, and at the head of which I sit. I am asking you a direct question and requiring a simple answer."

Paige looks at me. I look at the ground.

"We are seeking the full and final truth of a recent death," she says.

"Death of whom?"

"Crane, ma'am. A man named Mose Crane."

"Foul play?"

"No."

"Merely anomalous? Potentially?"

"That is—right. Correct."

"Where?"

Aysa's answers are coming quickly now, either out of deference or fear or some combination of the two.

"On Vermont Avenue. At Judge Sampson's home, ma'am."

"Ah," says Petras, and she tilts her head up and thinks. "Ah."

Mr. Doonan softly shuts the door, returning from the inner office. I don't recall seeing him leave. He passes a note to Petras, who writes on it and passes it back.

"Madam Expert," I begin, and Doonan stops me, pointing at the clock.

"Mr. and Ms. Speculator," he says blandly, "your time is up." I don't move. Aysa doesn't move. Doonan steps between us and Ms. Petras, drawing his suit coat together and buttoning it like he's closing a door. "The Expert is a busy woman, as you know, and your allotted time has long since elapsed."

"Sit down," Aysa tells him.

"Respectfully, miss," Doonan begins, and she says, "I said sit the fuck *down,*" and I hope she knows I love her—not with some goony-eyed romantic love but with the fierce, true love of respect. One Speculator to another. I love Ms. Paige fierce and true and I will love her forever.

"Go on and have a seat, Mr. Doonan," says Petras, and he does. She places her hands over her eyes, and when she removes them all of the tension is gone from her face. She smiles pleasantly, robotically, as if we are here after all to seek her expertise, to ask about appropriate strategies for sentencing or community policing.

"As you may be aware, Mr. Speculator," Petras begins, "we on the committee have certain prerogatives regarding matters of epistemological certainty."

"What?"

This is off topic. I don't know what this is, but I don't like it.

"That is, the State has vested in me the power to determine, under certain circumstances, when matters can be deemed inscrutable. Impossible to be weighed as true or not true, and therefore dangerous."

She gives me her bland smile. I know what she means, the ultimate power of the State, the authority to designate things as unknown and unknowable, beyond the reach of speculation. But I don't see what that has to do with this—until I do.

"Wait."

"Mr. Doonan would be happy to provide you with documentation of the statutory authority to which I refer."

I see it now—the danger that has entered the room in the slip-stream of her murmuring tone.

"Ms. Petras, hold on."

"Upon review of the case currently under discussion—"

"You haven't reviewed it. You—"

"—my office is taking the official step of declaring the matter of the death of Mose Crane—"

She is just reeling it off, chapter and verse, reciting it like Arlo would, except not to flaunt her knowledge of the Basic Law but to build it as a wall.

"Hold on."

The trap was not clear until it was too late—the ground did not shift until I stepped onto it. Oh. Oh *shit*.

"—as unknown and unknowable."

"Laszlo?" says Aysa, confused, uncertain. Mr. Doonan is still writing. There are three notebooks on his desk now, just the three. Outside the window of the bungalow, carts putter past, important people going from one important place to another, clutching folders bulging with important papers.

I have been carrying around the small light of my investigation, like a man cupping a candle under his palms, hoping for it to stay lit, and instead I've brought it to the one person with the power to snuff it out between two fingers. I don't even look at Ms. Paige right now. I can't. I can't bear to watch her realize what I've done. What an idiot I am.

"I declare the truth of the death of Mose Crane, and all matters flowing therefrom, to be unknowable." She nods at Doonan, who nods back at her. He is writing in his Day Book, a big silver number with silver-edged pages. The captures are rolling. It's all being lost, before my eyes. "All relevant truth that can be collected has been collected," she says.

"No," I say. "It hasn't."

"Well." She stands, and holds out her hand. "It has, though. And let me add, finally, also, on behalf of the Golden State: thank you for your efforts in this matter."

It is the end of the conversation. She holds out her pad for me to stamp, and I stamp it, and Paige stamps it too. Too late I have figured it out, too late to draw the line that I should have drawn already.

E is not for Elena at all. *E* is for Expert.

"Okay," says Petras brightly. "Was there anything else I can help you folks with today?"

17.

Everybody keeps everything. *Archiving is a bulwark.* You do it. I do it. We have to do it.

I do it now, down in the crawl space beneath my small house. I unpack all of the flat facts I've collected, the whole paper trail of the day that was, a day's worth of living. Conversation stamps and stamps of presence, the receipt from passing through the gate arm at the administrative campus, the receipt for every cup of coffee and doughnut consumed, the record of my interrogation by the regular police in the hallway outside Judge Sampson's chambers. The slip of stamped paper I was handed on the seventh floor of the Service building, when we turned over Sampson's Night Book to evidence processing.

I tear today's pages of notes clean from my Day Book, one at a time, careful to leave the carbons in place.

My motions are deliberate, slow, careful. I have performed this ritual many times. Once for every day of my adulthood. Those notes relating to Crane, to the death I was investigating and am not investigating any longer I fold in half, and then fold in half again, make of them a small hard square, a stiff packet with four sharp corners, and this I slide last into the bag and seal it. Mose Crane is dead, but his death is not an event for me. It is gone from my mind.

When I'm done, I don't get up. I stare at my boxes, thinking maybe I'll start opening things up. It's tempting. It's always tempting. I could just sit here for a while, rummaging through years gone by, digging up scraps of the past for consideration. People do it. I have done it. Sort through the old years, seek out certain incidents, key days, fragments of memory, spread them out on the ground and just wallow for a while, before sweeping it all back together and stamping the bags "Unsealed and resealed." I could waste hours in reflection, self-abasement, and recrimination. There are people who fall down that rabbit hole and never come up.

Not me. Not tonight.

I rise stiffly, keeping my body very still. Wriggle back out of the crawl space, walk slowly back up the stairs.

"Fuck."

I find my face in the mirror, in the darkness of my empty house. Silvie took a lot of the furniture when she left, but this standing mirror is still here, by the front door, leaning against the wall. "It might be fun to look at yourself in the morning sometimes," she used to say. "Before you leave the house."

There is blood still on my forehead, up by my hairline, at the level of the roots. Blood still in my eyebrows, small flecks like red dust.

I pass through the kitchen into the bedroom, peeling off the rest of my clothes as I go. Coat and pants, shirt and tie.

I knew a one-legged policeman once. When I was still on the regular force, before I followed my brother's lead and drifted into Service. His name was Rafael, and we used to drink together, after shift, at a bar on Grand Avenue north of downtown. He lost the leg, he told me, when he was a teenager, but he could still feel it. *"Sometimes I swear I could touch it. Sometimes I swear if I look away, and look back——"* He was pretty drunk. I was drunk too. He never told anyone, he said, about how he still felt like the leg was there. *"Please, Laz, keep it to yourself, okay? They'll jack me up on that shit,"* he whispered, beery breath in my ear. It was late at night, just taxis on the street outside. *"On that Clarify. They'll kick me the fuck over the wall."*

He still felt the leg and he liked to feel it. He liked to believe that it was real.

I will miss my case but my case is gone.

I stumble into the bathroom and piss and splash water on my face.

I come out into the bedroom and see a dark shape in the greater darkness of my unmade bed. Nested like a dead animal in the mass of rumpled sheets.

A book. The book. Still in the cover that says *The Everyday Citizen's Dictionary,* but I know what it is, I can see its true face through the mask. *The Prisoner: A Novel.* By Benjamin Wish. It's on my bed.

What the *fuck?*

It is open, facedown, spine bent, pages riffled, like a bird shot out of the sky.

It's impossible, of course. It's fucking impossible.

Because I jammed the book into the dresser this morning. Didn't I? I did. I think back, throw my mind out backward, like feeling behind you in the darkness. This morning. To the diner, to the office, Kelly Tarjin begging me for help, Silvie at the Record, the judge, the expert, the day replaying itself, but I know—I know—I *know that book was in the dresser when I left.*

It sings to me.

From the bed, it is singing.

I can hear it singing.

I left it in a drawer. Didn't I? I did. I know that I—

"No," the voice sings, the visiting voice. *"You—"*

I clutch at the side of my head. I'm in my T-shirt and underpants, alone in this room except that I'm on the Record. In this room there are three captures: one above the door, one embedded in the floor lamp, one on the ceiling fan. It's just lucky the jacket is still on the book, but if someone was in here—if someone came in—

No one came in.

I am staring at the book, and I take a step toward it.

I want you. The thought dances to life. Like a stranger, a visitor, an alien voice.

I turn my back on the book.

I take my weapon out of the bedside table and perform a careful circuit, room by room. I am seeking an intruder, but as I move slowly through the house, I begin to feel like I am the intruder myself, stalking through the handful of rooms in my little house and seeing each one anew. I can picture myself, as if from above, a dark figure, moving in shadow.

I don't find anything. In the kitchen, my juice glass is still on the kitchen counter, lightly stuck in the place where I left it, and my plate is in the sink. The light is on in the bathroom. My pile of last night's dirty clothes is still in the laundry room. I peer out each of the windows, checking for signs of entry. I crane my head up and down the street. Across the street is a wide field filled with lima beans and lettuces. Down the slope from my backyard is a four-lane road, and across the road are acres planted with avocado.

It doesn't matter how long I look: I won't find anything. Nobody's been here. The front door was undisturbed and no one has a key, and who would break in and take nothing, disturb nothing, only take out a book and not even take it—just open it and leave it on the bed?

No one. No one would do that.

So I return to the bedroom living in two realities at once—*We always are, aren't we, despite all our efforts we are*—believing and not believing that someone was or is in the house with me, knowing and not knowing that I am alone with *The Prisoner: A Novel.*

I know exactly what it wants. It wants me to read it. That can't be so, of course, because it is an inanimate object, possessing no impulses or desires of its own. The book does not carry intentionality. It simply is, but there it is, having somehow crawled from my drawer and thrown itself open on the bed, willful and desperate for attention.

I grab my head with both hands, press my flattened palms to my temples like I am trying to keep my head from toppling off, and growl.

The book wants me to read it, and I want that too. I want it very badly.

I should go to the fridge and find a beer and drink it, maybe drink another one. I should turn on my wall-mounted and watch some stream, any stream, fucking "Slipping on Sidewalk Cracks" or "Old Men Walking Dogs." Anything. I should brush my teeth and wash the blood from my hair, and fall into bed like a tree, get up in the morning, and see what Alvaro has written on the board for me to pursue.

Yes, there was a case at 3737 Vermont Avenue, there was a dead man on the ground at that address, there were certain associated anomalies, but all of that is gone now. That matter is unknown and unknowable, and that is a part of the job—it is part of living in the world. There are certain things that cannot be known and can never be known, and this must be accepted, our safety and our future depend upon it, and I am trying to bear it and depend upon it, and it is like knives, it is like holding the blades of knives.

Charlie could have done it. Charlie would have outsmarted them before he could be outsmarted, Charlie would have sensed the maneuverings of the gray man in the corner, seen the wall the Expert was building and tunneled under it, flown over it. Charlie would have come back laughing with the whole truth and nothing but, dangling from his clenched fist like a monster's severed head.

Every time I close my eyes my body hums for solace, and every time I open them I see the novel lying on the bed.

I put down my weapon. I pick up the book. I *need* it.

I start at page one.

"Listen, lady," said Shenk very slowly, shaking his head. "You're in the wrong place. Okay? You need to find yourself a lawyer."

"You are a lawyer."

"Yes. I'm a lawyer." Shenk smiled. He felt weary. He was tired of smiling. "But what you need is, you need a lawyer lawyer. A real lawyer. You understand?"

That's how it starts, page one, the page after the title page. A lawyer in his office, morose and deflated, visited by a needful stranger, and already I can feel the book's claws in me, the claws of fiction. Who is the lawyer and who is the woman, what is their past and future—

I put the fucking thing down. I put it down on the edge of the bed and then I pick it up again and throw it against the wall.

I stand up and grit my teeth and stare out the window at the sleeping city. The tops of palm trees, the distant movement of brake lights. Reality all around me.

I know what is going to happen already, I can feel it happening. I have been warned of this my whole life. We all have—I have and you have. I have spent my whole life protecting against alternate realities, and now this one is like an injection, it is like pushing poison directly into my veins, and I can't stand it, I can't allow this to happen, but then I yell "Fuck!" and I storm across the room and grab the book with greedy fingers and find the page I was on and start to read again.

The Prisoner is the story of a boy named Wesley Keener, who becomes gravely ill after a botched surgery, and it's about his family, desperate for his recovery, desperate and scared and sad, and it's about the lawyer that they hire—that's the lawyer from the opening passage—his name is Shenk, and he is a sad and furious man when we meet him but then we understand that he wasn't always that way, it was this case, this broken boy who made him so, and it's about the boy himself, who lies for most of the story in silence, in a vegetative state on a hospital bed with some sort of mysterious alien life moving inside him—that's the part I saw yesterday, the section I already read, the part I glanced at accidentally in my office. I charge on, I read and read. It's all happening in a city called Los Angeles, within a state called California, which is related somehow to the Golden State, bearing some similarities in the detailing, in weather and geography and here and there in street names, landmarks—which is disquieting and yet mesmerizing and the thing about the book is that none of it is true, nothing is confirmed or certain. The book speaks in the voice of various of its characters, and each of them—the lawyer, the boy's father and his mother, the doctor—has an opinion about what must have happened, each of them marching around shaking their own version like a fist, and so it is a riot of subjectivities, a violence of truths, and the fuck of it is—is that as I read I am beginning to cry, tears rolling hot down my heavy cheeks and disappearing into my beard because I do not understand this—

And then I feel like I do understand it, what it means, of course I do, but I can't think about it, it doesn't bear consideration, it—

The world as I have understood it is slipping out from under me and I ought to stop but I can't. I can't stop. I keep reading and as I read the book settles down over me, it *becomes* reality as I read it, the air becomes fuzzed, to the point that when I look up it is like *the reality of my room is less real than the reality inside the book.*

I read it for hours, curled forward over the small artifact of the book, sitting on the wood floor of my house, feeling the real world under my ass, leaning against the wall and feeling the steadying actualness of drywall and plaster against my back, and this extraordinary struggle plays out *inside the boy,* but really the novel revolves around the people outside him, who have no idea what's going on, just as I, reading it, have no idea *really* what is going on, and I want to know what is real even though I know that none of it is real, that a novel is just a book of lies, a bundle of falsehoods like sticks lashed together with sentences for wires, the boy invaded by alien intelligence and the doctor drinking himself sick over his failure and the father seeking his own truths in a maddening truth-diffusing system of systems called the Internet, and I can feel all of this non-sense, all of this not-true, it's all watering my eyes and itching my throat, burning me down from the inside, and still I can't stop—

I am approaching the end of the book. The stars have shifted the sky. The father and the doctor and the lawyer have traveled to a different city, a glittering vacation city, in search of a last chance, a hope they know to be a wild and impossible kind of hope. This city is called Las Vegas, and the author, Wish, describes it as "a place where, famously and dangerously, big gambles are known at times to pay off." And as I read, as I travel along with the people who love the boy, on their desperate mission to find the one man who might save him, as they barrel in an old car through the heat of what feels like an endless desert in search of this mirage of hope in this place Las Vegas, which cannot be real, I am as close as I have ever been to understanding what happened—what *really* happened—what laid us low—what cut the Golden State adrift and cloistered in its own truth at the edge of the world, as close as I have ever been to the old world that left us or we left, and it is like I am driving in a car through the desert toward the inscrutable past—

Toward the truth—

I read to the end, faster and faster, I can't stop, I keep reading, pushing forward through this dream of something that is Not So and never has been, and by the time I reach the final pages, however many hours later, I am curled up beside my bed as if in hiding from the world outside, hiding from the Moon, my back against the wall and my knees curled up against my chest. I am reading the end pages and not wanting it to end, I am shaking, my body in full revolt against all my manly efforts to hold it still.

Later on—much later, I don't know how much later—there's a noise.

I roll over and raise my head, confused and weary. Baffled. I'm on the floor, somehow, with the book beside me. I don't know where I am. I don't know how much later it is.

But then the noise, again. Something crashing against something else. It has a texture to it, a wooden thump.

I moan. *I'm in a hospital bed.*

I am an unconscious child.

I'm on the floor and the book is nearby, closed and angled away, its spine turned away from mine, like we are lovers who've quarreled in the night. False reality is clinging to me like the dust of an old world, gritty at the corners of my mind.

My family is clustered around my bed, consumed with worry.

I shake it away. I stand, slowly, and brush myself off, wiping bits of falsehood off my chest and my arms.

It's knocking, that's all. Someone is knocking at the door.

The Moon hangs like a lamp outside the window, shedding a grudging half-yellow light. I don't like the sound of the knocking. I find my gun and chamber a round. I get up, slow and deliberate, and, holding the gun in front of me, I walk to the door.

The pounding continues.

I am the father. It is the doctor at the door. He is here to lay scorn on my desperation for a cure, my sad need to pick and choose my own truth.

No. It's my son at the door, my boy, alive at last, back from the dead.

Come on, Laszlo. Come on. Get it the fuck together.

"Who is it?" I stand at the door, gun drawn but not aimed, just like I learned in the academy.

"It's me. Mr. Ratesic? Laszlo. It's *me*."

I keep my weapon drawn as I look through the peephole and there's my trainee, in jeans and a T-shirt, no pinhole, hair pulled back and tied, looking up into the door's eye with raw urgency on her young face.

I glance back into my bedroom, the sliver of it visible through the door. The novel just out of sight. And I think—what have I done?

18.

"**Okay,**" **says** Aysa, breathing heavily, nodding her head, gathering her thoughts. "Okay," she says. "Okay. So. I went back to the office to finish reviewing."

"Reviewing *what?*"

"The stretches. Can I come in?"

"What stretches, Ms. Paige, did you go back to finish reviewing?"

"On Crane's apartment. The stakeout stretches from Mose Crane's apartment. I never—I hadn't finished them."

She holds up her hand and a shiver cuts through me. She's got one tight in her fist, a slim rectangle of silver plastic. She's been back to the office, and not only was she watching the stretches, she made an echo of one: she burned it and stuck it in her pocket and brought it here.

"You weren't supposed to do that," I say, glancing up at the doorway capture, and I'm trying to be stern but I fear I sound like a child, like a small, scared child. "You can't have done that."

Of course I could be talking to myself. *The Prisoner* is in the bedroom, still quietly singing. Its alternate truth is still glimmering in here, glossing the furniture, fogging my vision. If she's broken the rules, then I certainly have too. When these stretches are played, when this reality is requisitioned, when this whole story enters the Record, it will be both of us who are found to have strayed.

"We were pulled from that case," I tell Aysa. "That is not a case."

"No, I know. Can I just come in? There's something you need to see."

"We can't look, Paige. There's nothing there."

"Well, Petras said so. But just because she says there's no anomaly, that doesn't mean there's no anomaly."

I'm stunned. I laugh. "Yes," I tell Paige. "That's exactly what it means. That's literally what it means. Petras was speaking for the State." The thing is determined. It is done. "We fucked it up." Catch it. Correct it. "*I* did. I fucked it up. Investigation complete."

She is shaking her head, gritting her teeth. She won't accept it—she can't. I wonder with a sudden horror whether Paige is sensing the presence of the novel in my house. She must be: with her discernment, her attention to falsehood, she must feel that it's here. Is she being polite? Deferential to my superior rank? Or can it be that she is so focused on the mission that brought her here, frantic in the dead of night, that she isn't catching it?

"Can I just show this to you? Can I just tell you what I'm looking at here?"

"No."

"Yes."

"Paige. No."

"*Yes.*"

She doesn't stamp her feet, but she might as well. She is like a defiant child, but somehow serious, more serious than me. She is more of a Spec than I have ever been, has more of whatever it is that puts a person in law enforcement—she has started and she can't stop. She cannot leave it be and that is her truth, bone truth, deep truth, she could not leave the matter of Mose Crane because that's who she is—and who am I? I'm the one who is told that it is over and says okay, it's over, just goes home and gives up. Abandons himself to a work of fiction, of all things, a malfeasant artifact. Hides his fearful face from the dangers of the real world.

And that's been it the whole time, hasn't it? Arlo told me to hold this young Speculator back, to ballast her, keep her calm and deliberate and cautious like I am calm and deliberate and cautious, but I never wanted to. I don't want to make another me. The parts of her I'm supposed to tamp down are the parts I like the best.

Paige went back to the office because she's not like me, she's like him, she's like Charlie, she is Charlie, and she won't stop. She can't.

"All right, kid," I say, and hold out my hand. She puts the stretch into it. "Let's see what you got."

Two minutes later we are crouched in front of my wall-mounted, in the center of the living room, staring at the front door of Mose Crane's apartment.

I glance at Aysa's somber face, blanketed in the light of the wall-mounted. She has not seemed to notice that I am in my underclothes, or that my house is a mess, and she certainly hasn't looked with curiosity into the bedroom and wondered why there's a copy of *The Everyday Citizen's Dictionary* lying on the floor like a spent shell.

On the screen is the familiar static shot of Crane's front door.

Ms. Paige says "Go" and "Fast," and reality races past, one minute, two minutes, three minutes passing in a rush, and then here he comes. "Slow it down," she says, and we watch him enter: a man in a suit, moving quickly, eyes cast down, holding his hat down on his head as he rushes up the stairs. The stretch does not show his face. I get as close as I can to the monitor but I can't see it.

"Do you see?" says Aysa.

"See what?"

"That's him."

"Who?"

She looks at me, and then back at the screen. I stare.

"Are you—sure?"

"One hundred percent."

"Stop," she says, and the image pauses and I recognize him in that instant—a face turned slightly to one side, a high brow, a chin tucked downward. It's Doonan, all right.

Do you know the figure, my right hand? Mr. Doonan is my right hand.

"When is this? Is this—is it during the missing two weeks?"

She shakes her head. "Laszlo. This is *yesterday*. Two hours and nine minutes after Crane falls off the roof."

"Wait," I say. "Wait." My mind is pinwheeling, turning over itself, but I can't keep up with Aysa Paige. "Go," she says, and Doonan goes, walks briskly up the steps and stands at Crane's door, his back to us, his face once again hidden from the capture by his hat, and he knocks, shifts on his heels a moment, and then the door opens. "Wait," I say again. "You said this was yesterday. Two hours and nine minutes after the fall. But doesn't that mean—"

"Yes," she says, snapping her fingers impatiently, pointing at the upper-right corner of the screen. "There's no one home. Look at the *time*." The stamp at the top right shows 10:54. "We're going to be there at eleven oh one."

"Who is?"

"You and me. Laszlo. Come on. It's yesterday. It's the day he died. It's ten fifty-four. He's already dead. He's at the morgue by now, and we're going to get to his apartment in a few minutes."

"And no one was home."

"That's correct."

"Aster comes up the stairs to the landing. She lets us in."

"Yeah, but watch. Back ten." The stretch backs up ten seconds and then resumes, and Doonan knocks again, and the door opens again. There is someone inside. A shadow of a person, and Doonan is laughing at whatever the person says, a murmur of low happy greeting, and then he steps inside.

"Whoa," I say. I'm leaning closer in my chair. We slow it down to watch it again, frame by frame.

Paige is good, but I'm good too, and I can see that what Petras's right hand is enacting here is a kind of dumb show. He is playing for the captures. He puts his hand on the handle, seemingly trying it but really picking the lock, working the cheap lock quickly and expertly with small tools. And then he stands back, makes a big show of checking his watch, and then the door opens, as if from inside, but it's really Doonan pushing it open, with the tip of one of those brown shoes he pushes the door open and turns his body to block the person at the door, because there is no one at the door. There is a shadow, and it is his own. He says hello to nobody, laughs at a pleasant word of welcome that nobody makes, and enters at nobody's invitation.

"Shit," I say, and Paige says, "I know," and then we watch it again slow. I explain to Paige how he does it, how Doonan, the soft unassuming administrator, is traveling with tools, hidden in his coat, secreted up his sleeve. He's breaking in, and he knows that the stretch will be watched. He's breaking in and he knows to make it look like he's not breaking in, and he knows how.

"He's there to take those days," I say. I stand. I start to pace, making tight circles in my narrow house, from wall to wall. I have shaken off the last tendrils of my dream, emerged from the world created by *The Prisoner*. It's like rising from a pool of water and shaking the droplets free.

"He's there to go down to that basement and steal days out of Mose Crane's Provisional Record."

"You think?"

"Yeah."

I don't just think. I know. I *know*. It strikes me with the force of certainty, as clear as daylight, as true as doors on houses. And other things are becoming clearer too.

"This is two hours after Crane dies? They know — Petras knows, Doonan knows — that the Specs are going to go search Crane's house, and they know what they're going to find. On those days in particular. If we were to go to the ninth floor and ask Woody Stone for the stretches from the alley outside — between the building and the Chinese place — five minutes after he goes in? We'd see Doonan coming out, putting the door back quick and careful and scurrying off."

Paige is pacing too; now we're pacing together, back and forth, making parallel grooves in my small front room. "He'd have to know, right?" she says. "That we would get into the dead man's boxes and find that days were missing? He'd have to know."

"So it must be — " I stop. Speculation is here — it's in the room — I feel it, a swell tide of darkness, speckled with possibility. "Whatever it is they're hiding. It is *worse*."

"Worse than missing days?"

"Yeah. Yes. Because — " I stop. I squeeze my eyes shut and live in the darkness with the truth as it appears. "Nobody would risk stealing two weeks of someone's days unless the risk of them being *found* was a thousand times worse than the risk of the theft."

The stretch is still rolling in the background, the light of the wall-mounted creating the only illumination in my barren house. And suddenly, as we're talking, we appear on the screen — a few minutes after Petras's man disappears inside, here we come up the steps. We almost saw him. We were just there. Then we appear on the screen, and Ms. Aster comes out, and we watch ourselves in conversation. The old versions of Ratesic and Paige, from the day before. Another reality. A different world. I stare at my own broad back on the screen with disgust, at the way I hold myself, how I loom with condescending satisfaction over Paige, who after all is so much smarter than me, so much the nimbler mind.

How I comport myself with the contemptuous affect of the senior Spec, moving with undeserved confidence through a world I think I understand.

"Stop," I say, and the images freeze on the monitor.

"Mr. Ratesic? Laz, are you okay—"

I would say yes, but she knows. It's already happening. It's happening and I can't stop it, speculation rolling me down into itself, into deeper and deeper darkness, and I want it—I let it. I feel it now.

A single candle's light kisses and winks to life in the dark room of my mind, and it burns warmer, sending out a radiance of light in which I can find the whole truth of this. The entirety of truth.

—*the right hand*—

　　—*Petras's right hand in Crane's doorway*—

　　　　—*Crane the blackmailer, Crane the obscure, skull split*—

All the things he knew and never said, all the small truths that flamed out and died along the lines of his neurons, died in his brain the moment he died too.

My eyes fly open.

"A construction worker," I say. Construction. Three syllables joined in a simple word. I say it just quietly, just to myself, stunned by the suddenness of my understanding, and liberated by it too. Liberated by the knowledge of what I have to do. Because in that moment I know. I know what it is. All of the pieces are flying into place, circling in like birds finding their roost.

"Laszlo?" Aysa stares at me, eyes wide and bright in the dimness.

"Do you remember when we talked to Renner?" I ask.

"At the death scene? Crane's boss?"

"Yes. Do you remember—he told us that Crane worked odd jobs." Renner, the construction manager in a sweaty panic, struggling to dig from his anxious mind every possible detail, spitting out facts as fast as he remembered them. "He said that Crane frequently did other jobs in his off-hours. That he was always coming from other work."

Working under the table on some mansion in the Hills . . .

"You read Petras's file, right?"

Nobody likes cheap labor more than the rich . . .

"Yes, sir. Yes, Laszlo."

"What was her address—the home address?"

"I forget the number. It's on Mulholland, though. Mulholland Drive. Laszlo—"

And now I'm seeing it in my mind's eye, a memory as clear as reality: a slim red binder, unmarked. Doonan sliding it soundlessly off Petras's shelf, hiding it away as the conversation approached a crisis.

"Laszlo. Where are we going?"

I am scrambling into my clothes. Jeans and a work shirt, whatever's at hand. Aysa isn't in her uniform and pinhole, and neither am I. I've got my car keys, I've got my weapon. I'm halfway out the door.

I ask Paige, as we head to the car: "Did Arlo ever tell you the whole story?"

"What whole story?"

"Of what happened to my brother. To Charlie."

MAIN TEXT (CONT.)

Charlie Ratesic paced restlessly before the glass windows of the Service, glaring out at the State. It was the middle of the night, and the buildings sparkled gloriously below, but all eyes were on the disheveled hero, rubbing the months of stubble on his chin, smoking cigarette after cigarette.

He had returned to the Service building after months undercover, and his colleagues had gathered to hear his report, to try to understand what it was he had been working on in darkest secrecy for all that time.

"They call themselves . . . the Golden State," he said.

We looked at each other in bafflement. Most of the unit was there, gathered around to listen: Carson and Burlington, Cullers, Alvaro. Laszlo Ratesic, our hero's younger brother, was leaning by the elevator wall, hands buried deep in his pockets.

"The Golden State?" I said slowly. "I had understood from your earlier reports, Mr. Ratesic, that this was a conspiracy *against* our good and golden State."

"Yeah." He pulled out another cigarette. Cigarette after cigarette. "See, the fuckers—they think it's funny, okay? To call themselves that." He sneered. "They think everything is *funny*."

He told us what he had learned, and we listened in horror. This criminal conspiracy, this self-styled Golden State, met nearly every night at the warehouse in Glendale, where they had removed all the captures and replaced them with duplicates. "Dummies" was the word Charlie used. Dummies. Machines cleverly styled to look like the recording devices that forge our reality, but which recorded nothing. Which are not connected to anything.

The whole building was dead to the eyes of the world so that lies could be told within its walls with impunity. This Golden State, Charlie told us, was meeting off the Record, disconnected from ongoing reality.

"But...why?" asked Carson, her face reflecting the fascinated horror that we were all feeling.

"To lie. Just to lie."

We could not conceive of it, the willful depravity of this place that Charlie had infiltrated: citizens parading about in full and luxuriant disregard for the truth, announcing themselves to have new names, telling each other that they were pirates, or millionaires, war heroes, thieves. Relating stories from their personal histories, reveling in changing the details every time they told them, making themselves funnier or braver or better-looking in retrospect. Making up stories willy-nilly about public figures and private friends.

They were spewing out so many and such extravagant lies that every time Charlie approached this warehouse, willing himself back into character as one of the conspirators, he could practically see the effusions of their dishonesty billowing out from behind the doors.

"It's fucked up," he told us. "These people are seriously fucked up."

"So what are we waiting for?" said Alvaro. "Let's bust in there and shut the place down."

"No!" shouted Charlie loudly, wheeling on poor Alvaro, who backed away, putting his hands in the air. Charlie's eyes were wild, red-rimmed. His hair was a mess, sticking out in all directions. "We can't."

"But Charlie," I said softly, trying to calm him. "Why not?"

The answer was simple, at least as he saw it: Charlie didn't want us to end the conspiracy because he had convinced himself that there was someone else involved he had not yet managed to identify. "Give me more time. A little more time. I have to find the monster."

We all looked at each other. Laszlo, over by the elevator, stood up straight.

"The monster?"

"That's right."

It was increasingly clear, the longer the great Charlie Ratesic stood there, staring at us, staring out the window, that something was wrong with him. Something was very wrong indeed. His lips were flecked with spittle. His eyes were wild.

"They say—" He ground out his cigarette, lit a new one. "These fuckers say that the Golden State—the real one, our one—is all bullshit. They say that the real golden state— 'state' like 'state of being,' 'state of understanding'—the real golden state is accepting that there is no such thing as truth. They think we're fooling ourselves to think we can be protected from lies. They say that all of it—the Record, the captures, the Service..." Ratesic was staring out the window again, out at the glittering majesty of the dark city. "They think it's some kind of fallacy, that we're, like—what do they say?—playing make-believe."

We were all looking at each other, looking at Charlie, trying to take the measure of what was happening inside his mind by the wildness in his eyes.

"They're writing a book," he said. Lighting a new cigarette with trembling hands. "A Night Book, they call it, because it's a book of real truth, truth underneath the truth. Just like a real Night Book, but...but it's a joke. It's a sick joke." Charlie took a deep drag of the new cigarette and launched again, a single long sentence curling out with the smoke. "They say the real truth is that there is no such thing as truth at all, there's only perception, okay, because everything you think is true can only be proved by pointing to some other truth, but *that* truth rests on another one too, and so on forever, and they say that what this means is that there *is* no permanent actual reality, there *is* no Objectively So, and all that we have built, the good and golden truth that surrounds us, is *nothing*." He stopped finally then, and stood trembling with tears in his eyes. "Not truth but its opposite. Its absence."

"Okay, Charlie," I said softly. "Okay."

"Don't do that, Vasouvian." He sprang back to life, snarling, and grabbed my collar. "Don't condescend to me. These assholes want to take the whole State off the Record. They say that whatever happened"—he let go of me and gestured wildly, gesturing to the ancient inscrutable past, the unknowable calamity that happened to the rest of the world—"that we oughta let it happen here. We oughta *make* it happen here."

"But that's impossible."

"It's not. It's not! There's a monster. There's a monster and the monster is going to make it happen. Unless we stop it."

"A monster. Charlie. Really?"

"What?" said Ratesic. "You think I'm lying?"

It was, I realized, time to talk alone. I took Charlie aside. We sat down at my desk and I poured us both coffee. The man had been undercover for six months, and I told him that in my expert opinion it was time for him to come in from the field. Monster or no monster.

"No," he said. He did not drink the coffee. "No, Arlo."

"What I'm afraid of, dear Charlie, is that the work—you being so exposed, for so long—I'm worried that it is affecting you."

"What? No. The work doesn't affect me. You know that. I don't get symptoms. I don't—"

"On the inside, Charlie. I'm afraid that it is affecting you inside." I didn't use the phrase that had occurred to me, as I looked with horror at the sallowness in his cheeks, the darkness in his eyes when he raved about his monster. I was afraid he had begun to rot from the inside out.

"I am worried, Charlie, that there is an alternate reality that has its hooks in you. As your superior—as your friend—"

"Enough." He slammed down his coffee cup. He grabbed his jacket. "I'm going back in there. I'm going to find the monster."

He stormed toward the elevator, wrestling himself back into his coat.

"Hey. Charlie?"

Laszlo Ratesic stopped his brother by the elevator door. He was bigger than Charlie by half a head, maybe, but you never really noticed him when Charlie was around. Charlie smiled to see him, though. He had his jacket on now. He was ready to go. "Yeah, buddy?"

"I just wanted to say be careful out there." Lazlo put his hand on Charlie's shoulder, but he did not try to stop him. He knew him too well. "Okay?"

Charlie nodded. "You got it." He patted his brother on the cheek, and stepped into the elevator. We watched the door close.

The next time we saw him he was in his hospital bed.

19.

"**Is that** all true?" says Paige.

"Everything is true," I tell her.

I've told her the whole story. And it is. It's all true.

The only part I left out was the distressing exultant feeling I got while I was listening to him that day, raving to old Arlo about this terrifying conspiracy he penetrated, this Golden State that was not the real Golden State, that wanted to make of us our inverse, build a world of pure thin truthlessness with no Record, no captures, everybody walking around with no burden of truth upon them, no prison of truth around them. How what I felt on hearing all this was a kind of inchoate sideways longing.

Wouldn't that be fucking great? is what I thought, watching the elevator door close behind Charlie. That's what I thought, a longing shadowed by the shame of that longing. Shame and fascination and fear.

Wouldn't that be something...

Same way I felt three hours ago, reading *The Prisoner,* immersing myself in alternate realities, soaking in them, in all these things that could be but aren't...

Come on, Laz. Come on. Get it together.

You can't see much of Petras's house from here. It is a modern structure, a single slab of deep gray, its frontage mostly hidden by hedgerow, its full shape obscured by moonlight. A thing of stone and glass, arrogantly defiant of gravity, built back from the road and cantilevered out over the valley below.

The house radiates. The house holds the monster. The house is a monster, looming, reaching into the darkness.

Paige has questions. One or two more questions formulating in that nonstop mind of hers, I see them bubbling in her, but more than that I can see the energy itself—she has questions but they're all incidental. Fuel for the fire. She is ready to roll. She is itching to go. *This is something, man*—that's what Ms. Paige is thinking.

I remember her on the bench outside the judge's chambers, my young partner, trying to puzzle out the judge's act of self-slaughter, her lip curling at the idea of such a radical reaction to something so *small.*

Whatever else she knows, she knows that this—the story I've told her, the story of Charlie, the story we're part of now—this is *not small.*

"Your brother went back into that house?"

"He did. There was no way to stop him. He thought he had to catch a monster." I look at her. She is looking through the windshield at Petras's house in the darkness. "He thought there was a monster."

"Not literally?"

"You know, I don't know. I was never really sure."

Using the information Charlie had gathered from his undercover efforts, Mr. Vasouvian along with Mr. Alvaro and the rest of us on the thirtieth floor planned a raid on the warehouse in Glendale. We waited for a week, two weeks; waited and hoped that my brother would come to his senses and get out of there. But an Off Record house could not be countenanced, and soon enough, with or without Charlie, it was time to act.

Three units of the Service went in together, with riot gear and heavy armaments, along with half a battalion of regular police. We arrested nine individuals, all of whom were subsequently charged with grave assault on the Objectively So and exiled for their crimes.

"And what about your brother?"

I just shake my head. I've reached the end of the story. I can't tell any more.

I don't know if he thought there was a literal monster or not, but here we are. Staring at Petras's house.

You were right, Charlie. You were always right.

For once I have a gut feeling, the kind Charlie got every day his whole life. There are only a handful of people in the State who could arrange the kind of careful unseen sabotage of the Record that Charlie was convinced had occurred, and Laura Petras is surely one of them. She did it before, and she escaped apprehension, and now she's doing it again.

Bringing another house off the Record. Her own house.

Mose Crane, itinerant construction man, freelance contractor, must have been among those who worked on the project. Maybe he knew and maybe he didn't know the nature of the alterations he had been asked to undertake on this property. Maybe it was later he figured it out.

But he did figure it out, I know he did, because six months later he decides to turn his knowledge into easy money, to use this piece of discovered truth like a crowbar, like a lockpick. To blackmail the judge and the Acknowledged Expert with what he knew. And that's what he's doing, prowling around the judge's house, when he slips and tumbles and dies, and in dying draws the attention of the Speculative Service. Petras and her allies have to work fast. They send Doonan scuttling to Crane's last known residence, two steps ahead of us, to remove all evidence of his connection to Petras.

That's plenty of explanation for Aysa Paige. She's in motion before I've finished talking, feeling for her weapon under her coat, opening her door. "All right," she says. "So let's go get her."

"No—wait," I say. "Stop."

"Why? We have to go now, don't we? We have to go right now."

"We are going to wait until she comes out. Tail her to work. Put her under surveillance. This is something we gotta do very carefully. As quietly and inconspicuously as possible. This isn't some kid we're talking about. This is one of our Acknowledged Experts."

"But—Laszlo." Aysa stares at me, stunned and agitated. Her voice is hot with urgency. "We have to work fast. We go in *now*. She knows we're on to her. She has to know."

"Or she thinks we think it's about Sampson, about Tester. Something small—"

"She's smarter than that, Laszlo. We gotta go in. Now."

"Just a second, Paige. Give it a second."

"No." She shakes her head. She hisses, *"Why?"*

She's right. I know she's right. I am sitting here doing what I'm always doing, which is trying to figure out what to do, and she is getting out of the car, patting her holster for her weapon, looking at me evenly through the window.

"Are you sure—in your heart, Laszlo, are you sure that this woman is what you think she is?"

I nod. *Monster monster monster.* I know. For once, I know.

"All right, then. Let's *go*."

Paige goes first and I stay close at her heels, matching her stride, directly behind her, an animal pack, a pack of two.

The air changes, I can feel it change, as we pass through the high hedgerow separating Mulholland Drive from the Expert's house. A short driveway, lined with wide flat pavers. A desert garden, the glistening knifepoints of succulent cactuses in the wan moonlight.

"Here," I say very quietly as soon as we step onto the lawn proper. I whistle softly to draw Aysa's attention, and then I crouch and point. *"Look."*

The capture is a remarkable forgery, specific in every detail. I snap my fingers in front of it and it moves, minutely, just like a real one. The lens blinks open and closed, open and closed, when I move my face; when I snap my fingers, the beak of the microphone jerks up, like a bird's. I look at Paige and can see that she is feeling what I am feeling, the wavering world, the air rippling and bending with the unacceptable reality: a dead capture. A forgery. A deliberate undermining of the foundation of the State.

It is galling. Horrifying to think of it—so much reality unrecorded, moments racing past. A hundred moments, two hundred. I stand here, counting. If you split each moment then you quickly reach infinity, all the moments in the world going unrecorded—a quantum of instants. A *forever* of reality, disappearing as it appears. I am standing in the center of a radius of absence. You don't realize what a comfort reality is until you leave it, what a good strong feeling is the truth under your feet and in the air around you, how nice it is to be surrounded at all times by the truth. To know that everything is being added to the ledger, that everything that is *is,* that everything that has happened has happened and will have happened forever.

I am terrified now. I feel like I might float up above the Earth, fly away, crash down into the sea somewhere. I look to Paige, staring at the dead captures, the row of dummies, and I know she is feeling what I am feeling, the world reeling, the sky becoming suffused with the thick truthless air. We are off the Record.

"Hey. *Hey,*" I say urgently. "Water is made of two hydrogens, one oxygen. *Hey.*"

She nods. Her eyes regain their focus. She stands up straight, whispers back to me, "Light is faster than sound."

"A million times faster."

"Yes indeed it is."

And we move on together, creeping like soldiers toward the front door, muttering facts, good solid facts, telling each other real things, solid true things.

The house is a stone tablet with tall panes of glass for doors and windows. The Moon hangs low; sunrise is close. There is a dog barking somewhere inside, urgent and nervous.

"Wait," whispers Paige. Holds up one finger. Tilts her head. "Listen."

Light noise from the back of the house. Barely audible. A murmuring sound, water running or someone laughing.

We look at each other, nod, lift our weapons.

And then, in that quiet moment, there is a minor seismological event somewhere deep inside the Earth. The ground rolls slightly, buckles—just a little bit. Just enough so you can feel it. The world adjusting itself to new realities.

It only lasts a second, a half second, and then the world settles again.

We lift our weapons. Paige goes first, and I follow.

We move silently around to the back of the house, where the sun has just crested the closest hill, the first beams of light, like a Peeping Tom peeking above a fence. The surface of a long pool sparkles, clean and blue, in the new sunlight, and the Expert is a shadow rushing through its depths.

The view from here is extraordinary, unimpeded nearly all the way around: this way are the glass towers of the distant downtown, this way the sprawl of the Valley, the long arteries of Ventura and Reseda dotted already with morning commuters. The house sits right on the crest, on the very spine of the hilltop. The first beams of sunlight reach over the fence and flare atop the pool.

A diaphanous bathrobe is draped over a deck chair. A simple breakfast is set up at a glass-topped table: a board with cheese and fruit, bread and a knife to cut it. A carafe of tea or coffee.

The bright form of Laura Petras breaks through the surface of light and she sees us, standing like pillars at the water's edge. Her head bobs at the waterline, her hair invisible under a tight swim cap, and she looks at us in puzzlement, but not in fear.

"Mr. and Ms. Speculator. May I ask what you are doing on my property?"

She flips up her goggles so they form a pair of eyes, inverse and bulging, on her forehead.

"I think you know," I say.

"I do not."

It is disconcerting to see a person dissemble so fluidly, so effortlessly. The look on her face is as carefully forged as the fake captures. A shiver of bad feeling rushes up my body. I keep my legs steady on the white pavement.

"Would you get out of the water please, ma'am?"

"If you tell me what you're doing here."

"No. First you get the fuck out, lady." That's Paige. Her gun is pointed directly at the suspect.

"I'm sorry," says Petras. "I've forgotten your name."

Paige does not move her gun. "Get *out*."

"Ms. Paige?" I say, ready with my usual note of caution, but Petras obeys. Slowly the Expert rises from the pool, flicking her eyes from one of us to the other. I hear the dog barking again, somewhere inside the house, sensible of something afoot.

Petras is in a plain one-piece bathing suit, her hair gathered tightly under the cap. She stands calmly, unafraid, dripping onto the white pool stone.

"If you want to discuss the Crane matter in more detail I am happy to oblige, but it will be in my office, at the appropriate time. And certainly not," she says, to Aysa, "at gunpoint."

The first full splash of sunlight reaches the house, reflecting off the second-story windows, making them momentarily into a wall of light.

"We're not here about Crane," I tell her.

"What?"

"We're here because you are in violation of subverting a bulwark of the Golden State."

"*What?*"

Her whole face has changed. Her whole body. She is caught and she knows it. I step forward, drop into the *vox officio*. "You are accused, Ms. Petras, of involvement with the Golden State conspiracy. You are accused of taking your home off the Record. You are accused of high crimes against the Objectively So."

With each iteration of the word "accused" her eyes widen further, and all the steel goes out of her stance. Suddenly she is like a fish hauled from the water, trembling, terrified. I have never seen anyone pretend to feel anything so earnestly, so naturally.

"But. But——" she says.

Aysa has had enough.

"Hands in the air," she says. "Hands in the fucking *air!*"

"Listen," says Petras, looking at me and then at Aysa, back and forth, trembling. "Listen, I *swear* to you——"

Aysa shouts, "No more talking!"

The ground trembles again, a mild follow-up seismic motion, just enough to make me momentarily unsteady. The surface of the pool ripples and trembles.

"I have done *nothing*."

"Shut up," says Paige, and I see on her face what I am feeling in my heart, the force of what Petras's stream of untruths is doing to the air, bending and tearing at it, pulling at its seams like fabric.

"It's not"—her eyes widen with feigned alarm—"it's not so. What you are saying, it is simply not so."

"It is so, ma'am," I tell her. "You were a conspirator in the plot initiated eleven years ago by Armond Kessler. You managed to escape justice, and now you have started again, replacing real captures with fakes."

"This is madness."

There are captures in the high palms, captures above the sliding doors connecting the poolside to the kitchen. But they're dummies, all of them. Connected to nothing, leaving no archive, creating no permanence. Charlie told me how astonishing it was to realize how easily a capture can be faked, and these are even better than the ones he encountered in Glendale. Their eyes blink like the real eyes of captures. They swivel to follow motion and catch sound. Masterful forgeries, perfect simulacra of the real thing.

"Nothing," Petras says. "I've done nothing."

Monster, I think. *Monster monster monster.* I am imagining the next steps of the terrible treason, imagining fake captures planted all over the Hills and the Valley, downtown and Mid-City, by the beaches and on the pier and in the parks. I am imagining the Record being undermined, one capture at a time, the truth going dark, the eyes of the Record blinking closed, one by one. *I did it,* I think. *I stopped her.* A powerful feeling floods through me, magic in my arms and legs. In time, just in time, we have saved the State.

"I promise you I have done nothing," says Petras. "I have executed the duties of my office. I have always been loyal to the State."

The more she speaks, the more I feel it, her lies tugging and pulling the air, bending the edges of the world all around me. My lungs fill up with it and my eyes are watering. The world is warping at all its edges, collapsing around me, cascading down the sides of the house. I am catching it everywhere, feeling it hard, as Petras cries out her innocence and Aysa tells her she's lying, and I know that's true, and I have my weapon out and aimed.

"Stop," I say, and lunge for her, and she raises one hand, and I jerk back, spin halfway around, and my first thought is that she can control reality itself, of course she can, and she has caused the searing pain in my shoulder with a sharp movement of her hand, but then there is another explosive sound from the house's second story and I understand that someone is shooting at us, she has signaled someone on the upper floor who has opened fire. *Is it Doonan?* I wonder, standing there like an idiot peering up, until Aysa grabs at me, pulls me down as she kicks over the glass-topped table to form a shield.

Petras is bolting back toward the house. A third bullet smashes into the tabletop, shattering it, glass exploding everywhere. The dog is barking, wherever it is.

I shout after Petras, over the lip of the inverted table: "Stop! Stop!"

Paige shoots up at the window and misses.

Petras is running, and I think wildly that I could shoot her, right in the back, shoot her and shoot the man upstairs, shoot the dog, burn the whole house down, and none of it would ever be known. This is the madness of living unrecorded, untethered to time. You can do anything and say it never happened. *Anything.*

Paige takes a second shot, clear through the window, and I see the shooter go down, spin backward as blood mists from the hole in his head.

"Stop!" I yell, and Petras stops. Paige rises unsteadily from behind the table.

"Turn around," I say, and Petras obeys. She has the knife that was on the breakfast board that was on the table: a knife with a long serrated blade, the handle clutched in her fist, the blade trembling frantically in the air before her.

She raises the knife's brutal edge to her throat. Tears form and fall from her eyes.

"I swear in the name of the State and my high position that I have committed no crime. Whatever kind of trick you are playing here, I will not have my life destroyed for it."

"Drop that knife, please," I say. The dog has stopped its barking. The sun has risen high enough that I can feel its heat. "Please drop it, Ms. Petras."

Her right eye flickers and jumps.

"No."

Aysa has her gun on Petras. I have my gun on her too. This is madness. But the problem is, it's not madness, because I have given this lady no choice and no chance. I have nothing to use as leverage, no power of mercy. The crimes with which I have just accused her, the crimes I know her to be guilty of, carry the maximum penalty, and she knows it the same as I do. The Golden State does not practice capital punishment, but everybody knows what it does, everybody knows what will happen.

She will be sent into the wilderness, of course. She will not only be toppled from her high position, she will be sent out past the wall and die there. So why would she cooperate?

"Drop the knife!" I shout again, but why would she drop the knife?

"Ms. Petras," says Paige, and she steps forward, and Petras steps forward too, and then jumps, and I shout "No!" but it's too late, Petras is jumping with the knife. I don't know what her plan is but she only gets as far as screaming and lunging, and Paige is firing her weapon, but she misses because Petras has slammed into her, buried the knife in her stomach. Paige misses but I don't. I catch Petras in her side just at the moment the knife slides in, and now both of them are bleeding—Petras gushing from her side, slumped forward, driving the blade deeper and deeper into poor Aysa, who is screaming, pushing at the other woman as she sinks down beneath her, the white stone disappearing under an opening curtain of blood.

"No," I say. I'm running across the slick pavement, slipping on their mingling blood. "No."

I am down on one knee, scrambling for Paige's wound, pressing the heels of my palms into it, holding her closed with my hands.

"Don't worry," I tell her, "it's going to be okay." I scramble for my radio, smash the buttons, raise the alarm, telling her, "It's going to be okay, it's going to be okay," and now it's my own lie that is rolling in the air, because I have no information to support my asseveration. Aysa's eyes are clouding. Her cheeks are losing their color. There is blood on my arms where I am holding her, a slick of blood expanding on the stone beneath us, dripping over the edge and expanding out onto the surface of the water, and it is not going to be okay.

"No." Too little, too late. "No."

Not good enough. Deep truth—bone true—true as daylight, true as doors on houses. Never good enough.

PART TWO

Our desire to know the whole truth is what makes us human. Our understanding that it can't be known is what keeps us alive.

—Various authors, *Past Is Prologue: A Novel of Our Good and Golden Beginnings*

20.

Death is the truest thing. Binary and unambiguous, permanent and forever.

The bells are ringing for Aysa Paige, one for each of her years, and I'm standing with my head ducked as rain sneaks into the collar of my coat. A miserable rain that drips over the brim of my pinhole, soaks into my beard, inches its way along the line of my neck and up the sleeves of my black coat.

The others in the crowd are holding umbrellas, most of them, but I'm not part of the crowd. Not really. They're over there, standing around the hole in the ground, the hole they're going to lower Aysa into. I stand with my head bent, far enough away to be at a distance. Charlie is here. He's right over there. I don't come and visit, because there's no reason to. I won't come and visit Aysa Paige either. Death is what it is.

The bells ring for the twenty-fourth time and then stop. The rain hisses on the leaves of the trees.

Today I am being hailed for my courage and dedication, for my valor and service to the State. It's heavily featured in the *Trusted Authority,* in both the print and radio editions, early reports of the extraordinary valor of two Speculators, one of whom was injured, the other of whom died. More details to emerge in time. There will be a novel. I will be one of its heroes.

That word "hero" is wrong. It *feels* wrong.

Charlie carried himself like a hero long before he was one. When we were kids I would tell him he was my hero, and he would wink and say you got that right. When in due time he became a hero for real, when they put the mantle on him, it fit perfectly and he wore it with ease, like his favorite jacket or his beat-up boots.

Me, though? The word "hero" sits heavily in my gut. It mewls and rolls. It disputes itself.

I spent this morning alone, staring out the window of my small house, trying to ignore the sour feeling in my stomach, the dark sense that any version of reality in which Laszlo Ratesic has become a hero, as a matter of Record, is a reality in which something is deeply fucked up.

My gut tried to convince me not to go to the funeral at all, to stay home and make myself frozen waffles and curl up in a corner and read the novel again: *The Prisoner* by Benjamin Wish.

But I had to come. I *needed* to, so I ignored my gut. I did make waffles, and I drowned them in syrup and ate them over the sink while I burned the novel in the toaster oven, and then I put on my black clothes. And now here I am, with rain dampening my beard, inside one of those moments when one's inmost truth sits in uneasy disagreement with the acknowledged truth of the world.

Charlie was a hero. *Aysa* was a hero. I am a skulker, a pretender, a fool. I got lucky, I was dragged by Aysa Paige to the scene of my heroism and now I am standing at a respectful distance from the hole they dug for her, clutching my wounded shoulder, rain collecting in my collar and in my pockets, and she's the one in the box.

The eulogies are short. Recitations of who Aysa was, where she came from. Among the speakers is a clutch of children. A small girl, holding a ragged teddy bear and blinking up at a microphone that has been angled down so she can reach it, has Aysa's same neatly arranged curly hair and big, expressive sweetheart eyes. A teenage boy, reciting a comical anecdote from Aysa's first day of high school, has her same proud chin and steel spine, her same way of seeming most upright and composed in the moment of highest distress.

There are captures even here, even among the headstones. Up in the trees, down in the bushes, pointing out from the dashboards of the cars parked in a ring around the site. A crew is out too, a three-person: main capture, aux capture, boom mic. The funeral is happening. Reality is in progress.

There's a pretty young woman in black pants and a black top and stiff black shoes that look brand-new, bought special for this miserable occasion. She looks stunned with grief, confused to find herself here, standing on the lip of a fresh-dug hole. I can't remember the name. *Do you have a sweetheart?* I'd asked Aysa, none of my business, and I can't even remember the name.

The main theme of all of the orations is that Aysa Paige was a clever and confident young woman, intuitive and direct, whose difficult childhood blossomed into a promising adulthood when her gift was recognized and she determined to join the Speculative Service. There are glances stolen in my direction. Here I am, avatar of that same Service, the culmination and embodiment of her dream fulfilled. I look down at my muddy black boots.

I cast my mind backward, backward to Petras's house. To the swimming pool, the bullets from the second-floor window. Our Acknowledged Expert in the Enforcement of the Laws, frantic and cornered, brandishing the knife. How had I let it happen? How had I let the brief story of Aysa Paige end this way?

Backward, backward. The sour mealy worm of speculation, crawling backward in search of better paths.

The last of the eulogists is a small and sturdy old dark-skinned woman, and she, too, has Aysa in her face, in the flicker of wry humor that accompanies even the saddest movements of her speech.

As she speaks, she never releases the arm of the equally ancient man who has helped her approach the microphone. The two of them are supporting each other through the ordeal of recalling the girl they raised.

Her parents are nowhere to be seen. *Fuck my parents.*

No one talks about what Aysa might have become one day. No one is going to dishonor the memory of the dead Speculator by speculating at her funeral.

But I do it in my mind. Nothing to stop me from standing and wondering. A glorious career, the heights of Service, the Arlo Vasouvian of her generation, or an early and sensible retirement, walking away while she could still walk on her own—a politician, an architect, an Expert. My pride in her will remain forever speculative. I can be proud of her in a thousand different alternate futures.

The machine makes a dull whirring sound as the coffin is levered downward into the greenery. It is the most hackneyed of clichés to compare a body being buried to a Record being sealed.

There are two gravediggers, waiting. They're both rail thin, bareheaded, in long black coats, like ragged Speculators moonlighting in a workman's trade. They are leaning on their shovels, waiting to finalize the transaction by heaping dirt onto the box when all of this talking is done. One smokes mutely, looking up at the fingers of the trees, while the other leans on his shovel handle, reading the *Authority*. Then he looks up at me, and nudges the other man.

The second one nods. He takes the page from his friend, runs one dirty finger along it, and then they begin to murmur to each other.

My gut was right.

My gut was on target, and the world is righting itself. It's happening now.

A black car pulls up to the outskirts, and three men get out, two from the front seat and two from the rear. One walks in front and the other two follow, moving quickly toward me across the muddy ground. The two in the back are regular policemen. I watch them come. Rain trickles down the side of my face. I have the avid attention of the gravediggers now, and of the rest of the funeral crowd: all of Aysa's look-alikes, older and younger, peering at my approaching visitors.

I detach myself from the crowd. Push my wet pinhole down onto my hair.

"Mr. Alvaro?"

"Mr. Ratesic."

My boss stops before me but does not put his hand out. His own pinhole is pushed down over his eyes, and when he pushes it up his eyes are unfamiliar. Wary. Distressed. But his voice does not waver.

"I need you to come with me."

"What are you talking about?" I rub my hand through my beard. "What for?"

I glance back at the grave. The machine is really whirring now, the low hum of the machine bearing Aysa into the ground.

"You gotta come with me right now."

"Tell me what's going on, Alvaro."

"It's the captures, Laszlo."

"What captures?"

The humming behind me stops. The operation is complete. She's in the ground. The gravediggers step forward but they don't start shoveling. They're listening.

"From your raid last night. You and—" He points behind me, toward the ground. "You and the kid. The house on Mulholland. We have the stretches."

The full meaning of this flat fact arrives all at once.

I'm staring at Alvaro and he's staring at me, but it's not him I'm seeing. I'm seeing the house. I'm seeing the driveway, dead captures looking up from the pavers, dead captures in the palm trees.

If what Alvaro is saying is true—and of course it is, it has to be, how can it be otherwise—then those captures weren't dead. They weren't dummies. Petras's house wasn't off the Record at all.

"It's five o'clock," says someone from over by the burial ground, and then suddenly everybody is saying it. "It's five o'clock." "It's just turned five." "It's an hour since four." Truth filling up the funeral yard.

Alvaro just waits, pointing to his car.

"Like I said, Laszlo. You gotta come with me."

My gut was right. I'm no hero.

The truth is a bulwark, until it's not anymore. Until it crumbles beneath your feet, slips out from under you, throws you sideways like seismological activity buried deep within a hillside.

On the thirtieth floor of the Service building, all the screens are showing the same thing. There is one stretch being played, but all the monitors are linked, and it's playing on everybody's desk. Everybody looks up when I come in, and then they go back to staring at their monitors.

Watching Paige and myself tiptoe as a team across the lawn on Mulholland Drive, very late last night, very early this morning. We creep together.

I watch the whole thing, beginning to end. I am conscious of everybody watching the stretch—all of them, Burlington and Carson, Cullers, Alvaro with his arms crossed. Everybody watching me watching myself, watching me lead Aysa to her doom. Watching me make the worst mistake anyone has ever made. Everybody is here. Everybody understands how bad this is. Nobody can understand what I did, but everybody understands what I've done.

Everybody is here, except for Arlo. Where is Arlo?

On the screen I crouch and point to the capture embedded among the footlights that line the driveway.

"Here," I watch myself say, on the screen. "Look."

"Fuck's sake," somebody mutters in the still air of the room. "For fuck's sake."

I command the stretch to go back, ten seconds back, and watch us again, me and Aysa doing our thing. It's a nice clean stretch, multiple angles, a good tapestry. We walk together across the lawn, crouch again to the capture, and again I listen to myself explaining to Aysa that it's dead, a dummy, that it's not recording.

We pause at the doorway, listen to the bark of the dog. A moment's hesitation, and we proceed around to the back.

And now here I am, accusing Laura Petras, Our Acknowledged Expert on the Enforcement of the Laws, of having participated in a conspiracy against the security of the Golden State, an assault on the Objectively So. And here is Petras, stunned and horrified, telling me I'm wrong, telling me it's a mistake, and here I am insisting, because she was lying—I *saw* that she was lying—except the captures have it all. It's all on the Record.

"Laszlo—" Alvaro puts a hand on my shoulder, but I shake him off.

On the stretch, the gunfire begins. We duck behind the table. Aysa leaps, the knife plunges into her stomach, and I say "Stop" to the screen and it stops.

Silence in the room. Cullers breathes out the words "Oh, Laz," just like that. "Oh."

I turn to Alvaro.

"How..."

I'm asking him the question that I know he can't answer. I take back *"How..."* I swallow *"How..."* Instead I say, "What next? What happens to me?"

"I'm not sure yet," says Alvaro, but then Burlington is up, arms raised.

"You? What happens to *you?*" Burlington with his bristle mustache and bald head, his scalp red with fury. "What happens to *you*, Laszlo? Fuck *you*."

"I mean, Laz. *Laz*. What *happened?*" Ms. Carson stands behind Cullers, her arms crossed. They're not all as worked up as Burlington, but no one is defending me either. Nobody understands. *I* don't understand.

"I had—proof . . ." I say, start to say, but the word crumbles on the edges of my lips. Proof? What proof did I have? What was I doing? Cullers is right: How could I do this? I'm supposed to be able to tell truth from lies; I'm supposed to be able to stare at the air and see where it's been bent by falsehood. We all are. So what did I see out there? What was happening? The mistake I made should have been impossible.

"Do you have any idea what's going on right now?" Burlington points to the glass windows, taking in the whole of the State. "This could be years of damage you've done. A decade at least. Public faith in our work is a bulwark. You ever heard that? Public trust is a fucking bulwark, you goddamn idiot."

"All right, people," says Alvaro. "Let's get to work."

"We can't," says Burlington, turning and grabbing his coat, storming toward the elevator. "That's the fucking point. We *can't*."

Alvaro shakes his head, sighing, as Burlington disappears behind the elevator door. "He's not wrong, you know. If people don't trust us, we can't do the job. They rely on our abilities. This . . ." He points at the screen. "This is bad. This is . . . it's very bad, Laszlo."

"I know," I say.

"Very bad."

And then he goes too. They all go. Out to do the work of the people. If they can.

I sit. I watch the stretch again. Ms. Aysa Paige and Mr. Laszlo Ratesic, creeping across the lawn. Waving their hands in front of the dead captures.

I stood in that house and I felt it, and Aysa felt it too, we stood there together, firm in our understanding of what we discovered. Petras was lying, and the more we pressed her the more fervently she lied, the more vividly we were aware of her lying. Those captures were fakes. The house was a new version of the old conspiracy, this was the final chapter of the case that my brother started—

Except it wasn't. I was wrong, and now it's exactly as Burlington said. Public trust is a bulwark, and I somehow have dealt that trust a catastrophic blow. So what happens now?

I am alone in the office. The sun is getting ready to set, and long shadows are painted on the sides of the Hills, dousing the gold glint of the skyscrapers one by one, like candles being blown out in turn.

I stare out the windows as I have done a thousand times, and I see that there is something new in the air, gently settling on the rooftops and on the streets. It may be my imagination—I don't know; it may not be. It's like dust, like grit, a particulate matter coming down slowly from the sky, sifted onto downtown in great slow drifts.

And I did this. It was me.

The phone rings on my desk and I leap for it. I have been waiting for Arlo to call. To tell me that this is going to be okay, and how.

"Hey, Mr. Speculator. You want to take a walk?"

I blink. The world spins and rights again. It's not Arlo.

"Silvie?"

"I'm in the lobby. Will you come down?"

"You didn't—have you not heard?"

"That you fucked up big-time? Oh, I heard. Come down to the lobby. Take me for a walk."

Silvie's tone is crisp, deadpan. I am staring out the window. The city is hazy, shrouded. The skyline, the mountains, the strip of gray sky. The air in the city has changed.

"I'm supposed to stay here," I tell Silvie. "I'm supposed to stay in my office."

"Did someone tell you that you can't leave?"

"No."

"Alvaro? Is that his name?"

"Yeah, Alvaro."

"He told you to stay."

"Not exactly."

"So come get some air with me."

"Why, Silvie?"

"Come down," she says again. "I'm in the lobby."

21.

There are dozens of Silvies waiting for me in the lobby. A hundred Silvies. A thousand. She waits in the long mirror-lined lobby of the Service, her reflections reflecting on each other, multiplying her and multiplying her again. Rows of Silvies smiling, waiting, each of them raising one hand in greeting.

I step off the elevator and lope toward the army of Silvies. One of them steps from the crowd and takes my hands.

"You look like shit, Laszlo."

"That's subjective."

"Not today it's not."

I manage a laugh.

"How's that shoulder?"

"It hurts."

"Should have thought of that before you got shot."

The Silvies turn and collapse back into one as she strides briskly from the lobby. "Come on. Let's go."

I might have thought the day couldn't tilt further from its axis. My ex-wife calling out of nowhere and inviting me for a stroll. There is still funeral dirt clinging to the insides of my shoes. There is still Burlington's red face, stern and huffing, vivid in my mind: "*You*, Laszlo? Fuck *you*."

The world is looking at me as we step out of the building, as Silvie takes my arm. The bustling crowd on the Plaza, the zealots on the steps of the Record, the businesspeople with their briefcases, the *Authority* hawker in his kiosk. Everybody staring, and I can read their minds.

"I should go back upstairs," I tell Silvie. "I want to go back upstairs."

"Five minutes, Laz."

"I should wait for Arlo."

"Hey. Laszlo. You need a friend right now. Let me be your friend."

She keeps her hand on the crook of my elbow, and we walk together, along the lip of the fountain, where the ducks regard us impassively. We move counterclockwise around the pond. I try not to look at people, at the good and golden citizens looking at me like I have betrayed them. Like I and my Service have betrayed each of them personally. Their anger and distrust are visible and invisible in the atmosphere, like motes of dust, and we walk through its unseen presence. If the Service can't be trusted, then why the *Authority*? What about the Record itself?

But Silvie's attitude is relentlessly normal, her cheerfulness is a thing of steel. She is holding my arm but it feels like it is she who is holding me up.

"You want to eat something?" she asks. "Should we find a food truck?"

"No."

"I think I saw that hot dog truck a bit ago."

"The Dirty Dog."

"Yes. Should we—"

"No."

I say "No," and also I think, *I should have kept loving you. I should have loved you forever. What happened?*

And then I remember. Judge Sampson comes crashing in. Sampson beaming, leering, opening his Night Book and laying down his finger on just the right page. I stop walking. I put my hand up over my eyes.

"Silvie," I say. "Silvie—"

She looks at me, smiling.

"Yes?"

"I—"

But I can't do it. I won't. Here she is, after all, having come to give me comfort in my darkest hour. There is this Silvie, and there is that one.

"Forget it."

"Forgotten."

We stop at an empty bench and she tells me to sit.

"Now. Mr. Speculator." She reaches into her bag. "I wanted to let you know the disposition of the matter you asked me to look into."

"The—what?"

"The what, he says. Come on, Laz. Scour your memory."

"Oh right. That."

"Yes. *That.* Mr. Mose Crane. A small apartment in University City. Worked as a roofer, odd jobs before that. Currently dead. All ringing a bell now?"

Her tone is absolutely normal, for her, for us: teasing, cutting, kind. My Silvie's voice. And yet—it isn't. It is new. How is it new?

"Listen," I tell her. "It doesn't matter. It's inscrutable. That whole case." I make a noise in my throat, some sort of laugh. Aysa is in the ground. I fucked it up. Somehow, I did. "Unknown and unknowable."

"Yes, so I understand," says Silvie with exaggerated sweetness. "Because, you know, I worked my ass off digging facts up for you. And then, just as I was reconstructing the days as requested, I received a communiqué from the Office of Our Acknowledged Expert on the Enforcement of the Laws."

"Yeah, no. I know."

"Turns out the circumstances of the man's death had been abruptly declared unknowable, and any investigative actions relating thereto were to be ceased immediately."

"Yeah, that's—that's my fault."

"Seems like everything is these days."

"Seems like it is." She's laughing, but there is something moving, some nestless truth active in her eyes. "But you know, Laszlo..."

I lean in closer. Light is reaching me as if from a distant star. We are sitting near the dead center of the Plaza, in the midday shadow of the Record itself, the Service behind us, *Trusted Authority* to the east.

"I'm sorry not to have more for you."

"No, *I'm* sorry," I say. "Sorry it was a...like you said. A waste of your time."

"Oh, Laz," she says. "Not like it was the first time."

We are speaking in a secret language. I don't know how else to explain it. You live with someone long enough, you have enough conversations, just the two of you, and a language builds itself underneath the actual words. Something—*something* is going on here. Something is being transmitted. Silvie is not here on a mission of sweet mercy, to drag me out of the far recesses of my depression: she is here to tell me something serious. She looks at me, and I look back at her.

"Silvie?"

"Yeah?"

"I appreciate it. I do in all seriousness appreciate it."

"Yeah," she says. She takes off my pinhole, touches my forehead with tenderness, tries to smooth my sweaty mass of hair down onto my scalp. "Hey, you know what? We should do the wall."

"What?"

She hops up, adjusts her skirt. Behind her, at the wall of the Record, the fervent and the zealous are doing their thing, tearing strips from their Day Books and inserting their small truths into the cracks and crevices.

"Come on, Laz. It'll be fun."

She turns, digging out her Day Book. I watch her, astonished. Papering truth into the wall is for day-trippers, fanatics. If Silvie and I ever discussed it, it was to roll our eyes at the very idea. But now I get up, move close to where she's standing by the wall, and watch her write, dashing words with her small pen onto one small corner of a fresh page. A scrap of truth, some small detail of her private heart. I wonder what it is, as I wondered the whole time we were together what was happening in those parts of her truth that were forever inaccessible to me and my grasping interest.

She tears out the page, one small corner, folds it up tight, and jams it into a crack in the wall.

And maybe it is because of the context, or maybe because I don't know where else my life is supposed to go, but in that moment, standing close to my ex-wife, I want her back. Fuck the judge. Fuck the past. Fuck everything that made the two of us impossible together. Surely the truth of right now weighs more than the truth of six months or a year ago. What is the rate of decay of old truths? When do they dissolve and disappear forever? Surrounded by strangers, hot and uncomfortable in the sunlight, I stand inside a powerful rush of longing for Silvie Ratesic. Watching her perform this small intimate act fills me with tenderness for her, a desire to know her secrets and protect them. She looks up and I look into her eyes, hoping, I suppose, to find some reciprocal desire.

But what her eyes bear, when I look closely, is something else entirely.

"Silvie?"

"Yes, Laszlo? What is it?"

There's a word I know, a word I heard in my training, but which I have not used or spoken since: "subterfuge."

I am pretty sure that if we were never in love, I wouldn't have known what to do next, but we were in love. It's one of the good strong truths of my life, a good piece of true that I keep fixed and firm, a thing of great and secret value, like a gold bar in the back of my closet: *Once I was in love with Silvie, and once she was in love with me.*

She's staring at the wall and I know what I'm supposed to do.

I write my own message, in a small corner of my own book. What I write is true—"I'm scared"—and I tear it out and fold it up small, and Sil is standing very close, and I put my message right next to where she put hers, and with the minutest tug, my body huddled around the paper to block the captures, I let her paper fall out into my hand, and we in this way engage in a small piece of private spy craft, use the old mechanism of love to exchange a secret truth before the very eyes of, and in the very citadel of, the Golden State.

And then, knowing the precipice upon which I am trembling, knowing that I brought her into it, thinking, therefore, somehow, that I owe her something now, I speak to her a piece of myself.

"I miss you."

"I miss you too." She reaches out and brushes my cheek. "A very little bit. Take care of yourself, Laszlo."

It is not until I am back in my car that I understand what she meant by *"Take care of yourself."* It is a phrase with multiple potential meanings faceted into it, and in this instance the meaning is clear:

by *"Take care of yourself"* she is not saying goodbye; she is saying *"Be careful."*

She is saying *"Watch out."*

On the paper, in her neat careful hand, in all capital letters, are the three words she conspired to keep from the eyes of the State.

"NO SUCH SOUL."

22.

While I drive I think about what it means, but I already know what it means. I understood the tiny slip of paper as soon as I read it, I understood "NO SUCH SOUL" immediately and completely. Mose Crane was not the victim of a robbery. Nobody snuck into his basement to spirit off two weeks of his days. It's not about the days that were stolen, it's about all the rest of them—all the days of a life that never existed at all.

Crane isn't real, and if there is no Crane, then the whole thing was a setup from the beginning. I was supposed to discover those missing days. I was supposed to be baffled by the mystery of Mose Crane. I was supposed to speculate, and to follow the trail of my speculation from Aster's basement to the judge's chambers, and from the judge to Laura Petras, and from Petras to my terrible mistake, when with blundering force I smashed the public trust in my Service, and dealt a blow to the foundation of the State.

But why would that happen?

No, not why, but who? Who set me on the trail? Who laid out the puzzle for me to solve?

And the truth is, the blood truth, bone truth, is that I know, I think I know, I don't want to know but I do, and I just drive. I just focus on the road, on the 10 west, and I drive.

There is this remarkable ability your mind has, sometimes, this trick it is able to play, where you have something figured out all the way, but you refuse to allow yourself to know it. When the flat fact is there in you but it remains below the clouded surface of the water, half drowned, waiting for you to dredge it up.

"NO SUCH SOUL" is a grand anomaly, radiant at the center of a circle of related anomalies, but I can't see it yet. I'm not ready yet to know. All I am ready now to know is that I am standing at a green door, heavy wood, hung in a red doorframe. A small house in Faircrest Heights, between a coffee shop and a drugstore, one of a handful of pretty houses on what is otherwise a commercial street. A half dozen modest one-family homes with fruit trees in the yard, each home painted its own pleasing color. I find the right house, an address I find I have memorized without setting out to do so. I am knocking and my whole body is trembling very slightly, recalling in me the barely discernible tremor of the small earthquake at Petras's house.

All I am capable of knowing right now is what is right in front of me, what I can feel with my hands, my calloused knuckles banging on a green door in a red doorframe. There is a little octagonal window set in the center of the door, and I shade my forehead and try to see in through the frosted glass, see if anybody is home. That's what I'm doing when the door flies open.

"Oh no." Ms. Tarjin is terrified to see me. She takes a stumbling half step backward, and a hand flies up to her mouth and she speaks through it. "It didn't work."

"What?"

"You were going to forgive him. You said the—the prosecuting attorney would drop it, if you forgave him."

"Oh. Right. No. Not forgive. *Absolve.*" I wince. Put up one hand. "Ms. Tarjin. It's okay."

"It is?"

"It is." My fears drove me here. I didn't stop to think of how it would make her feel, this poor lady, to find me washed up on her shore. "I contacted the PA's office, and I, uh—I formally absolved Todd of the false representation he made to me. Just like I said I would. Okay? Like I said."

She exhales, her hands trembling. "Oh—Okay. Okay." Then she steps back and tilts her head. "Then what...what are you doing here?"

"Well." I take off my pinhole, push a hand through my hair. "I need to ask you a question."

A few moments later, we are arranged in her small dining area.

I ground myself in the reality of the small house. A handsome wood dining table ringed by mismatched chairs, a low-hanging light fixture with six bulbs. Steam rising from teacups, the smell of baking bread. The wall-mounted plays in the kitchen behind us, turned to a stream called "Eating Lunch Outside." I'm across from Ms. Tarjin, who leans forward on her elbows, looks at me carefully. There are freckles across the bridge of her nose.

Eddie, the other son, is home. He emerged from the back of the house while Ms. Tarjin fixed tea, and now he's looking at me with plain distaste, arms crossed. He watches us, half hidden behind a room divider, anxiety and dislike plain in his eyes.

"What does he want?" he asks, and then, to me directly: "What do you want?"

"Help," I answer, over his mother's shoulders. "I need your help." I turn to Ms. Tarjin, who is trying to puzzle me out from across the table. "You and your mom."

Eddie doesn't come over. He stays where he is. "What kind of help?"

"Okay, so, the other morning," I say. "The other morning at the diner. At Terry's diner. I heard you. I heard you talking, and I—I stood up and I came over. And we talked for . . . for three minutes? Four minutes?"

"Yeah," says Eddie warily. Trying to figure this out. While we're talking the wall-mounted is cycling through short stretches: a picnic in Griffith Park, a barbecue at one of the crowded State beaches.

"Yeah. And—look, there is a radio on my belt. A radio." I am talking too fast. Tripping over myself, talking sideways. Tarjins, mother and son, exchange glances, trying to figure out what's going on here. "Do you remember?"

"Yes," says Ms. Tarjin.

The first anomaly—what was the first of the anomalies?

"When I approached you, in the restaurant—"

The first of the anomalies. Not on the lawn—

Ms. Tarjin leans forward, reaches past the cup of tea she has poured for me, and places a steadying hand on my shoulder. "Breathe. Hey. Mr. Speculator? You gotta breathe, okay?"

She is empathetic. Kind. I follow her instructions. I breathe.

"What do you need to ask us?"

"When I was—while we were talking, did my radio go off? The radio I wear on my hip—this." I point to it, the black box, black dials, red lights. I shift my body weight awkwardly forward to angle my hip toward them. "Did it make any noise? Was there a call that I ignored?" They look at each other again. "Please try to remember."

Ms. Tarjin puckers her lips. Unsure, unwilling to lie.

But Eddie is shaking his head. "No."

"Are you sure?"

"Yeah, I'm sure. You were—you didn't move. There was no radio call. I'd remember it. I remember thinking, *Well, that thing is cool.*"

"The radio?"

"Yeah. Even though I was scared, I was thinking, *That thing is cool. I wanted to see it work.*"

"And if it had gone off, you would have noticed."

"I would have noticed. Yeah."

"Are you sure?"

He nods. Of course he's sure. I'm sure too. I can see the truth that I feared, rising up slowly from below.

Ms. Tarjin stops me on the way out, calls my name at the green door.

"Are you okay?"

"No," I tell her. "I'm not."

"Are you in danger?"

"I—" It sounds so stupid. But it's the truth. "I am. And—we all are. I think the whole—" I shake my head at the enormity of it. The ridiculousness. "I think we may all be in danger."

"How?"

"I'm not sure yet. I don't know. But I'm going to try to stop it."

This is a strange thing to say, and surely it is a strange thing to hear said. But Ms. Tarjin just nods, looks at me, at the life of the State proceeding behind me. The coffee shop next door, the brightly painted small houses. One of those palms that stands taller than all the ones surrounding it, extending itself far above the world, as if straining with curiosity.

"Okay. Well." Ms. Tarjin smiles and places her hand on the side of my face. "Come back. Okay?"

"Okay," I say, and I linger just a moment more, just a half a moment, before I get back in my car.

Maybe there will be a world where that happens. Maybe the future will unfold in such a way that I do return, find my way back to the green door in the red frame. This moment, this flickering instant shared between two humans, will keep me going awhile. I know it will. I will live in a world for the next little while in which everything works out, and I come back like she said, and then who knows what happens after that?

For now I point the car back downtown, back toward the Plaza.

The anomalies did not start on the lawn in Los Feliz, and they did not start in the apartment building on Ellendale. The first of the anomalies was in my own fucking office.

The upstream untruth, from which all the others flowed, was the call I missed, about a car crash outside Grand Central. A case that, had I been dispatched to handle it, as I should have been, would have prevented me from being assigned to the Los Feliz case. To Mose Crane.

Supposedly he radioed but my receiver did not register the call, and that was the unaccountable event. That was the first anomaly.

"Oh no," I say, my hands tight on the steering wheel, the city racing past me. "Oh no."

Stone of the ninth floor, big Woodrow Stone, the Spec Service's Chief Liaison Officer to the Permanent Record, works at a big desk with a bowl of popcorn in front of him at all times. He pushes handfuls into his mouth with one hand while he runs his consoles with the other, staring at seven different screens at the same time, weaving together stretches with a magician's touch. He is a master of the various dials. He is an assembly artist. He is not a pleasant human being.

"Stop," he says when he sees me coming in, bringing whatever piece of reality he's watching to a sudden freeze frame. "What do you want?"

"There's a stretch I need to see."

He sighs, a heavy man's heavy sigh, making sure I know how irritated I have made him by my appearance. I tell Woody what I need, and he sighs again.

"Isn't that the same thing your partner was wanting? That girl?"

"Ms. Paige."

"Right, right. Well, guess what? It's already processed for return."

"But it's still here?"

"Yeah. Well...yes. Physically. But it's been processed." This is his fiefdom, his keep, and Woody in his sluggish way is active in its defense. There is a process that defines the request I've just made: officer engages with the Liaison, the Liaison files with the Record, the Record upon due consideration produces the desired stretch or stretches. Woody heaves himself up out of his chair, pulls open the filing cabinet behind him. "Lemme get you a G-9." He looks at his watch. "Actually, it's after six. So this'll be tomorrow. Or, actually—"

"*Actually,*" I say, "I need to see it right now. Where is it, Woody?"

"What?"

"I need to watch it now."

I reach across him, to the slot on the side of his screen, and eject whatever stretch it is he's been reviewing. Woody put his hands on his hips, and for a split second I imagine someone watching us, in some far future, in the basement of the Permanent Record, some officer or archivist who has requested this stretch for review, the reality being generated in this room, right now: *Laszlo Ratesic makes a rash demand of Woody Stone, who pushes back...*

"The fuck are you doing, Ratesic? Stop."

"Where is that stretch?"

"Ratesic. C'mon."

"Where is it?"

Woody's eyes make an unconscious flicker to the rolling cart parked in the corner, behind me, loaded with unsorted stretches marked for return. I can feel it in there, sense what I need.

"Woody," I say, forcing myself to be calm, forcing my voice to be soft. "Did you know that she's dead?"

"Who?"

"Ms. Paige, Woody. My partner."

"The . . ." His voice catches, he has to start again. "The girl?"

"Speculator," I say. "Agent. My partner." There are more words. Hero. Martyr. I skip them. I've got him already: Woody is gawping at me, his face slack with sad disbelief.

"That girl is dead? Dead how?"

"It was in the *Authority*."

"I didn't—" He looks at me imploringly, his thick chin trembling a little. "I didn't see it. I'm in here, man. I'm working. Will you tell me?"

He liked Aysa in their brief moments together, and he's stricken now. I take it. I use it.

"She and I cracked an anomaly, okay? A big one. There was a grave assault in progress, and we stopped it, but she died in the field."

"Wow." He shakes his head, and then, in his bafflement and grief, requests a two-step verification, confirmation of what he knows he heard. "She *died?*"

I nod. He keeps shaking his head. He's as big as I am, Woody Stone, maybe even a little bigger. Bigger around the middle, with a sagging gut and thick legs. Stubble and sallow cheeks, a life lived indoors, staring at screens. "But you cracked it? The anomaly you were working? You dug it down to the truth?"

I am silent. "I'm trying, Woody. I'm trying."

I wait. He grits his teeth. Glances up at the capture above his desk, bearing witness. "All right. Well—all right."

He goes over and crouches at the laden cart and paws through it. He scatters stretches like playing cards on his rug and sorts them until he finds the one I'm after. He slides it in and cues it and steps away, back into the far corner of his office, his mouth twisting in discomfort at his role in this malfeasance.

"Play," I tell the machine, and I watch it how Charlie would have watched it. I watch it how Aysa would have watched it: leaning forward, eyes narrowed, pulse active, alert and alive.

And then, before Woody can stop me, I tell it to play again.

Three times I watch Mose Crane crawl up the pitch, and three times he falls, flailing, and three times I stare at that shadow, which is after all just a stub. A smudge. It should be long, is the thing— what it should be, given the time that Crane was up there, is a daybreak shadow, a finger of shadow stretched out across the slanting roof. This small shadow makes no sense, except it does, because it is only there for me to see it. It is not a shadow cast by a person, it is not the shadow of the frame of the skylight. It was added to this stretch of reality, subsequent to its creation.

It is a clue that is its own solution. It was meant to be found. It was planted there for me to find it, to fall through it like a shadow, to slide off it like a roof.

The stretch is still rolling. I tell it to stop, just as Mose Crane hits the ground again, and the machine obeys and the room fills with the subsequent silence.

I wish I could say "Stop" to everything, to all of this, shout "Stop" and let reality hang in the balance for a minute, or forever. *Stop*, I think.

"Hey, Stone."

"Yeah?" His voice is hesitant. I don't know what I look like, what kind of wildness has come into my eyes, but I can tell I'm making Woody nervous.

"How does a stretch get changed?"

"What?"

"Reality, Woody. Is there a way to alter one of these stretches of reality, once they've been captured and transferred?"

Woody stares back at me, scratching his thick neck. I have reached the edge of his understanding. He looks at his machine. Dumbfounded. It is like I've asked if you can alter a dog so it can fly, or a fish so it can walk across a room.

"No," he says finally, a tremble in his voice.

"'No' because you *know* the answer to be no, based on evidence?"

"'No' because—'No' because—" Woody is stammering. It is like he is caught in a loop, a half hitch of reality, as if *his* reality has been altered, spooled around on itself to say "'No' because" and only "'No' because" forever.

"'No' because—" Finally, with a deep breath: "'No' because nobody would ever do that."

"I know," I say, but the problem is, yes, somebody *would* do that, and now I've come down hard on a bone truth, on the brutal bone truth that if there is ever anything that somebody could do— something violent, something perverse, something cruel and unconscionable—if there is ever anything that somebody could do, somebody is going to do it, somebody has already done it.

So of course someone has figured out how to alter stretches to make them reflect reality that never occurred. Someone has done it. Someone has done it to this one, the same person who invented Mose Crane so I might find him.

The only question is who did it, but that isn't a question anymore. I know it, I have known it, I can't not know it anymore.

"Woody?"

"Yeah? Yes?"

I'm an animal let loose in his small office, charging in circles. He doesn't know what I'm going to do next. "I need to do a live watch."

"Well—"

"Don't say no. I need to connect to live captures."

"Where?"

"The Record."

"I—come on. Laszlo. I *can't*."

"You can."

He can't because the world is watching. Because reality is always being captured. Because if anyone sees him do such a thing willingly, he will face the consequences. So he will have to do it unwillingly, that's all.

I draw my weapon and aim it at Woody. "A live feed. Right now. A tapestry. Basements one through twelve. *Now*."

Woody turns back to his deck and I keep the gun aimed at him until he presses a final button and the blackness of his screen lights up into a thousand subdivided screens. *The Record itself has eyes inside it, of course it does, the Record is on the Record*, and Woody the magician can open its eyes, all of those thousands of eyes at once. He turns his screen into a tapestry of screens, divided into a dozen boxes that then scroll, each of them, and we are suddenly everywhere inside of those famous basements, peering into the catacombic guts of reality itself.

It doesn't take long to find him. Arlo Vasouvian in the dim subbasement light, moving with deliberation along a narrow carpeted space between two file cabinets.

"What the fuck?" says Woody. As we watch, the old man peels the lid off a box. His bifocals are perched on the tip of his small nose; he's squinting, looking for something. "Is that—"

"Yes," I say. But I can't say the name. It is too painful. There would be glass in my throat. It is one thing to suspect that your heart has been broken, another thing to know.

"What floor is he on?" I croak. "Which capture are we looking at?"

Woody IDs it for me, then says, "What's he doing?"

"What's on sub nine?"

But before Woody can answer, Arlo turns to the capture that is watching him, turns and looks at us watching him, and smiles.

"What the *fuck?*" says Woody, pushing away from his machines and looking at the ground.

Arlo's smile widens into a grin as he looks right at the capture and raises one hand in greeting, because he knows we're watching. He can see us seeing him, and his cheery acknowledgment is as sharp and violent as a punch. He is inside reality, looking out.

I turn away from the screen at the sound I hear behind me, the sound of Woody being sick into the trash can beside his desk. I breathe deep and fight off the same unsettling need, because I am wobbling too, walking slow, dizzy, through a world shuddering under my feet.

CODA (SETUP FOR SEQUEL)

Agent Charlie Ratesic, the hero laid low, muttered from the depths of his unconsciousness while his head lolled back and forth in his hospital bed. The machines keeping him alive and free of pain beeped endlessly in the small room, their rhythm like a mechanical pulsebeat.

I was sitting on a chair by the edge of his bed, as I had been sitting for a week, keeping him company, telling him stories, waiting for him to wake.

"I'm sorry, Charles," I said, as much to myself as to him, as much to the captures in the room as to the person who lay before me, past the reach of hearing. "I am so dreadfully sorry."

I had said these words so many times already. Others had come and gone. Charlie's heartbroken parents, our colleagues bearing flowers, cards, the doughnuts they knew he loved, which at the end of each day I took out with me and distributed to the doctors and nurses. Poor Laszlo, Charlie's brother, had come every day, come and sat silently beside me for hours after his own shift was through.

Technically, I had little to apologize for. I had told Charlie not to return to that warehouse. Indeed, I had not only warned him but ordered him not to go. He knew that it would be my duty and my responsibility to shut it down: an Off Record house could not be abided any longer, and I had to act.

He knew we would be going in there, and that we would come in with weapons blazing.

And yet when the decisive day came, and we swept in with the full force of the State, there he was, still undercover, skulking among the conspirators, unable to free himself from the idea that there was a monster left for him to find.

He had been caught in the cross fire. Shot six times, including twice in the stomach and once in the chest—a bullet that pierced the lungs and brought him perilously close to dying right there, off the Record, on a dirty warehouse floor in Glendale.

And perhaps that would have been better, I thought with sadness as I listened to the machines breathing for him. As I watched the medicine dripping into his arm. *Drip, drip.*

"Arlo?"

I had fallen asleep, I suppose. My eyes opened to find his looking into mine. Charlie, dear Charlie. He spoke, clearly but with difficulty. "The monster," he said, and I closed my eyes. *Still.* "I have to..." He cleared his throat. Turned his head to one side. "Get the monster."

"Goodness, Charlie," I told him. I opened my eyes, leaned forward, and took poor Charlie's hand. "I wish you would take pleasure in your success."

"Success," he murmured. "Success."

It was like he could not accept the word. Like he was rolling it around in his mouth, tasting it, unsatisfied. The machines beeped and hummed.

"Yes, Charlie," I said. "*Success.* Numerous arrests were made. A grave assault on the Objectively So was thwarted. All because of you, Charlie. Because of you."

"The monster..." He couldn't stop. He wouldn't. My old friend, still in the thrall of this wild idea. What was to be done? He looked up at me. Desperate that someone believe him. "What if it were an Expert, Arlo? What if it were someone from the Office of the Record?"

"Or"—I stood up, wiped my hands, leaned as far over his bed as I could, whispered as quietly as possible—"a Speculator?"

23.

All four of them are dead, each with a single neat bullet hole through the center of the forehead.

I recognize them all, Librarians who worked the entrance of the Record, rigorous and polite and efficient. The duty team, caught unawares by a familiar face.

The first is just inside the door, thrown back against the wall, still wearing a stunned expression. Blood runs in a frozen trickle from the bullet hole down into the line of the eyebrows.

The second is centered in the lobby, slumped at the wanding station, thrown across the small desk with one hand outstretched, clutching his weapon as if caught just before he could fire.

The third is at the elevators, between the two shafts and just beneath the keypad, and she sits with legs extended and arms slack. Her face is turned toward the elevator just to her right, where the fourth of them is wedged between the elevator door and the wall of the car itself, half in and half out, keeping it from closing, inviting me in.

The lights in the elevator car are dim but I can see the button panel, and there is a dark red fingerprint on the button marked 9, a clue so glaring and egregious it has to have been purposeful. A taunt.

Subbasement nine. That's where you'll find me. Come along, now . . . down we go . . .

I push the button gingerly with my forefinger and it comes away tacky.

At the last minute, though, I don't take the elevator. I step off before the door can close, step around the fallen bodies of the Librarians, and use the spiral stairs instead.

I go down slowly, one floor at a time with my weapon drawn, listening at every floor. Pause at sub four, where Silvie's offices are tucked away. Pause again at sub five and then again, halfway between six and seven, where I hear or think I hear the minute click of a file drawer shifting open. The blood button was 9 and that may be where he is, or it may have been another artful misdirection, another signal rigged to catch my eye and hold it while worlds move in shadow all around me.

One more clue for me to find, one more part of the trap that was set for me, for my clumsy feet to stumble into.

With each footfall the ornate structure of the staircase shimmies beneath my heavy frame. The metal stairs are very old. There is gold detail at every balustrade.

I breathe heavily as I descend.

"I can hear you, Mr. Ratesic."

I'm halfway down, between sub eight and sub nine, and I stop on the edge of a stair. His gentle creak of a voice echoes from somewhere close by.

"You were never one for sneaking up."

There are no offices on sub nine. Just endless intersecting hallways, file rooms, review rooms. The hallways are dim, lit only by the cool red emergency lights of the Record after hours. Helpless to do otherwise, I go in the direction of Arlo's voice. And it is even easier than that: there is blood on the floor, dark fresh heel prints on the tile.

I follow those footsteps, still not believing, still not wanting to believe, that it's him I am following. Still unwilling to live in the world in which he is the villain at the end of the hall.

And yet here he is. Around a corner, the sixth door down. Seated at a table, examining a file. He looks up and squints behind his glasses, gives me his old fond smile as I come into the room with my gun raised and aimed at his head.

"Get up, Mr. Vasouvian."

He shakes his head and murmurs, "No, Mr. Ratesic."

The file on the review desk is deep blue: a CSE. I take two steps into the room. All around me are files. Cabinets full of folders; binders on shelves. Up to the ceiling, down to the floor. Collated truth, running from floor to ceiling and to the ends of the walls.

My gun is aimed at Arlo's head and I am deciding whether I would really do it.

"You have to get up, Mr. Vasouvian. You have to stand up and come with me."

"No, no. No, I'm not doing that."

He seems glad to see me; he seems as he always does. He smiles, and scratches his nose, and sighs. There are flecks of blood on his glasses, a smear on his necktie and on one rumpled lapel of his corduroy jacket. He has killed four people, and left their bodies for me to find.

"I'm not going to do that," he says. "This is not a normal situation. You can't think you are going to—what?—arrest me? No. What you will do is kill me. But not right away."

"Stop talking, Arlo."

He sighs again. "I'll tell you what. Come and sit down across from me and we can look at this together."

"Look at—what?"

"At the file." He taps it with two fingers, gazing at me evenly. As if he has been waiting here for me so we can discuss it. As if we had an appointment, and I am late.

"Come, Laszlo. I wish you would have a seat."

He points with his chin to the chair opposite his, and I can feel the energy in the room changing. I am the investigating officer who has come upon his prey, but at the same time I am the younger man, less experienced, a pupil in the presence of his tutor, a child in the presence of the adult.

I keep my gun up. "You are under arrest for——" I stop. For what, Laszlo? For everything. For all of it. "For murder in the first degree."

"Okay. I plead guilty. We will come to all of that, Mr. Ratesic. Justice will be done. Please. Sit."

There is a chair across from him. I sit, but I keep my gun out, in my hand.

"This is a CSE file, Laszlo. Do you know the nomenclature used down here? In the labyrinth?"

"CSE," I say. "Collated Significant Event."

"Very good." His smile brightens, gold star for me, and he begins reciting from memory, his favorite trick. "Incidents of self-evident public importance are to be cross-cataloged into a master file, to include all relevant information from all relevant captures, gathered together in a permanent and comprehensive manner to put on Record the full and final truth of the incident."

Arlo slides his glasses up on the bridge of his nose and turns the file around so I can see it more clearly. He lays one finger beside the title on the tab. *"The Death of Mr. Charles Ratesic of the Speculative Service."*

I look up sharply. "What the fuck is going on here, Arlo?"

"So many things, Laszlo. So many things."

He angles his head, peers at me thoughtfully. It's the same old head, the same old man, the large ears and small black eyes. His thin white hair is dappled with blood.

I open the file. I close it again, seized by a dark horror of what's inside.

It is cool in here, climate-controlled. I can hear every thump of my heartbeat. I can feel the dull whoosh of my blood.

"Go on now, son," says Arlo. "Have a look."

I open it again and begin to turn the pages inside. Transcripts of Charlie's fevered explanations on the thirtieth floor, describing the shocking extent of what he had discovered: the Off Record house, the ring of brazen liars, the clandestine organization calling itself the Golden State. Still photos, lifted from video captures, of Charlie in his hospital bed, struggling to survive the multiple gunshot wounds he suffered in the raid.

While I flip through it all, plunged back into this memory, Arlo speaks softly.

"I, of course, have had extraordinary access to this file. At-will access, so to speak. Firstly because I was the senior officer who brought Ratesic onto our force. Secondly because I was the man charged with overseeing his undercover efforts." He takes off his glasses, idly works at a freckle of blood with his thumbnail. "And lastly, of course, as the author of the novel inspired by these extraordinary events."

I turn over a page and stop, and read it, and read it again, and then I look up at Arlo, who is looking back at me carefully, very carefully, waiting to see what I will say. What I will *do*.

The page is a précis, a kind of executive summary, compiled from edited transcripts. It details how Charlie Ratesic was recovering from his injuries until he was murdered by his younger brother, Laszlo Ratesic, who willfully increased the dosage of Charlie's pain-reducing medication until he died.

"That's—" My head is shaking. I am shaking my head. "No. No, that's not right. I didn't do that. Why would I?"

Arlo turns the page over, and on the back side is a series of photographic stills, taken from the hospital room captures. There I am in the pictures. I am standing at Charlie's bedside. I am crouching at his bedside. I am examining the machines. I am turning the dials.

"I suppose you didn't know that I knew," says Arlo. "What you did, I mean. But I have always known, Laszlo. I have always known what you did."

"But it's not—" I find my voice. I say it loud. "That never happened." Louder. "It's not *So*."

"Come now, Laszlo. *It's on the Record.* We're looking at it." He puts his fingertips firmly on the photograph. It is black-and-white. My face is distinct. "Look!"

"Why?" I look at Arlo, my face hot with grief. "Why did I do that?"

"You were jealous of Charlie. You had always been jealous, and now—well, now, the man had become a genuine hero. The greatest hero the State has ever produced. You couldn't bear it, Laszlo. I am absolutely sympathetic, I have always been so. Which is why I have kept my silence for all these years."

"Oh." I say it again very softly: "Oh."

And I turn the page over and over again, the words on the front and the pictures on the back, turn them over and over, as if I can shake the letters and the images right off the paper, make it all go away, but it won't go away, because it is *true*. I remember it now. I spent these years unremembering it but now it is coming back, rushing back, grabbing at me, clutching at my heels like speculation: the bitter sting of envy I felt in Charlie's presence, the hatred for him that has always seethed below the surface of my adoration. How easy it suddenly seemed to be done with those feelings. Done with him, done with him *forever*. I remember the smell of the room, the beep of those machines, how easy it would be, how easy it *was*.

"Oh fuck, Arlo. Oh no." I tilt back from the table and turn my face away from him in the dim light of the Record and weep at what I did, at what I am. "Oh no."

"It will be all right." Arlo rises, comes over to my side of the review desk, and lays a hand down on top of mine while with the other hand he gently strokes my woolly head. "It will be okay. Look, Laszlo. *Look*."

There is another CSE on the table, beside the first one. I lean forward, baffled, pushing tears out of my eyes with my thick fingers. It is the same file, the same blue, the same label. Exactly the same. *"The Death of Mr. Charles Ratesic of the Speculative Service."*

"What?" I say. "What is this?"

"This is the file that lives here, on the Record. It is a forgery, Laszlo."

"Forgery": old word, dead word. The word itself an artifact.

"The file that you just read—that one"—he points at the first file, the one in which Laszlo Ratesic betrays his beloved brother—"*this* file has lived for all these years at my home, Laszlo. I could not bring myself to destroy a piece of the Record, but it does not live here. I replaced it with this one."

He lifts this second file and places it precisely on top of the first one, hiding the first from view. We sit in the silence of the enormity of this crime of forgery, of purposefully removing truth from the Record and replacing it with false. Rewriting the Record. A grave assault upon the Objectively So. And for what? For *me*. I flip open this second file. It tells the story that I knew and have known for the last decade, the story I have long taken for truth. It shows how Charlie was injured in the raid, how he struggled to survive for days and then weeks, how the doctors were able to stabilize but never reverse the course of the opportunistic infections that ultimately claimed his life. There is no murder in this file. No envious Laszlo, stopping to tamper with the dials. The man was wounded, and then he died from his wounds. A martyr.

"I replaced this file"—Arlo lifts a corner of the new file, gives a quick furtive glimpse of the old one before covering it again— "with this. Because I believed that we would be better off with you in the world than not in it. To defend our world and protect it. Especially with Charlie gone. I made that call. I made that decision."

"Oh, Arlo. Thank you." I reach out across the table, new tears on my cheeks, and I grab his shoulders, push my forehead against his. "Thank you."

He pulls from my grasp. He stares at me. His eyes behind his glasses are dark with sadness.

"I cannot believe it." His voice is a weary rasp. "Every time I see it I still cannot believe it."

"Believe—" I peer at him. "Believe what?"

"You saw it, didn't you? In your mind. You *saw yourself murdering your brother.* It was true inside your heart, that you killed the one person you love more than anyone in the world. Oh, Laszlo. I have spent a melancholy lifetime contemplating the impermanence of reality, and yet I am constantly stunned anew."

With small, deliberate movements, Arlo lifts first the forged file and then the real one—and yet another file is revealed. And this new file is the same again, the same CSE a third time through: *"The Death of Mr. Charles Ratesic of the Speculative Service."*

I look at Arlo. I look at the file. I open it.

Murder again. The text and the pictures together tell the story: Charlie, incapacitated and vulnerable, is defenseless against the stealthy approach of the monster... except the monster is Arlo. It is Arlo Vasouvian who lurks at the bedside, Arlo Vasouvian who crouches, and then Arlo Vasouvian with the dials in his hands.

Memories drop out of my head. The truth reverses itself, scrambles and re-forms. I pick up my gun again. Arlo leans back and stares at me, not like a friend now. Like a scientist, examining, considering. I raise the gun and he does not flinch. Around us hangs the solemn stillness of the Record.

"That file is the real one," I say.

"Yes."

"You killed Charlie."

"I did." Arlo, blood-splattered, gentle-eyed, stares back at me evenly. "That is accurate. To the extent that that word owns a definition." The three blue files are still on the desk, and now, as he talks, Arlo shifts them around, places a palm down on one and moves it in an idle circle, then does the same with the others, rearranging and rearranging their places, shuffling and reshuffling their order. "He was good at his job. Very good. I never thought—" He shakes his head in wonderment. "Never for a moment did I think that his undercover operation would be a success, but as you know, it was. With long effort and clever skill he destroyed nearly all we had built, and he had found nearly every member of our Golden State. As it was constituted, I should say, at that time. I could not let him find me too. He was, of course, a very talented man."

"Arlo Vasouvian," I say, summoning the voice I need, "you are under arrest."

"No," he says, "I'm not."

"You just confessed. It's all—" I look around the room, gesturing up at the captures. "It's all on the Record."

"Oh, right. The Record. Inviolable. Impregnable." He sighs. "You're not listening, Mr. Ratesic. Or you're listening but wishing not to hear." His hands pause in their card-trick motions. He picks the file that ended up on top, flips it open. It's me, in the photograph, me crouched to the dials.

"But that's not—"

"Real!" He stands abruptly and snarls, contorted with contempt. "Would you stop it? Would you *stop?* With 'real' and 'not real,' 'fake' and 'not fake,' 'true' and 'not true.' Stop!" He sweeps all three files from the desk and rushes out of the room, and I go after him.

He is moving quicker than I've ever seen him, flying from narrow hallway to narrow hallway in the weak light. I follow his footfalls, follow his thin shadow. At the stairway shaft he turns and snarls, holding all the files up, clutching them to his chest like a shield.

"Do you know why they built the Record underground?"

There is a true answer to that question, as true as two and two, and I give it automatically: "Because it provides infinite room for expansion."

"No. Bullshit! It's a metaphor. Everything is a fucking metaphor." He holds the files out, over the side of the railing. A couple of pages slide out, flap and flutter down into the empty air of the stairwell. "They built it belowground so everyone could walk around feeling like the truth was beneath their feet. You see? We—we here, I mean—we in this dumb and blinded land, we live our lives believing that beneath us there is *foundation.* That there is *something there.* Permanence. A record. *'The Record.'*" He puts the phrase in sneering quotes. "But it's not so!" He flings one of the files downward, one of the three official versions of *"The Death of Mr. Charles Ratesic of the Speculative Service."* I watch it as it flies and then falls, spilling end over end into the descending darkness of the empty stairwell.

"Under us is nothing, Laszlo. *Nothing.*"

"And so what—what—" Fury of my own is rising. My body is trembling. My face bends into a snarl. "You want what? Nothing? You think it would be better to have no truth at all?"

"No. No, poor Laszlo. Dear Laz. Laszlo, my love." He lets go another of the files and it flaps open, empties as it falls, its two wings bending upward like a bird's. "Letting go of the fantasy of objective and provable truth would not be better or worse. It would be accepting reality and figuring out what to do next."

There is only one of the three files left now. He holds it up. "Shall we open it, Laszlo? See what the truth ended up being?"

I don't take the bait. I have taken too much bait, been too easily led. "You are under arrest, Arlo Vasouvian."

"You're not going to arrest me," he says. "I already told you that. You will let me go, or you will shoot me dead."

"How do you know?"

He smiles sadly, looks across the darkness. "I am only speculating."

I'm not going to shoot him. I won't do that. I can't. But I step toward him with the gun still raised, reaching for the cuffs on my belt. I am going to do this correctly. I will take him in. He will confess. The truth will be rebuilt. There must be a mechanism to do that. There must be a form that can be filled out, a process that can be initiated, to reconstitute that file, reinstitute the events, remake reality as it was. There will be a way.

"It was her idea, you know," says Arlo, as if something has just occurred to him. "To use you in this way. Once we had concluded that starting again with Off Record houses was too simple, too literal, too small. Once we had decided we needed to achieve something larger—to send a shiver through the bulwarks, as they say. It was her idea. This piece of it. This marvel of string pulling that brought you along."

I stop. "Her": Silvie? "Her": Tester? *Her*—

He is watching me. Narrow-eyed, examining. Watching my face as this miserable new truth breaks through. "Ms. Paige."

"Yes, Laszlo. Aysa is ours. She was always ours. Her parents were ours and so was she."

I close my eyes. No more. I can't take any more.

"I had told her all about you," he says, "during her training. I told her all about brave Charlie's poor kid brother who never measured up. This sad unfortunate younger man, who doted upon and resented heroic Charlie in equal parts. And Aysa thought—it's really quite remarkable—Aysa thought, well goodness. Perhaps this younger brother will be eager to finish what his brother began. How hungry he must be for his own moment in the sun. In the good and golden sun."

I am shaking my head. I am back at the house on Mulholland, beside the pool with my junior partner, the two of us in silent wonder at the lies to which we were bearing witness, and not just witnessing but feeling, and not just feeling but *seeing*.

"But she saw them just like I did," I tell Arlo. "She saw Petras's lies and denials. The same as I did, she saw them."

"You saw her *say* she felt Petras lying. You saw her *say* she saw it."

I blink, trying to grab hold of my own memories, corner my own mind. I am not the hero, confronting the villain. I am a lost and tiny man, diminished and confused and uncertain. I am nothing.

"So she was, what, an actor? She was acting?"

"Actor." "Acting." Old words from an old world, concepts with dim ancient references, half hidden by time. The old world, not to be known.

"Yes. Just so," says Arlo. "An actor. Like Crane, the roofer, whose name was really Ortega, by the way, except it's not, not really. It's Ortega, it's Crane, sometimes it's Mortenson. Once, for a week, we called him Joe Dill, just to see how that felt. He practiced so often how to throw himself off a roof and make it look like he fell. See? See, Laszlo? Can you imagine doing that? Just that moment of letting go, letting your body slide? To him it was worth it. Aysa allowed herself to be sacrificed, just like quote-unquote Crane, who taught himself to fall off a roof. And both of them knew what I know, which is that it was worth it. *Worth it.*"

"No. It can't—none of this can be true."

"Yes!" He laughs, a short burst of happy laughter, and brings his hands together. "Now you see it. That's the whole point, Laszlo: that's the whole point." He rushes forward and grabs my arm, smiling, eyes wide with delight. "Laszlo—I'm not even standing here right now."

"What—what are you talking about?"

"The figure you are talking to is a projection. I am hidden somewhere else in this building, preparing to make my escape." He says it in a melodramatic voice, making a face, playing a game. "Unwilling to risk capture at this late moment in my long-planned scheme."

"That's impossible. That's insane. Something out of a—"

"Out of a what, Laszlo?" He steps closer. "A novel? Why can't it be true, Laszlo, if all the rest of it is true? I have power over stretches, I have power over people. Why not power over the air itself?"

"It's a lie, Arlo."

"Okay, then. If it's a lie, can you see it?"

"See..."

"Can you see the lie?"

I look wildly around the room. I step backward from Arlo and I look at the air around us and I don't feel it and I don't see it. No crackle in the atmosphere, no bending at the edges. Nothing.

"I'll say it again, dear Laszlo. A firm declaration, posited as fact." He makes his hands into a bullhorn, trumpets it: "*I'm not really standing here. I'm a hologram.* Well? Now? Are you *discerning* anything now?"

He says it with plain contempt, mocking the idea on which I have based my life.

"If I'm lying, you'd be feeling it, right? *Right?*"

He's right. I would see it. Wavelets of telltale in the atmosphere, ripples in the very air—I would be *feeling* it, just as he says, and now I do not, now the air is crystalline and calm, just Arlo walking toward me saying he is not, after all, Arlo, proving his bastard point, showing me that I cannot trust in what I know. I am discerning nothing. I hold the gun steady, hold it up straight.

Now, very slowly, he pulls out his own gun and aims it at me, as I am aiming mine at him.

The cold air of the basement is perfectly still.

"I doctored all of those stretches," says Arlo. "I put a forgery on the Record. I convinced two people, two that you know of, to sacrifice their lives, knowing that it was worth it. What makes you think I couldn't create a hologram of myself, and it's the hologram you are talking to now?"

"No," I tell him. "Yes. I don't—I don't know."

"So if I'm telling the truth, then you can shoot me."

"What?"

"I'm not here." He takes a step closer. His gun is pointed at my face. "It's not me. So shoot. Go on. Shoot—"

I pull the trigger and I feel the kick of discharge, and Arlo's chest explodes in a red blur and he flies backward and slams into the stair rail. I run to him, and I don't know if I'm crying because he is my friend, my oldest friend, and I love him and he is dying in my arms, or because of what has happened. He is cradled in my arms, his real body, no hologram, the real Arlo, his real flesh body. Then I hear footsteps crashing down toward us, the whole staircase is shuddering with the force, and now it all makes itself clear to me in retrospect, every inch of this nightmare playing itself out in reverse and filling in its details, right up to this moment—*this* moment right now! He never stopped playing mastermind, arranging details, right up until this moment, with the regular police pouring off the stairs and him bleeding in my arms—

"Freeze," they are shouting. "Do not move!"

Captain Elena Tester and six other officers, a small army of regular police filling up the narrow space around the stairs, surrounding us with guns drawn.

"Wait," I say, turning, body hot with confusion and fear. "Wait."

Tester and her officers crowd around me, closing in. She is staring, astonished; Arlo is collapsed in my arms, sprawled across my lap.

"Laszlo," she says. "What have you *done?*"

"Nothing. I haven't done anything. It was . . . He . . ."

They step closer, one step at a time, guns raised. Arlo, in my arms, bends his body upward slowly. Brings his lips up to my ear and says, *"Worth it."*

Tester circles me warily, keeping the gun leveled at my face, and the other officers fan out behind her. Arlo is cradled in my lap, his blood on my pants, his blood on my arms and on my face, his blood all over my black coat. What am I going to say? He tricked me. He said he wasn't real. He said that shooting him wasn't shooting a real person.

I feel that there is nothing I can do but explain myself, and that I would be a fool at the very least not to try. So I tell Captain Tester she's making a mistake.

I tell her that Arlo Vasouvian rigged the whole thing, that he is trying to frame the Speculative Service, that he is purposefully attempting to erode trust in our Basic Laws. I tell her he is at the head of an elaborate plot to kick away the pillars that support society, to smash in the walls that have kept us safe inside the Objectively So. While Arlo's body lies in my arms and Tester's officers keep their guns trained on my face, I say, "You have to believe me, you have to believe me"—I say all the things that are the only things I can say, and she reacts exactly as I would have predicted.

"You know, Laszlo," she says flatly, "that sounds like the wildest bunch of lies that I have ever heard. But *you* tell *me*." She crouches beside me, pulls out her handcuffs. "You're the expert."

PART THREE

"Look. Look!" Shenk had him by the arm at this point, had him in his clutches, and he wasn't letting go. "If this kid thinks that he's an alien from outer space, and he *does things* based on this belief? That he's an alien? Then, I mean, on a certain level, guess what? The kid's a fucking alien."

—Benjamin Wish, *The Prisoner*

24.

Hey! I think. As loud as a thought can get, which after all is not all that fucking loud. *I'm in here. Hey!* I can't see out the windows of the truck because the windows are blacked out, tinted over, so I do what I can do, which is stare into them and beam my thoughts out uselessly into the passing world as the truck rumbles along: *Help.*

I'm in here.

Help!

No one can hear. No one can help.

The people out there are dim shapes on the street corners. Faceless creatures behind the wheels of their vehicles, glancing with disinterest at the truck and then away.

I am strapped to my seat. A metal pole runs from floor to ceiling in front of me, and I am shackled to it at wrist and ankle.

The truck has been stripped of the artifacts of its old design. All that's telling me where I am is the old stink of cooking water and the shape of the vehicle, tubular, low and long. I am inside a truck that is shaped like a hot dog, and I am both inside this machine, shackled to a plastic bench by my wrists and ankles, and outside it, looking longingly at it as it cruises past. I could not have known, the many times I looked with keen interest at the Dirty Dog cruising the city, that it is out of service. It has been decommissioned and repurposed as a mobile prison, delivering the exiled to their exile.

No wonder, I think stupidly. *No wonder it never stops.*

Even in the state of dull bafflement with which I have suffered the last two weeks, of trial and sentence, of confusion and fear, of public approbation and private pain, even in my raw confused condition, I can pick up the old scents of boiled meat, of relish and mustard and pickle. I take some very small comfort in the pleasant ancient smells of condiments and meat. And I take comfort, too, in the thought of all the people out there, my good and golden fellow citizens, watching the black truck with the pink piping as it sharks past, wondering idly as I have for years, *How come it never stops?*

I can see where the refrigerator once was, up there behind the captain's-chair-style driver's seat. I can see where they had a row of compact metal containers for the various condiments, and probably a steam tray for the hot dogs themselves. But now all of these culinary accessories have been replaced by monitor screens, a bank of dials, a map of the city covered in beeping lights and lines.

One of these dots, it is easy to understand, is us. This vehicle I'm captive inside of. That is easy to figure. Requires zero speculation. We are moving fast now, and the dot is moving fast.

It's just me in the truck—me and the driver and the man seated across from me, a narrow ugly man in a tan coat and sunglasses, with a gun in his lap. The gun and the ugly man are both staring at my face.

"Excuse me?" I say to the man, but he doesn't answer. He looks like a Librarian, except for the sunglasses. He has the same set expression in his bearing, in his posture. Passive, still, exuding his grim authority.

I'm in a hunched position, because of how I've been bound, tied to the pole with a set of sleek plastic tethers. I have not been put into any sort of jumpsuit, nor even stripped of my Speculator blacks. Only my pinhole has been taken from me. Otherwise I am still me. There is heat on the back of my neck.

I feel miserable, a result of how much I now understand that I never did before, how much I've learned in these last days and how much dissonance I'm suffering now; or it might just be because the air inside the decommissioned hot dog truck is stale and close and pungent. It's hot, and where I'm going it's only getting hotter.

"You can lower your weapon," I tell the man across from me. I don't know if he's really a Librarian, but he has become one in my mind. "I'm not going to do anything." I tug at my restraints, demonstrating how tightly my hands are lashed to the pole. "I can't."

He doesn't answer. The gun does not move. The driver, absurdly, begins to whistle. The back of his neck is closely shaved, bristling with small dark hairs.

The truck banks into a turn, and I am shifted to the right, and then the truck speeds up, and I feel it rising, moving uphill, and then it turns again. I don't know if we're close or if we're almost there. I don't know where *there* is or how far away it is, or what is going to happen to me, or how I will die.

Help, I think again, radiate my desperate fear out through the sides of the truck toward whoever might be out there, but this is useless—it's ridiculous. I am living in a pretend world where empathy has secret supernatural power, where it can fly on wings and burrow into the secret hearts of strangers. And even if my message could sing out through these blackened windows, the truth is, I'm not the good guy. I am not the hero of this novel. I have not been kidnapped by nefarious crooks or dirty liars. I am the crook and I am the dirty liar. I have been tried and convicted for my assault against reality. I have left a trail of blood behind me, and my exile, now underway, is necessary to the ongoing security of the State.

It has all happened. However I remember it, whatever my own personal truth, it all happened. What is So is So forever. It's all on the Record.

The truck's engine makes its steady rumble. Time passes. Minutes of it, and then hours; there is no clock on the truck. Miserable and terrified as I am, in time my eyes get heavy and the hot dog truck becomes the big blue bus my brother and I used to take down to the beach on Saturday afternoons, when we were children still, still in that young and dreaming part of life. We were just teens, experimenting with what kind of adults we were going to be. Shirtless and self-conscious, already thick around the middle, I am clutching my surfboard at the bus stop before sunup. Charlie, bouncing from foot to foot, T-shirt wrapped around his forehead like a privateer, is whistling cheerfully at the sunrise.

I blink. Shift in my seat. I am on this hot dog truck driving farther from the city, deeper into the wild, with my hands and feet shackled, and I am also an awkward teenager on the bus to the beach. I exist in two places at once, listening to the rumble of the truck and listening to Charlie, whistling through his teeth.

No, though—no. It's the driver, still whistling. I jerk awake. The driver's head bobbles slightly as he whistles. My body aches from the shape it has been forced into, for however long it's been.

I think we're going downhill now. I can feel the truck's pneumatics shifting underneath me. The Librarian seated across from me rises, walks the two paces across the truck, and sits beside me, his right leg pressed against my left.

"Where are your identifications?"

"In my pocket," I say. "Right side."

He reaches across my lap, unconcerned with the intimacy, and wriggles his hand into my pocket. It all comes out: birth cert, five-years card, adulthood card, work card, home address attestation. A parade of Laszlo faces, one after the other. Growing older, uglier, fleshier; a flip-book of my dissolution.

The driver keeps on whistling.

"Is that everything?" says the man, and he sniffs. He's not a Librarian—no. Some special branch of service?

I nod. "Yeah."

"All right."

He gets up again. He's got a little screwdriver in one of his pockets, and he uses it to open a panel on the metal wall behind him. Behind the panel is a shallow drawer.

"What—" He slides my documents into the drawer. "What are you doing?"

He doesn't answer. Maybe he *is* a Librarian: he's got a wand. He puts the screwdriver back in his pocket and takes out the slim metal tube, black metal with silver caps on either end, and I feel an instinctual revulsion. What is going on? I draw back, pull as far away as I can from the pole to which I'm tethered, but he's not aiming the wand at me. He places my documents in the flat drawer and slowly passes the wand over them, front to back, a slow steady movement, like he's wanding someone's forehead, and there is a hissing noise from inside the drawer, and smoke rises from it in a disappearing puff.

"Hey," I say. "Hey."

But it's already done. He tilts the drawer forward so I can see the ashes inside, and then he tilts it further, so they scatter on the floor of the hot dog truck.

"Okay," he says, and the driver stops whistling long enough to say it too: "Okay."

"Now. What's your name?"

"Laszlo Ratesic."

The truck jerks to a stop, as if we've hit something, and I fly forward off the bench and slam face-first into the pole. And the man who is not a policeman, not a Librarian, who must be some sort of special officer, an officer of some kind of border service known only to those in its employment, he's up and out of his seat, and so is the driver, and the two men begin to kick me, one and then the other.

"Liar!" shouts the borderman, kicking me in the center of my stomach.

"Liar!" shouts the driver, kicking me in the neck.

"What is your name?"

"What's your fucking name?"

"I don't—" I'm no dummy. "None! I have no name."

The kicking stops. The driver winks and walks back to his captain's chair. "Now you're getting it."

The other man, though, the borderman in his tan suit, still stands over me, looking down. The truck starts up again. I feel the muscle of its engine thrum along the length of my body.

"What year were you born?" says the borderman.

"I—I—" I hesitate. I swallow. It hurts. A bruise is developing on my throat—inside or outside it, or both. My wounded shoulder has burst back into hot pain from the kicks.

"What *year*," he says again, staring directly into my face, "were you *born?*"

"I was never born."

I wince, but that's it. That was the right answer. The borderman braces himself and lifts me by the armpits and heaves me back to my feet, shoves me back in my seat. The truck keeps rolling, rolling downhill now, gaining speed, slowing only for the occasional sharp turns that tell me we are switchbacking down the far side of the mountain. Some mountain.

I slump and the tethers bite into my wrists.

My gut hurts. My throat, my head, my shoulder.

For all of my life, exile was just a word, an idea rather than a process, a wall erected around certain behaviors, not an actual thing that happens, not a series of actual physical events. These are those events. This is how it happens.

If I ever thought of it, I guess I thought of checkpoints. Some kind of physical barrier between this world and the next one—a wall or a partition. Men with long guns up high on parapets, angling their rifle noses down toward attempted incursion.

But there is no barrier. The truck never stops; the driver never rolls down his window to exchange words or money or documents with some guard at some fence.

No physical barrier separates our world from the outside. We simply rise up into the Hills and then down again, a winding path that I have given up on trying to memorize.

My eyes fall closed and Charlie is calling my name as he bounds off the old bus, telling me I'd better hurry the fuck up and grab my board and get off, and in the memory I can't recall what the actual name is. *"Hey——"* says Charlie, and there is a mute moment, like glitches in audio dropping out of a stretch. *"Come on."* My own name has elided from my head. A welt is rising on the side of my forehead from where I got kicked. This is how fast the truth can change— one hard kick from a heavy boot and everything is erased.

The brakes hiss and the body of the truck shudders as it stops. A dragon sighing as it settles.

The two men rise, the borderman from his seat and the driver from his, and they huddle at the side door of the truck. They ignore me, push their foreheads together, and murmur to each other.

"Two and two is four."

"The word 'serrated' means 'lined with jagged teeth.'"

"A hummingbird is of the family Trochilidae."

They speak very quietly, hushed as if fearful, hushed as if in prayer, preparing for battle. Murmuring true statements into each other's hearing. They are doing exactly what Aysa and I did during our approach to Mulholland Drive, chanting facts, girding ourselves with small pieces of reality like strung beads. Every "is" and "are," every flat declaration of a true fact, is like a piece of armor, and they are assembling it around themselves.

I start to do the same, catching up, following their lead.

"Bricks are heavy," I say. "Twelve inches to a foot," I say, and the driver grabs me by the back of the neck, opening the door with his other hand, and I say "Limestone is a sedimentary rock," and he pushes me, hard, down the short exit staircase, off the truck and down onto the road.

"Night adders are venomous," I say, and gasp because the air is thin and it is so bright that I can barely see. I squint up at the brutal desert sky: endless, baked blue, the sun a merciless glare above it.

The borderman and the driver rush down off the truck after me. They move quickly. The borderman squats at the roadside, digs into his pocket and comes out with a knife, a short effective blade that slashes the binds on my hands and on my feet.

He nods at the driver and the driver nods at him. Done. Mission accomplished.

I rise to a feeble seated position, blink helplessly in the brightness. "Wait," I say. "Don't. Listen. This is a mistake."

"Liar," says the borderman.

"I'm not a liar," I say.

"Liar," says the driver, and he kicks me away from the truck and I tumble backward, land on my ass. The concrete is hotter than the sand.

"There's a plot," I say, and turn up my palms, for mercy. "A plot to destroy the Golden State."

"Yours," says the borderman, and catches me under the chin. "Your plot."

He kicks again, and my face flies backward, and I'm on the

ground again, blood pouring from my nose. "We're in danger," I say, and he kicks me again, a hard one, again in the center of my stomach, and I moan "Danger," and he says "Liar," and then the driver catches me in the small of the back—"Liar!"—and the other one does, and then both of them together, over and over, and the individual words begin to blur and rise together, into the single word, loud as anything, true as doors on houses, louder and stronger: "Liar! Liar! Liar!"

And then they move swiftly back up the steps onto the truck to escape from the air, which is already baking me inside my suit.

A blur of sounds—"Liarliarliarliar"—a whirl of inward-collapsing sound, which rings in my ears and hangs in the air and mingles with the retreating hum of the truck, driving back to the good and golden world, leaving me here in the sand.

25.

This is what it's like outside the Golden State.

Now I know. A new piece of truth to add to my personal store, to carry along with me for however long it is before I collapse out here and die.

The fate of the exiled is unknown and unknowable, until you are added to their number. Until you get put on a truck and kicked off the truck in the hot, empty air of the world outside the world. The fate of the exiled is unknown until the knowledge is all around you like a carpet of heat, shifting under your footsteps like burning sand, stinging your eyes like windblown grit.

I gotta get up. That's the first thing. Get up. *Rise, you dumb brute, rise.*

So I do, I struggle up, arrange my feet underneath me, shake off the pulse of pain in my kidneys and in my shoulder and my head, and start to walk. The air is fiery yellow, it's ash-streaked gray, it's billows of angry red at the horizon's farthest edge.

I walk along the road that is just a strip of uneven asphalt through an endless landscape of hardscrabble dirt and desert sand.

Every direction I look the air is warped and shimmering with heat.

This is what it's like. This is what we have protected ourselves from, in there, at home, but now I'm out here. I'm gone from home and I have to get back.

So I go. I walk. One step and then another one and then one more. It hurts but I go. Back toward home.

I fucked it all up and now I have to get home and put it right. Save the State.

Past brown desert plants, dead or dying. Through low drifts of sand that come across the road in dry rivulets. Clutching my side, wincing, breathing hard. Past stands of bent cactus and clusters of rocks in tottering piles, crusted with old dirt.

I'm walking, I am, but it's not easy. Staying upright and ambulatory. Performing the basic mechanics of forward motion. Not easy at all.

I follow the road.

The sky is all sun. A wash of reds and yellows. It is hard to hold up my head, so I don't, I stare at my feet while I walk, keep my head hung, my chin pressed into my clavicle. I clear my throat and spit on the ground, or actually what happens is I try to spit and manage only a thin clot of dried-out mucus, which dribbles from my lower lip into my beard. There is a steady pulse of pain from my wounded shoulder, and I keep falling into the pulses' cadence, walking to the dull rhythm, one footfall for every angry throb. My kidneys hurt bad, from where the men's boots slammed into me, so I clutch my side and walk stooped, bent, one step after the other, as individual drops of blood form and fall from my nose.

I think one of my eyes has come loose. That's what it feels like, like it's loose or swollen somehow. I can feel it getting bigger inside the socket, threatening to burst.

About a half mile from where I got tossed off the truck the road is blocked by an old highway sign, green with white detailing, fallen from its mooring and covering the road, bent up at a sharp angle and shimmering lines of heat.

I try to step over the broken sign and misjudge it severely, because

I can't see because of my fucking eye, and I scrape my shin on the sign's edge and pitch forward onto its face, sliding forward like an awkward kid on a playground slide, down the blistering hot surface of the sign until I land in a heap at the bottom.

I get up. I keep going.

I've gotta get home, that's all. Get back.

Although first what I'd really love is a drink of water. My tongue is fat inside my mouth, and my throat is burning, bristly, thick with sand and dirt.

I keep thinking I hear laughing voices, or cars coming, or my radio singing out, but I'm always wrong. I carry no radio. I have no identifications.

I stop walking and stand still in the heat. Just for a second. I raise a hand to my brow, try to block the sun from scouring my eyeballs. I wipe blood and phlegm out of my beard. I just gotta stop a second, that's all. Try to get my bearings. Make sure I'm walking in the right direction.

I'm not. I'm walking in the wrong direction. *Fuck.*

I got fooled. I got turned around. When I fell across the downed sign, or maybe earlier, maybe all along. It's just—it's really hard to say. The sky is all one sky, all one ugly swirling pale gray, a color that is no color. The air is tremulous, coruscated at its edges. It's like— it's like all the lies I have ever seen, all the times I've watched the air bend and ripple, all the dissonance of the atmosphere, it's all gathered around me now, thick and getting thicker.

I don't know which way to walk. The road is lined with Joshua trees, speckled with their small hearty blooms, bristling with prickles, standing with their hands in the air. The sky is just heat, a wall of glass heat, and such a sky cannot guide my way. There is horizon in all directions.

I go back the way I came. Retrace my stumbling steps. My feet are burning, swollen and itching with heat inside the leather of my shoes. Intolerable. I stop and my whole body nearly pitches forward with the teetering momentum, and I sit down to wrestle off the shoes. I get the left shoe off okay but there is a knot in the lace of the right one, a miserable tight little bastard that my thick fingers cannot possibly undo, and the sweat makes it impossible to even see, so I end up tearing the damn shoe off entirely, wrestling the whole thing off in one furious gesture, like tearing the skin off an animal, and then I fall backward, staring up, my head in the impossible heat of the sand, and start screaming at the sky.

In the silence, when my voice runs out, I again hear sounds in the distance. Or — do I? They are not even sounds but the echoes of sounds, toy sounds. A truck's horn blowing. The jingle of small music.

My mind drifts upward, feeling around in the absence of breathable air. It is the lies themselves that have done this to the atmosphere out here, out past the reach of the State. Absent the bulwarks, without the bedrock of the Record beneath it and the sheltering fortress of full and permanent truth above, this is what happens to the world, it gets to be so shot through with lies that it traps in heat and multiplies it, sears the ground and poisons the air.

Maybe this, after all, is the history of the world.

Exactly as feared. Exactly as we have been warned. An unlivable world, outside our boundaries, east of the mountains — this is what the world has become. Has become and remains. A sky alive with lies, constantly rolling and billowing, boiling in on itself. Here is a sky that is no sky. Here is a world that is a vacuum of itself. The sun is a fiery liar, burning into me, burning me down.

I hear a voice and it's Arlo's voice, whispering cruelly as he did in the bowels of the Record, telling me how it's all a metaphor, *lies like heat* and *the truth as a shelter*, it's all a system of metaphor we have talked ourselves into believing, except now look! Look, you old asshole. You traitor! Look at it out here! The sun is burning my skin, the sky will bake me alive, so fuck you with your metaphors.

I get back up. I keep going. There is no reason to keep walking except if I stop it will be forever. I will lie down and the sand will rise up slowly and cover me over.

So I keep walking, barefoot now, starting to pick up some speed, moving in what I am now just fucking hoping is the right direction, bearing my melting bulk back toward the Golden State. Because Arlo arranged my exile for a reason. Our defenses are weakened. Public trust in the Service has been grievously assaulted, and now he's going to . . .

. . . fuck, though. I can't remember.

I can't remember what he's going to do next. But I have to get back. I have to stop him.

Shit.

Wait. *Shit.*

I don't know which way to walk. I turn around, a half-turn, scratch my head. Sand drifts out of my hair. I start walking the opposite way, because, yes, *this* is the right way, this way is south. I think. I press forward, one step after the last, moving automatically.

After a while I take off my coat, walk with it folded over my arm for a few paces, like I'm going to find a chairback out here somewhere to sling it over. Then I fling it into the desert, watch it unfold like a winged beast and fall dead to the ground, and I laugh, the sound of my own laughter a haunted croak. I think maybe I was walking the right way before, and now I fucked it up. I'm just not sure.

I stop.

This is how it ends: you just stop.

You keep walking until you see a sign by the side of the road, a tall pole listing aimlessly to the left, an oval pitched on top of it with words in it—a word and a letter. It says "FLYING J." That doesn't mean anything. The sun has baked sense out of my mind.

I pitch forward off the road, toward the sign, and as I reach for the metal pole I imagine somehow that it is going to be cold to the touch, but it burns me when I grab it. My fingers start to cook and I shout and let go, draw back, totter, and fall.

I wake up only because I have no choice.

"Hey," I say.

Someone is peeling my eyes open. I mean literally digging their fingers into my eyes and peeling back the lids.

"Hey," I say again, or maybe I just *try* to say it—my throat is clogged with dust and heat. My lips don't work. I say a noise that sounds like "Hey" while this lady forces my eyes open with her nails. She is squatting over my chest, straddling me with her heels pushed into the sand, scrabbling at my eyelids with all ten fingers, hissing, trying to get my eyes open.

"Hey," I say, really *say* this time, getting the word out with an effortful croak. I try to rock myself up, but I can't move. I'm big but weak. I'm a downed bear in the dirt with this lady on top of me, laughing, her face matted with grit.

I can feel her weight and her fingers in my eyes, but I don't trust that she is real. It's a vision, or a dream. This is the way it works out here, outside the State, in the thin air of the truthless world: you wake with a demon squatting on your chest and she scrapes away your skin until your flesh is raw to the world.

"Smoke smoke smoke," says the woman, and her voice is familiar in its tone and its rhythm. "You smoke, yeah? A smoker and a joker, that's my boy. You got any?"

Her breath is outrageously bad, a stale reek blowing right into my nose and mouth. I bat her away with the back of my hand and she grabs on to my wrist, slaps me in the face with my own hand, and giggles, witchy.

"Stop hitting yourself," she says. "Stop."

The light slashes into my brain and all I can see is her face, leering with want, her tongue clucking. I have seen this face before. A round face, high cheeks, laughing mouth. Now that my eyes are open she has switched to my cheek, dragging her ragged nails through my beard, digging hard. I feel cuts opening, feel blood blossoming out into my beard.

"Come on," I say. "Stop it."

"Where you keeping 'em?"

She *is* real and I do know her.

"Hey," I say one more time, and manage to angle my torso up and get my elbows propped beneath me. The lady tumbles off into the sand, and both of us struggle to our feet and stare at each other.

"I was just asking for a cigarette," she says.

"Lemme see."

I abandoned my coat miles ago, but the pack is in my right front pocket, three cigarettes still inside. I shake one out and hand it over. She pokes it into the corner of her mouth and it dangles there. She doesn't ask for a light, just stands with the cigarette at a raked angle in the corner of her pursed lips. As hot as I feel, she looks hotter, wearing three or four layers of skirts, wearing a jumble of overlapping T-shirts and vests, like she was wearing when I saw her in Judge Sampson's courtroom.

You're not alone, out here in exile. That's not how it works. Not with so many having been exiled before you. A whole universe of wanderers out here, farther and farther from home.

"How did you——" My question makes no sense, but I finish it anyway. "How did you find me?"

"Wasn't looking. Just good luck. What about you?"

"What?"

"How did *you* find *me?*"

She laughs, crazily, but I am gathering the impression that she is not crazy, or not as crazy as she was. It's also possible that I can't tell anymore, because I'm crazy myself. The heat is a monster hunched above us, the heat that is bloated, greasy with untruth, the heat that has us both trapped inside it.

"You have to help me," I tell her.

"Oh yeah?"

"We have to get back," I say. "We have to . . . "

She's waiting. Gaping mouth curved up, ready to laugh, and I know why. What am I about to say? *We have to foil the plot! We have to defeat the Golden State and save the Golden State!* Lunatic slogans. Idiot ravings. Nothing is real.

"Where are we?" I ask her instead. "What is this place?"

" 'This place,' 'this place,' " she says, parroting my voice. She holds up both hands, like a Joshua tree, and turns in a rapid circle, like I saw her doing in the courtroom. "America. Just America." Then she points one hand toward the sprawling, low-ceilinged building behind us. "*This* place is Flying J. Okay? A truck stop! Magazines, prostitutes, and cigarettes. Fried eggs and waffles, playing cards and gum." Her voice has rolled over into a giggling singsong, and she is dancing from one foot to the other, and now she starts singing outright in a low croon: " 'And I think to myself . . . what a wonderful world . . . ' "

Ms. Wells is tapping at her hips and then her chest, frisking herself for something, which she then finds, deep within some pocket: a small plastic cigarette lighter.

"Oh," she says, holding it up. "Here we go."

She lights the cigarette, and I'm thinking how awful it looks to be smoking in this terrible heat, surrounded as we already are by the choking misery of a thousand lies, when Ms. Wells abruptly spins around and trots toward the building.

"Hey," I say. "Wait."

I lumber after her, but it's too late, she's already slipped inside the truck stop, and I can see her through the glass—the whole front of the place is glass, the doors are glass—doing her mad dance through the empty aisles, puffing on the cigarette, hopping from foot to foot.

I try the door. She locked it. I bang on the glass.

"Hey," I say. "Hey!"

She stops dancing. The shelves are almost entirely empty, an empty shop in the emptied-out world, but there are a couple of things in there. Ms. Wells grabs a red plastic can. A gas can. She unscrews the stopper and begins to empty it out, swinging her arm to splatter and splash the liquid all over the filthy tile floors of the Flying J.

I watch, astonished, as she moves through the store, rushing up and down the aisles while gas streams out of the can and splatters on the floor, until finally she turns the can upside down and taps out the last drops and dribbles. She tosses the can itself at the front of the store and it bangs off the glass and back toward her.

She looks at me and does not look crazy. Her pale eyes are lucid. She is calm.

"What the fuck?" I shout, trying to make myself loud enough to be heard, as if she can't see me clearly enough. "What the fuck are you doing?"

She drops the cigarette. It spins end over end from her two fingers to the floor and by some miracle doesn't land in the gas, but bounces and continues to burn, harmless, on the floor.

So Ms. Wells crouches, squints at the butt like she is inspecting a small insect, and then gives it a small push with one finger, and in an instant the store turns red with living fire, flames bursting up in the center of the floor and rushing out in all directions. I scream. The fire spreads with astonishing force, racing along the floors and up the walls, consuming the cheap plastic shelves in an instant. I see Ms. Wells with her arms up, grimacing, shaking her head from side to side and moving toward the center of the fire, disappearing inside it like curtains are closing around her. What is she—*what the fuck?*

I run up to the building and then back away, shielding my eyes, turning my face away from the inferno. When I'm able to look again I can still see her, just barely, perfectly still in the center of the fire as it engulfs her, and it is her own deliberate doing, I watched her do it, but I can't just turn away. She is a person born of flesh, as am I. I left my identifications on the hot dog truck but I'm still a person, and so I'm casting about, spinning around in a desperate circle. I see a pile of buckets beside the row of gas pumps, buckets full of squeegees for windshields, a thousand years old.

I grab the topmost bucket and dump the squeegees out onto the ground. I jam the bucket onto my head and I choke at the miniature rain shower of dust that sprinkles into my eyes and mouth even as I bear down and run toward the building, head bent forward, hurling myself like a truck, like a missile, like a bear with his head inside a bucket, and slam into the glass.

I am flown backward by the impact, and I land, grunting, on the ground. It hurts like hell: my shoulder, my head, my spine where I smashed into the ground. I sit up, groaning, lift the bucket off my head, and Ms. Wells is not on fire but she is about to be, so I put the bucket back on and I start from farther back. I give out a wild animal yell, making of myself a battering ram, hurtling toward the glass, and this time it smashes open. I hurl the bucket off my head, kicking through the broken glass while the fire is billowing out, gathering force as it feeds on the rush of oxygen from out here in the rest of the universe, and I find the lady, Ms. Wells, just as the fire reaches her, and I grab her and lift her roughly and carry her from the fire, out into the slightly lesser heat of the rest of the world.

Then, for a long time, we are on the ground, sprawled beside each other and breathing heavily. Still as lizards. Cooking in the heat.

I don't know how she is still living. She should have died in the fire, but then again, so should have I.

"Are you a hologram?" I ask her.

"No."

"I had a friend," I tell her, "who said he was a hologram."

"Oh yeah?"

"I killed him."

"Whoa," she says. Her eyes are closed. My eyes are also closed. "That's crazy."

"Why did you do that?"

"Do what?"

"Come on," I say. I open one eye to look at her and find that she has also opened one eye to look at me. "Why did you almost kill yourself? Set yourself on fire. Were you—what, were you testing me?"

"Do you think I was?"

"Yes. Did I pass?"

"Well. Let's see." She tugs on her hair, and then nods, satisfied. "I'm alive. I had to know, you see. If you were still human. I don't mean, are you a hologram? Or a robot, or—anything like that. I mean, 'Is he still human?' Like, possessed of a good and golden heart. I thought you were, we thought you were, but—" She sighs. "I had to see."

The word "we" catches me. I open my other eye. She is still talking, on and on, with no trace left of madness in her voice or mien. "A lot of people, you know, they lose their identity, they are decoupled from the truth, and something happens to them. Everything gets—burned away. You, on the other hand, you appeared to me as remaining still essentially ... present. Still human."

"But what if I failed the test? You would have died."

"I was very confident in my analysis."

"Come on. Come *on*. Can't you talk straight for one second?"

"Oh, you mean like they talk straight in there? Twelve and twelve is twenty-four, and north is the opposite of south, and all of that? All of that 'truth'?"

I'm ready to say yes, exactly, all of that truth, but she isn't stopping.

"There is truth in scripture," Ms. Wells tells me. "There is truth in the Brothers Grimm. There is truth in any old map you find. Any old mooted map, with a skull for a compass rose, 'Beyond here there be dragons' and all of that. You got truth in that too."

She stands up. She starts walking away from the wreck of the Flying J, which has more or less finished burning down and stands as a desiccated hulk, a black and irradiated heap adding new lines of heat to the wavering world around it. I trot clumsily in the wake of Ms. Wells, staggering to keep up with her, my feet burning on the sand. Now we've arrived at a small car, bright green, reflecting viciously bright beams of sunlight from all its chromed edges. The car says "VW" above the rear license plate, and it is painted with flowers and speckled with rust.

"Is this your car?" I say, and she doesn't answer. "Can I take this car?"

"Oh yes," she says. "You're going to take it. You have to." She opens the trunk and pulls out a bottle of water. "Here. Drink."

I finish the bottle in a swallow and she hands me another one, and I drink that too.

"Okay," she says. "Listen. Do you want the world?"

"Yes."

She points. "It's that way." She fishes in one of the pockets of one of her shirts and holds up a single silver key. "Go and get it."

"Are you serious?"

She puts the key in my hand. "It's all yours."

"Is there enough gas? To get me home?"

"Home? Is that where you're going?"

"Wait—what does that mean?"

But she's already gone. I get in the small car. I crane my neck out the open window.

"Hey," I call. "Are you coming?"

"Coming?" She is already twenty steps away, striding with purpose. "I'm a sweeper, boy child. I gotta keep sweeping."

And she's gone.

26.

The city, my city, when at last it appears, is a dim gleam on the horizon: a collection of fairy lights in the desert, yellow on yellow, showing itself through the heat and haze as I crest yet another low rise.

I jam the accelerator and Ms. Wells's little car rushes, ratting, forward.

And then I see a cluster of buildings, the tops of buildings, just barely visible above the rolling dunes, just their tips peeking up, and I follow a long bend in the road, until all at once it is unveiled: the Golden State, bright late-day sun glinting off the glass surfaces of the world, returned to me. I grin, jubilant, my dry lips cracking from the effort, and I yelp and smack the center of the steering wheel, a grateful holler to ricochet back across the silent desert to mad Ms. Wells.

I smash down on the gas pedal again, and my heart kicks into double time.

I did not believe you, Ms. Wells, I did not know what you were, but I should not have doubted your fluttery and sporting mind. Because there it is, here it is, the Golden State getting taller and clearer as I close out the miles, and just in time, because the gas needle is inching perilously close to empty.

I'm home. I'm back. Oh, Ms. Wells, I'll never doubt you again.

I come into the city on a broad avenue I don't yet recognize, three wide and empty lanes in either direction, running between towering buildings, and I am trying to figure out what district I'm in, what section, and I've just about decided I'm downtown, it has to be downtown — but what part of downtown? — when one of the car's front tires explodes and the steering wheel jumps out of my hand.

"Shit," I say as the car skids and flies, bounces with a rattling bang off a street lamp and careens in a new direction, totally out of my control. I struggle to get the wheel steady in my hands but it shivers and rolls, flying through my fingers. The car caroms to the other side of the road and my head cracks against the driver's side window, sending a bright flash of pain across my skull.

"*Fuck,*" I say, rolling back from the blow. "*Fuck.*"

The car sputters and stops, perpendicular to the roadway, steam hissing out from under the hood. The air-conditioning dies along with the engine, and in an instant the car becomes a furnace. I take deep breaths, fighting to steady my shaking hands. The sun is blinding, burning, intensified by the glass of the windshield. There is an ominous hiss coming from somewhere in the guts of the car. Blood is trickling into my right eye. I must have cut my head when it hit the window.

"Get out of the vehicle."

The voice is mechanized. Loud. Coming through a bullhorn or a speaker, some kind of amplification system. I look through the wreck of the windshield, rubbing blood out of my eye with my knuckles, trying to see who's addressing me. My head is a thick knot of pain.

"Get out of the vehicle."

I grasp the door handle, take a breath, and step out into the blasting heat.

An even, flat expanse of asphalt spreads in either direction. A long street, dotted with street lamps, lined with buildings. I still don't know where I am, exactly, just that I'm home. I peer up at the street lamps, looking for captures. I had forgotten that I'm barefoot. It was okay driving but now the pavement sears the soles of my feet.

"Hello?" I call feebly, hands in the air, turning in a slow circle. I don't see anyone. If somebody shot out my tire, I don't see the shooter. Enormous buildings, majestic constructions of concrete and glass, rise on either side of me, up and down the street, each of them with its own giant-scale architectural style. There's a building that is itself an entire skyline, each of its dozen individual towers fashioned to look like the top of a downtown skyscraper. To one side of me is a pyramid, its front-facing sides made of sheer black glass, rising many stories into the air.

I keep my hands in the air. I walk gingerly from where my car stopped to the traffic island at the center of the lanes.

There are no buildings like this downtown. Maybe I'm *not* downtown. Maybe I'm up in Pasadena or Glendale, or down in the beach cities. Some reach of the State where my travels rarely took me.

"Stay exactly where you are. Keep your hands visible."

The voice again, from nowhere and everywhere.

"Okay," I say. Now, squinting upward into the haze, I can make out a kind of catwalk, an elevated hallway with a glass bottom, suspended over the road and spanning it, connecting one of the massive buildings on one side to one on the other. I squint up at the catwalk, in search of the source of the voice. I think I can spot figures shifting about up there, dark shadows floating above the roadway, but I can't be sure.

"Don't shoot me," I say to whoever it is. Wherever they are. "I don't want to die."

I do, though. A little bit, I do. It hurts to speak. My feet are burning and bleeding. My face is peeling, flakes of hot skin coming off my cheeks above my beard.

"You can't be out here," says the voice.

I spin around. I don't know where the voice is coming from. "Okay," I say.

Then I see them. Two of them, coming across the road toward me, with guns aimed at my head. They are Speculators, is what they are—black suits, black shoes, black hats—and I am about to call out in happy greeting, ask them their unit, tell them who I am, but then I see that they're also wearing thick aprons that cover the whole midsection. Plus black helmets with tinted visors pulled down over their faces.

The words come to me again, and the truth of the words: *I don't know where I am.*

The Speculators approach me swiftly, growing closer like shadows, like creatures risen from some impossible deep to come and claim me and drag me away. There is a crispness in their movements, a panther-like military integrity that reminds me sadly that I'm standing here barefoot, broken, bleeding from my head.

"Please don't shoot me," I say. "Please."

They stop, guns still drawn and aimed, and the taller of the two raises the faceplate and holds up a stubby bullhorn. It's a woman, pale-faced, staring at me impassively.

"We will not shoot you unless you give us a reason."

"Okay," I say. And then, ridiculously: "That's great."

"Please provide your identification."

"I don't have any."

"What do you mean?"

"I mean, I don't have any."

"None?"

I shake my head.

She is stymied. Irritated, even. Leaving her faceplate up, she turns to her partner to confer. He is shorter than her, broad around the middle, and when he flips up his own faceplate I see a round, pocked face. They press their foreheads together and talk so I can't hear them. Figures are moving on the catwalks, clustering. Dozens of people. Staring at me. I turn to one of the glass buildings, on one side of the street, and I am being watched from there too. And from the building on the opposite side. Hundreds of pairs of eyes, thousands, maybe, are watching.

I know at last where I am. A skyline that is not a skyline but a cluster of overlapping skylines. I know it from *The Prisoner*, from when, toward the end, the desperate father of the ailing boy arrives with the others in that glittering and hopeful city in search of the old man who may or may not hold the secret that can save the child. When they get there, it's late at night, and the father drives his car down a broad avenue—this same broad avenue—past throbbing crowds of partygoers and happy revelers, and his own grief and panic are drawn in sharp contrast to the footloose alcoholic joy of those he is forced to pass through en route to his salvation and that of his family.

The whole world of the book returns to me in a flash, a world layered over this one, Dave Keener unable to deal with the traffic, throngs of cars going on either side, so he pulls over and gets out on the side of the road and climbs up on top of his car, scanning in both directions, while the exhaust of a hundred cars blows up into his eyes and coats his throat.

I am in Las Vegas. Las Vegas, as it turns out, is a real place.

The two officers have come to some sort of disagreement, presumably about my fate. The short fat one raises his gun and points it at me, and the other one, the one who spoke to me, pushes it down. I step off my traffic island and head toward the Speculators—

or officers, or soldiers, or whatever they are—hoping to engage them, but they ignore me, continue their squabbling. Their voices float over to me in patches, ribbons of conversation.

"...I don't know what you want me to do—"

"You know what you have to do. Directorate *just* issued new instructions on this."

"What directorate are you fucking talking about?"

"*Main* Directorate."

"Main Directorate of *Identification,* or Main Directorate of *Border Security?*"

"I don't know!"

"You just said you did know!"

"Can we just call it in? Let's call it in."

"Fine. *Fine,* Rick."

Rick holsters his gun and digs under his heavy apron and comes out with a radio, a small black box of a make I've never seen before. He murmurs into it while his partner watches, and then the three of us stand there sweltering.

"Hey," I say, realizing suddenly how brutally thirsty I am. "Can I—"

"Remain where you are."

"Remain where you *are.*"

"Do not move."

"Do *not* move."

"Stay."

So I wait, unmoving, under the watchful eyes of the two officers in their thick lead aprons and black face masks, and under the eyes of everybody in those hotels that line the street, because that's what they are. Hotels. I know them from *The Prisoner,* I have been given a map in advance: a guidebook. That's Luxor, Caesars Palace, New York–New York. Purpose-built simulacra of real places, once built for pleasure. Inside them now, I think, I presume, are people—the people who live in Las Vegas now, who live here now in the present like there are people who live in the Golden State. These people, the Las Vegas people, were never real to me before this instant—but neither were they unreal. I had no reason to conceive of their existence, nor reason to doubt it. They were unknown and unknowable.

But now they are real, and I can feel their eyes staring from the glass windows above and around me.

Sweat is running in streams from my brow down into my beard. Blood has caked in the corner of my eye, and it flakes off the cracked blisters on my lips.

Two cars pull up at the same moment, from opposite directions, one on either side of the traffic island where I'm standing. The cars are yellow, each with the word "TAXI" stenciled on its side. Nobody gets out of the cars. The woman remains with her gun pointed at me, while the other, the one named Rick, hustles over to the window of one of the taxis.

For a long moment he talks to whoever is in there, and then he trots back over to his partner as the door opens and a new officer comes out—a tall, thin woman, no apron, no mask, dressed all in blue.

She has a bullhorn, and she lifts it to her lips.

"Take off your clothes."

"What?"

She doesn't repeat herself. She just waits, watching. My fingers are clumsy, swollen, wrestling with the buttons of my shirt. While I struggle out of my clothes, an officer emerges from the second taxi and methodically puts down four traffic cones in a square around me. There is yet another cop inside *his* car, watching him tensely from behind the steering wheel. My pants are burned onto my skin, and I have to fight them off, wrestle them down, unpeel myself from myself. When the new officer, who is older, black, with a thin gray mustache, is done with the traffic cones, he strings yellow caution tape from cone to cone, cordoning me off.

At last I stand in my underpants, the sun flaying my broad red back.

I am becoming aware of life in the corners of this picture. A man and a woman sit on a decorative concrete wall in front of one of the hotels, dangling their feet. A little boy is on a bicycle, swooping in curious circles closer and closer to the conversation. Half a block up there's a statue of a towering figure in a draped toga or cape, lording proudly above the intersection.

The first officer keeps her gun on me while Rick waits beside her along the perimeter. He takes off his hat and wipes sweat from his brow while the tall woman, the one with no mask and no apron, lifts her bullhorn again.

"We're going to need to know your name."

I start to answer, but then I don't want to. I can't. My kidneys ache from the thud of the boots in my side in the hot dog truck. "I don't have a name."

"Look," she says. "If we don't know who you are, you're danger-ous. If you're dangerous, we have to handle you as we handle any threat."

As if to underscore the tall woman's point, the officer with the gun raises it a little higher. Rick brushes his fingertips along the hol-ster of his own weapon but doesn't draw. The last of the officers, the perimeter man with the thin gray mustache, has his hands in his pockets, but he's looking at me closely.

I am going to die here, I think. *Wherever this is—one way or another—I'm going to die.* I might as well go out with my name on.

"My name is Laszlo Ratesic," I say.

"You're Golden State?"

"Yes."

She says it like that, not *"Are you from the Golden State?"* but *"You're Golden State?"* and I wonder what that means.

"You're a refugee?"

"I—I'm sorry. I—"

"Exile." She interrupts, impatient. "You're an exile."

I squint. I can't hear her clearly. Maybe she said "in." You're "in exile" or you're "an exile."

"Yes," I say, the answer is the same either way, and feel the pain of longing for my homeland, which strangely enough appears to me as the pleading, earnest face of Kelly Tarjin, whom I only met three days ago. I think of her in the doorway of her small home in Faircrest Heights, her face worn with care. I recall her telling me to come back and me saying okay. I imagine her now with a stab of regret, imagine her waiting, imagine arrogantly that she cares, that she's standing in her doorway in fruitless anticipation of my return. The weakest form of speculation: fantasy.

I miss her. I never really met her. "Home" is a word with no fixed and permanent definition.

Meanwhile, the mustache guy trots over to the captain and mutters in her ear. She looks baffled, but then she shrugs and hands him the bullhorn. He starts to talk, it doesn't work, he puzzles at the mechanism and starts again.

"Hey, would you say the name again?"

"Laszlo," I say.

"The whole name."

The captain is watching him. He's watching me.

"Laszlo Ratesic."

He confers with the captain, and then with the other two cops, who lift their visors to join the conversation, until he speaks again into the bullhorn. "Good news. We will not be killing you for the time being."

The dark-skinned cop with the gray mustache has a partner too, a young woman with a black ponytail. She's driving and he's in the shotgun seat, and I'm in the back, and they don't talk while they take me wherever we're going. It's a short ride down the avenue— the Strip, is what it's called. That's what Wish calls it in *The Prisoner*; I remember it now. In their easy comfort with each other, in the clear mutual respect I sense between the two, I am reminded helplessly of Aysa Paige, my old friend, my first and last and only partner.

My thick head lolls back and maybe I sleep a little, in the air-conditioned back seat of this taxicab that is a police car, in this city that did not exist until half an hour ago. I drift off to sleep deciding that the best thing to do is remember Aysa forever as the Aysa I knew first, the one who never betrayed me and never intended to. Let that truth be the one that lasts, let that be the real bone truth of her and me.

When the cops open the back door, we're at a hotel called the Mirage. It's a simpler, shabbier building than some of the others—a pair of identical buildings, each a massive rectangular slab of concrete, striped with glass, angled backward toward a tower in the center that connects them. It looks like a book open to the street.

In the parking lot, as we get closer to the rear door, there is what looks very much like a giant pile of rotting pumpkins, hundreds of pumpkins smashed to pieces in a shifting pile, covered in flies.

I don't ask. I am done, for now, with questions. I follow my escorts inside, and I am overwhelmed by noise: a vigorous open-air bazaar is in full swing in the lobby of the Mirage, with market stalls set up and lines of customers haggling over clothing and food and small housewares.

"Six bucks? Fuck you," says a beefy guy, shaking his head at a small woman with wiry hair and a handkerchief over the lower half of her face. They are arguing, it seems, over a cardboard box filled with steak knives.

"No," she says, tugging down the kerchief so she can enunciate better, "fuck *you*."

The beefy guy steps up to the lady, making fists of both hands. The cop with the mustache steps toward the confrontation, but his partner, the young woman, stops him. "Don't worry," she says. "I got it."

She strides over, hand on her gun, as I dodge a wheelbarrow laden with bicycle wheels. Mustache takes my arm.

"You doing okay?"

"No," I say.

"Yeah," he says. "I bet you're not. C'mon."

He leads us through the lobby, past the elevator bank, into a quiet dark room, and the feeling of the place is immediate and unmistakable: across all space and time, in whatever universe I may stumble into, the smell and feel of being in a bar remains the same. People are scattered at small tables throughout the room, nursing bottles or small glasses, and there's a bored-looking bartender, a guy with spiky hair, reading a book with the paper cover folded back. Before him, across the bar, is a man in a gigantic motorized wheelchair.

"Hey," says the cop, and everybody looks up. But he's talking to the guy in the wheelchair. "Hey, Charlie. I believe this man belongs to you."

The man in the wheelchair moves his right hand, just his right hand, to work a device on his armrest. Slowly the machine turns, and I can see his face.

"Charlie," I say. "Oh, Charlie."

The chair moves slowly toward me, and I walk toward him, almost as slowly as he comes toward me, so baffled am I, so weighted with astonishment. My feet plant and lift themselves one heavy step at a time as he rolls across the tile floor of the bar, the mechanics of his chair whirring as he comes. The cop steps back and crosses his arms, watching our reunion, and the bartender goes back to his book. Halfway across the bar, the front wheel of Charlie's chair catches on a lip of tile, and the whole thing nearly totters over backward. He stops, fusses with his buttons, and navigates the obstacle.

"Lashed to the mast." The phrase appears in my head. My long-lost brother, living still.

We meet in the center of the room, and I crouch before him and put my hands on his narrow shoulders.

He cannot move his neck.

He says something, but I can't hear him. His mouth barely moves and the words are faint and garbled. I bend closer.

"Heya, dickhead," he whispers.

I follow him as he moves across the hotel, through the crush of people in the market. Old decommissioned casino games are shoved against the walls, unplugged. Felt tables have been made into market tables laden with goods. Way up above me are hotel rooms, doors hung with wreaths. Clotheslines are drawn between the mezzanine railings.

I stand beside Charlie in the elevator. His whole physical self is gone, his broad swaggering body is blasted and burned and shriveled, but I would know him anywhere. I would know him a thousand times.

*   *   *

"Welcome to"

Charlie writes those two words and I take the paper and wait while he writes more.

"my swinging"

I am smiling already, but I wait for it, for the third scrap of paper. He holds the nub of a pencil in his hand, between middle and pointer fingers, clutching it fiercely between two knuckles, and it trembles wildly as he writes.

"bachelor pad"

I laugh. His face does not move. He is frozen. His face is a mess of old scars and burn marks, pocked and pitted and locked in place. His mouth is a sideways oval, a bent O angled toward his right cheek.

Charlie can't talk. Not really. Each word he utters is a triumph of sustained effort and still comes out as a strangled, unearthly whisper.

"Charlie," I keep saying, tears rushing down my cheeks, a hot rush. I feel like a dummy.

He has a sheaf of loose papers balanced in his lap. He writes, holds up papers for me, one at a time.

"Knock it off"

And then:

"you baby"

I would knock it off if I could. Instead I crouch down before him and hug his withered legs. His body is a coil of wire, bent up into a seated shape. He is impossibly thin, slumped into the movable chair, head fixed in a half tilt, the muscles of his face unmoving.

I have presumed my brother dead for so long, though, and here he is, alive. There is terrified joyful movement inside my chest, small birds opening their wings.

The balcony of Charlie's room has a view of the central courtyard of the hotel. You can look across at other rooms just like it. The bazaar I walked through on my way in continues down below: as we talk, occasional snatches of haggling, contentious commerce drift up and reach us.

The room is full of paper. There are the loose pages scattered on Charlie's lap for these small conversational notes, but that's just the beginning of it. His coat is overflowing with paper, his jacket pockets stuffed. The room is full of filing cabinets, shelves, boxes, and they're all full of paper.

"You OK?"

I shake my head. "Not really. I went to your funeral, Charlie."

He writes. The pencil jiggles between his knuckles.

"Me too"

I laugh. He's still writing, writing two words at a time, writing—

"Arlo: smart"

I read it and his fingers are curling for me to give the note back. I do, and he scribbles, crosses out and amends, and hands it back.

"Me: smarter"

I don't have to ask him about what happened next, once he disappeared from the Golden State. I spent twenty-four hours, give or take, in exile, in the desert between the Golden State and this place. I know how I feel now, burned and blasted, twisted and wracked. My throat still feels dry and full of sand. So here's my Charlie, after my day in the desert, plus months. Plus years. However long until he made it here.

He's looking at me while I look at him, and then he does his effortful writing again, creating just one word:

"Beard?"

"Oh. Yeah," I say. I put my hands up to my face self-consciously. "I started it after you were gone. I dunno why. Just—I dunno."

His eyes don't move. They are settled on my face. His chin ducks down then, very slightly, which seems to be the extent of movement he's got, as far as moving his head. I crouch down before him, put my ear to his thin lips.

"It looks like shit."

I laugh. He is not laughing but I know that he is.

"Fuck, Charlie," I tell him. "You cheated death."

His pencil moves across the paper. I wait for it.

"No. The"

I wait. Listen to the noise of the bazaar. Look around the cluttered, paper-ridden room.

"other way around"

It takes a long time for Charlie to explain everything that he wants me to understand. And it is a mark of how much Charlie remains Charlie—world-beating, stubborn, domineering Charlie—that he does not give a shit how long it takes.

Whatever he has to say, it is worth waiting for, because it is Charlie who is saying it.

Charlie was in the desert for a long time. He doesn't know how long. He does not know how close he came to dying, but he knows it was damn close.

And then at last he made it here. It took him a lot longer than it took me, because there was no Ms. Wells then, no outrider from Vegas making sorties into the State, finding exiles and pointing them in the right direction.

"What is this place? Why is everything indoors?"

Charlie writes.

"Under my ass."

"What?"

He points to the paper again. *"Under my ass."*

I crouch before him and perform the peculiar intimate act of reaching under the fragile structure of his body, leveraging him up slightly with one hand while I feel around with the other under his bony rear end until I find the wiry spirals of a notebook. More paper. Paper everywhere.

The cover of the notebook is blank. Still squatting, I flip it open and read it.

It is the provisional understanding of the people of Las Vegas that at some (currently) indeterminate time in the past, an enemy (???) of what was then known as "THE UNITED STATES OF AMERICA" (with "enemy" to be [provisionally] defined as EITHER an external adversary OR an internal adversary OR some combination of the two) did inflict (EITHER over time OR "at a strike") irrevocable damage upon "THE UNITED STATES OF AMERICA."

The text in the notebook is hard to read. There are many strike-outs and erasures, with some passages in pen and others in pencil, and with much of it written in, over, and around earlier text. There are arrows at the ends of lines, directing the reader to skip a paragraph or turn the page over to find the thought continued on the back. Each notebook page is a patchwork of smaller pages, smaller pieces of paper, taped and stapled on.

This (postulated) irrevocable damage done to "THE UNITED STATES OF AMERICA" was realized by taking advantage of the nation's highly interconnected energy infrastructure, coupled with the (near-??) total reliance of that "grid" (term?) on computerized control mechanisms

which were highly vulnerable to interference ("sabotage"). The postu-
lated "enemy" (internal OR external OR combined, as noted above) was
thus able to take advantage of

A) "systemic flaws" in this "grid" AND/OR

B) "systemic flaws" in the general population's ATTITUDE TO-
WARD authority, i.e., DISTRUST for any statement issued by the
"government" (including, FOR EXAMPLE, an announcement relating
to an attack on the "grid") AND/OR

C) "systemic flaws" in the population's ATTITUDE TOWARD the
"media" (term?), such that—

I close the notebook for a second and take a look at Charlie. It's
hard to tell but he might have fallen asleep. His mighty presence has
momentarily departed the room. I try to find my place in the book
but it's hard, among the wandering lines of texts, the arrows and
cross-outs and redirects. So I just pick a page, a few pages on from
where I was.

—a BLAST RADIUS measuring dozens (hundreds? +++?) of
miles in diameter. The effects of this accident (term?) were COM-
POUNDED by the inability/unwillingness of survivors to communi-
cate [i.e., severe distrust toward fellow survivors, refusal to accept or
solicit assistance, presumption of "enemy intent"]. Lacking the tools
to measure, we can feel uncertain—

Someone had written "we can feel certain," and someone else, or
maybe the same person having second thoughts, had gone back and
made "certain" into "uncertain."

—that despite the intervening passage of [???] years, the environ-
mental hazard that was the result of the explosion(s) still pervades

the atmosphere in (some but not all) of "THE UNITED STATES OF
AMERICA."

That's the last word on that page, "America," and then it skips
down a few lines and someone else in different handwriting has
written, in parentheses and in very small letters, "(term?)."

It goes on. I can't read any more. I sit with the book in my lap,
looking out the window of Charlie's little room. The sky isn't poisoned with lies, you idiot. It's poisoned with poison.

"Hey," says Charlie, working hard to get the word out. "Hey."

He is holding out his working hand for the notebook, and I hand
it to him. He flips back to the first page, takes his pencil and presses
down hard, underlining a single word, the fourth word in the paragraph: "provisional."

The roof of the Mirage is all farmland.

I followed Charlie up here in the elevator, and now I lope behind
him through yet another alternate universe, a landscape of self-
sufficiency rolled out high above the street.

The rooftop has been covered in soil, built over with greenhouses
and silos. I follow in Charlie's wake as he maneuvers past patches
of unsown field, cornstalks growing in bent rows. He ably navigates
the bulk of his chair between piles of mulch and a clatter of unused
shovels and rakes. Dark soil is laid out right to the lip of the roof,
with roots twisting into it deep, with the bulging, uneven bulbs of
pumpkins twisting up out of the dirt.

Charlie writes.

"Mine all mine," his note says.

He owns the pumpkin patch. He has papers for it. Other pieces of
this common garden are owned by other people, all of it pipelined
to the bazaar down below. The people of Las Vegas determined, one

way or another, to create a civilization, dragging themselves along as they go.

Charlie angles his chair very close to the edge of the building to show me what he wants me to see: a wooden machine that he built, or maybe had built, right at the lip of the roof. It's a very simple structure, just a plank of wood balanced on a triangle, like a teeter-totter, suspended in place with a thick elastic band. And there's a pumpkin placed, delicately, at the near end of the plank. It's a cata-pult, and it's loaded. Waiting to fire.

We regard this primitive invention for a moment in silence. I feel the heat of the day finally starting to dissipate as it gets closer to nighttime.

Charlie writes one of his notes, and I bend over him to read it:

"What happens?"

"What do you mean?"

But he doesn't write any more. He holds up the same paper again. *"What happens?"*

Meaning, I gather at last, dense Laszlo, what happens when you fire it? When you let loose the pumpkin? *What happens?*

"It'll—it'll go down. Fly over the side." He waits. I look at his rickety machine, and then back at Charlie, still holding his paper, the scrap of interlocution, patient, insistent. "It'll fly down and then smash on the ground below."

I peek over the edge of the hotel, shade my eyes. Down there is the parking lot, littered with the smashed carcasses of pumpkins.

I step up to the machine. I haven't seen him do it before, and I would have said it was impossible, but Charlie arches his eyebrows: mischievous. Daring.

So I fire the pumpkin. Release the band, step back, and watch it fly off the board and disappear over the edge. Together we watch it go: hurtling down and down, arcing outward, tracing a long wobbling parabola until it makes its satisfying smack, loud on the pavement, and bursts into gore, atop and around the existing pile.

I look at Charlie. I'm grinning, weirdly exuberant. He's already writing.

"Again"

"Again?"

"Again"

We fire the gun over and over. Six pumpkins, ten. The orange corpses pile up far below us.

I'm trying to figure out what the point of this is, what Charlie wants me to see by showing me his jury-rigged pumpkin-firing machine. But after the third or fourth pumpkin I'm mainly lost in the spectacle, holding my breath each time we launch a new projectile and it flips and spins in its ballistic descent toward the climax, the explosive moment of contact with the hard, flat parking lot, the bursting into chunks and lumps of stringy goo. And I laugh with delight and turn to Charlie and he's waiting, head angled toward the pile, waiting for me to load the next one. This is not just fun, this is a demonstration of some kind, I'm sure, some lesson to be learned about the Golden State, about how we have huddled fearfully away from the edge of the world, burrowing mole-like inside our small store of truth, blinding ourselves to the possibility of more. Or maybe the idea here is something even more elemental, more base—Charlie sphinx-like in his wheelchair, watching me work the machine, waiting for me to get it—maybe the message is that Arlo and his revolutionaries, with their contempt for the very *idea* of truth, that they are wrong, too, and that they are even *wronger.* Maybe what Charlie wants me to get is just that when you shoot a fucking pumpkin off a roof the same thing happens every time. Every single time.

But then when we're done, when we've depleted our whole pile of pumpkins, before we go back to the elevator, my brother struggles his one working hand off the armrest, lifts one finger to jab me in the center of the chest. He pushes at my sternum, above my heart, with a push that is surprisingly firm. Then he takes the same finger and slowly pushes it into his own chest. Drawing an invisible line between his heart and my own.

This is a novel.

Some of the words in it are true and a lot of them are not and a lot of them are of that indeterminate third category for which there is no good name. But you can say that it is an amalgam of true and false events, true and false impressions, a series of imagined and actual experiences that have been strung together in a particular order to provide access to a kind of truth that might otherwise be unavailable. And more precious for it.

Blindly, blindly, we are feeling our way toward something.

Okay?

My name is Laszlo Ratesic and I am fifty-four years old, formerly of the Speculative Service, formerly a citizen of the Golden State.

I am writing these words in a notebook my brother, Charlie, gave me. The first of nineteen empty notebooks I found inside this yellow taxicab he requisitioned for my journey.

I am at a roadside hamburger restaurant off Highway 8, en route to a town that is called Vancouver, or that was once called Vancouver. There are inquirers in Las Vegas, my adopted hometown, who believe, provisionally, that there are people living in Vancouver who are relatively healthy and stable, who have built a new world, and with whom a profitable exchange of ideas and/or commerce might be arranged.

Or there might not be. I will find out. Or I won't.

The roadside hamburger restaurant, as I sadly concluded when I saw it, is nonoperational, and probably has been that way for many generations. I only know it was a hamburger restaurant because it is shaped like an actual hamburger. This is a metaphor.

Once, many many years ago, a man named Arnold Ramirez ordered something called the Dinosaur Burger and ate the whole thing, an achievement that entitled him to get the meal for free, and to have his picture hung in a frame on the wall of the restaurant. After some internal debate, during which I contemplated the photograph of Mr. Ramirez and his clean plate, I took the picture down, carefully opened the frame and slipped it from the glass, and taped it inside the notebook you are now reading. (See appended.)

Charlie is not able to come to Vancouver, so I am going for him.

He has filled up this car with paper. He has instructed me to fill the paper with truth and bring it back to him.

Some of it will be right and some of it will be wrong.

I will do as my brother has instructed me, and open up the covers of my books like the lids of jars, fill them up with truth and bring them home.

Right now I'm smoking in the night, looking up at a sky full of glimmering pinpricks of light, and I know them to be stars and also diamonds.

ACKNOWLEDGMENTS

I am very grateful to Joshua Kendall at Mulholland Books, and also to my literary agent, Joelle Delbourgo. Both were so smart, and so *patient,* as I wound my way through many alternate universes until I found this novel. Thanks also to Emily Griffin and her team at Century/Arrow in the UK.

Thanks to Nell Beram, who copyedited the hell out of the final manuscript, and to Ben Allen for shepherding its production. Thanks to Amanda Brower for a crucial early read. Thanks to Jenny Meyer for carrying my banner overseas. Thanks to Joel Begleiter for being charmingly, relentlessly Joel Begleiter.

Thank you to the law professor Larry Sager at the University of Texas, and the political scientist Adam Berinsky at MIT, for elucidating conversations about law and truth.

Thank you to everyone at Mulholland and the wider world of Little, Brown, especially Sabrina Callahan, Pamela Brown, Alyssa Persons, and Reagan Arthur.

Thanks most of all and forever to Diana Winters, Rosalie Winters, Ike Winters, and Milly Winters. I love you guys so much, and that's the truest thing I know.

ABOUT THE AUTHOR

Ben H. Winters is the *New York Times* best-selling author of *Underground Airlines* and the Last Policeman trilogy. He is a winner of the Philip K. Dick Award and the Edgar Award, and he has been nominated for an ITW Thriller of the Year Award. Winters lives with his family in Los Angeles.

MULHOLLAND BOOKS

You won't be able to put down these Mulholland books.

SF
WINTERS
2019

1552991